PHILLIPS, JAYNE ANNE
QUIET DELL

QUIET DELL

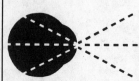

QUIET DELL

JAYNE ANNE PHILLIPS

THORNDIKE PRESS
A part of Gale, Cengage Learning

GALE
CENGAGE Learning

Detroit • New York • San Francisco • New Haven, Conn • Waterville, Maine • London

Thorndike Press® Large Print Basic.
The text of this Large Print edition is unabridged.
Other aspects of the book may vary from the original edition.
Set in 16 pt. Plantin.

LIBRARY OF CONGRESS CATALOGING-IN-PUBLICATION DATA

Phillips, Jayne Anne, 1952–
    Quiet dell / by Jayne Anne Phillips. — Large print edition.
    pages ; cm. — (Thorndike Press large print basic)
    ISBN 978-1-4104-6607-5 (hardcover) — ISBN 1-4104-6607-8 (hardcover) 1. Women journalists—Fiction. 2. Murder—Investigation—Fiction. 3. Chicago Metropolitan Area (Ill.)—Fiction. 4. Large type books. I. Title.
PS3566.H479Q54 2014
813'.54—dc23   2013040313

Published in 2014 by arrangement with Scribner, a division of Simon & Schuster, Inc.

Printed in Mexico
1 2 3 4 5 6 7 18 17 16 15 14

for Annabel Eicher

AUTHOR'S NOTE

This novel is based on the true story of a crime that took place in Quiet Dell, West Virginia, over eighty years ago. The names of the characters whose lives the crime claimed or influenced are real: their thoughts, perceptions, and relationships are imagined. Their letters, the trial transcript, and various excerpted newspaper articles are quoted exactly from original documents. Minor day/ date discrepancies reflect discrepancies in the original coverage or documents.

CONTENTS

I.

This book is intended to be of wholesome helpfulness to mankind, and not to engender morbid desire or taint human souls.

— E. A. Bartlett, *Love Murders of Harry F. Powers (Beware Such Bluebeards)*

(Special) — In the backyard of the Eicher home at Park Ridge, a suburb of Chicago, stands a little marker, with the inscription, "Graveyard for Animals," scribbled in the childish handwriting of Annabel Eicher, 9. There the Eicher children had buried a bird, playmates said.

— *The Clarksburg Telegram,*
December 9, 1931

Cost of Living, 1931

New house $6,796.00
Average income per year . . . $1,858.00
New car $640.00
Average rent per month $18.00
— Remember When . . . 1931,
A Nostalgic Look Back in Time

CHRISTMAS EVE
DECEMBER 24, 1930
PARK RIDGE, ILLINOIS

ANNABEL BEGINS

When the year turns, there are bells on the wind. All the old years fall on the ground in lights. When you walk across those lights, it sounds like walking on all the piled-up leaves of giant trees. But up high the bells are ringing for everyone alive. There are silver and gold and glass bells you can see through, and sleigh bells a hundred years old. My grandmother said there was a whisper for each one dead that year, and a feather drifting for each one waiting to be born.

My mother says that's just a story, but I always do hear the bells, even in my sleep, and everything in front of me is all white and open like a field. Then I start dreaming.

The trees in my dream sparkle. It's quiet in the dark, and I'm indoors, on a stage. The trees are behind me but they are alive, touching limbs and stirred just so. A silent spirit seems to move among them, and the light has found me. It's a large theater, rows and rows before me, and a balcony I glimpse through a gleam that dazzles me. The audience is quiet, waiting for me to speak. Perhaps they are watching a play, my play, or a play in which I perform. I can't make out faces beyond the footlights, but I see the tilt of heads and the shapes of ladies' hats, and a glow seems to float amongst them. There's a hum of admiration or excitement, and a swell of whisper like applause. Then the lights on the stage darken. I hear people weeping, so moved are they by the production.

Grandmother used to say that I might find myself upon a stage one day, as an actor ("don't say 'actress,' " she told me, "the word garners no respect"), or the author of a play. Grandmother admired the suffragettes and said they would open all fields of endeavor to women. If she were younger, she said, and not required at the bosom of her family, she would have joined their movement, to help them fight their war of argument and reason. She was required because Heinrich died. Her "beloved Heinrich" was my father, an only child. We called him Papa. He called Grethe "Miss" or "Missy," and he called me "little Nell," though my name is Annabel. I try very hard to remember him, but I don't, not really. Papa is his portrait, in the gold frame over the parlor mantel ("That is not a photograph, my dear, that is a portrait in oils"), and he is the man in the wedding picture with Mother.

One day he didn't come home. I was four years old. Nothing was said that evening to alarm the children. Betty, our nursemaid, sat with us at dinner and put us to bed, for the police had summoned Mother and Grandmother.

Papa was struck by a streetcar in the Loop, just after dusk. He was walking from his club to the station.

I believe there was a crowd, jostling and shoving, distracted by the siren of a passing fire truck, or startled by sudden rain. He was a fine designer of silver in our own backyard workshop, and an actuary for Metropolitan Insurance and Casualty Company of Chicago. He advised on odds and probabilities. This was the irony, Grandmother said, for no one could ever have predicted the sudden death of a man so strong and healthy, who never smoked or drank and was well liked and much respected. He did business at his club because that was where business was done, and was an artist at evenings and weekends, a man known for his talent and easeful charm. He performed in theatricals at university and sang a fine tenor, but pursued mathematics. One job his entire working life, Grandmother says, and head of actuaries when he died, as well as Mother's adviser and manager in the art of silver design. One home from the time Grethe was born, and Grandmother sold their Chicago apartment

17

to relocate with the family. Papa wanted fresh air for the children, and fine schools, and a garden with a barn for his workshop, and a stable for a pony, and the park nearby, where we float our boats and walk through forest paths to the meadow. The meadow is high in spring and mown in summer, and Papa helped us fly kites.

I think I do remember the kites.

Grethe was eight then, and he told her to take off her glasses and run, run straight out and follow the tug of the string; there was no one in the meadow but us and the wind was high. I was little and he held me on his shoulders, clasping my knees, while the kite went up and up. The string played out in his hand against my leg.

I felt so tall, with the grass so far below me, and the kite so far above, dipping and bounding. I was holding on to Papa's hair, which was dark and thick and combed straight back, but blowing that day, blown up like the wide collar of my dress and the ribbons on the kites. I can't see Papa's face, or his eyes near mine, but sometimes, when I'm alone and I think hard, I can feel his hair in my fingers, cold and coarse, and I clinch my fists to hold on.

I know all of Grandmother's stories about Papa, but the kites are not her story. Her stories are in the photograph box that she kept on her dressing table. It's a tall wooden

18

box and the sides are four glass frames: the photographs slide right in. Heinrich, a baby in a blousy dress. Heinrich, ten years old, with Grandmother and Grandfather Eicher ("Like you, Annabel, he read the dictionary, and wrote out new words"). Heinrich in his graduation portrait. Heinrich in military uniform ("To have survived the Great War, and be killed by a streetcar in his prime"). The carved top of the box lifts up, and the other photos fit neatly, each thick card snug in the velvet-lined inside.

The box is mine now. Grethe never looks at photographs. The faces are too small for her to see, and she doesn't care for stories. She had measles and a high fever when she was two. They nearly lost her, Grandmother said, and the crisis affected her eyes and concentration ("Due to her limitations, it's best she's not imaginative. Grethe can learn to run a home and she will marry. Until then we must protect her"). Grethe doesn't go to school any longer; she is quite as tall as Mother and goes with her to the shops and the bank. She helps plan meals, and Mother instructs her on etiquette.

Grethe is delicate. Her hair is dark like Papa's. If she doesn't remember things, I must remember for her. She plays the princess or the pilgrim in my plays and dioramas. I say the lines and she acts them out, for she has a calm slow way of moving and can hold quite still. Hart ruins the dioramas and rouses Duty to barking and running about. My brother Hart is very quick and I must give him long speeches and grave actions. He must be the hero or the villain, and lay flowers at Mother's feet by the end.

Duty is our Boston terrier that follows Hart everywhere and sleeps on our beds by turns. Betty brought him from the pound and Mother let him stay. The pony had been sold by then, to a family on a farm. Duty was already trained, Betty said, because he'd lost his family in a tornado, and a boy needed a dog. Hart wanted to call him Topper because he has a white spot around one eye like a gentleman with a monocle. But Duty wore a collar with letters sewn on and wouldn't answer to any other name. Just as well, Mother said. A pet needs walking and feeding, and his name will serve to instruct. Duty knows to sit, and Hart taught him to fetch and dance. When Grandmother was sick, Duty lay at her door. The nurse was coming and going with trays and said that dog would trip her, he must be shut up.

Duty is in my dream. I stand upon the stage before the trees and Duty is there, sitting just at the edge of the light. His little legs are stubby and his chest is broad and his short brown coat shines like a mirror. Duty's eyes are wide apart and he can seem to gaze in two directions, but he only looks off toward the wings, to where no one can see.

Grandmother always told me that our dreams are wishes or fancies, gifts of the dream fairies that guide and care for us in our sleep. She said that poems and stories are the whisperings of angels we cannot see, beings once like you and me, who know more than we can know while we are here. "Address me in your mind when I am gone," Grandmother told me. "I will hear you always, and will send a reply in the sounds of the grass and the wind, and other little signs, for we no longer speak in words when we have slipped away."

The nurse didn't come on Thanksgiving. I think Grandmother was glad. Mr. Charles O'Boyle, our former roomer, would come for dinner, and the Verbergs from next door, who were bringing the turkey and the chestnut dressing. Mother was making the vegetables and her gelatin surprise, and Charles would bring the pies. Charles is a great one for making pies. He baked them every Sunday, the years he roomed with us, before the Dunnegan Company posted him back to Chicago. Grethe was setting table with the Haviland china and Hart was to lay fires in the dining room and parlor grates. We roast marshmallows on the long forks at Thanksgiving, and figs with chocolate. It was my turn to sit with Grandmother. I brought up tea for one.

"My dear," she said. "You gladden every heart."

I fed her with the teaspoon. She could not hold the cup.

She talked about the silken cord that binds her soul to mine. She slept and woke and slept and woke.

The cord is a real cord and I keep it under my pillow. Not all of it. Once it was very long, the last of the silk braid Mother used on the sofa pillows and parlor drapes, and Grandmother made a game of it for walking through the park. She invented games for us after Papa died, and took us everywhere, to the circus and the moving pictures, but always to the park ("So near it is like our own backyard"). Betty was seeing to Mother and Mother was settling accounts. We children went, afternoons, with Grandmother, single file, holding to the cord. She used to say there was one of her and three of us, we children must hold to the cord just so. She fashioned one large knot for each right hand, and I was first behind her. Then came Grethe, and then Hart, our gentleman protector, with Duty at his heels. We walked two blocks to the park and the arched gates, past the fountain and the pools, into the woods where the trees grow close. We held to the cord in silence, for Grandmother liked us to hear small sounds — the cricket and the mantis, and grasses moving in the meadow beyond the pines.

Sound travels even in the cord we hold, Grandmother said, for the heart beats in the hand.

The cord that's left is but a curl wrapped round a knot and tied in double bows. Now if we go to the park, I tie it round Mrs. Pomeroy, who is only a rag doll, no bigger than my two hands, so the cord goes round her waist four times like a golden belt. She was a gift from Papa. We all have our beloved companions, Grandmother said. Where I found such a name she did not know, as I could barely lisp the words when I was two.

Hart says Papa brought him to the park to ride the pony on winter Sundays, and led him all around the meadow. Grethe has asthma and the air was too cold, but Papa and Hart dressed warmly, like explorers on an expedition. Their breath was white as smoke and the afternoons were blue.

I was too young to ride. I don't remember the pony, but he was dear to Grethe, to Hart, and all his friends. A Shetland, Hart says, small as a big dog, with his mane in his eyes, and long eyelashes like Mrs. Pomeroy's, though hers are sewn in thread. One could lead him about the yard with a carrot ("A farmer's son brought hay and feed, cleaned the stall, exercised the animal in bad weather. Your father would have that pony, but the expense was too much, you see, after he died"). There were fine parties at birthdays and May Day, with mimes and jugglers, pony rides and rolling hoops.

Now we have balloons and Mother makes ice cream.

There wasn't ice cream on Thanksgiving.

It was understood I would sit for the blessing. Then Charles carried my plate upstairs. Mother brought a clear broth for Grandmother, but Grandmother was asleep.

"You are not like others," Grandmother liked to tell me. "Your dreams see past us."

Once she bade me close my eyes and touch my forehead to her cool, dry mouth. She kissed me and blessed me and said, whispering, not to ponder the pictures I see, but to hear and see and feel them. Their stories are truths, she told me, for each foretells the eternal garden in which we'll all walk together.

I wonder if that garden is earth or air, if one hungers there, or feeds on nurture that renews itself, like the dew and the wind, like the bells, ringing the old year into the dark, snow swelling every sound.

I asked Grandmother, did she remember Denmark. *Min lille svale,* she said, and slept.

I ate my dinner. Snow fell past the windows like a picture in a book.

Duty does not really dance. Hart calls it dancing and taught him with bits of meat. Duty stands and moves forward, then back, holding his front paws up before him. Like a

24

suitor at a soiree, Grandmother said. Not such an old dog, Mother said, if he can learn new tricks.

The trees in my dream shine like trees on a glittery valentine. The sparkle looks like snow, catching light, or drops of rain held fast. It is a wonderful effect. Living trees could stand upon a stage in pots of earth, and the limbs might move on wires, gently, as though stirred by a breath.

Grandmother woke and said, "I fear your mother has not been entirely provident."

Then she slept.

Betty has been gone some time now, as we are too old for a nurse. Mrs. Abernathy was a medical nurse, and very strict. She wore a uniform and kept me out of the room. Grandmother told everyone I was the only nurse she needed, but I was not allowed. I could hold her hand at certain times, or read aloud the speeches from my plays.

Mrs. Pomeroy is old and soft. Her arms and legs are mended. She will wear the silken cord in my Christmas play and I will voice her words. She will be Grandmother and speak as Grandmother speaks.

We took turns at Grandmother's bedside on Thanksgiving. I stayed longest, and scarcely left her side. Grandmother told me, when she was still up and sitting in her chair, that she would sleep longer and longer, and then not wake up. She said her death would be a blessed death and one she wished for me when I am very old. She told me a poem to write down, and I wrote each line exactly. I read the poem out for her two times. Then she told me to put the paper in her bedside table, and to open it again when she was gone ("Death is not sad if one has lived a long life, and been of service").

I wanted to look at the poem, but I knew the words.

What lies behind is not myself
But a shell or carapace
Cast off, an earthly taste.
I have gone on you see
To make a place for thee.

Grandmother can hear me. I do believe so. And I hear her voice in the words of her poem, and in other words that come to me.

Perhaps she has sent me the dream about the trees. I could hear a sigh in the branches, a bare whisper. No doubt there was a fan offstage, blowing a breath of motion.

Grandmother used to say, so little can move so much.

■ ■ ■ ■

II.

■ ■ ■ ■

In the partial darkness he imagined he saw the form of a young man standing under a dripping tree. Other forms were near. . . . He was conscious of, but could not apprehend, their wayward and flickering existence. . . . His soul swooned slowly as he heard the snow falling faintly. . . .

— James Joyce, "The Dead"

CHRISTMAS DAY
DECEMBER 25, 1930
PARK RIDGE, ILLINOIS

CHARLES O'BOYLE CONSIDERS

He woke at dawn, certain of a course of action.

They understood one another. Asta was not like others, and would never condemn him. She was the sister he'd wished for, sensible, stalwart, and they were the family he returned to, every holiday, and nearly once a month. The boxes in the garage, his tools, books, drawing implements, the archery set he planned to pass on to Hart, held his place. His job and promotion at Dunnegan were secure; he could put most of his salary toward keeping the family afloat. He must convince her, plead his suit gravely, lovingly, for he could not live as he did forever, and she could not go on as she was. Anna, Asta, Anna! It was madness to sell the house in the middle of winter, in this grim economic climate that showed no signs of abating. What she'd said last night had really quite disturbed him. To move the children from their neighborhood, their schools, and with what means of support? And in the aftermath of Lavinia's death, which had surely wakened memories of the sudden loss of their father, memories nearly unconscious for Annabel, who was so young at the time, and clearly a highly imaginative child.

Asta was not thinking such. Early in their friendship, she'd offered him the privilege of addressing her by her pet name, Anna. It was that girl within the woman he must now protect.

He lay back in bed, considering. The air at the windows was white and mist obscured any view. He felt marooned and comforted, afloat in the fairy-tale world he associated with this home in which art and music quietly underscored the players: Lavinia, old world grandmother, matriarch of dwindling fortune; Asta, artist widow, aging Cinderella abandoned by any prince; innocent Grethe, whose steadfast gaze belied her lost acuity; intrepid Hart, equally adept at playing the clown or the explorer; and Annabel, recording all in her childish tableaus and plays, reciting and remarking, strewing her bright optimism before her like bread crumbs across a frozen steppe.

This Park Ridge enclave of Lutherans was so determinedly American; the Eichers no longer referenced their Northern European heritage, but Andersen and Grimm had originated their horrific tales in Denmark and Germany. Grim indeed, Charles considered them: seductive trickery, leading little children to the slaughter like fattened lambs. Make-believe encouraged the fantasy that virtue was finally rewarded: Charles knew it was not.

His own mother's innocence had victimized them both. Had she not possessed her small inheritance, they'd have lived in penury. Undeterred by the approaching birth of his child, her husband had left her, disappearing almost professionally when he realized his lawyers could not break the terms of her trust. Devoted to son and church, she taught Charles her own father's belief in ambition, hard work, husbandry, for poverty was the end of safety, a casting upon the waters. Her trust assured her a decent life and protected her into middle age; she sold bonds to pay for Charles' education at Notre Dame: engineering — solid, architectural, eminently useful. His fine arts instructors encouraged him, invited him into their circles, but he demurred, consciously denying the father whose chiseled profile, stylistic flair, and dark good looks were his only legacy. Charles modeled his behavior, if not his meticulous dress, on the portly maternal grandfather who'd provided for him even in death. He went to work immediately after graduation, easily supporting his mother and himself until her last illness depleted all. Charles borrowed to assure that she was privately nursed and died in her own bed. Then he broke up the house, sold everything to cover the debt, accepted Dunnegan's transfer to Park Ridge. He'd begun again, and found rooms with the Eichers.

Lavinia had opened the door to him, smilingly remarking that he resembled the Arrow collar man just then familiar from advertisements. No, he'd assured her, he made an honest living with the respected Dunnegan Company, and he held before him the newspaper in which Asta's notice had appeared. "I am Charles O'Boyle," he told Lavinia, "the gentleman roomer you seek."

He became Asta's confidant, her trusted friend.

They knew one another's secrets. Asta was German, not Danish, brought up in London and schooled in Copenhagen. She'd met Heinrich at the Artists League and married into his secular Jewish family. The Eichers were moneyed, assimilated intellectuals, all of them passed away, save Lavinia, who managed an inheritance at the behest of her only son. They'd emigrated in luxury on the *Queen Mary,* a wedding trip: husband, wife, and the husband's elegant mother, a kindly dowager whose every remonstrance to her new daughter was couched in compliments. Lavinia had purchased the Chicago apartment, then the

Park Ridge Victorian with the expansive barn; she supported the growing family with deepest pleasure. The children didn't know they were half-Jewish. It was collusion Heinrich had framed and sealed in his marriage to a Lutheran. Asta insisted on Lutheran religious education for her children; they'd chosen Park Ridge for its Lutheran community and the artisans' collective husband and wife immediately joined, as much as for Heinrich's ongoing insurance employment in Chicago. The inheritance wouldn't last forever, though it might have ensured good schools for the children had Heinrich lived.

He had not. The Eichers were a charmed and beautiful village on which dark stars fell. Misfortune was common, of course, but the family persevered with such well-bred patience, and made of pretense a brave and moral art.

The holidays made much of celestial markers. Wonder. Light. *Royal beauty bright.* Charles had spent every Christmas Day, the past four years, in this house. Yes, it was that long now. Usually he arrived for tea, arms laden, and stayed for dinner. Good he'd allowed more time this year. Yesterday was calmer, time alone with Anna to talk, observe. He hadn't seen them since Thanksgiving. Lavinia had died that night, and he'd canceled his appointments, stayed on to help with arrangements, sleeping in the room he'd

33

left two years ago. Yesterday, on his arrival, Anna made a point of directing Hart to "the guest room" with Charles' bag. Annabel of course followed, carrying the parcels of presents, except for the very large one, which he'd left on the porch behind the wicker swing. Anna watched approvingly as the children clambered up the stairs. He'd glanced at her, surprised, and she nodded, indicating that yes, he would sleep in Lavinia's room, undoubtedly the first "guest" to occupy it.

"Charles," she said, and took his arm. "Let Hart settle you in. I'll take your overcoat, and that lovely white scarf. There's tea in the dining room."

Perhaps, when they'd come to their arrangement, she would address him differently. My dear, she would say, and he would answer, My darling Anna, my dear Anna, for she was very dear to him. Making money, flying as though driven, he'd lost sight of what mattered, including her, and this home, even the idea of home. Sending the children souvenirs, postcards, valentines, from Mexico, Canada, California, as though to reserve what he couldn't embrace, he knew his attentions pleased Anna; his every remembrance of the children was a gift to her.

He rose now from Lavinia's bed, a strange thought, though everything in the room was changed. The closets were empty. Anna had told him she'd discarded the sheets and bedding, even the curtains and rug, warning Annabel days in advance. Her grandmother no longer needed a room; she did not need earthly things; a room was not a shrine. The floor was bare, the bedspread a simple muslin coverlet. Wooden half-shutters afforded privacy. The room could house a maid or cook. Or not yet. Let them all first adjust to other changes: to his permanent residence, to a marriage and sacred contract, and the easing of financial burdens. He would free Anna, fund her work, upgrade the studio barn behind the house, which was now so shabby and run-down.

Charles had resources. Yes, he must make that point strongly. He'd prospered, invested well, risen in his profession, and he wanted to protect this family, cosset them, as much for his own sake. Theirs was the only unspoiled world he'd ever encountered. He would give generously, gladly. Money should mean more than discretion and foreign hotels. Far from home, he pursued his indulgences voraciously but avoided youth who might attach themselves, and anyone who spoke English, never revealing personal information, or even his name. He returned dazed and satiated from these sojourns, plunging into a work schedule grueling enough to provoke exhaustion and dreamless sleep.

This Christmas was bitterly cold. The radiators hissed.

Charles went to the window in his night-clothes, glimpsing the backyard outbuildings through denuded trees. The playhouse windows were partially shuttered. The studio behind, an expanded barn, sagged visibly. Quite an operation in its time, a thriving, part-time cooperative, numerous artisans forging Eicher designs marked with the lovely inverted EAE. He remembered Anna working when he'd roomed with the family, small pieces, but she couldn't support her design business after she was widowed.

He'd thought Lavinia's death a release for the family, as well as a sorrow, that her resources would go to Anna and the children. Now he knew that Lavinia's funds were exhausted. Years ago, she'd purchased the Cedar Street property with the understanding that her son would support her. Anna had mortgaged the house to pay expenses, and used Lavinia's savings to pay for medical bills and private nursing those last months. Charles should have known. He'd worked from home half a year, supervising his mother's care. But Anna had no income. And so this decision to sell her house, the only home her children had known, and do what?

His breath fogged the glass, and he placed his hand upon it. Instantly, the condensation withdrew and the laden pines appeared, their limbs piled with snow near the window. A

36

few strands of metallic tinsel, tangled in the branches, blowing wildly, no doubt bespoke Annabel's attempts to decorate the playhouse. Heinrich had built it when Grethe was a baby, anticipating the lively daughter she might have been. Now the starlike fissures in the playhouse window glittered with ice. Heinrich's death, yes. Sudden. Away from home, Charles recalled. An accident — a streetcar, a rail station. Exactly as might happen to anyone, to Charles, tomorrow or in ten years' time, and no one to care or bury him, unless he made a change.

He opened Lavinia's window wide and leaned forward onto the sill, chest deep in cold suspended air. The silence seemed doleful, eerie and total, the air very still. He fancied he heard, distantly, the jingling of bells. No, it was the dog, the skittering click of the terrier's nails as Duty made his way across floor and carpet runner, from Grethe's room to Hart's, to Charles' room, the guest room, for Charles was a guest.

The dog nudged his door, waiting. Charles shut the window and admitted his visitor. Duty walked briskly to the bed and jumped up, settling against the pillows before peering at him attentively. The baleful, slightly wall-eyed gaze seemed disconcertingly human. Charles leaned down to stroke the dog's short, alert ears and wondered guiltily if his leave-taking two years ago, necessary as it was, had contributed to Anna's present financial crisis. Selfishly, visiting on the odd weekend, he hadn't noticed the leaner look of things. Anna had sold most of the silver, Heinrich's designs and her own. The clocks from the mantels were gone, the German music box with the bell jar casing, and the lovely Danish cabinet with the blue tiles. Charles himself had purchased a tea set with classic, masculine lines, an early piece of Anna's she obviously valued, when he moved back to Chicago. He would bring it home; it belonged here. He could not restore what Anna had surrendered, but he could assure her safety.

He must shave. Go down early and speak with Anna, before the children wakened. The dog yipped at him once as though in reproof, and settled closer against the pillows.

Charles lathered his face, regarding himself in the mirror. Hart had arranged Charles' mug and shaving brush, just so beside the soap, as though to make him welcome. It wasn't ideal, a lone boy among women. And Hart, so aware he was the man of the house, would struggle in future to mitigate the needs of three females whose characters and requirements were so disparate.

Charles understood, especially on this day. Christmas moved, saddened, excited him. He'd loved the holiday as a child. All of

Chicago lit up. Mother took him skating before Christmas tea at one of the fine hotels, and he was confirmed near Christmas, an altar boy whose priest spoke of "our Father who will never forsake us." Mother adored Father Kerrigan and urged her son toward him, the better to supply Charles with good and holy influence. Innocently, Charles accepted the priest's attentions; he learned subterfuge, hypocrisy, secrecy at Father Kerrigan's knee, at his hands. He learned to hate the man's diminutive physical stature, his peppermint smell. The sound of his footsteps, the rustle of his vestments and surplice, provoked a sick, gnawing shame. Charles left the Church at fourteen, embraced academics, track, archery. Later, throughout the years at Notre Dame, he avoided services except at Advent and the Festival of Epiphany. The words of the Latin hymns, so familiar from childhood, made betrayal seem universal, his own confusions relative and unimportant.

Gaudete! Gaudete!
Christus est natus ex Maria virgine!
Gaudete!

He could, almost, rejoice, and his mother stood beside him, proud of his success, his excellent marks, his athletic prowess. A sprinter, he sailed over hurdles at all-conference meets, an acknowledged champion whose long legs flashed like blades. His mother had relocated to Bloomington and displayed his trophies there before their return to Chicago and the start of his career. But that home was gone, and Charles' apartment was not a home.

He ran the water hot, filling the small room with steam and shaving the lather from his face. He was needed here. He could have children. Not squalling infants but these very well-brought-up girls and boy with their European manners and courtesy, children whom he already regarded as family, like nieces and nephews. He would never interfere, of course, or presume to take their father's place, but Charles was not a stranger. Surely they'd accept him as their mother's husband, someone to care for her, and he did, truly. Grethe, at fourteen, was adolescent now; she would need protection, someone to see she met the right sort of man someday, or no man. Let the three of them go on happily, Asta, Charles, and Grethe, as Hart went off to school, and Annabel, the charming minx, opened a theater company. Joking. Perhaps she could become a librarian, settle her head-in-the-clouds sensibility. She was still young, chunky and solid, but would grow slender and tall, like Grethe, who was plain, thank God. Annabel, though, would be lovely, quick: that round, catlike face and high cheekbones, and sparkling hazel eyes.

Charles leaned into the mirror. He was still virile, attractive, but he'd torn himself on one shoal after another these last years, and righted the wreckage, never obvious, considerate of his job, his position, yet he'd aged, his face was fleshier, while Anna looked exactly as she'd looked five years ago. As she would look five years hence.

The age difference was not so great. He was nearly thirty-seven. Anna was forty-five.

He bent to wash off the last of the soap in the basin and thought of Hart, learning to shave soon, taught by whom? Charles knew the reality of widows and children, families drawn closer by the dampened fire. Perhaps it was why the Eicher home had so appealed. He'd recognized the tenor of feeling immediately. Intent on becoming a man of means, he'd arrived on Anna's doorstep, an aging orphan whose inclinations set him apart.

Inclinations: Anna's word. She saw his desires, his compulsions, as inclination, nothing more. Years ago, she'd spoken to him frankly, understanding all he didn't say. *Charles, you're getting older. The senses bank their fires. Other things grow more important.* Her dear, good face, her strength, her lovely gray eyes! And then she'd touched his wrist and whispered, beseeching him: *You must be careful. Promise me you'll be cautious.*

41

Amazing what women knew if they cared for one.

Anna, what depths were yours? What tortured you? He would know. She would tell him as they lay side by side, her hands in his. He would install his gramophone on the large corner table in her room, his record collection on the shelf below, and play for her all those sweeps and phrases that set his mind aflame. He was certain he could perform if called upon. Yes, why not? If that was what she wanted.

A man was not one thing.

The pathology of hiding and shame was the harmful element. The Greeks had not regarded love and morality within modernity's narrow frame. And he carried Catholicism's weight. He'd not told his mother of his experience, his helpless anger, but she knew or suspected, or she'd never have accepted his lapse of faith, his refusal to enter any sacristy. He'd walk her to confession if he was at home, and sit smoking outside on the broad bench beside the street. He imagined that boys coming and going from services glanced at him, and once a tall young priest met his eyes openly, then turned away without speaking. Charles' temples burned, thinking of it.

The risks he'd allowed himself. The devastation he'd narrowly escaped, or not entirely. But that was past, must all be past.

He bathed his eyes in the water once more and toweled his moist skin dry. He'd taken care. None of it would follow him, but he could not combat his tendencies alone, nor trace the confusion to one cause. He must gain focus, stability, reason to live differently.

Now he stood at the bedside, listening. The dog yawned and stretched on the coverlet, watching him. Charles chose a pleated shirt with French cuffs from his open suitcase and dressed carefully in a suit made for him in the Loop by a London tailor. He thought of Anna in her room, awake, he was certain, lying still before the tumult of the day. Snow was falling steadily. Last night, after Anna went up, he'd placed his presents for them under the lavishly ornamented tree, retrieving the large one from the porch. He'd purchased a fine gold locket for Anna, and a set of tortoiseshell combs, but he wished he'd bought her a ring, an engagement ring. Better if he'd planned his proposal, rather than reacted to news of her rash plans. No — best to be completely honest. He could say, honestly, that they were the only family he knew, that he loved her deeply and more devotedly than any mere paramour could or would, that he cared for her children as she did. He'd no idea her circumstances were so dire. He would make it up to her, to the children, to himself.

Why should all be denied him? He felt

confident, hopeful; he would display that confidence and hope. Their faces shone before him. He'd left prayer behind, forcibly, forever, but his soul turned toward them.

He sat on the bed, the smell of his clean face and throat like flowers near him. Too early to go down, perhaps. He pulled the dog onto his lap. "There, there," he said, "Duty, you silly creature. We shall see."

ANNA, ASTA, ANNA

"Annabel, darling, we simply can't have candles burning in rows across the living room carpet. You may mark off the space with blocks or books, and the curtain will make a border for the stage." Asta, checking Grethe's table settings, moved a water goblet slightly higher, to the tip of the knife.

Annabel turned to regard her mother and said, in a conversational tone, "The rooms where Grandmother's gone are very dark."

Why did she say such things? Asta touched her palm to Annabel's forehead: no fever. She stroked her daughter's soft, tousled bangs, and kept her tone even. "Annabel, your grandmother is surely in heaven, and heaven, surely, is not dark. Don't speak that way, and on Christmas, and before company." Asta looked to Charles, sitting companionably near her, his chair pushed back from the long table.

"I'm not company," Charles offered, "but

you should listen to your mother."

Annabel stood motionless, as though declaiming to them both. "The rooms lead one to another, down below. Outside there's a meadow full of sounds and creatures. Crickets, whirring and buzzing. And birds, singing and clicking."

"It must be summer there," Charles said.

"Annabel, that's enough." Asta pretended to consternation with the punch bowl, which she was about to fill for the sideboard. "Go and help your sister plate the figs and chocolate."

"She doesn't like me to help with her settings."

"Nonsense. Go on now, and Charles will be in shortly to help with your theater curtain."

Annabel gave her mother a long look, then turned on her heel. Goodness, that child! Asta watched her leave the dining room, touching a hand along the high back of every chair, her lace curtain cloak drawn about her. Her short dark hair, grown now to the nape of her neck, glimmered like a silken cap.

Charles stood to help with the crystal bowl, holding it steady while Asta poured it full from pitchers of cream soda and seltzer. "I must say, I like the short haircut. Very stylish. Has our Annabel been reading about flappers and gin joints?"

"No, but it does suit her." She didn't mention Annabel's dramatic gesture, two days after Lavinia's funeral. She'd cut her braids off just at her ears, and taken them in her pockets to lay atop her grandmother's grave at St. Luke's cemetery, three blocks away. Charles had left for the city, and Asta had not sent word, lest he rush back, when he'd already spent a week helping them. "I'm putting out six cups, Charles. Annabel will want one for Mrs. Pomeroy, who — just to prepare you — plays Lavinia in the pageant."

"Our girl is fanciful," Charles said, "and misses her grandmother."

"Yes, she does." There'd been nothing for it but to send Hart to retrieve the braids while Asta sat Annabel on a high stool in the kitchen and cut her hair, feathering it at the chopped bits with Lavinia's sharpest sewing shears. Very short hair, troubadour style, was the fashion, she announced, aware that Annabel understood the term and would repeat it next day in school. She didn't want her daughter teased. She'd spoken to Annabel's teacher so frequently; she hadn't the heart to discuss the haircut as well, but noticed, at a class concert the next weekend, that several other girls had cut their hair short, in imitation or adulation.

"Punch!" Charles announced, "but I won't ice it yet." He turned to Asta. "How are the children doing, really, do you think?"

"Grethe is helpful. Hart does very well at

school, tries to be perfect. Annabel seems cheerful enough, but she brings her grandmother into everything. It worries me. I tried to get her to use Christmas colors in her pageant, but she insists everyone wear white, and has dragged out the contents of one of Lavinia's chests. We shall be surprised at what manner of thing adorns the players. Tablecloths, curtains, sheets with monograms, doilies perhaps — time will tell!"

"Annabel does need time, Asta. All of you do. Her plays are a way to see things through. Better she chooses white than black. And let her have her candles. Just give me some paper lunch sacks. I'll fill them with sand from the bucket on the porch, and arrange them as luminarias, placed just as she directs. Let her have her way and feel she's made a success."

"I suppose, but she's nine years old, precocious, and so preoccupied with fairies and spirits and pronouncements. Hart says she talks in her sleep, and I often hear her, perfectly alone in her room, whispering away."

"The plays are her games. She's her own society. And she *is* providing our only after-dinner entertainment. The more elaborate, I say, the better." He reached to touch her hand. "Anna, Anna. I'd love to see you smile."

Looking at him, so tall and handsome and beloved, she did smile. He wore a man's oilcloth apron that Heinrich had worn in the workshop, years ago. Those aprons were indestructible, unlike so much else. But all that could change. She thought of the letters in her bureau drawer, tied with silk twine, one nearly every day for the past weeks. Still smiling, she felt a blush rise to her face, and her eyes moistened.

"That's better," Charles said. Noticing her warm glance at his attire, he untied the apron and thrust it into her arms.

She laughed, folding the thick thing in squares, smaller and smaller, just as she had years ago, walking through the grass from the workshop on summer evenings with Heinrich. They worked hard on weekends while Lavinia entertained the children, then stayed up late *en famille,* eating fine meals Betty kept in the warmer, hand-turning ice cream, playing croquet by lamplight, listening to gramophone records. Heinrich loved teaching them ballroom dancing and boxing postures. Annabel was his poppet, his Nell, and Hart followed him everywhere. There were good things to remember, things she must hold fast.

Charles had followed her into the kitchen. "Madam?" He put his gold cuff links in her hand and held up his wrists like a cooperative prisoner.

Anna fastened the French cuffs of his shirt and watched approvingly as he pulled on his suit coat. He was fine and dear and she would miss him. But surely he would forgive her someday, and visit them often. He seemed much valued at Dunnegan, and came and went as business dictated. He would stay for holidays, just as now. Cornelius' Iowa holdings were not so far from Chicago, and she would write to Charles from the property in the South, explaining all. Better to tell him by letter. All was so clear when one held a letter in one's hand. One's handwriting was intimate, a reflection of one's deepest nature. Cornelius had spoken volumes; page after page of his flowing script had comforted and led and reassured her; he'd questioned with her, answered, deepened their bond to one of lasting strength.

"Anna." Charles touched her hair, smoothing it back from her face. "Sit down with me. We've been working from the moment we lay eyes on one another this morning. The bird is in one oven and the vegetables in the other. Everything must cook. And I insist we have a glass of wine."

"Yes, let's do. Where shall we have it?"

"In the dining room, at our own Christmas table."

His warm touch was on her shoulders. Dear Charles. He'd insisted on ordering in all the provisions, for he knew the local tradesmen, apologizing that he hadn't time to actually bake the pies this year but thought the children would appreciate apple and cherry tarts, as well as a chocolate *bûche de Noël* and another treat he'd kept fastened in a cardboard cake box. A surprise, he'd said.

"I must speak with you now, Anna. You must give me leave." He turned her to face him, and looked quite grave. There was a high color in his cheeks.

A chill gripped her heart. He might be ill. She knew this happened. Lavinia's husband, Heinrich's father, had died young, hidden away in a sanatorium, poisoned with the mercury antidote to his disease. Lavinia had known, never reproached him, and stayed with him to the end. "Of course, Charles," Anna said. "What is it? You're not ill?"

He smiled to reassure her, and put his mouth against her hair. They stood quite still for a moment. "No, of course I'm not ill," he said.

Anna was too relieved to speak. Such a catastrophe would have canceled everything. She could not have left Charles, alone and facing terrible difficulty. She felt him take her hand and followed him to the dining room.

"Shall we?" He held the opened wine, and touched her fingers to his mouth.

She laughed. "Charles, you're such a storybook character today."

"My dear," he said behind her, "we live storybook lives. Do open your eyes and observe."

The dining room before them was transformed. Clearly, Charles had been under

50

orders to distract her in the kitchen while Grethe and Annabel, who stood expectantly at the end of the table, finished preparing their tableau. The votive candles inside the cardboard houses and church of the Christmas village were lit, and the little houses glowed in a long row down the length of the table beyond the place settings. Grethe had arranged pine boughs and cotton snow, mirrors for skating ponds, the miniature flocked trees. Annabel had no doubt placed the little porcelain figures, ice skaters and shopkeepers, children with sleds, men in top hats, women carrying parcels. They were Lavinia's fine hand-painted German Christmas sets, and they stood about in conversational groups, glided motionless atop their reflections, or bent to their work, all in concert.

"Girls, it's so beautiful." Anna felt Charles gently embrace her from behind and was glad, for she was almost faint. The chandelier's teardrop crystals caught the dipping sparkle of the candles and the gold of the stenciled border on the cranberry walls. Such a warm color for a dining room, Lavinia had said, and stood on a ladder to paint the stenciled pattern, a filigree of barely present fleur-de-lis.

"Mother, I lit the candles for Grethe." Annabel held out a stump of matchbook, beaming. Anna could see the soot on her fingertips, and a dark little smear on her cheek.

"I'm very glad I dressed appropriately," Charles said into Anna's hair. "This is the most beautiful Christmas table ever seen by man or angels."

"Man or angels," Annabel repeated, clearly impressed with the phrase.

"She did very well," Grethe said, "but she wouldn't use the kitchen matches. She wanted to use the old matchbooks from Grandmother's collection."

"Never mind," Charles said. "That's fine, Grethe. And now your mother and I will have a glass of wine, and enjoy your work while you guess what's in those presents."

The girls, under strict orders never to leave candles burning in a room, turned away to finish their preparations. Anna sat gratefully. Charles pulled his chair close beside hers, and offered his handkerchief. "There, you see? Everything is going to be all right, Anna."

She took the wine he poured for her and felt its warmth in her mouth. "Annabel insists on keeping Lavinia's old matchbooks. She found a cache of them and won't let me throw them out. She likes to arrange them in rows on the kitchen table."

"They're interesting," Charles said. "Little pictures of Copenhagen and London, names of exotic restaurants, but I'm surprised the matches still light. Look, our dramatist has written the place cards with great style."

Annabel had written their names in script that approximated Lavinia's, with swooping serifs on all the capital letters. Well, let her. Charles was right. She must express it all, somehow. Anna saw that Grethe had assigned Charles the seat at the head of the table, with Asta to his right, and Hart to his left, and the two girls opposite one another. They were all so happy to see him. She herself was so glad she'd not invited the Verbergs or the Breedloves, neighbors who would have kindly provided distraction, given Lavinia's death a month ago. Anna wanted this last Christmas in their home to be just for the five of them.

"All right?" Charles asked.

She nodded. She'd told Charles of her plan to sell the house; she would tell the children in the spring, after Cornelius visited; she'd no wish to involve the neighbors and their gossiping. She and Cornelius would protect their privacy and minimize the upset to the children. She glanced out the casement windows to the right of the long room. "Such snow," she told Charles. "So good that you arrived yesterday."

He held his wineglass to hers. "*Salud,* Anna. To the storm. It's lovely, because everyone we love is here."

Not everyone, Anna knew. But soon, in April, she hoped, when spring allowed easy travel and she could see to real estate decisions. Snow whipped against the house, drifting in the yard. Grethe had lit the gas sconces and the room glowed like a refuge.

"Anna," Charles was saying, "this is the perfect time and place to say what I have been wanting to say to you."

"Of course, then," Anna said. "What have you to say to me? Shall I drink my wine down first?"

He looked at her with shining eyes and seemed to contemplate the question. "Umm, yes, have a bit more wine. And don't forget this drop." He put a finger gently to the corner of her mouth and drew it across her lips.

She smiled into his face. He'd seemed to her a handsome younger brother when they first met. Now he was her counterpart and adviser, and so attentive and courtly today. She felt as though they were playing a scene together, a scene in which she was young and whole and knew nothing, and he was her well-intentioned suitor.

Holding her gaze, he took her hands. "Anna, there is no one I can or would love as I love you. You are right to think of change, but the change should be ours. Let us be together, Anna, always and completely."

"Charles, what are you proposing?"

"I'm proposing marriage, Anna. Marry me and let me take care of you. You are my family and I am yours. If I can't be a father to your children, I can be their friend and guardian and constant support, and love them as my own."

"Charles —" She could not answer. He'd thought on this, to help them, and was quite serious, and would be deeply wounded.

He took her response as encouragement. "I'm doing very well, and will do even better when this wretched Depression ends. There is no need to sell the house. Let me support and help you as one who loves you, as your husband, Anna, devoted only to you. Let us truly be a family."

She leaned toward him, her heart pounding. "But, Charles. Wait, please —"

"Yes, Anna? Yes?" He put his face gently against hers.

Her temple fit against his smooth, warm cheek, and she felt the tense, strong line of his jaw. Fleetingly, she thought, If only he was different. But he was not. "Oh, Charles," she whispered, "what you suggest entails such sacrifice. I cannot let you."

He whispered in kind, in a rush of emotion. "That is over, Anna, that is over. It has not made me happy and it is over." He pulled away to look at her. "Understand that I dedicate myself to you and the children completely; I will not deceive you or myself, ever, ever again. I pledge my fidelity and my means and my life." He saw that she was crying, looking at him as though stricken. "I will make you happy, Anna. I love you completely. I can be a husband to you, in every way. Let me."

Anna gripped his arm. The room, the very air, seemed to pull her backward as though into a deep well. "Heinrich once denied himself, and sacrificed his true desire at my request, completely and for always, and then he died, Charles, he died. But for me, oh, I know he would have lived —"

"Anna, what are you saying? It was an accident, a motorcar —"

"A streetcar, Charles, in the Loop. Yes, in the snow. There was a great deal of snow, on the tracks and everywhere, and the crowd —" She stood suddenly.

"Shhhh, Anna, be quiet, be quiet and try to breathe."

They were in the kitchen. He was holding her in his arms at the sink and bathing her face with cold water, icy water that tasted of salt. He pushed her sleeves up and held her wrists under water that dropped in galloping clumps into the deep double sink.

"Anna, sit down." He helped her into a kitchen chair and knelt beside her. "You aren't making sense."

"You are so good, Charles, so good to me, and I thank God for my good fortune, that I am not required to accept your sacrifice, but I ask you to wait —" She pushed him a little away, bracing her arms against him. "Trust me, for I will explain in time, and you will be my good friend, just as you are now —"

"Of course I'm your friend. And you must listen to me. Heinrich died in an accident. Whatever was between you had nothing to do with it. Do you hear me?"

"Yes." Her eyes were wet and dark.

"You are confusing regret with responsibility. It was reasonless. That is the meaning of 'accident.' " He paused. "Anna, why have you never told me of these feelings? Why did you never speak of this?"

She looked past him, into the room. "So much is becoming clear to me. A great change must happen. Is about to happen."

"Anna, the change should be that I am here with you, and we are married. Promise me that you will not dismiss me. Think on what I've said, when you are calmer. And you must not make any decisions that we don't discuss. Look at me, Anna."

She took the wet, squeezed towel with which he'd bathed her forehead, and held it to her face. She would not tell him, and she would not take advantage of him. His offer had moved her, blinding her with remembrance. "Yes, all right. I'm all right, Charles. I don't know what came over me."

"It's very hard to be alone," he said.

"Yes, it's hard." She smiled at him tenderly, knowing she was not alone. The letters in her room were a presence, constant and deep.

"I'll stay a few days. We'll think it through," Charles said. "Do you mind?"

"Of course not; you're welcome to stay." She drew him to her and kissed his forehead. How would he, how could he ever, find the heart's companion she had found? The world would not allow him.

He stood and lifted her to her feet. "Are you recovered?" He sighed as she nodded affirmation. "Anna, I feel as though we have traveled a great distance. I've surprised you, I know, but I've told you of my deepest hope. Anna, depend on me."

"Charles." She realized he must have carried her into the kitchen like one of Annabel's pageant heroes, and touched her palm to his face. "We love you very much. It would never be Christmas here without you."

A crash resounded from the living room. They heard Hart's cries of "Duty! Duty! Give it up!"

"I'll go," Charles said. "We'd best have the pageant soon."

Annabel has taken off her shoes in order to stand on the camelback sofa and attempt to hang the theater curtain for her pageant play. Grandmother had made the curtain long ago, for what Annabel can't remember; it is red velvet in two floor-to-ceiling panels. Grandmother kept it rolled like a rug around a cardboard tube between shows, to prevent it wrinkling, and now Annabel is in charge of it. Last night Charles fetched a length of rope from his trunk in the garage and helped her thread it through the sewn panel at the top. Rope will hang it so much better than cord, and reach from one wall sconce to the other, across the living room. If only she had a piece of white organdy, big as a bedspread, gauzy and see-through, to hang as a backdrop with the Christmas tree's lit candles shining through: heaven behind the players in the glade. It is the sort of idea Grandmother would have liked, and Annabel imagines Lavinia, just for a moment, standing as she did on Christmas mornings, in her vanilla wool robe with the silk cuffs. Her pink leather slippers were patterned after ballet shoes and fit so nicely, with one silk strap across. They are *palest rose,* and French. Annabel has them still, under her bed in a special box. She has put them on her feet, but they are far too big; Grandmother was vain of her long thin feet and high arches. Some nights, Annabel sleeps with them, for the kid soles are clean and smooth. Turned in together, they are the size of a thin doll tucked under her arm; Duty would sneeze at the lavender scent when he lay his head upon them. *Heaven is certain,* Grandmother had said. So it will appear in today's pageant.

She reconsiders: a backdrop would only mute the effect. The players are in a forest, their backs to the glowing candles and tinsel shimmer. Annabel gazes around the room, balanced on the sofa back. "Hart," she calls out. "Come and help me tie up the curtain."

He appears from the hallway, tossing his juggling balls. Duty runs at his heels, ready to fetch one when it drops, for it always does. Hart glances at Annabel. "You'd better hope Mother doesn't see you there."

"It's angled against the wall," she says, "and won't tip. You don't have on your costume."

"I'm not putting it on until the last minute."

"Hart, you said one should wear one's costume beforehand, to get into character."

"It's a window curtain. God's sake, I'm not going to walk around in it."

"It's embroidered in gold and hangs quite nicely, if you'll pin it like I said. And Mother doesn't like you talking that way. Did you practice the voices?"

"Sister, I practiced for hours. What's here? Your shoes? Thrown down just where I'm walking. I might have tripped!" He's field goal kicker as well as quarterback on the freshman football team, and takes aim in perfect form, arms outspread, kicking one of her Mary Janes hard into the air. Duty is immediately after it, barking wildly. The shoe skims shining through the prisms of the chandelier and bounces off the wooden baseboard under the window, hitting the dog in the face. Duty snarls and grasps it by the strap, shaking it viciously.

"Hart, he's going to mark it with his teeth, and make it filthy wet!"

Hart is after him, eyes alight. He catches the cord of the heavy brass floor lamp, which crashes to the floor resoundingly as he leaps over it. "Duty! Duty! Give it up!" The terrier races away with the shoe, skittering behind the sofa and out in a burst of speed.

Charles comes rapidly in from the kitchen. "Annabel, get down from there! I told you I'd hang the curtain. What fell? What's going on? Anything broken here? Are *you* broken?"

"Nooooo." She lifts her chin and peers at him through her lashes.

"Aren't you the coquette. Did you tease Duty to mischief?" He helps her alight, as though from a coach.

She looks up, wide-eyed. "I never, Charles. Hart kicked my shoe to be smart."

"And he is, very smart, but I hope he hasn't broken your mother's favorite lamp." Charles rights the pink silk shade, reaching up under the fringe to feel for the bulb. "Ah, there. It was only loose." He twists it tight, and the lamp glows again, lighting up the Chinese scene embroidered in the silk. "You'll undermine your own play," he tells her seriously, "with all this drama."

"We haven't hung the curtain or got the costumes on, or even lit the tree yet," she says. "They'll forget."

"You're not actually nine years old, are you?"

"My teacher says I'm more ten than nine, and might have skipped a grade." She picks up her shoe and displays it on her palm. "I like your winter scarf, that you wore yesterday. It's white."

"You're more thirty than twenty," Charles says, "and yes, my scarf is white silk. You want it for your play."

"Everyone is in white. Like angels."

"Hall closet," Charles says, "in the sleeve of my overcoat. As long as you won't have the dog mauling it."

She knew he would say yes. She hears Duty rush past again in the hallway, round the corner at the banister, and start upstairs, slowed by his ascent. He's big chested and strong jowled, but short in the legs and sausage shaped; Hart will catch him easily.

Her mother stands in the doorway, holding Hart by the arm. "Are we put to rights here? Hart, be still. Let Duty go. He's running because you're chasing him. He'll drop the shoe as soon as he thinks you've stopped playing. Charles, here are the paper sacks for the luminarias. Eight should certainly be enough, and I have glass holders for the votive candles."

"What are luminarias?" Annabel, pleased, smoothes her lace-curtain cape.

"For your footlights. Charles' idea. And

you're to do exactly as he says." Her mother steps over to give Charles the sacks, and he drapes an arm around her, pulling her companionably close. Annabel notes that her mother fits under Charles' arm, exactly as the woman should fit to the man. Perhaps she will write a play for grown-ups, and her mother and Charles will perform it. She could dispense with a narrator and write herself a part at last.

"I'll find Duty," Hart says.

"No," Charles replies. "I'll find Duty. Fill these sacks half full with sand from the bucket on the porch. Then you will take them carefully to the kitchen, and your mother will set the candles. You must all make haste. Dinner is served at noon sharp."

"Charles," asks Annabel, "what is in that very big box behind the tree? I know you won't tell. Do you know, Mother?"

"I have no idea." She steps over to have a look. "Heavens, Charles, when did you bring in such a big box?"

"Last night. You were all dreaming of sugarplums. It's for the children."

"It's a race car with a motor," Hart says. "Or a team of sled dogs, asleep and folded up."

Charles gives him the sacks. "To your task, my man."

"Hart, your costume is on your bed," Annabel prompts him. "For when you come in from the porch." She knows what their mother will say next.

"Put on your coat and hat," their mother tells Hart. "It's snowing to beat the band."

Annabel, her shoe in her hand, gazes at the crèche atop the shiny piano. She's quite disappointed that the Verbergs aren't coming, for they always clap loudly and make exclamations. And she will have to put up with Hart's additions and tricks, as he must amuse himself. Grethe, her stalwart, can be counted upon to strike the right attitudes while Annabel says her words. They always have flowers at the end for Mother, but today there are no flowers. Hart said he had no allowance to spend on them; in fact, they've all made their presents for one another this year. Mother said this was the true spirit of Christmas, but Annabel knows they are being provident.

The piano is shut to save the keys, and Annabel places her shoe there. The living and dining room sconces are gaslit and scarcely used, but one glows now above the crèche, day and night, until Epiphany. Grethe said it means the eternal flame, a phrase Annabel noticed but hadn't time to question. Her present to her mother, in response to direct request, must be her "Play for Christmas," and Annabel has typed the words, key by key, on the old Corona typewriter Charles had left in the back bedroom. The pages look well enough, with the cutouts of doves pasted on. Hart consented to type in the lines he planned to ad-lib, though he didn't promise to say exactly those, for *ad-lib* meant to improvise, and one could never tell if Duty would perform as instructed. She told him he was so annoying to ruin her play and he lectured her about setting off the serious bits with humor, if she insisted on using a rag doll as a character. To make it up, he stapled the pages into a cover. The glade, he said, was a good idea, at least.

Annabel leans in to peer at the crèche and wishes for a magnifying glass, to see the faces on the figures. Only Grethe is trusted with the crèche; she prizes the Holy Family, the kings, the shepherds, the angel holding the banner, the sheep and cows that stand and lie in real straw. It was their mother's crèche, in her childhood. Annabel looks closely at the white feet and delineated toes of Mary and Joseph, who are barefoot; the kings' and shepherds' feet are covered by layered robes and tunics. The colors were painted in Italy long ago; the white of the bisque seems to glow from within the pinks and browns and blues and scarlets.

Dreamily, Annabel scoops a handful of straw from within the stable and stuffs it loosely into the shoe she holds in her hand. She folds under the strap and puts the Baby

Jesus, who lies molded in his swaddling clothes, into her shoe amongst the straw. She pulls her lace cloak around the Christ protectively and takes him to the big window, standing close against the glass to let him feel the cold. The Palladian window in the living room is like a door of falling snow, for the window starts at her knees and runs upward nearly to the ceiling. Annabel breathes with the snow, holding the shoe to her chest, until she hears sounds upstairs. Quickly she covers the Christ with her hand and moves to the piano. The crèche scene is much changed. Joseph's flared fingers are alarmed. Even the animals gaze pointedly at the empty porcelain hole, and Mary's prayerful expression strikes in Annabel a tiny thrill of fear. She puts back the Christ, which fits snugly in, porcelain lip to lip, like one tray inside another.

She sees that her glade must be littered with straw, and the lights off but for the gaslit sconces, and reaches behind the crèche, where Grethe has heaped the extra straw. She sweeps it all into her arms. The players will be barefoot, of course. It would have been ridiculous otherwise. She will write in her final changes.

Outside, Hart is shoveling, clearing the walk. Be sure it's clear to the street, his mother kept telling him, as though anyone would arrive in the middle of a storm, and on Christmas. The Verbergs and Breedloves have gone away to relatives and their porch lights glow eerily in the snowy whirl. Lit trees twinkle in the parlor windows of houses up and down Cedar Street. All is deserted. The snow is so deep that he will have to rescue Duty if the dog even walks into the yard.

"Stay there, Duty," Hart calls. "Stay on the porch."

Snow falls in pieces and great puffs, like a magic show. He still has to fill the luminarias, and put on the round tablecloth Annabel says is his costume. God, how they cater to Annabel, but she's the closest he has to a brother and at least gets up to things, while Grethe is more and more quiet, as Mother presses her into more cleaning and arranging. Nothing must be moved or touched in the whole downstairs, or she puts it back again. Irritating how she has gotten so pious, and is a full head taller than he.

Girls made presents, it was easy for them, but what was he to make?

By accident, he'd gotten something nice for everyone.

Grethe will like her beads, strung on knotted string with a cross. Lutherans had no need of rosaries, his mother said when he showed her, but these were Venetian beads, and a real gold cross; wherever did he find it? She insisted he say. He told her about the Catholic church rummage sale, on Saturday mornings. He didn't tell her about the girls that ran it. The one with auburn hair said he must look her up when he was out of knickers. They were cheeky girls, and let him look through boxes in the back. He traded his jar of cat's-eye marbles for a pair of tarnished cuff links — Charles always wore posh shirts with turned-back cuffs. And he gave his Tom Mix books for a doll's celluloid vanity and chair. It was yellowish, like vanilla ice cream, and would fit Mrs. Pomeroy, Annabel's daft rag doll. The girls prized the vanity and wrapped it carefully in layers of pink tissue from the hatboxes that toppled everywhere in leaning tiers.

Duty is barking, biting at snow blown on the wind. Hart rounds off the opening to the street between the hedges and starts back, running the shovel before him, sliding and skidding.

He's in a quandary about the present he found for his mother — a silver ladle, tarnished nearly black, tossed on a tray of unsorted dinnerware at the Catholic rummage, but he'd picked it up and felt the raised A on the handle, then saw her mark on the back. He'd asked how much. Oh, have it, said the girl, and dropped it in the box with the doll furniture, the cuff links in their velvet ring box, the rosary in its hosiery pouch. Hart polished the cuff links and ladle, with rags and the strong-smelling salve in the garage, until they shone; he knew to wear gloves, and he liked how the dark lifted off in oily smears. His mother would love having the ladle she made come back to her, as she didn't make anything anymore, but where would he say he'd gotten it? She can't know that someone threw it out, or worse, died and lost it to a rummage sale. And she will know unless he lies, for she knows where he got the rosary. He has nothing else to give her.

"God," he says aloud, and "God!" again, in frustration.

On his knees, he begins filling the luminaria sacks with sand. The wind gusts and he ducks his head, squinting, pulling the open bags closer to the front door. Halfway full, Charles said. Hart spades sand into one bag after another, using his mother's garden trowel to throw sand, every other spadeful, over Duty's head onto the icing steps. Duty rushes to and fro, chasing it.

Snow swirls and the sun is a dull glow. Hart looks out and sees headlights, searching slowly along the unplowed street. A flower delivery van stops just at their walk; a red-faced man emerges, coatless, wearing a stocking cap and coveralls.

The man comes inside the hedge, leaving the van running and the door open. "This the Eicher residence?" he shouts. "Asta Eicher?"

"This is the forest glade and luminaria factory," Hart calls back. "It is my glade and my factory."

"Are ye drunk, boy? Shall I ring the bell?"

"No, it's my house." Hart stands, brushing the sand from his jacket. "I'm Hart Eicher."

The deliveryman produces a swathed object, stepping along the snowy walk in an odd, dancelike gait until he stands at the bottom of the steps. "Well, come here then, lad, and give these to your sister, that's a good lad. I've miles to go. The devilish truck is full."

Hart breathes in the roar of the man's breath. He's the one who's drunk, and thrusts the vase into Hart's arms. Turning, he gains the van and slams the door. The van rumbles and lurches off into the middle of the drifted street.

The flowers look to Hart like a bandaged head on a pedestal. He rips off the paper, pocketing the small sealed envelope that falls out. They're red carnations, a slew of them, perfect for Annabel's purposes. Charles has certainly sent them, and won't mind if they're delivered as part of the pageant. Hart is cheered, for he will put the flowers under the sofa and produce them at the end in a flourish.

He hears a sound then, an immense groan overhead, and a crack like a rifle shot. A tall bent pine near the house breaks before his eyes, dropping a slide of snow, throwing off clouds of spray. The tree lands soundlessly across the drifts and the front walk. One long branch reaches up onto the porch like a finger.

The pageant was put off, for the goose was done and cooling before the children could ready themselves, and everyone was hungry. Charles carved the bird as they passed the plates, while Asta served vegetables: the garlic mashed and brandied sweets, the peas and green beans, the oyster dressing, cranberry relish, and onion chutney, and hot giblet gravy for every plate. The children sipped punch from their cups, water from their goblets, clear cream soda from their wineglasses, drinking toasts. Grethe and Annabel cleared and rinsed the Haviland dishes while Hart was told which dessert plates to take from the good china. The Cambridge glass with the gold rims, yes, would look best with the bright tarts, while the *bûche de Noël* elicited sighs. No sooner had Charles sliced the chocolate, giving a meringue mushroom to each child, than he brought out the surprise: swans that were cream puff pastries, their flaky wings dusted in powdered sugar, their long regal necks and proud heads a perfect first bite. Everyone cheered. Only Annabel placed her swan before her like a prize and said she would keep it always. Her mother told her it would spoil, but she maintained she would freeze it in a block of ice and keep it in the snow.

Finally, all was in readiness.

Annabel insisted Charles draw the heavy drapes across the windows, for snow had ceased falling and the afternoon light had gone brighter. The candles were lit on the Christmas tree behind the players, and the luminaria arranged in front like half-circle footlights. The setting was a forest glade on the last night of the year.

Asta settled herself. Charles looked at her, raising an eyebrow as he and Annabel stood back-to-back, each holding an edge of red curtain. *Presenting, a Play for Christmas,* Annabel announced, as she and Charles revealed the scene. Scattered straw softened the bare floor, and the twilit space before the tree did look a bit like a glade. Hart stood in place, looking off to the right. He was barefoot and bare legged, though his cloak, white damask embroidered in metallic gold thread, hung nearly to the floor. Jingling bells sounded softly as Grethe entered from the left. She looked quite lovely in her white velvet chorister's robe. Where had Lavinia gotten such a thing?

Annabel's play had to do with cold and snow and a wandering pilgrim on New Year's Eve. The angelic traveler had saved some unfortunate birds from a fox, thanks to her brave dog. Mrs. Pomeroy's toy high chair sat midstage, heaped about with straw. Hart worked in a few tricks for Duty, who performed rather well, and Annabel intoned offstage as Grethe struck her poses. Asta followed her every movement and quiet expression; Grethe was so practiced and comfortable in Annabel's tableaus.

Her sweet, quiet girl. Grethe puzzled at what her younger siblings understood so quickly. She didn't laugh at jokes and avoided children her own age, for which Asta was grateful. Grethe had attained her willowy height by age eleven, and her open face and guileless eyes prompted the wrong interest. Asta remembered her relief when Charles came to them, replacing those young men who'd rented rooms before him. Asta had caught one of them, Grethe close beside him on the sofa, showing her an art book featuring Rodin's marble sculptures.

Now Grethe produced Mrs. Pomeroy from beneath her cloak. Hart remarked on the Grandmother's small stature; the swaddled doll, a white veil covering her yarn hair, sat attentively in her chair. Asta took Charles' arm, aware that Annabel could see her, and laughed politely when Duty exceeded direction, knocking Mrs. Pomeroy on her face. She heard Lavinia's expressions in the lines, and her thoughts drifted anxiously to Grethe.

"Don't warn that child off men," Lavinia had hissed, "don't frighten her. How can we expect to find her a husband if you turn her from what she might enjoy?"

Lavinia had no inkling. Her physical relations with Heinrich's father had been genteel and infrequent, while he exercised his passions elsewhere; Heinrich had spoken of music tutors and tennis coaches, minor royalty and society men. The bedroom was truly a private chamber into which no mother gazed. Who would be kind to childlike Grethe, whose mind was that of the average eight-year-old? A religious vocation might be best; it would shelter and protect Grethe, allow her to be of service in some simple way. She loved ceremony, and knowing the order of events before they happened.

Confusingly, Annabel's shoes were onstage and Hart was wearing Charles' fedora and scarf. Oh yes, the actuary, who wrapped the white scarf about Grethe's neck. *Go onward now, for there is much to see and know.* Well, Asta would read the pages later and praise the author. Annabel could be so optimistic and so morbid, by turns! She now appeared, flushed with pleasure, for the singing. She had the good sense to always end her Christmas pageants with a carol. Annabel struck her triangle, a pure, true tone; they sang of sweet silver bells and cares thrown away.

Grethe stepped out for her solo, her voice as clear as running water, while Hart sang his lyrics in an assumed baritone, racing to tell the tale dramatically and lifting his arms to raise the sound, which set Duty to running and barking. The children joined hands. *All sing in jolly fashion,* directed the program. And indeed, the singers leaned toward the audience, overenunciating every joyful note. Charles beamed, and Duty, unbidden, executed the circle trick, turning about completely on his short bandy legs.

The players paused and stepped back. Annabel struck the triangle; the tone reverberated like the strike of a clock. The notes were true, sustained one to the other, and unbearably sad, for each opened the heart a little deeper.

Ding
dong
ding
dong

A beat of silence reigned, as though holding all concerned. Asta felt her breath return and found herself on her feet, cheering and applauding with Charles, who hugged the children all together and opened his arms to her. "Stupendous, incredible," Charles was shouting, and Duty ran wildly about, barking and jumping.

Hart reached under the sofa, drawing out dozens of brilliantly red carnations, which he plunged into Asta's arms, nearly upsetting her. The girls sighed their admiration and reached to touch; the flowers were layered depths of red blossoms and fern. "For you, Mother!" Hart exclaimed, dropping to one knee and sweeping off Charles' fedora like the plumed hat of a prince. "You don't mind, do you, Charles?" He stood to shed his cloak and return Charles' fedora.

"Mind? Certainly not," Charles said. "My compliments on the perfect gesture. Need help with those, Anna?"

Asta looked at him in thanks and knew instantly he had not sent them. She smiled happily and asked Grethe to get the large vase from the china cabinet. She would question Hart in private. The children were calling out, "Presents, presents," but Charles clapped his hands for order.

"You may open one present," Charles said, "and we'll do the rest later. No need to change costumes or disassemble the set. Now — which present?" He pretended surprise when they called enthusiastically for the very large one, and helped Hart move it from behind the tree.

Asta moved through the open pocket doors to the dining room table and put down the flowers, pouring the remains of the water goblets into the vase. There were fifty carnations at least. She'd not seen such a profusion of flowers in one arrangement since Heinrich's funeral. Lavinia's service had been small and private, but Heinrich's death had occasioned such an outpouring of surprise and grief. Huge bouquets kept arriving until she put a sign on the door asking that deliverymen take flowers directly to the church.

"Mother! Mother! Come along now, they're waiting!"

Asta looked up, startled. Heinrich had often addressed her as Mother in the children's presence, while he called his own mother by her given name, as though she were his contemporary, but today it was Charles, gesturing for Asta to join them. The children sat poised around the gift, which was wrapped in simple brown paper and a big red bow; she moved toward them as they tore the paper away in great ripping swaths.

She proceeded smoothly, by instinct almost, for she felt tremendous fatigue. She stopped Hart in the hallway, while the girls were upstairs changing and Charles outside, dragging the fallen pine tree from the walk. "Do you have something for me, Hart? The card, from the flowers?"

"Mother! A toboggan from Canada! I can take the fellows sledding!"

She stood waiting, wearing a benign expression, her open palm before her.

He reached into his pocket and thrust a small envelope into her hand. "I hate those hats though. Do I have to wear one? I have a winter cap."

"Oh, indulge him," Asta said, holding the card to her breast. "They're from Quebec, and quite warm and smart. He wants to photograph you three on the sled."

"They look like girls' hats."

"Well, look fierce. You heard Charles. They're patterned on French naval caps, and they do have a military air. Now, put on your galoshes. And bring the girls' boots to the front porch, as well."

"What takes girls so long?" he said, rushing past her.

Charles was coming in the front door, stomping his feet on the tiles of the entry. "Perfect snow for sledding! I've got the toboggan set. Where are the girls?" He stepped to the staircase. "Annabel? Bring my camera as you come down? On the bed in the . . . guest room. That's right. Don't drop it."

"Was it a large branch that fell, Charles?" Asta slipped the envelope into her shirtwaist.

"A small tree, I'd say. I'll saw it up tomorrow. Now, then. Are we ready?"

The girls appeared in their winter gear, and Hart in his; they put on the blousy winter hats, which were tight across the forehead and bound with thin red bands. They filed outside and Charles arranged them according to height, which he said was the balanced way to sled in a Canadian racing toboggan.

78

Asta followed, onto the porch, and watched him snap their picture. The wind whipped snow into her eyes and the children shielded their faces. The sky was a dark, bruised blue. Snow fell slowly, almost haphazardly.

"You won't stay too long, now, will you?" she called down.

"Everyone out till we get to the park," Charles said. "Hart, you can pull the sled." He was rushing up the steps to give Asta the camera. "Don't worry," he said quietly when he reached her. "They're with me. Go and rest. And don't touch a dish. They're rinsed, and Grethe and I will wash them later."

"You are dear, Charles. They're so excited."

"I'm excited." He was clambering back down the steps, and waved to her as they set off. "Go and rest."

"I will," she said, and went in, shutting the door behind her.

Beautiful, Useful, Enduring

Each day, she gives herself this moment alone. Often the mail has just arrived. She lies on her neatly made bed, thinking of him, holding his words in her hands. She will read them once and again, and place them in the bureau drawer now emptied of all but the careful bundles tied in specific order, and the photographs laid out like solitaire, each in its place. This being Christmas, there will be no mail, but yesterday's letter promised she would hear from him, that despite the snows or weather, his fondest wish will reach her, his deepest longing, his knowledge that the new year will bring great changes for them both, and generous love such as only mature and nurturing individuals might find in one another. She takes the small pink envelope from her clothes and draws the message from inside.

All cares cease! Joyful Noel!
I love thee.

(Your) C.

It is not his script, of course, for he phoned in the order to a Park Ridge florist, but the words are his, and the phrasing so clearly the written voice she's come to know. He has taken time and trouble to reach her; perhaps he is alone in his rooms, watching the storm, or dining in the restaurant of the fine hotel where he lives. He travels frequently, seeing to his business dealings and holdings; the Fairmont Hotel, he writes, is a fine establishment but can never be home. She reads the card again. Yes, her cares will cease. "C." In late spring, perhaps sooner, they will meet for the first time, though she knows his soul so deeply. She will look into his eyes and see his words within them.

She knows certain passages of his letters by heart. From the beginning, he has addressed the gulf between them, the loneliness that led them to correspond, his desire to marry, his standards and means.

My dear unknown friend: My wife can have anything within reason that money can buy, but above all I expect her to give that true love and devotion everyone of us craves.

She is not unattractive, but she is past her youth. She fears she looks careworn, drab, for she cannot afford the smart clothes and fine shoes, the appointments with hairdressers and manicurists, that might show her to better advantage. She's not grown stout, at least; in fact, since Lavinia's death, she's lost weight. Such have been her worries and concerns, concerns she dares not confide, lest he think her a burden or question her motives. He must not know the depth of her exhaustion, for his words are the source of her renewal and stir in her the warmth of trust, and even, after so long, the anticipation of gentle touch.

Each day is vividly alive with keen interest and it is you, Dear, who has given me the inspiration. Before you, life was prosaic and commonplace. No longer!

Cornelius plans a future based upon her

and she will not disappoint. The photographs, seated portraits taken in professional studios, show a man of no great height, well fleshed, immaculately dressed. His round gold spectacles and bow tie imply discernment. He is not handsome, but his gaze is direct, his eyes kind; perhaps he is shy, and less eloquent in person than on paper. It does not matter. She requires only his fidelity and support, his consideration, for he seems a gentleman, and takes such time and care. An ardent and faithful correspondent, he writes two letters for every one of hers, yet never reproaches her.

I am trying in this manner to find my only One. . . . I have no financial worries, but, dear, it does not satisfy the heart. I need a good, true, affectionate wife; one who will love me and make home a paradise.

The children, he knows, require her time and attention. Their grandmother's recent passing has surely grieved them, reminding them anew of their father's early death, but children are resilient. She has tried to make them known to him; she tells him that they are deserving and good, and not just because she loves them; adults who know them admire them, and they are well liked by the neighborhood children. Cornelius, a widower, is childless, and a man longs for a son. She believes he feels a special sympathy for her boy, who is twelve, nearly a young man. She's written Hart's name on the backs of photographs enclosed in her letters, and Cornelius responded so warmly, supplying a pet name for a boy he has yet to meet.

I am indeed very proud of Buster. He looks like a splendid young chap, and the two girls, too, they look like fine children. They will have the opportunities that they deserve and they will be able to develop into whatever their inclinations may call for.

Whose children will inhabit the dilapidated playhouse when they have gone, and hide their treasures in the broken-down workshop? Perhaps both will be razed, and a garden grown on the open land. All will be open. She will take her husband's arm as they cross streets in the South, in the gentle mountain clime Cornelius describes, and in Cedar Rapids, where he owns a city home and a farm, hundreds of acres of Iowa land, lying flat beneath the sun. She imagines the land, arable and plowed as far as the eye can see, with a great cloud passing over it.

The cloud is an image of her evasion and lack of candor. This she knows. Someday she will tell Cornelius all, the secrets she holds close, the shame, how the shock of Heinrich's death was preceded by the trial of his betrayal, the long wrangling arguments, discussions, pleading, for he believed he had the right to betray her, to respond to his heart's call, to end, he said, the dishonesty that undermined them both. He would say yes to Dora Hulck, née Dora Scholes, a divorcée who had ended her childless ten-year marriage and left the coal merchant whose funds had established her business. The Hallo Shop, a thriving enterprise, produced hand-wrought silver flatware, hollowware, and jewelry, just two blocks from their own barn workshop on Cedar Street, and employed many of the same artisans who designed for the Eicher enterprise. Now Dora would move her shop to Chicago. She wanted Heinrich to manage the expanding business and be her partner in all things, for she had taken him to her bed; they were lovers truly matched and would create Hallo's Norse Line, a collection of Scandinavian-influenced silver. "Beautiful, Useful, Enduring," the Hallo motto, would set an industry standard; they would make permanent impress on silver design in America, their adopted country; they would do important work.

Yes? Work?

Anna imagined Heinrich leaving her, and his mother with him, taking the children, for Lavinia believed herself as much a mother to them as Anna, and believed in her only son absolutely. Anna would be destitute. She'd no sense of how to run a business, how to plead a case through the courts, no means to hire lawyers, no presence of mind but to beg him not to think of this, to beg Lavinia to counsel him, demand of him . . . but Lavinia prided herself on her disregard for bourgeois convention. She saw her son's gifts unrealized, his talent wasted. His streetcar commute and his work in the city, actuary for Metropolitan Insurance and Casualty Co., were beneath him; he excelled of course, for his mind was precise and sharp and he inspired confidence, but business was not Art. He was finer than commerce, meant for better things, meant to foreman the major studio they'd all envisioned and could not support. Dora Scholes had offered him the opportunity he deserved. Lavinia refused Asta counsel and retired to her room at the first sound of marital argument.

Asta begged Heinrich to consider their marriage of more than twelve years, their own struggling but solvent enterprise, his years of seniority at the firm that employed him, and their children, their children! Was his life so unbearable? Had he no feeling at all for her?

He said, in a tense, quiet voice, "I'm leaving you."

"Why?" Asta shouted. "Why Dora? Is it her business, the money?"

He looked at her, stunned, then advanced

upon her, enraged. "Why Dora? Why do you think? Shall I show you why? Throw off your clothes, as she does! Start on your knees! Take me to mine!"

They were alone, for the children were at school, and Lavinia would not intervene. Asta tried to flee the room.

But he took hold of her, and dragged her to this bedroom. He forced her against the wall, there, by the mirror, and held her wrists above her head. He stood nearly against her, as though he would kiss or fondle her. She turned her face from him and closed her eyes, but he spoke against her throat, hissing his anger, and she felt each word enter her. "I must work, and work, and work, to even begin with you. I am a man! I am this man! I am not a villain, despoiling you. And I am not your teacher! You do not learn!"

She opened her eyes and saw that his other hand was fisted, that he shook with restraint, lest he beat her senseless. And then he turned and left the house, taking with him the valise he'd left packed at the front door.

Lavinia spoke frankly of Heinrich's infidelity only once, late that night over tea at the kitchen table, when the children were asleep. The room was shadowy in the snowy, windy night.

Lavinia, appearing regal, kindly, poured the tea. "Asta, hear me out. In this world in which women have so little freedom and enjoy so little regard, it is not always a bad thing to share a man, openly or not, if all are happy, and it is not such an unusual arrangement among artistic people, that alliances be discreet, particularly when there are children involved, over whom aspersions must not be cast."

"Children? Aspersions? How dare you, Lavinia —"

She held up a thin hand in caution. "I will tell you now that I counseled Heinrich, most seriously, never to tell you and wound you so, and to demand discretion of Dora, if she loved him, discretion that would have preserved your home and even your marriage. He might simply have taken the job as foreman at Hallo, maintained a room in Chicago for the sake of appearances, satisfied his passion for Dora, which would have cooled in time, I assure you, and remained a husband and father finally able to provide for his family; be the artist he was and yet allay your cares, allow you time to do your own work. That he should even think of dragging his children through such a scandal! No, I did not agree! But Dora Hulck is working-class Dutch, and childless, and older than Heinrich, remember; she divorced a wealthy, disagreeable man, and she wants my son to marry her."

Asta steeled herself; she was determined not to weep. "I thought you would have taken the children, and gone with them."

Lavinia shook her head, and reached for Asta's hand. "I could not live with Dora Hulck, nor would she allow my presence. She is shrewd, but not the right sort of influence for the children, nor has she any interest in them. Oh, dear Asta. She requires his genius and is blindly, passionately in love with him, but she hasn't the breeding or education for the discretion that might have made it all possible."

Asta pulled away and spoke in an angry whisper; she wanted to shout and throw the tea against the wall. "Lavinia, you are wicked, wicked, to think I would live in a shell of a marriage while my husband opens Hallo Shops in New York and Boston —"

"Dora will not have children; she is obviously barren. Asta, you had only to be patient for a year, five years . . . you have every advantage to press. Heinrich's love for these children is limitless; he's devoted to them. You must welcome and encourage his devotion, as Dora will not —"

"Stop it! Stop it!"

She would not. "And to you, Asta. He's devoted to you, their mother who loves them, and never deserved the wavering of his affections."

"Then why? Why?" Emotion choked her, for she knew why, and surmised that Lavinia did not; Heinrich had allowed them, at least, the privacy of their intimate relations.

Lavinia leaned forward into the small nimbus of light and spoke fiercely, insistently. "We do not get what we deserve! Never! If we did, the world would be just! We get what we work for, or what we're born to, if fortune does not intervene to take it from us! Talent grows if it is exercised. And passion, like hunger and thirst, demands satisfaction."

"That is certainly your son's assertion!" Asta could not stop herself, though the wind rattling the windowpanes seemed to mock her. "And fidelity, Lavinia? Sacred vows taken before God?"

Lavinia sat back, enveloped in shadow. "Yes, I know you are religious. But, my dear, you are a mature woman. Surely you have wanted, at some time, something or someone forbidden you, something your soul recognizes as its own true counterpart, for whatever reason, or reasons unknown to you."

Asta met her eyes. "I loved Heinrich!"

"And he loved you. But he denied himself in support of you and the children. You met as artists, did you not?"

"Oh, reproach me because he works at a career —"

"It is not a career, Asta. It is a job, but he is not resentful. He accepts, absolutely, his responsibilities. And he admires and respects and loves you. I can assure you that he reproaches himself bitterly over Dora, oh, so bitterly —"

"As I reproach you, Lavinia! For not telling him never to see her again!"

Lavinia leaned forward to grasp Asta's hand. "My dear Asta, listen to me. Love is . . . inarguable. Passion is a capability with which one is born, or not. Passion can destroy, yes, but it seeks and must have. That is its nature. You know my experience. Yet Heinrich's father was my soul's companion, and gave me the son I love. We maintained our home and our regard for one another. He was tortured by his own needs. Would I torture him as well? I cared for him too deeply. And he adored me. I did not encourage him to hate himself for needs he could not deny."

Asta clinched Lavinia's small hand in her own. "Lavinia, *you* must listen. I will not allow or condone Heinrich's need for Dora."

They were silent. The tea, untouched, was cold.

Lavinia allowed no more discussion of Heinrich's infidelity. She spoke to her son in confidence, divulged no further opinion, and told the children their father was on a business trip. Heinrich disappeared for nearly a week. He came back on the Saturday of a snowstorm, never addressing Asta, and took Hart to the park on the pony. The animal was grown shaggy in his thick winter pelt and long mane, and neighed clouds into the air, feasting on apples that Heinrich pulled from his pockets as he led them down the street.

They were gone for what seemed hours. The snow today reminds her of that day. How heavily it fell, coating every branch and blade! And then Heinrich returned and came upstairs to their bedroom while Lavinia supervised the help, and dinner for the children. He would stay, he told her; his heart was torn but he would not leave his family; he was no longer an artist; an artist who did not work was not an artist; he was a manager, both here in their workshop enterprise and at Metropolitan Insurance and Casualty; he had let Dora go, he had lost her; she had berated him for his lack of nerve and forsaken him.

Anna flew to him and fell on her knees before him and kissed his hands and stopped his mouth, doing with him and to him all the things that he liked her to do, even those things that she often refused him. He took her again and again, wild with sorrow, and forced her response, first with anger, as though he would drive himself through her loins to the base of her spine and into her throat, and then with tears, holding her where she bruised most easily, sucking and biting at her, turning her, pushing into her slowly, hot and wet and searing, for his unnatural pleasure that was her sacrifice. He'd whispered, in past encounters petitioned or commanded, that women who'd had children must give their men this secrecy, this tight resistant embrace that prevented childbirth yet offered complete possession; she must only open and be taken. He pulled her against him to stand as men stand, bending her forward until she held her own ankles; she urged him deeper, her gown fallen about her as he pushed it from her. They could not talk of this but it was what he most desired.

She washed him as they lay on the tile of the lavatory, sponges and warm soapy water, her hands and her mouth, until he turned her and began again, bracing them both against the hard porcelain edge of the tub. She was not herself to him thus, faceless, bent and spread to receive him. He held her weight completely in his arms, his fingers against her pubis as he fit himself slowly, urgently, inside her privacy, squeezing her mind completely from her. Silent, he worked for his paralyzed shudder of release, sustained even as he softened within her and carried her, like his own appendage, to the bed to lay against her, pressing tight into her, pulsing in some state of unconscious appetite until he slowly withdrew. She knew he wanted to sleep, holding her so, but she crept from him to pour a bath. She lay on towels beside the tub, utilizing the slender wand, the red tubing attached to the enamel pitcher she kept hidden in the bathroom cabinet. Numb and shamed, she positioned the pitcher above her in the basin, imagining the pour of water filling her, wanting the unbearable pressure that rinsed her clean.

After, she lay in the deep bath in steaming, fragrant water, easing her soreness, weeping with relief and gratitude. He would not leave her. She would do as he asked whenever he asked and pose no questions and it would be as though he had never left her. Daily, she changed their sheets, scrubbing the pale gold stains with bleach. Her complete dependence was established anew between them. The safety of her home and children and her only hope lay in his hands that bruised and caressed and demanded an animal intimacy. They must be creatures feasting on one another. His desires demeaned and humiliated her; she performed base actions and lost all sense, for he dissolved all boundaries by which she kept herself apart. She could only surmise, throbbing in the hot bath, that childless Dora pleased him in all ways, that Dora welcomed and encouraged him, while Asta had forced him to deny himself, had evaded and denied. She would never again deny him.

The accident was four days later. A streetcar, in the Loop, in darkening, swirling snow. Instantaneous, she was told. He did not suffer.

Suffer? A chasm opened before her and she stood on a precipice, surveying vast dimensions, for there was no way to cross over. His life insurance of two thousand dollars was smaller than expected, for he had taken his commissions in cash and not reinvested a percentage. Lavinia's funds were set aside to educate the children. The house, free and clear, was their only other asset. They would borrow against it, even as they rented out rooms and lowered expenses.

Mr. Malone at the bank was most kind. He first met with her in the week after the funeral, leaning toward her over his broad desk. "Mrs. Eicher, may I ask the ages of your children?"

"Why, Annabel is four, Hart seven, and Grethe, the eldest, is nine."

"Yes, and the life insurance has been paid you, and how long can you make it last?"

"I think, a year or more."

"His firm offered no other help?"

"They paid the funeral expenses, which they stressed was a generosity. Heinrich was engaged in the commission of his work, but it was after hours, the accident."

"I see. Are these your account books?"

"Yes, my husband's account books. I'm sure you are far more familiar with the figures than I, as Heinrich did not share such details. We had a very traditional marriage . . ."

Here she blushed, in remembrance of her own actions the afternoon Heinrich returned to her, and in the nights following. It occurred to her now, sitting opposite Mr. Malone, that perhaps Heinrich had pretended she was Dora, that he missed Dora and wanted Dora.

"Yes." Mr. Malone looked at her intently, as though to focus her attention. "The traditional arrangement of finances is quite common, Mrs. Eicher, though I'm not sure it's wise. Heinrich was in excellent health and, like many men in their prime, had no reason to suspect a shortened life. He was an athlete in his youth, wasn't he? A boxer?"

"Yes. He won trophies, in Europe, at twenty, before we met."

"Yes, he spoke of it." Malone took off his glasses, folded his hands. His eyes were brown, warmly golden, his thick dark hair silver at the temples. "I'm so sorry for your loss."

"Thank you, Mr. Malone. I do appreciate your frank advisement." Her voice caught slightly, and he rose to get her a glass of water. He was tall and broad in the shoulders; Heinrich had said Mr. Malone rode horses, that they sometimes saw him in the park, cantering a long-limbed roan, as they walked the pony. Lavinia said he was Catholic, and childless; his wife was not well.

He set the glass of water, poured from a covered glass carafe, before her. "I do advise my clients to set aside far more than life insurance, but Heinrich looked forward to full-time engagement in your mutual design business, and he put monies toward it, understanding there would not be immediate return."

She pushed the account books toward him. "I know the books show expenses for my business, which was only breaking even. I shall finish my present commissions, curtail my work, and try to rent the studio space. We will also rent rooms, to gentlemen exclusively, and provide board. That will be our income, and will allow us to stay in our home."

"Yes," he said carefully, "initially, at least, but let us think forward, beyond this next year. I'm aware that your daughter Grethe requires special consideration."

Anna nodded. "Yes, a childhood fever left her compromised. She is trusting and good, but not perceptive. She needs protection."

Malone paused, and continued. "We must think in terms of the next fifteen years, until such time as your son reaches adulthood, and will I'm sure provide for you. He must be educated. I will of course grant you a mortgage on your house, but I suggest you consider selling Cedar Street and buying a smaller home with less land, a town house perhaps, and live off the capital until such time as —" He saw her stricken look, and went on. "Or you could sell the parcel of land behind the house; there's frontage on the street back of the property, adjacent to Mayor McKee's home, which makes the land attractive to an investor or builder."

"Fifteen years," Anna said. She reached for the water, but could not bring herself to raise the glass to her mouth.

"It's difficult to make decisions now. Unfortunately, it will be necessary at some point. Mortgaging the home incurs debt, while selling it could provide you with careful income." He waited, observing her. "Would you like some hot tea?" His gaze took in her untouched water glass, and her gloves twisted in her hands.

"No, thank you, Mr. Malone." Shame suffused her like a warm glow. She probably seemed quite stupid, to cling to a house she could not afford. Odd, the clarity of her thoughts that day, which concerned not this meeting, for which she had tried to prepare, but Heinrich, whom she saw as clearly as though he were beside her. He would stand at the window in their dark bedroom. Moonlight bathed his face and bare chest. He was just her height, and the muscles of his arms and thighs stood out like ropes. He tensed as though bearing a great weight, then came to her for his solace. He began, knowing she would not limit, hinder, resist. Nearly faint in a banker's office chair, she could feel Heinrich lift her off her feet, and saw in his eyes the complete desolation she'd refused to acknowledge.

Yes, he was desolate, desperate.

"Mrs. Eicher?"

Asta forced herself to meet Malone's gaze. "Yes, Mr. Malone?"

"You're a silversmith, aren't you, Mrs. Eicher, as was Heinrich. You are an expert on silver and design. Given that Heinrich's mother lives with you and can help with the children, might you consider inquiring about employment in that realm? Perhaps with a firm downtown?"

"My mother-in-law is nearly seventy, Mr. Malone, and my children are young. When I worked at our own enterprise, I was near them, in the backyard studio, always supervising." Others never understood that Lavinia entertained the children but indulged odd enthusiasms. She was shattered by Heinrich's death, and would make a martyr of him; she needed distraction. Asta planned to rent both back bedrooms, have nice young men coming and going, provide board. Lavinia would go on with the children's piano lessons and theatricals and walks, and help with the cooking. "No, I shall simply have to try to make it work."

"I see. Well, then, I shall do all in my power to help you."

When she took her leave, Mr. Malone clasped her hand in his two hands, which were deep and fleshy and warm, and dwarfed her own. He was soft-spoken, gentle, as though, being a big man, he took care not to overwhelm. The unwelcome thought that his wife was fortunate flickered in Asta's mind, for a man that size possessed of Heinrich's appetites would surely kill a delicate woman.

She flees her thoughts by reciting Cornelius' letters; he writes of women with deepest respect and admiration. Particular lines are her comfort. The cadences run like rhyme, familiar, assenting, protective, assuring her that her correspondent respects her widowhood, believes women worthy, holds Christian attitudes.

Woman's holy courage was first revealed to me in my mother. I first saw it at my father's deathbed. . . . Dear, love can never be a light thing with me with such memories. My boyish heart was thus early impressed, sealed by the enduring strength of love. I shall never forget . . . the profound seriousness of the right love of the one man for the one woman, and vice versa.

He is truly fine. How fortunate that he, of all others, found interest in her words. The American Friendship Society, located in Detroit and possessed of good reputation, was the only firm to which she'd sent a carefully worded request for "correspondence, leading to true friendship, fidelity, and matrimony." Some who responded listed motherless progeny or a frank need for a helpmate.

None reflected Cornelius' education, ideals, or means. She had not mentioned love in her initial notice; she wanted to communicate modest virtue and discourage philandering opportunists, who might use the mails to prey on women. Neither had she mentioned her children or her name, or even her correct initials. She must secure lives for her children, and stability, and she dared hope, at last, for her own soul's companion, a man for whom no sacrifice was necessary, to whom she could turn openly and trust as she had trusted no one.

To think of her state of mind at that time, a mere month ago! She'd placed her notice only weeks before Lavinia died. The second mortgage she'd taken on the house would see them through winter and satisfy some of the creditors. Snow fell at Thanksgiving just as now. Images of Heinrich's death, recalled so intensely, haunted her. The snow seemed a visitation of the same snow that fell upon his end, five years ago, blanketing their home that fateful week, just as on the night Lavinia died. Asta nursed her, for she'd had to discharge Abernathy just as the crisis approached. Lavinia, as though she knew resources were gone, slipped quickly into a coma. The children, home from school before Thanksgiving, sat vigil by day. At night, her chair drawn close to Lavinia's bed, Anna imagined the loud screech of a streetcar's brakes and sudden, total oblivion. She could afford herself no such luxury, yet she wanted to go and stand amongst the crowds in the Loop, just at the crossing of the tracks.

Cornelius' letters, first addressing "My Unknown Friend," began arriving, telling of himself, his past, his hopes for a family, despite his age and widowhood. He, too, was cautious; they determined they would not meet for six months, nor would they speak on the telephone, but would write exclusively until such time as they might proceed decisively, based on trust, loving attraction, and abiding knowledge of their mutual beliefs. He deliberated with her on the children, extolling the wholesome influence of rural life in the gentle Appalachians, yet pointing out that Cedar Rapids, where they would also have a home, was a growing metropolis, and not so far from Chicago, where they could find a fine school for Hart, and a finishing school for Annabel, somewhere their youngest girl would meet sophisticated, quick people to her liking. Grethe, of course, would live at home.

Cornelius was a widower of long duration; Anna would compete with no ghost. His affections would be open to her. She was so young when she'd accepted Heinrich, so inexperienced, despite her knowledge of languages and careful education. Like him, she was an only child. He saw in her a pliable, well-bred girl whose talent he respected, who would give him the family he desired. Anna had believed herself in love with Heinrich; perhaps she loved him still, fearfully, anxiously, yet she could never reach him or satisfy him; he would not be her easy companion and approving friend, as Charles was; nor would he speak to her at length, deeply, as Cornelius did, in script now familiar to her as her own hand:

> The great trouble is that men are so ignorant that they do not know that women must be gently caressed. . . . There are still some true marriages, dear. Two individualities come together, maintain their separate individuality, if they have the proper spirit, but their life streams merge, become one, and are never divisible again, even when death seems to strike them asunder. It was I believe this lovely and tender and mystical spirit that gave my mother the proud and beautiful strength she had when my father's earthly presence passed away from her. She knew what she knew.

Anna opens her bedside drawer and places the small pink envelope among its fellows. How rare is the man who loves women, yet feels no need to control and dominate, who responds to worlds beyond this one, and practices fidelity as a basis of trust, as the demand of his own moral character. Cornelius' mother had been his inspiration, not his compatriot; his parents' marriage, a sacred ideal to which he aspires.

So thinking, she takes up Annabel's play, which the child had placed beside her mother's pillow. Yet Asta does not read the words; she gazes into the snow that falls so thickly past her windows. Charles and the children will soon return from sledding. She must build up the parlor fire. They will roast the last of the marshmallows and crisp the graham crackers. Asta will grate chocolate and nutmeg onto the ballooned, sticky sugar.

One moment more. She closes her eyes and tries to hear Cornelius' voice in his words. She sees his lines on the page, thinks again of the phrase about his mother: *She knew what she knew.* What did it mean? Asta sits up, suddenly alert, wondering. Snow, icy and needling, tossed on some errant gust, whirls at the windows. She grips the pages of Annabel's play and peers into the glittering maw of the storm, which seems to fly at itself, endlessly, furiously circling! She feels herself drawn within it and catches her breath, only to find herself gazing intently at the pages of her daughter's earnest words.

A PLAY FOR CHRISTMAS
by ANNABEL EICHER

DECEMBER 25, 1930
In honor of Mrs. Heinrich Eicher

The Players

The Pilgrim . . . . . Miss Grethe Eicher
(voiced by Annabel Eicher)
The Stranger . . . . . Master Hart Eicher
The Actuary . . . . . Master Hart Eicher
Duty, Faithful Companion . . . . . Duty
(if he behaves)
The Grandmother . . . . . Mrs. Pomeroy
(voiced by Annabel Eicher)

Guests: Mrs. Heinrich Eicher,
Mr. Charles O'Boyle

A Play for Christmas

The Setting: A Forest Glade

Narrator: It was cold and dark on the last night of the old year, and snow was falling. A poor pure Pilgrim walked through the forest glade, looking for sticks to sell. Her feet were bare and her hair was covered with snow. She looked up to see a Stranger before her.

Stranger: Young Pilgrim, where are your shoes?

Pilgrim: I left them, fine sir. Two small birds had fallen from their nest. I filled my shoes with straw and hid the baby birds inside, and my shoes in the crook of a tree, for the mother bird to find when the Fox has passed.

Stranger: What of the Fox now? Are you afraid?

Pilgrim: No, kind sir, for my Faithful Companion has chased the Fox to its den. Duty! Offer your greetings.

Stranger: (shakes Duty's paw) I see that your dog is exceedingly brave. And what do you carry in your apron, young Pilgrim?

Pilgrim: Matches, sir. May I light a fire to warm us? For the wind howls and I must warm my Grandmother. I carry her with me, for she cannot walk any longer. (Grethe takes Mrs. Pomeroy from her cloak, and puts her in the doll chair between them.)

Stranger: Your Grandmother is quite small.

Grandmother: Yes, I am small, but my voice is in every breeze and leaf, just as I promised.

Pilgrim: Listen! What is that sound, by those trees?

Stranger: Come, Duty. We shall see. (The Stranger and Duty exit.)

Grandmother: The true in heart walk abroad, for the last night of the year is a magic night. (The Actuary enters, with

Duty, dressed in the same white cloak but wearing a fedora hat and white silk neck scarf.)

Actuary: What is this place? Duty has brought me here.

Pilgrim (to Grandmother): Mother said that his name would serve to instruct.

Actuary: And so it has! He is a fine animal. Sit, Duty. (Actuary falls to his knees.) Grandmother, you remind me of my own mother, who taught me to advise on odds and probabilities.

Pilgrim: But, you speak with the voice of the Stranger. Who have you become?

Actuary: Child, I am your own dear father, waiting for you in the life after this one. And here is your loving Grandmother, who abides with me. We have found your shoes that saved the birds from the Fox (places the shoes before her). Here too is a pure white scarf to warm you (puts the scarf around her neck).

Pilgrim: It is soft and light as warm snow.

Grandmother: You must pull this charmed garment close around you, for there is much to see and know. Triumph belongs to the Pilgrim, and goodness is your measure and delight.

Pilgrim: But how will I hear from you again, or know that you await?

Grandmother: Listen to the rain and the wind, the snow and the sounds of bells. All of these speak for us, just as when you sing:

(End with "Carol of the Bells," all sing.)

Asta lowers the pages to her chest. Of course she will compliment Annabel, but the play saddens her utterly, despite its ringing conclusion. Few pilgrims encountered triumph, Asta reflects; triumph was so seldom even a factor.

Well, Annabel must study literature, and read the classics, and board at a school for young ladies that offers rigorous instruction. She must be challenged intellectually, not encouraged to commune with spirits, and kept apart from men until she is of age. She is far too forward, trusting, inquisitive. Lavinia had nearly ruined Annabel, and Asta is far less sanguine about her influence than Charles. The problem of Annabel is the true cost of Lavinia's help and support; Lavinia had claimed Annabel, in recompense, no doubt, for her own loneliness.

Asta well imagined elements of that loneliness. The same man had preoccupied them, but Lavinia's close alignment with her son was not confusing, not demanding or exhausting. Her mourning did not leave shame and desire in its wake, long nights in which shame was desirous, and desire shameful. Heinrich had demanded Asta's complicity, not merely her submission. She'd thought her shame necessary, central to his satisfaction, but no, it was simply an inconvenience. Dora had required no urging, no demands.

Today, in the wake of Charles' generous proposal, the knowledge she'd denied had welled up inside her. She'd refused, in all these years, to see the truth. Heinrich had come back to her, yes; he had forsworn Dora, and the prospect of artistic support and success. But he stood in the snow that day in the Loop, next to the tracks, and saw the streetcar approach at full speed. It came on, sparking the wires like a dragon in the snowy air. He knew that no one would say it was suicide. All was resolved. Only strangers would attend him. His mother was healthy, vital; she would help raise his children and her money would see them educated.

Or perhaps he thought nothing. Perhaps he didn't need to think. He stepped onto the tracks, his timing perfect. No witnesses claimed to see the moment of impact; his body was dragged some distance. Afterward a crowd gathered, surging forward against the implacable, motionless streetcar, whose passengers made haste to disembark.

Asta looks into her room, hers alone for nearly five years. She knows, she knows, and falls instantly asleep. The thin pages of

Annabel's "Play for Christmas" slip aside, and the rose Tiffany shade of the bedside lamp casts the only light. She moves through a passage of veils that opens onto the cold, crowded confusion of the rail station in Chicago's Loop. The approaching trolley shrieks and the gleaming rails crackle with electric fire. There's Heinrich, walking toward the streetcar in the snow. She reaches for him, but Lavinia comes between them, her words blazing up in the steam of the trolley's burning, whining brakes . . . *adore me . . . needs he could not deny . . .* Asta screams at her in the gathering crowd: *As I denied Heinrich! You knew he walked in front of that train! You knew and pretended not to know!* But Lavinia has hold of her: *No, Anna! That is your fear and suspicion. Heinrich would never leave his children fatherless and unprotected! Never!* She is here beside Asta on the bed. *Don't think such faithless thoughts. We have been unlucky. That is all.* The older woman's delicate, lined face comes very near. *We must think clearly now, and persevere, and raise these children as he would have wished.* Asta opens her eyes then, for the words are billowing drafts of snowy air. A loose catch has given way and the window beside the bed is blown completely open. Annabel's play is scattered across the floor as though drawn to the open window and the wind.

■ ■ ■ ■

III.

■ ■ ■ ■

Personal Ad: Civil Engineer. College Education. Worth $150,000 or more. Has income
from $400 to $3000 per month. He writes:
My business enterprises prevent me from
making many social contacts. I am, there-
fore, unable to make the acquaintances of
the right kind of women. As my properties
are located through the Middle West, I
believe I will settle there when married. Am
an Elk and a Mason. Own a beautiful 10-
room home, completely furnished. My wife
would have her own car and plenty of
spending money. Would have nothing to do
but enjoy herself, but she must be strictly a

one-man's woman.

> — Cornelius O. Pierson,
> P.O. Box 227, Clarksburg, W.Va.

June 24, 1931
Park Ridge, Illinois

A VISITATION
Everything was prepared. Cornelius was motoring from the South in his new automobile and should arrive for a late supper.

Asta Darling:
Just a few lines, dearest, as I expect to leave here next Sunday and arrive Monday.

When I come I want to see you alone — tell the children anything you like. I will come at night.

Do not let the neighbors know I am coming. Leave all business transactions to me.

Your faithful Cornelius

Of course she wouldn't start talk among the neighbors, but she'd warned him the children were excited to meet him. She explained that she couldn't leave on "business" without introducing him, for she'd never left the children, even overnight. She hadn't the opportunity, since that first long journey to America, to travel. And to enjoy, Cornelius reminded her gently. Of course he would meet the children, and they would leave quite early the next day, without good-byes, for it was not good-bye. A quick departure would lessen any anxiety. She'd engaged Mrs. Abernathy, Lavinia's medical nurse, to stay the week. The children would be busy; she would write them daily, and be back for them, with Cornelius, as soon as affairs were settled. They would begin their family life, a prospect so dear to his heart; she could not know how dear.

It was unseasonably warm for June. The table was set as though for a banquet: Cornelius must know of her taste and refinement, that she honored him and would provide a gracious home. Soon enough, he would know her financial straits. Grethe and Hart had savings accounts to which Charles made birthday deposits, and Hart made pocket money bagging groceries on weekends. Their savings exceeded her own funds, for she had none, and would have to borrow some small sum from Hart, for the trip. Cornelius had said he would see to her every need, just as he would going forward, but it wouldn't do to have absolutely nothing, like a child.

Nothing. She sat at the kitchen table, and put her face in her hands.

She wouldn't allow Charles to pay her bills

or know the extent of her situation: that would be double betrayal, for he expected to return in July and discuss his suit again, on any terms she liked, he said, but she would not burden him with the well-being of her entire family, or allow him to embrace a life he would surely find incomplete. She'd arranged with Malone that the bank pay the mortgage going forward, adding to the debt to be settled when the house was sold.

Cornelius would see to everything. He was a businessman. Careful men like Cornelius, financially astute, steady, warmly polite, were the true Americans. Men like Malone, in his bank. She imagined, for a moment, Malone and Cornelius, settling her affairs congenially, in the very office in which Malone had advised her, most recently, to accept the bank as trustee until she could sell her home.

She opened the icebox to check that the aspic had taken the mold. She'd poured it a bit late, being occupied with the tea sandwiches, her own fresh dill and cucumbers, sliced paper thin, and the cold chicken, arranged in slices, with her own corn relish; she'd found the last of Lavinia's canned green beans, her beets with mustard seed, in the pantry, and a jar of her bread and butter pickles, that Hart loved so. She'd made the noodle kugel, Lavinia's recipe, early, before the heat; she could serve it hot or cold, depending on Cornelius' wish . . . depending

115

on his wish. Was she a fool? She shut the icebox and latched the door.

She must continue to believe in him and not lose her nerve; she imagined herself in his fine new car, the road opening before them, the world speeding by as they conversed . . . he was on his way, ever closer, in this moment!

She prayed he would forgive her lack of candor. They would meet and she would explain. So many weeks and months, so much in common. Hope had silenced her, she would tell him, but she promised herself she would not leave with him until he knew part of the truth, lest he question her altogether.

Where was Hart? The bank closed at five. She would ask him for ten dollars, no small sum, and for him, poor boy, it was a third of his savings —

And where was Abernathy? She'd promised to arrive by three with her valise, and to serve dinner this once, from the kitchen, though *she was a nurse, not a servant.* How fortunate she'd no medical cases and was clearly hard-pressed; she'd accepted partial payment for a week's work, and would stay over in the guest room. Grethe would do the shopping under Abernathy's supervision, on credit, and help with the cooking. Hart would walk and feed Duty. Annabel and Hart were obliged to attend Bible School each morning at St. Luke's Church down the block, which provided lunches for the children. Hart would be most annoyed; she would have to talk with him.

If he would understand! He must be educated and meet a station in life equal to his talents and abilities, and the girls must be protected. To depend solely on a man, with no recourse to family solvency, as she must, was an unacceptable risk, as surely for Annabel as for Grethe . . . but that was far off. Cornelius said that of course Grethe would remain with them for the foreseeable future, safe and happy —

When they were married. If they carried out their intentions, which despite their fond letters must wait on their meeting, on the chance to spend days alone together, in travel, for they were journeying from one life to another, were they not? He would experience her home, and she his, observing proprieties, she'd no doubt, until they were wed. He seemed to view convention as a moral code to be observed with decorum and appreciation.

He needn't know of Heinrich's demands and needs. But he knew of Heinrich's affair, his infidelity, his months and weeks of indecision while Asta suffered — this she'd confided in her letters, for she found that she could not give an account of herself, her sorrows and hopes, without speaking of it. In fact, Cornelius' own mention of certain words, in his first letter, drew her, like balm to an open wound: his wife *must be strictly a one-man's woman. I would not tolerate infidelity.* He'd not yet confided as much, but perhaps Cornelius too had found his heart stripped of comfort by a sudden, devastating revelation.

She startled as the front door slammed open, bouncing against the doorstop, and the screen door squealed on its spring. Duty ran full tilt through to the kitchen and buried his muzzle in his water bowl. Hart came after, whistling as though he hadn't a care in the world.

His mother wore her lace collar, her cameo brooch and earrings, and her kitchen apron; she looked not herself, her hair falling down in strands on one side. He couldn't believe what she was saying. "Why can't I bag groceries every day, like I do on Saturdays, and make more money?"

"Hart —" she began.

"I know we need money." He glared at her. "We can't buy on credit forever, like you bought all this." Still holding his catcher's mitt, he swept his arm out wildly to indicate the long table, with its place settings and glassware. It looked set for a party, all for this Cornelius.

"Hart, I regret that you must even think about credit, or the fact we need it." She put her hands on his shoulders.

He could feel her steady herself, and that

scared him. He squared his stance, and tried to remember his anger.

"But don't talk of credit," she said, "and most certainly not today. It's common to discuss money, and soon the bills will be paid." She met his eyes. "I have made decisions that affect us all and I ask for your patience and help. Son, with your grandmother gone, I depend on you more than anyone."

"I don't mind," he said quietly. She was barely taller than he. The whites of her gray eyes were faintly reddened, and her mouth had a sort of pinch. She seemed always to be thinking of something that worried or distracted her. "Is Charles coming for lunch as well?" he asked.

"No, they'll meet another time. You know Charles is traveling all month." She took his arm in hers. "Now, I've told you that Cornelius is coming quite a distance to be with us, to meet you children. He wants only to be your friend and adviser, to ease the way for all of us."

Hart only nodded.

"We'll be gone a week or so. Then we'll be back for you, and we'll all take a lovely trip together, to see his home. We've not gone on a trip for ever so long, have we?"

Gravely, Hart looked at her, and wished himself back at the ball field in the park, amongst his friends who would hoot and cheer as he struck out another batter. It was only teams chosen by lot, neighborhood boys, but he was fiercely desired for his pitching arm. The pounded grass smelled wet in the early mornings, when they began. He thought of the smell and how good it was.

"I need you to watch over Annabel. She's so distractible and imaginative. You must take responsibility until I return. Can you do that?" She paused. "You know I can't ask Grethe."

"Abernathy will be here," he said.

"But Annabel doesn't much like her. And you know how your sister looks up to you, and listens to you." Her gaze softened. "And well she should, my fine, grown-up boy."

Her hand brushed his hair, light as a leaf, and he was about to tell her that he would take care of them all before long, that all must stay as it was, but the doorbell rang and his mother stepped past him. "There's Abernathy. I must speak to her." She turned. "I nearly forgot. I know you're hot and thirsty — have some lemonade. Then wash up and go down to the bank, will you, and withdraw ten dollars for me. I haven't asked you often, and this is the last time, I promise."

"It's fine," he said.

"Thank you, Hart. Don't tarry, it's nearly three. And Grethe wants to go, for the walk. Take her with you?" Then she was gone.

Miserable, Hart walked through the kitchen

to the small back porch, and hung his mitt on a nail in the eave of the roof. Duty's mangled tennis ball lay abandoned on the top step and Hart sat down beside it, seeing the backyard as he supposed a stranger would. Inside, the house was tended like a museum, but their mother took no interest in the back, which was littered with Annabel's toys. The small rock mound of the graveyard, as she called it, where last week she'd managed the neighborhood children in a funeral for a baby barn swallow, had fallen aside. The homemade sign looked woebegone.

They weren't allowed inside the long studio barn anymore. Boards had dropped along the front and it was too dangerous, his mother said, but Hart went in alone now and then, to stand quietly. There were still massive workbenches to either side, and a great open expanse down the middle. The floor was covered in sawdust. Swallows nested along the roof beams. He didn't quite remember the workshop, when it was full of people in long aprons and protective glasses, and there was heat and glow and noise. He tried to feel his father standing close in front of him, but the emptiness stayed empty.

He heard Annabel then before he saw her, in the playhouse. It was off-limits as well, and needed repair. Annabel had swung the front window fully open, also forbidden, because the six mullioned panes were pocked and cracked, and bits of glass had popped out onto the grass. She was wearing Charles' long white scarf, pretending she was a lady or a geisha, carrying Duty here and there like a potentate, for she made a fuss over the paintings on the walls, which showed a Japanese scene. Their mother had painted the mural long ago, when Grethe was a baby. The small square houses were submerged in greenery, and the uneven dirt road, smaller and then larger, opened toward the viewer. Ladies walked there in Japanese kimonos with wide sleeves and sashes; one man in a wide hat pulled a cart. There were tall palm trees and faraway snowcapped mountains. It was noplace and nowhere, for none of them had ever been to Japan, but Hart had always imagined that the cart was full of ice from the mountains. The man in the hat had drawn it down a long, long road, and he was still pulling it.

Hart picked up the muzzy tennis ball and threw it hard. Duty jumped from Annabel's arms and ran joyously after it, barking wildly, his short legs a blur of motion.

Asta remembered to lay her apron aside, and smooth her hair. "Mrs. Abernathy, how good of you to come. Was the streetcar delayed? On hot days, the cars get so full —"

"Oh, Mrs., I got to the station and needed a cab, the valise, you see, I couldn't manage,

I'll have to charge you transport, Mrs., I'm sorry."

"Yes, of course. Let me take your bag." Asta led the way up the carpeted stairs, pleased the valise was, indeed, a substantial weight, and promised commitment, for they had not stipulated a specific end date. "Up this way to your room, the guest room, the front one, with its own bath." Asta looked behind her to see Abernathy, a tall thin woman with a rather gray pallor, following, removing her hat. But Abernathy knew the room, of course. Lavinia's marble-topped dresser was cleared and empty. "Next week it will be seven months. We've gotten through the winter."

Abernathy nodded curtly, as though there were any choice in the matter. "I was sorry to be discharged before she passed. Thanksgiving, it was."

"Yes, I was sorry as well."

Abernathy stood, hat and hatpins in hand. "Fine. I'll just unpack then, Mrs. I know you want me to serve dinner. Six on the dot, I remember it used to be. When is the guest expected?"

Asta had moved a small writing table and two comfortable chairs to one wall. She indicated the chairs now. "I'm not certain. He's driving a long distance. I know you want to freshen up, but could we talk for just a moment?"

"If you like." She sat, her hat on her lap.

Asta composed herself and began. "I trust you'll keep the terms of our arrangement private, Mrs. Abernathy, and any knowledge of my finances, confidential. Most especially this evening. Mr. Pierson is an old friend whom I don't want to trouble with any sense of my difficulties, and the children, of course, must feel secure as I see to our affairs." She paused, aware of Abernathy's expressionless gaze. Asta had paid her the last of Lavinia's savings as an advance, half the fee.

Abernathy remained motionless. Finally, as though considering a verbal response unnecessary, she nodded.

Asta dropped her voice. "You know, I've never left the children, but I must see to important matters." She wanted to reach for Abernathy's hand, to seal some bargain. Surely Abernathy knew, having nursed Lavinia for weeks, how completely Asta lived for her children. "Things, unexpected, thrust upon us — the financial reversals and difficult choices brought on by illness, by widowhood. You're a widow yourself, I believe."

"Certainly, Mrs., for twenty years. And forced to make a living, a better living than my husband ever earned, driving a streetcar and drinking half he made."

A streetcar? Drinking, Asta thought. Irish. But twenty years ago. She looked out Lavinia's window to see Annabel in the playhouse, and Duty launching himself from her arms through the window, which was swung fully open. Grethe, then, came into view beside her. Grethe disobeyed very rarely, and today of all times! Annabel was far too persuasive for a child her age. She knew better. Asta would go over all the rules, everything, again, in no uncertain terms. But she turned first to Abernathy, not to seem abrupt. "I thank you for your discretion, Mrs. Abernathy. Come down when you're settled."

Abernathy nodded, and gazed into the room. "You've made quite a change here, Mrs."

"Yes, I thought it best, for the children . . . that they not, see it as a shrine, or continue to . . ."

"Death is a business," Abernathy said, looking around her.

Downstairs, Asta sent Hart and Grethe off to the bank, and Annabel to the parlor, to await a frank talk, but considered Abernathy's remark. How odd the woman was. Death was Abernathy's business, one supposed, but what a strange, unaccountable statement. God save anyone from such a life, moving one desperate illness to another as someone lay wasting away. Abernathy was competent, never ruffled. Asta could trust that nothing would go wrong; all would remain in order, and for a week or a bit more, that was all she required.

"Annabel?" Asta found her in the dining room, surveying the table settings. They didn't often have company. "Does it look nice, darling?"

"Oh yes. Mr. Pierson is sure to appreciate a lovely dinner after his long drive." She fixed a hand to each high rounded point of one of the tall ladder-back chairs. "You can tell by his spectacles that he likes fine things."

She'd wanted to see his photograph. Just this morning, Asta had obliged. "I'm sure he does, dear. And I'm certain he will appreciate you. You might recite something for him, I think. From your *Child's Garden,* perhaps?"

"I know what I shall recite."

"It must be short, Annabel."

"Oh, yes. Grandmother told me, never try the patience of one's audience."

Asta concealed her irritation at the mention of Lavinia. "Annabel, I asked you to wait for me in the parlor."

"I was just going there," Annabel said.

Asta went to the kitchen to get the child a glass of milk and a few of the icebox cookies she'd baked fresh. She didn't want to antagonize Annabel, who was her mother's only supporter in this venture, for she didn't remember a father, and loved the idea of a business adviser, a very close friend. Sometimes, she'd pointed out, friends became suitors, as happened in *Little Women,* between

126

Laurie, the rich neighbor, and Amy, the youngest sister, who was Annabel's favorite over Jo, the tomboy; Amy was a painter, and her suitor, like a prince. Mr. Pierson was not a prince, Asta had said, only a very nice man.

She fetched a cut-glass tray for their repast, for Annabel loved such things. Lavinia had certainly taught her to value "fine things," and if reality was not so fine, to construct stories and fantasies.

But fantasy was of no use. Had Cornelius not offered his help, not grown to revere Asta as his heart's desire, where would she have turned? She would surely have accepted Charles' proposal and been another man's disappointment. So, the milk and cookies. Annabel would be waiting as though for a visitor, pretending her behavior was not the issue. Asta took the tray into the parlor.

Annabel looked up with a brilliant smile and Asta felt herself lighten, as though some edge of happiness touched her. Was it so unbelievable that a good man existed? Mature people who had endured life's struggles surely deserved happiness, and appreciated good fortune far more than the young.

The bank was open another half hour, despite their mother's haste. She'd rushed them off in their clean clothes, insisting Hart wear a tie. They'd plenty of time, Hart assured Grethe, who walked quickly, regardless, exactly in the middle of the sidewalk. She wouldn't cross streets until there were no cars in sight, even if the light was solidly red. He knew better than to argue.

He searched his mind for a remark of no consequence. "That's a nice dress you're wearing," he told her.

"Do you know it was Grandmother's? Mother did it up. She says I'm just Grandmother's size."

"You're wearing Grandmother's clothes?"

"I must wear them now because I might grow too tall soon. And this is Grandmother's hat." She touched her straw boater, and the navy ribbons that hung by her chin.

Hart was perplexed. What right had his mother to dress Grethe in these clothes? He remembered silks and taffetas and parasols, and tasseled shawls that shimmered at holidays. Was Grethe to go about in all that? Were they so poor that Grethe couldn't have her own clothes? He couldn't ask her if she minded; that would only make her think she should. "Well, you look very nice," he said. They were opposite the bank, and he took her arm.

"Mother put my hair up," she said. "A little girl doesn't wear this sort of hat."

"I suppose not," Hart said. His mother said Grethe would always be a little girl, but here she was, dressed up like an older woman. "Look here," he said, "take my arm, like so,

128

because I'm your brother. But don't take any other fellow's arm. You know not to, don't you, no matter what he says about your hat."

"My hat," she repeated. She looked at the light fixedly. The sun was glaring, and the color was hard to make out.

He drew her across Main Street, into the bank. The marble floor and walls were markedly cool and the big clock glowered down. He saw the minute hand jerk. There was a long queue, but only two tellers serving customers. Hart indicated three chairs to the left, by the wall. "Sit just there and wait for me, Grethe. Don't talk to anyone."

"What are you mad about?"

"I'm not mad. Only just wait for me." He stood in line and looked back as she settled herself, like a bird lit on a cushion, sitting forward as though she might rise any minute, knees together, feet flat on the floor, as their mother had taught her. So many rules made Grethe anxious, for she had to remember them all. She was born normal but she was special now. Their mother had said this so long ago that Hart couldn't remember not knowing. It couldn't happen to Hart, she'd explained, or to Annabel, because these fevers only afflicted small babies, and changed how the brain might grow. Grethe would always need their protection.

He made sure no one teased her at school, and helped her with her homework. She couldn't memorize the Gettysburg Address for graduation to fourth grade, no matter how many times he repeated each phrase, and so she hadn't gone to fifth grade, and was schooled at home. She walked about with a book on her head, and went with their mother now, to stores, the post office, the bank. This bank.

He looked back at her; a tall gentleman was talking to her.

The man, dressed in a fine suit, leaned over her. "Excuse me, are you Miss Eicher?"

He could hear what they were saying, for the bank was like a church. Hushed voices carried. Hart was two from the front; she'd be waiting far longer if he left the line now. He looked directly at her, trying to get her attention.

"Yes," she was saying in her practiced way, "I'm Grethe Eicher."

"I thought so. I'm William Malone, president of this bank and a friend of your mother's. She speaks so highly of you." He was nodding at Grethe, pleased. At least he wasn't trying to shake her hand.

Grethe looked at him, and never once looked at Hart.

"How old are you now, Grethe?" the man asked her.

"I'm fourteen." She gave her serious, studious smile. "I have an account at this bank."

There she was, giving out personal information, just because some man spoke to her. Hart cleared his throat and looked over at the teller, who was taking an uncommonly long time with the old lady in front.

"Charles opens a savings account for us when we are ten," Grethe was saying, "for our gift money and pocket money. He makes our first deposit. Twenty dollars."

"Does he?" Malone said. "A young person should have a savings to look after. Charles must be a very good man." Now he sat in the chair next to Grethe, as though to have a proper conversation.

Grethe was obliging, attentive, concentrating, no doubt. "Oh yes, he was our roomer, and comes to see us quite often."

"Excellent." Now Malone looked over at Hart. Grethe followed his gaze as though coming out of a spell. "Would you children like to come to the office, have some lemonade or cold water? Very warm today, isn't it?"

Hart was finally at the cashier's window, but turned to look hard at Grethe and said, perhaps too loudly, "No thank you, sir. We must be getting home." He gave Malone a clipped nod and turned his back, leaning on the teller's counter, hunching his shoulders as though to protect some privacy. He slid his bankbook forward and heard Malone take his leave. He knew Grethe had never moved, or shifted her feet, only turned her head and smiled at the nice gentleman. He knew she wondered what she'd done wrong, to make Hart mad at her again.

"Now, Annabel," Asta began. "You know I count on you, this coming week, to do exactly as I asked, just as if I were here with you."

She sat with her knees together, on the sofa, very prim. "I know, Mama."

"I was very disappointed to see you defy my instructions. What would Mr. Pierson think, if he saw you behaving so?"

"I . . . don't know, Mama."

"Why were you in the playhouse, when I forbade it?"

"I had to go inside today, just for one time."

"What do you mean? And did I see you in Charles' white scarf? Have you had it since Christmas? Why ever didn't you give it back to him?"

Annabel widened her eyes and spoke in a rush of pleasure. "Because he said it was the loveliest silk and should stay with me, because it was in my Christmas play, the best play, he said, ever, of all my pageants."

"Well do bring it in. It can't hang out there in the heat and damp."

"It belongs there. It's listening."

"Annabel, listening to what?"

"To the ladies, walking about, the Japanese ladies and what they say about us."

"What they say?"

"About everything spread out in the yard,

like a marketplace, and everyone milling around."

"Milling around? What do you mean?"

"A party or a social in the yard, while we're gone. Ever so many people, in and out."

"Annabel! Stop this nonsense. You are not to be in the playhouse, and you know it. And why did you encourage Grethe to disobey?"

"I . . . I shouldn't have. But she is one of the ladies in the painting and should wear the scarf before them, where they see her in *their* world, not *our* world, because *their* world —"

"Hush! You are very, very selfish to ask Grethe to do what I expressly forbid! Don't talk to me of this and that world! The painting is just an illustration, a picture; I painted it myself! The glass in the playhouse window is broken and could cut someone. Someone could be very badly hurt —" She stopped herself, for Annabel was leaning forward, hanging on her every word.

"Yes," she breathed. "But the light of the world shall quell all hurt and lift away the fortress of the dark."

Quickly, Asta rose and touched the back of her hand to Annabel's forehead. The child was flushed, her cheeks bright red, as though she'd stood before a fire. Asta pulled her close, and lifted the cold milk to her mouth. "Here, drink this." Annabel was parroting words she'd heard at church. The big painting of Jesus and the children at St. Luke's said something about the light of the world, and the homage to Martin Luther was emblazoned with a legend about a mighty fortress. "Better?" Asta put a cookie in her hand. "Eat this. There are raisins and nuts in it."

Annabel nodded, and took the second cookie her mother offered.

"As for the light and the world, you can bring all that up tomorrow at Bible School. That's just what Bible School is about. And you'll make stained-glass windows with wax paper and crayons, and the teacher will iron them to melt the colors."

Annabel leaned her head on her mother's shoulder and clasped her hand.

"Now, you'll stay out of the playhouse, absolutely, while I'm gone." She felt Annabel nod her assent. "I want you to go to your room, where it's cool, and have a nap. Then wash up and put on the dress I left on your chair. The heat has tired you out. And Duty too." Asta had to move the dog; Duty lay like a dead weight across Annabel's feet. Asta walked her daughter to the stairs and set her moving up them, Duty trailing behind. Annabel would allow him on the bed and he would put his snub-nosed head on the pillow beside hers. Abernathy would forbid it, but Asta knew that Duty, while she was away, would wait until Abernathy shut her door at night to choose which child to guard.

■ ■ ■ ■

Asta went to the living room to compose herself. Lavinia's ornate, inlaid desk still radiated her presence. To think that the desk, and the tall highboy with its carved garlands and original glass, had crossed safely from Copenhagen in the hold of that tossing ship and were here still, unmarked, with Lavinia and Heinrich gone and she herself so changed. She could not look too closely at this house just now! In her heart, she wished Cornelius would fall in love with it, decide to purchase it, even as a rental property, for the children's sake . . . the walls, the floors, the Palladian windows in their frames, the ceilings with their moldings and stenciled borders, were haven and anchor, and all fallen to her. It was after five. The drapes and sheers and needlepoint shades of the tall windows blocked the worst of the heat. Asta turned on the gaslights and sank into one of the embroidered, overstuffed chairs. The sconces, subtle as candlelight, cast a pure vanilla glow. Stunned with fatigue, she leaned back to wait.

It was six; it was seven, and eight, just dark of a warm summer evening. It had rained hard, only briefly, enough to wet the streets and refresh the gardens. The long curved sides of the black Chevrolet coupe looked

135

shiny and freshly washed. He cut the engine and pulled silently to the front of the house. It was a good neighborhood, a fine house, undoubtedly full of fine possessions. A welcoming light shone above the door.

He took from his pocket a white linen handkerchief and removed his round gold spectacles. He cleaned the lenses carefully and folded the handkerchief, replacing it in his front suit pocket so that one corner crisply protruded. He regarded himself in the driver's rearview mirror and smoothed his bow tie. Then he got out of the automobile and walked quickly to the front porch.

■ ■ ■ ■ ■

IV.

■ ■ ■ ■ ■

Lights were shining from every window, and there was a savory smell of roast goose. . . . She sank down and huddled herself together. She had drawn her little feet under her, but she could not keep off the cold; and she dared not go home, for she had sold no matches, and could not take home even a penny of money.

— Hans Christian Andersen,
"The Little Match Girl"

My dear Grethe,
    You do not mind for me to address you by your given name? You see, your mother has told me so many lovely things about

you that it would seem so distant for me to be calling you by the formal title of Miss Eicher — and then we are not strangers — Are we, dear?

Your mother always has so many lovely things to tell me about you . . . and I love you, dear, because I believe you are all that your mother tells me you are. I would be very proud to have you as my own girl. Tell me — would you like to have me as your daddy? You could then have ever so many lovely things and we would have lots of fun together — wouldn't we, dear?

I know you are a great help there until I come for you. I am very anxious to see how well you are doing and to know exactly what you are doing at any time of the day —

Do write me today some time, dear,
with love, Cornelius

JULY 2, 1931
PARK RIDGE, ILLINOIS

A CHILD'S JOURNEY

Annabel was awake first, and saw the black car parked below. She was sleeping in Grethe's room, for the bed was large enough, and they both slept better so, with Mother away. They wore beach pajamas; the nights were stifling, and they did as they liked after Abernathy shut her door at 8:00 P.M. It was Mr. Pierson's car, Annabel was certain, as shiny and clean as though it had never moved. "Grethe! Get up. The week is over and Mother is here! And Mr. Pierson! I'm going down."

Grethe was rubbing her eyes. "Should you? It's quite early, isn't it?"

"Mother is here! Abernathy will leave!" Annabel ran to wash her face. She must not say she was miserable. She quite liked Bible School, but Abernathy had them occupied all afternoon, polishing silverware, folding laundry, while Hart joined his friends at games and must be home by dinner. It was tiresome, for he took Duty with him, and the girls hadn't even the diversion of going to the park. Duty returned parched, and napped all evening, then wandered disconsolate when the house was dark and he found Annabel's bed empty. She would hear the click of his nails along the hallway, until she stood drowsily in Grethe's doorway to announce herself. She would have to pick him up and lie down with her hand upon him, or he would stand, terrier-fierce, pulling at her clothes, intent she go to her place.

Her place was with Mother in Mr. Pierson's automobile, gliding beside waterfalls and rivers, wearing Charles' long silk scarf perhaps, her hair blowing back. They would be every bit as jolly as Frog and Toad in their motorcar. Her mother read *Wind in the Willows* aloud to her every summer, with Annabel doing the voices. Rat, her favorite, was the smart one. Always conniving, Mother said, it's what rats were, no matter how charming. Mother liked Badger, for he was the sage. And why were there no girl animals? Her mother sighed, for it was a question Annabel must always ask.

Grethe was calling her. "Annabel, shouldn't we put something on, if Mr. Pierson is here?"

"I'll choose you something. Only let's hurry." They opened Grethe's closet, in which Mother stored the things she'd saved from Grandmother's armoire. The dotted Swiss, the peach silk, the black lace. "This one," Annabel said, and took the black.

"But that's Grandmother's mourning dress. It's for funerals."

"It's ever so pretty though, with the cut-out lace for sleeves." She tossed her head. "Wear it for a robe, or wear what you want. I'm going down!"

She raced for the stairs, skipping every other one, Duty at her heels. Rounding the landing, she slid a hand along the wide banister for balance and plummeted forward.

"Good morning, my dear. You're awake early, and I'm so glad." He was standing just below her, instantly, one foot on the stairs and his pocket watch open in his hand, like the rabbit in *Alice's Adventures in Wonderland*. Annabel thought to jump into his arms and surprise him, as she had many times surprised her father in thoughts that were not really dreams. But the watch gave her pause. She fancied she heard it ticking.

"Oh, Mr. Pierson! Where is Mother?"

"She's waiting for you, dear, in our new home, and wants us to get on the road right away."

"She's not here?" Annabel stopped on the stairs.

Mr. Pierson stepped close to her, the banister between them. Bathed in the light from the landing window, his eyes were very blue. "Your mother misses you terribly and

141

can't wait for you to join us. I've come for you, you see."

Annabel rushed past him, out the front door to the porch. The street was empty. Only the porch swing trembled on its chains, for it always swayed when someone opened the door too fast. She had smelled her mother's scent, below her, then above and before her. It was very curious. She reflected that the scent had weight, as the wind has weight, or force, to blow here and there; it had moved past her unaware, as though in a great hurry, not knowing her. Suddenly her head hurt very much, and she sat down in the empty porch swing.

She felt him sit in the swing beside her.

"Your mother has found you a very pretty pony," he said. "A pet for all of you, but yours to ride, I think, because he's no taller at the shoulder than this." And he touched the top of her head. "Would you like to know the color of the pretty pony?"

Annabel felt him turn her face toward him, and direct her gaze.

"It is a white pony, with white mane, and a black star just here." His hand was heavy on her head, and now he touched her forehead with his thumb. "Here, a black star." He pressed a warm circle on her flesh.

The headache eased. She forgot it and felt drowsy, as though lifted from a hot bath. "Mother has gone," she said.

"Our secret. Let the others be surprised."
He stroked her brow. "About the pony." His
eyes widened on hers; he swung them gently
in the swing.

Annabel felt a bit sleepy, smaller and
younger. She looked down at her open hands,
in her lap. Her palms looked very white, like
a drawing she saw from far away.

"Now then," he said, and clapped once.
"It's a lovely morning to travel."

Annabel wished the neighbors might see
her on the porch with Mr. Pierson. He looked
very nice in his suit, and less formal without
his bow tie, his spectacles in his jacket pocket.
"We're going soon then," Annabel said.

"Yes indeed," he said.

"Mr. Pierson, can I make a picnic?"

"Yes, my dear, why don't you. What a good
idea. Be quick about it though. We have a
long drive and shall leave in the cool of the
day. And you may call me Cornelius, as your
dear mother does. After all, we are not strangers, are we, dear?" He stood from the swing
and held the front door open for her as she
flew through to the kitchen.

She passed Grethe, standing on the stairs
in Grandmother's black lace dress, and Mrs.
Abernathy behind her, pulling tight the sash
of her wrapper. "We're going!" Annabel
shouted. "I'm making a picnic!"

Grethe could feel Mrs. Abernathy behind her,

bristling with irritation at the early hour, at Grethe's attire, at Mr. Pierson, for he'd sent no word of his arrival.

"Good morning, Grethe," he said warmly, as though she alone stood before him.

"Mr. Pierson, good morning." She could not bring herself to call him Cornelius, as his letter bade her do.

Now he looked above her at Mrs. Abernathy, who never came downstairs in her wrapper. "Good morning, Mrs. Abernathy. How have you fared? No problems, I hope."

"No," Abernathy said, disapproving. "Not a one."

"A reflection of your excellent supervision, I'm sure. Mrs. Eicher will be so pleased. But we must get an early start. Would you be so kind as to wake Buster, Hart, that is, and make a hot breakfast for the children? No need to dress, unless you insist, for we are all family here, and this is the start of our promised trip south."

Abernathy went back upstairs without a word. Mr. Pierson smiled at Grethe. "She *will* dress, though, won't she, Grethe?"

"Oh yes," Grethe said.

"Yes, it will take her a moment. Come here, my dear." He took her hand as she walked down the two or three stairs to where he stood, as if she alighted from a carriage and he received her.

She thought they might be going to sit

alone in the living room and discuss something important. But he put his hands lightly on her shoulders, and fixed his eyes on hers. "Grethe, your mother wishes you to go to the bank, right away, and withdraw funds that she requires. Her directions are written clearly in a note entrusted to me, which I will give you."

"Shall I go then? Myself?"

"Of course you shall, my dear. This is private between us. Your mother trusts you to go to the bank. You're the eldest, aren't you, and so it's most appropriate."

"Now? I should go now?"

"Yes, of course. The bank is open and won't be crowded this early. Don't tarry, and speak to no one, as your mother has told you."

"Yes. She tells me that. And to wear my hat."

He nodded in agreement. "Wear what is usual for you."

She'd slipped on her Sunday shoes, respecting Grandmother's dress, with no socks, which felt quite odd. "Oh, then I must change —"

"No, you look quite nice as you are. Only, where's your hat?"

Her hat hung on the tall Victorian hat rack. She liked its many pegs and diamond-shape mirror, and the glove drawer below. "Just there," she said, pointing behind him, "beside Duty's leash."

He swept her hat from the rack, and the leash clanked to the floor. Somewhere upstairs, Duty began barking, for he thought it was time for his walk. Cornelius, or Mr. Pierson, put her hat gently on her head.

She remembered that her hair was down, not up, and that she wore her bathing pajamas under Grandmother's dress. They were short trouser pajamas, to her knees; no one could see them, or her camisole, on top. But she felt quite strange, without her undergarments. She couldn't possibly go out of the house this way, yet she must.

Cornelius seemed pleased. "It's true what your mother says. You are a young lady now, and very capable."

Grethe, despite her dilemma, tried to smile, for Cornelius was smiling. He stood very near; his blue gaze warmed her inside her throat.

"All set, dear?" he said encouragingly. "Fasten your hat —"

"It . . . doesn't fasten, you see. The ribbons only hang, like so, they're navy ribbons —"

"Of course, very nice. And here is the note for the bank." Her name was written across in flowing script. "It's private, addressed to the bank, and you must not show it to anyone, or speak of it. Simply hand it to the teller at the window. You have your purse? They will give you an envelope, which you must bring straight back to me."

She took her purse from the banister, where it hung by its strap, and held it open before him.

He put the note snugly inside the zippered pocket. "Do you have your glasses?" he asked. "Will you need them at the bank? Or on the walk?"

"I keep them in my purse, in their case." She hung her purse across her chest, which she should have done before putting on the hat, but the strap was long and only grazed the brim. "I never wear them walking, no." The thick lenses had caused her much distress, until Mother let her study at home, and children no longer called her names.

He straightened her hat, and tapped the thin gold rims of his spectacles. "Glasses give one an intelligent air. Those who do nothing have no need of them!" He beamed at her. "Isn't that so? I shall take you to my optometrist and order you fine, light, gold frames like my own, with lenses ground to special order. Would you like that, Grethe dear?"

"Oh yes," she said, and was thinking of it as he steered her out the door. She was down the steps. "Quickly now," she heard behind her, but the door was shut when she looked back, and no one was watching through the curtain, as Mother watched when Grethe had gone to the downtown shops with Grandmother, or Hart.

She'd not gone to the bank alone, or anywhere, alone, that she remembered, except for the corner grocery.

Cornelius was ever so kind. He treated her as the others should treat her. She walked briskly, as usual. Her black dress was a mourning dress, she knew, but it was silky against her, and cool in the early morning, with the lace sleeves. She faltered, remembering: *navy with navy and gray, black with all but navy.* The ribbons of her hat were not right. Her hair was down, not up. She hadn't gloves, which one should wear with such a dress. Shapes approached on the sidewalk, took clearer form, and passed by her; she counted corners, listening to the traffic, and was on the third corner, which had no traffic light.

Here she must wait longest, looking side to side.

The cars passing in the street were dark colors, one after another. A woman brushed past her, heels clicking, stepping into the street. She followed the woman and was in the street; a horn blared at her. Grethe stopped in the middle; cars passed before and behind her. She looked for the woman, walking away, but she was not there. Then suddenly the woman appeared, smiling, and raised an arm for Grethe to follow. Looking neither right nor left, Grethe crossed, nearly running until she felt the safety of the curb under her shoe, and the broad sidewalk. The woman was gone, very quickly it seemed, and Grethe walked quickly as well, for she was only one stoplight and a crossing from the bank.

Hart is riding the pony as his father leads it across the meadow. His feet don't reach the stirrups, but he grips the horn of the saddle and the pony's long mane. Rider's mane is coarse and combed, and the color of cocoa. His father adjusts the bit in the pony's mouth, speaking quietly. The pony turns his soft ears as though they're engaged in conversation. The words are important but Hart cannot hear them. They walk over pale new grass, under blossoming trees. The meadow is limitless before them, open, but the grass grows higher, and higher still, to Rider's flanks, to his father's waist. The sharp, numberless blades part before them and register no passage. Hart sees his father's muscular back, for now he is shirtless in the heat, in suspenders and trousers. The light is warm but not unpleasant, bright yellow and then brighter still.

Leaves begin blowing about wildly, flying up in clattering swarms. The air, crisp and cool, smells of woodsmoke. The pony walks over layers of dry leaves that crackle like crumpled paper. The meadow is low and the trees nearly naked. Hart sees, far off, his mother and sisters, parading with parasols.

They're walking together happily, all listening to Grethe, who speaks with felicity and wit, having never fallen ill. Rider tosses his head, for there is a bonfire in the cleared center of the meadow. His father, in a fine suit now, calms the pony. Hart knows they will pass by, though his mother and sisters and grandmother sit round the fire on café chairs, roasting their figs and chocolate on long sticks. Hart hears their laughter, tinkling like distant chimes, but nothing is funny, for time is short.

Snow begins falling, powdering the sleeves of Hart's jacket. The snow thickens, falling so heavily, coating his leggings and boots. He is roped to his saddle, his hands in bulky mittens. Rider steps slowly, deliberately, for the wind is blowing and the snow is shank-high. They are headed to the open meadow where the snow is unbroken, shining on its surface. Hart sees his father, holding the lead, grasping the pony about the neck in a half-embrace.

A shape approaches in the snow, a tall man on a fine horse. The man wears formal riding clothes, jodhpurs and jacket, and nods as he moves past. As though observing some genial custom, the men greet one another's horses. "Rider," says the tall man, inclining his shoulders far above them. "Traveller," says Hart's father, nodding. Hart hears the big horse walk past, begin to canter, and then to gallop. The sound of its hooves grows louder and louder until one roar of wind envelops all.

Desperately, he wants his father to turn to him. He wants to call out but his scarf is pulled high across his mouth. His father stops Rider and feels his way along the pony's back to Hart, in the cutting, swirling snow. Hart pitches forward out of the saddle, into his father's arms. His father's face fills his vision and he remembers, perfectly, the last time his father took him to the park on the pony. He knows his father's eyes and smell, his mustache and full mouth, his strong, compact hands, for he has thrown off his gloves and pulled Hart close to him. Hart is crying and his father begins to cry, unashamedly, saying that he went away but he has come back, he will never leave Hart again, ever, unless I take you with me, my dear sweet child my only boy my one.

Hart holds on to his father's neck very hard, but someone is shaking him, pulling them apart. "No!" he shouts to his father, but it is Mrs. Abernathy, saying Hart must get up, for his mother has sent for him and Mr. Pierson is here with the automobile.

So early, just as Cornelius promised, there was no line at the bank. Grethe gave the note to the teller, who looked at her, and back at the note. "Excuse me, one moment." She then stepped to another teller's window. Grethe saw them pick up the telephone and make a call. She knew she must have done something wrong. Were they calling her mother? But her mother was not at home. Grethe held her purse to the center of her chest. She hoped she would not have to put on her glasses and read the note before the teller. She could do so, of course, but she must always practice before she read aloud.

"Miss Eicher . . ." The teller was back, and leaned forward, as though inviting a confidence.

"Yes?"

"I'm afraid we cannot honor this note. It is not your mother's signature, you see."

"It's . . ." Grethe waited.

"Do you understand me, dear?"

Grethe was about to say that Cornelius might have written the note, for he had surely written her name across in that lovely script. She wished that she could write her name like that.

The teller leaned closer. "Mr. Malone would like to speak with you, but he is in meetings all day in the city. Can you come back tomorrow with the note? He asks that you allow him to help you, personally, first thing tomorrow morning."

"Yes," Grethe said, and turned to go, but the teller called her back, for she had forgotten to take the note.

She waited a moment outside the bank. She must concentrate, for she was anxious. The signature. She must remember, for he would ask her. Funds were money and Mother wanted money, and he did, for their trip. Perhaps now they would not go on their trip, and she would not see her mother very soon. She felt tears prick her eyes. Still, she must hurry. She hugged her purse to her chest and saw the note still in her hand. Quickly, she put it inside the purse, relieved, for she might have dropped it and never known. She crossed the first street with the light, and came to the second corner, the broad avenue.

Traffic blurred, unbroken.

She wondered, if she put on her glasses, would the traffic stop for her. No, one thing had nothing to do with the other. She wished she might see the woman at the crossing, but she saw no one, only the cars passing in angry streaks, until she glimpsed Hart on the other side of the street. He would be very upset with her, even if he knew that Mr. Pierson had told her to go to the bank. She listened, looking from right to left to right. One car was coming, far off, but she crossed in time.

She turned one way and another, but Hart had gone on ahead; she hurried to catch up. She would not mention that Mr. Malone wanted to help her personally. If Mr. Pierson should tell her to return tomorrow, Hart would go with her and stand just beside her. He was very protective, Mother said. Grethe thought she saw him, always a corner ahead of her, and walked faster.

Hart pulled a shirt on over his pajamas and found the canvas shoes he wore as slippers. He knew, vaguely, that he had dreamed about the pony and his father, and he was angry with Abernathy for coming into his room and waking him.

He saw the car then, gleaming in front of the house, incongruous as an ocean liner. Hart had never seen it in daylight, for his mother's friend had arrived after dark, and they'd set off together near dawn a week ago, before the children woke. But now Mr. Pierson was back, and they would ride along with the chrome trim flashing. He wondered about the color of the seats and visors, and smelled pancakes as he ran for the stairs.

"Ah, Buster!" Mr. Pierson smiled up at him, clapping him on the shoulder as he reached the landing. "You shall be copilot, my boy. We're leaving quite soon, so you must have breakfast."

"I'm sitting in the front, then?"

"Absolutely. I know the way, of course, but you will track our progress on the maps, and decide when we stop for ice cream. What do you say?"

"Mr. Pierson, can Duty ride up front with me? He's ridden in cars before. He's very good at cars."

"No, no, my boy. We haven't room and it's much too long a journey for a dog, in such hot weather. Duty will stay with Abernathy until our return. He's a good watch dog, isn't he, and we can't leave Abernathy here by herself, can we?"

"But she doesn't even like Duty," Hart said.

"Ah. You wait. By the time we return, they'll be friends. She has him shut up in the pantry now, due to all the rushing about." Mr. Pierson inclined his head, considering. "You must explain to Duty that you'll be back quite soon. People think animals don't understand, but I disagree. They hear a tone of voice; they know things, in their way."

"Yes, they know," Hart said, and saw, in his mind's eye, his father and the pony, walking before him in the gently falling snow.

"I'm very glad to have you along, Buster. You are such a good lad and your mother and I are very proud of you. Now have your breakfast, and be quick."

Hart felt himself nodding and turned, for he heard Duty barking wildly. He felt very odd and wondered why he hadn't heard the barking all along. Abernathy, frowning, gave him a plate of scrambled eggs and pancakes. Annabel was packing the picnic basket, emptying the icebox. Hart went into the pantry, where Duty at last fell silent. Hart, his back to the wall, slid down to sit on the floor. "Duty, it's all right." The dog licked his face and scratched at the heavy door. "I know, never mind," Hart said. "Look here, you have the eggs. I'll have the pancakes."

Duty, diverted, fell to work. Hart folded the pancakes in half and ate them, dripping syrup on the plate. Absently, he kept one hand on Duty's sleek head, for his palm fit the dog's hard, flat brow. "I have to be gone for a bit," he said. "You'll stay here and watch over things. I know you won't like it, all of us going at once."

His father and the pony had disappeared at nearly the same time, or so it had seemed to Hart. His mother and grandmother took the children to the funeral parlor, where they all knelt, touching the closed box. They were judged too young to attend the service, but the house was a blur of people and flowers and food laid out. Soon after, the pony was sold to the farmer who'd supplied hay and feed; a good home, his mother said, with pasture and a lake. Hart wanted to go with the pony, to the pasture and the lake; later he didn't remember kicking and hitting, and screaming until his throat was raw. Then he lay wrapped in quilts, a cold cloth on his forehead. His mother told him that she would never punish him for what he could not remember doing.

Hart stroked Duty's shoulders and back, where his hide wrinkled in shiny folds over his muscles. He was small but strong, with jaws like a trap, and a quivering, astute nose: he found rabbits in their nests, and mice in their holes. Once in the clinch, he never backed down. There was no punishing him for all that, but leaving him was punishment. "I'll take you to the park when I get back," Hart said, "but the fellows will miss us. There's not another decent pitcher."

Duty looked up from the eggs, then licked the plate, nudging it aside. He turned a tight circle and sat on his haunches next to Hart, as though they were spectators at the same event.

Mr. Pierson was standing at the door as Grethe came up the front steps. "My dear?" he said quietly.

Grethe thought it would be hard to tell him, but the words came easily. "Mr. Pierson, they wouldn't give me the money. They said it was not my mother's writing."

"The signature, do you mean? How tiresome. Your mother won't be pleased, but never mind. Get the children. We'll leave immediately."

"Right now? I'll ask Mrs. Abernathy to help pack —"

"No need. We'll be back for all that later. In

any case, your mother has clothes for all of you in her trunk."

"She does?" Grethe had helped pack the trunk: her mother's best clothes, and numerous mementos, but —

"The note, my dear."

She gave it to him gratefully, and saw that Hart had come up behind them, holding a plate of eggs and pancakes.

"Grethe hasn't had breakfast," he said.

"Quite right," Mr. Pierson said. "Give her that plate, for the car. It's your second, isn't it? You've a good appetite! The picnic is in the backseat. Come along, Annabel!" He motioned her forward.

"I told Duty I will bring him back something special," Annabel said, "and send him messages. Dogs hear what we do not!" She was holding her rag doll, Mrs. Pomeroy.

They could hear Duty barking, from the pantry.

"We will be back soon enough! Quickly now!" Mr. Pierson widened his blue eyes at Hart, and smiled happily. "When we're far enough east, my boy, south into the beautiful hills, I shall give you a driving lesson. There is one stretch seldom traveled, where the stream runs along beside the road and the turns are gentle. There you shall take the wheel, with my assistance of course."

"I'm going to drive?"

"Oh, yes. A boy your age should know how

to drive. Be quick now, your cap!"

They were all out the door, into the car, rolling down the windows and remarking on the plush seats. Grethe saw that Mr. Pierson, Cornelius, she must call him, was still in the house. Perhaps he had forgotten the note. But then he was on the porch and down the steps, and they were all clapping and cheering. He turned the key and the motor growled as the gears engaged. Hart wanted to blow the horn to tell the neighbors good-bye, but Cornelius drove them smoothly away. The journey was begun.

■ ■ ■ ■

V.

■ ■ ■ ■

Whenever the moon and stars are set,
Whenever the wind is high,
All night long in the dark and wet,
A man goes riding by.
Late in the night, when the fires are out,
Why does he gallop and gallop about?
                    — Robert Louis Stevenson,
                              "Windy Nights,"
                    A Child's Garden of Verses

July 3, 1931
Quiet Dell, West Virginia

WINDY NIGHTS

West Virginia seemed to Hart a magical preserve of forest and trees, deep valleys, high vistas where hawks wheeled, and few people, for they passed frame houses and small hamlets, isolated barns, and no towns of any size. There would be fireworks in Park Ridge. He wondered if he would see lights tomorrow night from somewhere in the mountains.

Hart had never seen mountains. He'd never traveled in an automobile, for they rode the streetcar to Chicago. He was used to the city, with tracks and noise and telegraph wires swooping from pole to pole. Mr. Pierson's farm was in Quiet Dell, with many acres of fields and woodlands, a pond for fishing, and a house with a broad front porch and double porch swings. A room for each of them, and a good dinner their mother was cooking. She would make a pie, Mr. Pierson was sure, for blueberries were in season and falling off the bushes.

Hart must have closed his eyes, for he saw the berries falling onto many confusing paths. He saw then the road in the playhouse mural, curving its way so far from the snowcapped peaks, and the man in the coolie hat, pulling the cart with the piles of shapes. The cart was full of ice for baby Grethe, too late, for her fever was raging and the damage done.

"Buster, my boy, are you sleeping?" Mr. Pierson's hand was on Hart's knee. "My copilot must stay awake."

"Am I going to drive the car soon?" He rubbed his eyes.

"Ah yes, you've been most patient. I believe we'll do that tomorrow, as your mother expects us for supper. We're pressed to arrive in time, and look at that sky. Rain, I think."

Annabel was reciting poems in the backseat, with Grethe grading each performance, needlessly, for Annabel started over unless she was perfectly satisfied. She repeated "The Swing" again, but Hart could barely hear the words over the rushing of air from the open windows. The sky up ahead did look dark, but just now there were blue patches, and the green depth of the trees on either side looked lit and brilliant.

Three gasoline pumps stood sentinel before a storefront. They were like robots, Hart thought, with big dials on their chests and round silver heads proclaiming their names in circular letters: *American Ethyl Gasoline, American New Action Gas, Amoco-Gas.* Their straight silver tanks repeated the names on oval badges, and the hoses looped from one shoulder to the other. The building itself was weathered. Bright metal signs glinted from every surface: *Kendall, The 2000 Mile Oil; Treat Yourself To A Good Chew, Mail Pouch Tobacco; Postal Telegraph Here.* The garage bay door was open, but Hart didn't see anyone. Then two men came out of the storefront and sat down casually on the long bench in front of the big window.

Mr. Pierson turned to the girls in the back-seat. "I happen to know they sell ice cream here. Anyone for ice cream? Annabel?"

"Oh yes. I want vanilla, with a cherry."

"Strawberry?" ventured Grethe.

"I know Hart wants chocolate, don't you, Hart?" Annabel said.

Hart only yawned. They'd slept very little the night before, their naps punctuated with games and songs that Mr. Pierson said were just the thing to keep them alert. Twice yesterday, again this morning, they'd stopped along the road with the picnic basket, once in a farmer's meadow, then in a shady glade along a railroad tracks, and last, at a deserted outlook with tables. Mr. Pierson praised Annabel for bringing such a lot of food. They ate from china plates Annabel had packed, which was why the blasted basket was so heavy. Mr. Pierson told the children to move around a bit, encouraged games of tag, and led rounds of Simon Says. Now the food was gone. Mr. Pierson bought snacks each time they stopped for gas.

He was in the store now, paying for the fuel.

"I hope Mother won't be mad about the plates," Grethe was telling Annabel. "You shouldn't have packed her good china."

"Then what would we have eaten from? It was ever so nice, with real plates and utensils, and the tablecloth to sit on." She sighed. "Anyway, it wasn't my fault."

None of them said more, for the plates and the basket were gone. It was so curious. Mr. Pierson had shown them the view from the outlook, pointing out the rills of water tumbling into a ravine far below, and the hairpin turns in the road, looping here and there like bright stripes suddenly visible between the tops of trees. He'd carefully put everything back into the basket after their meal and walked across the highway to the outlook, as though to see the vista once again, carrying the basket. He stood even beyond the sign, with the basket at his feet. Then he turned suddenly, sending it over the edge with his foot.

The girls didn't see; they were behind a stand of rocks, performing necessities. Hart saw. He'd watched Mr. Pierson approach the very edge with the basket and wondered if he would jump. But Mr. Pierson had only kicked the basket over and done a kind of pirouette affecting surprise, as though he knew Hart was watching, and then looked down again, as if to see that the basket had really vanished.

"How clumsy of me," he'd said. "I shall have to buy your mother a beautiful new basket. It does give you girls a lot more room, however, to lie down and nap, for we will certainly get in after dark."

He was back at the window of the coupe. "We're fueled up. Now, then. Annabel, you come with me to help with the ice cream." He winked at the girls. "They have all the flavors, and I've made special arrangements about the cherry."

They were gone, into the store.

"Hart," Grethe said in the quiet. "I miss Mother. I wonder why she didn't telephone us, all the time she was away."

Hart watched the two men who sat talking on the long bench by the store window. He might get out and ask them why a man would throw a basket of dishes and silverware into a ravine. He might send a postal telegram to Charles, but they'd left so quickly that Hart had not withdrawn his money from the bank. He had only a few coins in his shirt pocket, which he'd grabbed from the tin in the kitchen. Suppose his mother needed another loan?

"Did she say she'd call?" Hart asked.

"No. They sent those postcards."

The cards were in the mail tray at home. They didn't sound like his mother, and weren't in her hand. Hart supposed she'd asked Mr. Pierson to be friendly and send them mail, but why pretend to be her, and sign her name, with "Mr. Pierson says hello" off to the side?

"It's starting to rain," Grethe said, "with the sun out. There might be a rainbow."

The wooden roof over the gas pumps was bright white in the darkening light, and the cement block of the building was painted silver. *Gibson Motor Company,* read the big white letters, *Norwood, West Virginia.*

Later, near evening, the rain is drenching. He can barely see the turn onto the narrow dirt road. The children are asleep, lulled by the pounding rain. He slows the coupe, not to startle them, easing the car onto mud, for Quiet Dell road is standing water and the creek along one side is nearly to its banks. The garage is near, and there's no other habitation for a mile since he burned the tenants out, months ago. He steers to the left side of the road and imagines the car afloat, riding the stream to Clarksburg, but he sees the garage, a simple hulk with a flat slant roof, intricate enough belowground. He will assure their sleep with the chloroform and

168

rag in the glove box, open the garage door, and back the car inside. His blood is singing. He's entered that outer region in which it all begins; a penumbra around his head pulses like the charged gray emanation of a sunspot. He peers into a cloudiness in which flashes of brilliant red appear. *Nederlandse koninklijke purpura,* his father used to say, Dutch Royal purple, a *kneuzing* well deserved, the color of his backside if not his face, each time, for only a *nestbeschmutzer,* a diseased cur, shits in its own cage, betrays its own. *Schaamte schaamte schaamte.* He feels a surge and grips the wheel, but the coupe slides to the right and halts, subtly tilted, the back right wheel in mud to the axle. The arcs of the headlights appear to fly into the downpour at a rakish angle; he leaves the engine engaged, an essential vibration, and applies the brake. The boy first, and when he is senseless, the girls, while he gets the boy inside, down the ladder to the cell. He takes the bottle of liquid from the glove box, grips the rag, inhales deeply, not to be affected in the close interior of the car. He holds his breath then, and begins.

A sick smell, prickly sweet, fists her shut, until the car door opens like a bottom and drops her out. The sluice of water is on her face and all around her, for she has fallen into a lake and someone pulls her roughly through long drowned grass that clings and tries to hold her. The car door slams. She gasps, swallowing rain. She is in his arms, crushed close.

"Where is Hart? Where is Grethe?"

"Inside, my dear, out of the rain."

"What is this place?"

"One of my properties. I'm afraid you're carsick. Would you like to walk or shall I carry you? This mud will ruin your shoes."

He is nearly shouting over the rain and she is dizzy, the downpour tumbling around her. She struggles to stand and he lets her lean against the car.

"We'll just wait where it's dry, until I can rescue our automobile from the ditch." He keeps his hand upon her.

Annabel sees the garage building through driving rain in the dark and knows about the basement rooms. It's like a shoe box cut in squares, deep down inside where he was pounding. Driving nails, making the walls thick and black. Stairs steep as a ladder go below. She sees it from above, with the roof ripped off and the smell steaming out, a butcher shop smell pouring out like a pot boiling over. She sees the trapdoor standing open, and Pierson pushing someone she can't see down the hole.

She begins to run, dodging his hand, and he chases her, grabs her by her clothes as her shoes fly off in the mud. He hits her so hard that she flies back against the car. There's a shattering inside her, glass flying apart in splinters too small to count. She sees then, from above, Pierson stuffing her muddy shoes in his pocket; she herself moves easily, high above him, as though a string of yarn, unwinding from a skein, might connect her to that other girl below. She sees that she is wearing her grandmother's slippers, but they fit perfectly, and are no longer worn but look new; they shine and bear her up. There is no rain here, though she sees the rain, a shifting, downward mass of transparent color. She finds herself in some new element, moving as a swimmer might tread water, and rises farther still. She thinks to call for her mother but knows her mother is not here.

Grethe and Hart, though, perhaps are here.

She sees Pierson, dark, hunched and wet, a furry, swollen spider sidled here and there by the mud that rises in ridges when he tries to pass. Then he's a ragged, fattened wolf, lurching to one side, for he has dropped her shoes out of a pouch in his belly. His belly drags the ground, heavy, filled with rocks that he has swallowed one by one. He pulls a girl by her bound hands. That is not she, Annabel knows, for she is looking down at him. She can see the bright rain and smell the mud, clinging to itself like the mercury that fell out of Grandmother's broken thermometer. Rain floods the muddy clearing and dense green woods, separating and running in rivulets, tossing and stirring and dredging up the ground that is black and thick as chocolate.

Then she's on the road with Pierson before her. She moves toward him, trying to reach the girl, to slide her from him, but there is only a trace of motion when she moves her hand, a shimmer. He pulls the child by the rope that binds her wrists, feeling around in the mud with his other hand for her shoes, to stuff them back in his pockets. The shoes fall into the mud again, bewitched or slippery, hard to hold. Annabel sees, across the road, Mrs. Pomeroy, in wet mud beside the car, where she fell when Pierson pulled Annabel out, for the doll had been her pillow. Annabel must have her. She moves close in a terrible slow drift but cannot grasp the belted dress or fabric face; her hand disappears in what she sees. She thinks about the inside of the car, somewhere dry and safe, and sees Mrs. Pomeroy wedged deep into the fold of the backseat. His hand will not find her; she is only cotton batting, crushed and squeezed so small. The golden cord about her waist is Grandmother's golden cord, the cord that binds one soul to another.

Annabel sees the cord then, longer, thicker, shining, tied to a rafter in the garage ceiling, for she is inside the dim garage. Rain hammers the roof. A long trapdoor lies flung open, and rough wooden steps disappear into the dark below. Annabel touches the cord and feels instead her grandmother's silken hand, reaching for her as though across a great distance. The air around her swells and brightens. Her own grandmother is here, clear and luminous.

Annabel sees in the shadowy garage, as though by candlelight, a mess of clothes and objects on the floor, open boxes and trunks, but her grandmother has only to move her arm and beckon to pull Annabel near and lift them up, high and higher, above the hulk of the building, the muddy road, the rain.

Annabel sees forests and meadows, green swaths and deep valleys, half lit in sunlight, shading darkest near the garage and its hidden rooms. She hears the meadow creatures and their sounds, clicks and whirs of song and flight, rise and flow all around her, so distinctly, though she is high above. The dark is gone.

She is here, with Grandmother near and all about her. But where are the others?

Annabel remembers what Grandmother told her: *When I am gone.* Is Annabel gone, then, though she is not old, or been of service, or lived the long life Grandmother wished for her?

Her grandmother's image shimmers as though disturbed. Her gown, flung wider, casts warmth like the glow of a hearth, and Annabel feels her words in realms of quiet color: *I have found you. You are not there, below.*

Is this my death? she wants to ask.

My darling, there is no death, not as we suppose, as some still fear.

But where are they, then, where are the others? Annabel tries to see below, but she cannot open her eyes. She feels Lavinia touch her face.

Child, look. Her grandmother's open palms are full of small shimmering gems, like crystals, like diamonds. Each one is perfect, clarified. Annabel sees that tears are real in this place. Tears can be petals or pollen, or mist or rain, her grandmother tells her, but the tears of grief are stones of light.

Annabel sees them falling, shining as they drop.

Never mind. Her grandmother's hand upon her bears her up, to show her that the others are wherever she wants to see them, *for you are a child, and see easily. Know they may see you, just as clearly.*

Annabel sees Hart with a bandage on his head, running below her through the buzzing pasture with Duty, yelling triumphantly. There is a lake, and summer and winter together, and a pony with a cocoa mane and dappled flanks.

She sees Grethe, younger, the capable ten-year-old she never was, walking by the stream in Quiet Dell on their father's arm. It is really Grethe; their father has come for her and happiness lies round them, moving over the grass of the densely green banks, into the trees that are wreathed in vines.

Annabel looks for her mother and sees her parents in their wedding clothes, walking along the Krystalgade to their reception at Copenhagen's Royal Hotel. Annabel, borne up, wheels over them as they stand on the windy deck of an ocean liner, dressed in jackets and hats. Her mother's scarf is a froth of white chiffon that suddenly blows up and away, beyond the sea, until it is Charles' white silk scarf draped about Annabel's shoulders; the turbulent sea grows smaller and smaller, calms and stills, to become the tea in her mother's cup. The cup is atop the piano in their own living room on Cedar Street. Her mother sits with baby Grethe, who bangs on the piano, so loud, before her illness! Then Mother is bathing her in cold water to bring down the fever; baby Grethe screams and Father holds her still. Mother weeps into the water, and the edge of the tin basin floating with ice becomes the gleaming handle of a fine perambulator. Her mother pushes the carriage, a fancy one with a velvet hood, Hart the child within, and Grethe, four years old, very proud of her new eyeglasses, skips ahead of their father.

Annabel feels the feathery weight of

Charles' long white scarf and pulls it close about her. She senses her grandmother's touch and hears her voice: *Remember they cannot see or hear you. You see what has been and what will be. You are not bound by time.*

Alone, she flies above the beautiful, unfamiliar hills. She sees all of Quiet Dell, the dirt road leading deeper into country, the creek nearby, warbling its music, pulling light from dark, for she has flown from night to day. Bluegill and minnows dart within the falling, leaping water, each a transparent sliver with a beating heart. Quiet Dell is beautiful, the trees at once gently riffling their great canopies, leading like stair steps up the sides of densely scented hills, ridge over ridge, as far as she can see. She looks back to find the others, but the garage building is a black hole. She hovers there and sees grasses and roots grow toward it at lightning speed, rushing and meeting and growing up, a fountain of green, for years are passing and the urgent land hums and flows, erasing the harrowing dark.

She turns to get away, far away. Lights in the hills blink small as fireflies. She can see through the roofs of houses deep in the hollows. A boy sits beside his mother's bed, feeding her soup with a teaspoon. The boy wipes her mouth and a shock of dark hair falls in his eyes. It must be cool and damp, for he has put a coat and many rude grain sacks over his mother's quilt. Annabel is about to throw down her white scarf, for its warmth is surely greater from so far, but she is standing in Broad Oaks of a summer evening. What is Broad Oaks? The street is brick, the sidewalk a tilted strip along a bank of grass. Small wood houses, and a storefront with a board marquee standing straight and bare above the roof. That is Quincy Street, and the Powers' Grocery, Annabel thinks, but the names mean nothing to her.

She longs for home and sees her mother and Mr. Malone, sitting opposite one another in his office at the bank. His name is on the desk in brass. How odd that she can hear the tick of the big bank clock on the wall by the tellers' windows. The clock ticks until the sound is submerged in the evening sounds of Quiet Dell, a chorus of birdsong and crickets, and the whirl of insects past her ears. She sees Mr. Malone turn toward her mother, concerned, and then it is not her mother, but another woman, younger, her hair pulled up and fastened chignon style, writing Malone's words in a notebook. Malone stands to be near her, and the woman stands nearly against him. They look at one another and do not speak.

Annabel hears a clatter of hoof beats. A horse of some weight travels fast over hard ground. There is no ground, but this world contains every sound, and the mission is urgent. Yes, urgent, and as though she rides upon the horse, feeling its weight and the bellows of its breath, a night sky opens to receive her. She knows the constellations and begins to count their stars.

VI.

Come up here, O dusty feet!
Here is fairy bread to eat.
Here in my retiring room,
Children, you may dine
On the golden smell of broom
And the shade of pine;
And when you have eaten well,
Fairy stories hear and tell.
— Robert Louis Stevenson,
"Fairy Bread,"
A Child's Garden of Verses

AUGUST 27, 1931
PARK RIDGE AND
CHICAGO, ILLINOIS

EMILY BEGINS

Emily Thornhill must present herself to William Malone, bank president, who with Mayor McKee and Chief Harold Johnson of the Park Ridge police, seems in charge of official inquiries concerning the Eicher family. So, Park Ridge in late August — a veritable paradise, by the look of the ordered, shady streets, even here in the heart of downtown. Well heeled. Thriving, even. Homes of stockbrokers, medical men, professors and their lovely wives and perfect children.

She parks her borrowed automobile across from the First National Bank and attaches her press credential to the handle of her bag. She carries a briefcase as well, containing research, notes, accessed public records, but never opens it before subjects, and keeps information to herself in interviews: public records are misleading, sparse, often wrong. She takes her notebook from her bag and offers herself to subjects as a supremely competent professional, a blank slate interested only in factual elements. Of course, she is interested in far more. She has an instinct for play, for reading what the subject doesn't know, but could, or might.

She looks across the street at the bank. It might be the entrance of a theater. Marble facade, columns, double brass doors, as though a crowd might need to enter and exit at once, as required at performances. Banking and business are theater, most assuredly.

Interesting that Malone asked the *Tribune* to send through her résumé, despite Mrs. Verberg's and Mrs. McKee's personal recommendations. He required professionalism in all things. Her accomplishments, seven years now full-time at the *Tribune,* were impressive enough. Perhaps he is one of those who suspect successful workingwomen of flighty temperaments. Perhaps he resents independent women who require nothing of men like him.

Very well. She is Emily Thornhill, thirty-five years old, of good family, "finished" at Miss Porter's School, in Farmington, Connecticut, graduate of the University of Chicago, journalist for the *Chicago Tribune.* Summers with her paternal grandparents in rural Iowa after her father's death, when she was seven. A daddy's girl, and then her grandfather's, certainly. Seldom saw her mother, who was nervous, "not well"; who employed a governess, early on, and later, widowed, hired an "assistant" to manage details, including Emily's visits home and her coming out, a proper society debut. Emily supports her mother now with funds from a family trust, in a genteel facility with views of the lake. She no longer knows Emily's name, but greets her as a social equal with whom she is distantly acquainted. Emily is her family's sole heir; there is enough to ensure comfort, if not luxury. Her father's parents, who loved her father and his only child, were her true home; she lived for those summer months and the train rides to Cedar Rapids. Her grandparents met her in the wagon, with a basket full of sandwiches and cookies, until Grandmam was ill, and then Granddad. They'd died, two years apart, during Emily's summers off from college, when she was there to nurse them; she counted herself fortunate and did not pine for a different life. She is happily unmarried, though she is not a maiden, and lives in a doorman building. *Working girl* still applies, in Emily's estimation, for there are few terms to describe someone like herself; *spinster* is inadequate in her case. Her hairdresser says they will dye her hair, subtly, when the time comes, but never cut it, the light brown color is so lovely against her complexion, and her thick curls are easily concealed in tight chignons or the Gibson girl styles she favors: old fashioned, respectable, to soften her smart suits.

She checks her image in the rearview mirror, and carefully wipes any trace of lipstick from her mouth. Malone is not the first to require that she substantiate her qualifications.

He stood as she entered his office. "Mayor McKee asked me to meet with you, Miss . . . Thornhill?"

"Yes. Mr. Malone." She advanced to shake his hand across the desk. He was a tall man, handsome, distinguished even, with strong hands. His palm was cushioned and fleshy, powerful, and the instant of contact was disorienting, like the minute shift of a room. She was glad the desk remained between them, and stepped back, irritated with herself. Perhaps he had this effect generally. She did not typically succumb to general effects.

He regarded her, then indicated a chair at a round table to the right of his desk.

She took her notebook from her bag and began writing. *Mahogany paneling, deep blue carpet, massive desk. Tasteful, not opulent. Side entrance exit. Malone, as described.*

He was speaking. "The story will break quite soon. No one can stop that process, which will take on a life of its own. Mayor McKee feels the community can trust you to be factual, yet sensitive, particularly to the family." He took in her attire, her posture in his upholstered office chair, her face, her eyes, her gaze, intently focused on the notebook in which she was writing. "The *Tribune*," he said, "the most influential newspaper in the metropolitan area, will set the tone."

"That is my intent, Mr. Malone." She felt his gaze and wondered what he saw. Her hair was up; she had not worn a hat, as it was a warm day. She looked at him evenly. "As you know, Mrs. Verberg arranged that I interview the housekeeper, Mrs. Abernathy, today at the Eicher home. I will interview Mr. Charles O'Boyle this evening in Chicago, before departing for West Virginia. I should arrive there a day after the Park Ridge police whose travel you funded." She wrote, *noble, protective, skeptical.*

"I did not fund them, Miss Thornhill. I merely supplemented town funds in the interest of time. We are all neighbors in Park Ridge." Silence. He waited to catch her eye and then held her gaze, as though demanding she acknowledge the point. "Their presence in Clarksburg was necessary in order to effect Pierson's arrest, on the basis of numerous letters to Mrs. Eicher, found at the Eicher home. He fled in haste after police questioned him here, a week or so ago, nearly eight weeks after the family disappeared."

"Understood, Mr. Malone." She understood that he felt some responsibility, far more deeply than did the neighbor women. He was childless, they'd told her. These were fatherless children beyond the realm of protection. She herself had glimpsed that realm. If not for her grandparents, she would have lived within it, despite any material advantage. "Do excuse me," she said. "The neighbor, Mrs. Verberg, is a member of my Chicago travel club, as is Mrs. McKee. They asked me to become involved. I do investigative reporting — mostly political and social issues. Their accounts, as well as my phone conversation with Mr. O'Boyle, indicate that concern is warranted. O'Boyle was apparently the first to contact the police about — Pierson, is it?"

"Yes, Pierson. I never met him and can't comment on neighborhood talk; I live on the other side of the park."

"But you were the Eichers' banker for many years? You, perhaps, advised Mrs. Eicher on financial matters?"

"Yes. I knew her husband, Heinrich Eicher, a businessman — insurance — a silversmith as well, who ran his wife's enterprise, a crafts workshop, silverwork mostly, on their property."

"You knew them socially, as well?" She fixed her gaze on her notebook. His hair was thick, chestnut, silver at the temples. He wore it rather long.

186

"No. Mrs. Malone is an invalid. We don't socialize. But I met with Heinrich Eicher several times in this office, over the years. After his death, a sudden death, a streetcar accident, five or six years ago, I met with Mrs. Eicher, and continued to do so."

"You advised her in the wake of Heinrich's death." It was a statement. Emily could feel Malone's presence in the room. Masculine. A hint of delicate, musky fragrance, like crushed flowers. She glanced at his desk and wrote, *cologne? subtle. No ashtray/pipe stand, photographs, keepsakes. Trays of papers, correspondence, three deep, perfectly organized. Invalid wife. Streetcar, sudden death.* She could easily check records on Heinrich Eicher.

"Heinrich did not leave her well situated. They'd invested in the workshop, her fine arts business, but the lack of resources after she was widowed, and then of course the Crash, finished that. The children were young. There was Heinrich's mother, Lavinia, to help, but she died after an illness of some months, this past Thanksgiving."

"Leaving only Mrs. Eicher, Asta, to raise the children, support the household. And to do that —"

"Miss Thornhill, these are confidential matters. I'm sharing information with you only because Mayor McKee asked me to do so." He stood and paced, behind his desk. "I am

187

not optimistic. A woman, middle-aged, goes off with a man no one knows. She tells her neighbor she's to be married to a man of means."

"And what did she tell you, Mr. Malone?"

"Nothing. I would have asked to meet the man for a frank talk, with Mrs. Eicher's permission, of course. Any honorable man would have agreed to such a meeting, even requested it." He stood and walked to the window, which looked out on the alley passage beside the bank. "She wanted to stay in her home until the children were of age, and asked, last January, that the bank take over the mortgage and lend her a small sum. The debt, as well as the mortgage owed, would be paid when the house was sold." He turned to face Emily. "She had not accepted my advice in the past. I'm afraid she did not confide in me because she believed I would think her . . . unwise."

Emily allowed herself to look at his hands. A ring, of course, though Emily doubted a wedding ring daunted certain Park Ridge ladies. A sterling reputation, Mrs. McKee had said, and the wife, delicate. Catholic, though Malone was not. Her priest, apparently, called on her at home. "And did you, Mr. Malone, think Mrs. Eicher unwise?"

"She would not sell the house, reduce her circumstances, conserve her resources. She felt she could not seek employment outside

188

the home, though she was a skilled artisan."

"But, for income —"

"Mrs. Eicher took in roomers, the past five years, until Lavinia's illness."

"And this past spring, in late June, she left her home with Pierson."

Malone turned from the window. "I'm told Pierson looked respectable, but the discovery of these letters, obviously left in haste, is ominous. I should have stopped him, saved the children, or at least tried."

"You?"

He sat at his desk, quietly addressing the room. "The day they left, I was in Chicago on banking business. My employee reached me by telephone early on July second. She said Grethe Eicher was at the window, with a note, purportedly from Mrs. Eicher, requesting one thousand dollars cash. I asked her, was Grethe alone. Yes, Grethe was alone."

"That was unusual?"

"Very much so. Grethe was often in the bank, but always with her mother. Once, just before the children disappeared, with her brother." He paused. "She was, too trusting. Slow — an illness, as a baby."

He had lovely brown eyes, golden almost.

"Sad," Emily said.

"More than sad. I told the teller to *say* it was not her mother's signature, and in case Grethe didn't know what that meant, to ask her to return to the bank, early the next morning, when I would help her personally. Someone was forging a note, but I had no idea Pierson was at the house, no idea of the urgency. If I'd been here that day, I would have accompanied Grethe home, to confront him. If I'd phoned the police from Chicago immediately, and dispatched them, on a hunch, to the Eicher home —"

"The police," she said quietly, "would have detained him, on a word from you?"

"I don't make spurious requests of the police," he said. "They could have detained him, in fact, if I'd had the note in hand, but the teller, another mistake, gave it back to Grethe. Still, the police might have prompted him to leave without the children."

"At that point, though — early July — Pierson was thought to be Mrs. Eicher's fiancé. I'm told that Abernathy gave the police a letter in Asta's hand, saying that Pierson was coming for the children."

"Yes." Resigned, he bowed his head slightly, and touched the fingertips of one hand to his brow. It was a deeply mournful gesture.

She judged him near fifty, perhaps, but his bearing was that of a younger man. Broad chest and shoulders. Riding, Mrs. McKee had said. Large home and grounds, his own barn and groom, a few acres of pasture, a pond. City Council member, pillar of the community. He certainly seemed so.

Silent, he leaned back in the chair, lost in

some middle distance. Then he said, "Do you ride, Miss Thornhill?"

"I do, Mr. Malone, though not for some time."

"No?"

She felt such heaviness emanating from him, but pressed on for his sake. "I learned dressage at finishing school, but spent summers on my grandparents' Iowa farm. My grandfather raised quarter horses, and he was determined I ride like the wind."

"Ah. Good man."

"He was a very good man. I still miss him."

Malone said softly, "You are going there, to that place."

"Yes. Tomorrow." She felt herself on some precipice above a raging sea, that he was standing beside her, had arrived before her.

"Have you covered this sort of case before?" His tone was personal now, as though opening some ground between them.

"I do what you might call the woman's angle on hard news — I've seen some horrific things, children who've died of neglect or preventable illness in the settlement houses, gamblers shot in hotels, murders of wives, or husbands. Mine is not a lady's profession, I'm often told, but I enjoy membership in the Junior League, the Women's Travel Club —"

"I ask you to be in touch with me, Miss Thornhill. While you are gone, and after your interviews today. I would like to send an instruction, to Mrs. Abernathy, that she surrender her key to the Eicher residence, to you. I ask that you return it to me, here, in this office, after concluding your interview. Would that be a terrible imposition?"

"No, Mr. Malone. And I would be happy for your consultation, going forward."

He sealed a note addressed to Mrs. Elizabeth Abernathy, and gave it to Emily. "I would accompany you, to deliver this note and accept the key personally, but you'll want to see through the house, and Mrs. Abernathy may be more forthcoming if you are alone. Lock the house when you leave. Nothing must be disturbed."

"I will not touch, or disturb, anything. I merely want to take notes, and . . . . stand in the rooms."

Such an admission was unlike her. She suddenly felt they'd been talking for hours. In fact, it was less than thirty minutes.

"I shall wait for you, here," Malone said. "You can park your automobile in back, as I do. Ring the bell at this side entrance, and I will let you in."

She had closed her notebook, packed up her bag. "Mr. Malone, one more question, if I might. Do you think she went with him, willingly?"

"Oh yes, I have no doubt."

"Why? Was she reckless?"

Malone stood and moved to the front of his desk, not two feet from her. "Not at all. She was artistic, well bred, careful, even a bit reclusive. But emotionally desperate for some years, I think. And then financially so. Desperate people see a chance, and take it. Some of them are quite unlucky."

She met his gaze openly and felt him near her, like a force. "Only desperate people take risks, Mr. Malone?"

"Risk can seem compelling, even necessary. If asked, Miss Thornhill, I counsel deliberation, always, no matter how painful." He stepped toward her.

Immediately, she stood and moved close to him. The fragrance, so subtle, was the smell of his skin. It was as though she'd stepped into some inchoate sympathy, charged and alive, between them. They stood so, looking at one another, and did not need to speak.

She found the Eicher home easily, a mere seven blocks away. Abernathy, tall, thin, her gray hair pulled back in a severe bun, stood waiting by the front steps. She held a dog's leash in one hand, and the dog, small, dark brown, stocky, sat panting at her feet, beside a square basket. Emily, locking the car, took a look at the house, a pretty place with grounds behind, and waved at Abernathy, a gesture of acknowledgment.

Abernathy made no response, but the dog

tore suddenly forward, dragging its leash, to greet Emily effusively. Jumping up, paws on her skirt, it backed off to execute a kind of circle on its hind legs. "Goodness," Emily said. "Very pleased to meet you." The dog was coughing, seemingly, as though overexcited or asthmatic. Emily leaned down, and the terrier jumped into her arms. It was about the size and heft of a twelve-pound bag of flour, thicker than it looked, solid, and sat still, comfortably adjusting itself to the crook of her arm and the brace of her hip.

"You've a very friendly dog," she said, by way of greeting.

"That is not my dog," Abernathy said. "It is the Eichers' dog."

"Was it choking, before?"

"No, it was barking. That is, it can't bark."

"Oh." Emily put the dog down, and it ran up the front steps, leash trailing. It was funny looking, a Boston terrier with eyes that bulged to the sides like marbles, and ears that seemed too big for its head. "I'm very pleased to meet you, Mrs. Abernathy, and I thank you for coming."

"Yes, Mrs.," Abernathy said.

Emily made no move to shake her hand. Abernathy didn't appear to want to be touched. "Mrs. Abernathy, I am acquainted with Mr. Malone, president of First National Bank in Park Ridge, and with Mr. Charles O'Boyle, friend of the Eicher family, and you know that I want to interview you concerning the Eichers, and Pierson, Cornelius Pierson."

"Yes, and I'm to let you into the house."

"That's right. I am allowed to see through the house. And I have a note from Mr. Malone on bank letterhead, authorizing you to surrender your key to me, which I will deliver to him." She gave Malone's letter to Abernathy and looked up at the entrance, where the dog stood, nose pressed to the front door. "So, the dog hasn't been here since you left, some weeks ago?"

"No." Abernathy opened the note and scanned it briefly. They were walking up the front steps, to the porch. Abernathy put the basket by the front door. Some sort of conveyance for the dog, it seemed a home-made contraption: a square wicker basket with leather handles, and a pillow inside. The top was a doubled layer of chicken wire that fastened snugly. "Did you make that?" Emily asked.

Abernathy looked at her as though she were daft. "Heavens no. It was in the pantry. It was the only thing I took from the house, to transport the dog."

"Of course. Before we go in, Mrs. Abernathy, let me ask — you have keys, as do the police. Would you know, who else has keys?"

"Why, Mrs. Eicher, of course, has her keys." Emily caught herself. The fact that detectives were en route to effect Pierson's arrest was not generally known, but surely, after so many weeks, Abernathy must think something amiss. Or perhaps she was invested in not thinking. "The neighbors? Mr. O'Boyle?"

"No. Mrs. Verberg said not. Mr. O'Boyle asked me for the key, on the telephone, when he called. He was very surprised Mrs. Eicher had gone, and then the children, with no mention to him, and his things, he said, are stored in the garage."

"But you didn't give him the key."

She turned to look at Emily. "Mrs. Eicher did not instruct me to give anyone keys. Mr. Pierson had a key. I did not let him in."

Emily nodded. He had Asta Eicher's keys, of course. "I'm told you had a letter from Mrs. Eicher, saying that Pierson was coming for the children."

Abernathy turned to unlock the door. "But not when he was coming, or what time. I could not prepare, Mrs."

"I'm not a Mrs. actually," Emily said, "never married. Nor a Miss — too old. I'm a journalist."

"Yes'm."

They were in the front hallway. It was a lovely Victorian house, once grand, now a bit run-down. There were signs of disturbance: furniture had been moved about, and the rugs in the parlor and living room were rolled up. The tall ornate walnut hat rack had been

196

turned sideways, its diamond-shape mirror agleam in the sunlight falling through the front door window.

Emily took the leash off the dog. It walked straight through into the kitchen, barking its silent, chuffing barks, then began circling through the rooms as though engaged in some determined mission. "You left the house, when? With the dog."

"They left morning of second July. I stayed, near a week —"

"And was the house like this, things moved, missing —"

"Certainly not. I kept the key and waited to hear from one of them. Mrs. Verberg phoned me a week ago, to say that Mr. Pierson was back, readying the house for sale, and the Mrs. had taken the children to see relatives out West. He came and went, and never contacted me. What was I to do with the dog? Not that he concerned himself."

"Could we go upstairs?"

Emily followed Abernathy, the dog running before them. The children's rooms faced the front street, and the girls' rooms had a door through, one to the other. They were generous, but not luxurious, and shared a bath. The beds were neatly made.

"I made the beds that same day," Abernathy said. Her expression never changed.

A pity, Emily thought. She'd wanted to see the rooms as they'd left them, sheets tossed back, clothes strewn, toys thrown down —

They went room to room, not speaking. Emily felt a brilliant rage harden inside her. She must remember everything: details accumulated like filings to a magnet. There was Hart's catcher's mitt, a baseball with faded red stitching nestled against the leather thumb. Grethe's room was rather plain: her parents' likenesses framed on her bureau, a handkerchief box, closed, a cross-stitched sampler over the bed: *Now I lay me down to sleep, I pray the Lord my soul to keep.* Annabel's table was piled with pages of writing and illustrations cut from books — Rackham, Wyeth, Eulalie. Others, from Grimms' and Andersen's fairy tales, the Uncle Wiggly books, *A Child's Garden,* were taped to the doorframes and dark wainscoting, along with many childish watercolors and drawings.

Emily looked at Abernathy, who stood in the doorway as though unwilling to enter. "These drawings, are they original?"

"Ma'am?"

"Are they Annabel's drawings?"

"Oh. Yes'm. She fancied herself an artist, like her mother. Always darting here and there. I'd never have kept track of her, had I let her wander the neighborhood."

"So, when you were here, the girls stayed at home?"

"Yes'm. Or in the yard, unless I took them with me shopping."

"And the boy?"

"He took the dog to the park, baseball, whatever. Boys take care of themselves, is my experience."

Emily looked closely at Annabel's drawings. Many were pencil sketches of sprites or fairies, wearing leaves or flower petals, accented with colored inks, and they were charming, really. Each figure held a sort of long wand or stick, like witch hazel or forsythia, arched, with buds. The wands were living branches, it seemed. Tiny starlike spirals hovered at the end of each, dabbed with yellow. Emily wished she might have one of the drawings — they communicated so directly the child's frame of mind. She felt the dog nudge her ankle. The creature seemed to attend her every movement.

She looked over at Abernathy. "I don't mean to keep you. Shall we sit in the kitchen to talk?"

They settled at the kitchen table. Emily opened her notebook. With Abernathy, it would be just the facts. This woman did not embroider or conjecture. Emily decided to be blunt.

"I want to ask, Mrs. Abernathy. You were employed as the children's nurse, responsible for their welfare. And it was Mrs. Eicher, their mother, no one else, who employed you, yes?"

"Yes'm."

"Did you question . . . letting them leave with Pierson, when you had not heard from Mrs. Eicher in over a week, except the one letter, saying he was coming for them?"

"I thought it surprising he appeared so sudden, so early, and let himself in without waking us. But he spoke for the two of them."

Emily looked at Abernathy, quizzical. "What made you think so?"

Calmly, she smoothed her hair. "He paid me exactly what was owed, to the penny, without my asking, and a week forward."

"A week forward? I see. He paid you in cash?"

"In bills, from her billfold."

Emily felt a cold point tighten behind her eyes. "From Mrs. Eicher's billfold?"

Abernathy nodded. "A red leather billfold. She paid a deposit, was when I saw it before."

"In her hands."

"Of course, in her hands, ma'am."

"And why would Pierson have her billfold? Women keep such things very close to them, don't they? And if she were furnishing a house in another place —"

"Well, she wouldn't be doing that with her money. She told me not to mention . . . her situation, the mortgages on her house. I didn't think about it that morning, I was so busy getting the breakfast. He pulled me aside and gave me the money, very quick, and I was dishing out the food, with the little one underfoot, packing a basket with what-ever was cold, from the icebox — and then the older girl coming back, when I hadn't known she'd gone. She wasn't sensible, she wasn't allowed out by herself, anyone will tell you —"

"You mean Grethe? She went out? Where?"

"She came into the kitchen, where they were all eating, and said, 'I went to the bank.' 'You did what?' I said. She looked . . . confused, all teary — and he took her down the hallway to talk to her."

The note, at the bank. "Did you hear what he said?"

"No. The children were talking about Quiet Dell, a farm, a pony. Then he was calling for them, and they were gone."

"To Quiet Dell," Emily said, "in West Virginia?"

"I suppose, in West Virginia."

"What do you mean, they were gone?"

"The boy had taken the basket — the little one had packed it so full, she couldn't lift it — to the porch, and I heard them in the front room. I was washing dishes in the kitchen, running the water, thinking I would pack their bags. I had told the boy —"

"Hart."

"Yes, to get their suitcases. He, Mr. Pier-son, said they'd likely be back in a week, and told me to fasten up the dog, to stop it rush-ing about. I said what about their things, and he said they'd buy clothes on the way, and toys, and ice cream. I heard him saying this, in the hallway, with the children cheering. So they didn't even dress; they weren't dressed for travel. The younger ones were wearing their pajamas. And he gave me no instructions. He'd paid up that day, July second, forward to July ninth. It seemed I was to stay in the house, only to take care of the dog." She paused. "Then the dog was hurt, somehow."

Emily looked down, and the dog jumped easily into her lap, as though aware it was an object of discussion. "Hurt? But didn't you say the dog was fastened up?"

"Shut up in the pantry. Yes. It's a swinging door, very heavy, but somehow it worried the door and squeezed through. Raced past me like a shot. I had the feeling it rushed the front door and hit the door as it shut. It lay in the middle of the rug, gasping. And they were gone. The car was gone."

In the silence, Emily heard a faint sound, exactly in front of her. "What was that?" she said. "Did you hear it?"

Abernathy only looked confused.

"Did you hear that sound?" Emily pointed. "There. Do you see it? On the floor."

Abernathy picked up something small and held it to the light. "It's a tiny nail," she said, "or a pin, but not a dress pin."

"I heard it fall," Emily said, "but from where?"

Abernathy came closer, squinting, it seemed, at the breast pocket of Emily's Oxford shirt, but she was looking at the dog in Emily's arms. She touched the dog's collar, turning it round. "It's here, see, from his collar. One of the pins holding the letters to his collar."

Emily looked. Four small metal squares were fastened on the dog's leather collar. D U T Y, they read, in capital letters. "Oh." She took the pin from Abernathy and, not knowing what else to do with it, put it in her shirt pocket. She felt, her hand brushing her blouse, the fullness of her breast under the white cotton cloth, and the thud of her heart. "I'm not clear," Emily said. "You say the dog was injured?" She was thinking that she must write; she must take notes properly.

"Running to catch them up, to go with them."

Emily rubbed the dog's ears, and put one hand flat against its barrel chest. "Were you hurt, Duty?" The dog looked up, and she saw two short, parallel lines of scar in the short hair of its throat. "Was he bleeding then, from the mouth, or ears —"

"No, from there, where you see that scar. A swollen kind of wound. I wasn't about to move an animal. I went over to Mrs. Verberg's, the neighbor. She came back with me and we put a thickness of clean sheet in the dog's basket, that basket, there by the stove, and moved it near. The dog was breathing a bit easier and lay in the basket, looking pitiful. Mrs. Verberg said to get the disinfectant, and she put a cloth just under, and poured iodine over the wound."

"Ouch," said Emily. "I'm sure that hurt, Duty."

The dog, hearing its name, turned its ears and held still.

"So it stayed in the basket a day or two, then began walking about the house, out to the front and the back, in and out. On patrol, Mrs. Verberg said. I saw to the wound twice a day, cleaned it. It healed, but after, the dog didn't bark, only makes that sound you heard."

"Duty, do you mind? Let's have another look." She turned the dog's head toward her, and carefully felt the scar. "It's very regular, the scar, like the lines of, oh, the side of a shovel." Emily put the dog on the floor, and it went to its basket and lay down, its head on its paws, and gazed at them inquiringly.

Abernathy sat down. "Or the edge of a door, sharp and hard enough, if it smashed just so."

Or the tip of a man's shoe, Emily thought. Perhaps the side of his shoe. No, the tip, cutting the skin at that angle. The dog went after him when no one saw, and he kicked it hard enough to break its neck. Except it was this thick-necked little terrier — but he silenced the witness. She wrote in her notebook, *Vicious. Dog would know him.* "So, after a week, you went back to your own home? With the dog?"

"What was I to do? The neighbors wouldn't take him — Mrs. Verberg has cats and Mrs. Breedlove is allergic. I can't have pets, with my hours. I've no fondness for animals, but I couldn't just have the dog destroyed. I had a case, then another, near my own building, and I've kept the dog this long, but no longer."

"You took good care of him, Mrs. Abernathy. You may even have saved his life."

"It wouldn't be the first I've saved," she said stiffly.

Emily remembered Malone's comment — a nurse tending those privileged to die in their own beds. Hopelessly grim, this woman. Emily saw before her William Malone's brown eyes, and his gaze that seemed to enfold her, and felt wildly alive. "I do like animals," she told Abernathy. "I grew up on a farm, partly."

"Whereabouts, ma'am?"

"Iowa."

"Not so far, then. Perhaps, someone there —"

"No, I'll take him. I work long hours and I wasn't looking for a dog, but then, sometimes we don't know what we're looking for, do we?"

Abernathy looked through her. "I'm sure I don't know what you mean."

WILLIAM MALONE, TRAVELLER

He told the bank manager he was not to be disturbed; he would work through lunch. He locked the door, and sat in the chair in which she'd sat. He felt the warmth of her, for she'd left not three minutes ago.

Emily Thornhill. The name rang in his mind like a bell.

He'd never experienced anything remotely similar. It had to do with terrible things, things he referred to in his mind as "the children" that had suddenly, in the past week, opened like a chasm under him. Words he remembered telling her, *urgency, desperate people, saved the children,* were vast and deep as lagoons within him. And the thought of Emily Thornhill, nearing those depths, finding the dark in which the children lay, and he'd no doubt she would find them, and stand near what remained of them —

It was too late now, not to find them. They remained in his mind's eye forever and he'd thought there was no one, no one, to whom he could speak of them. He was fifty-one years old. He was married, yet he was alone. Emily Thornhill had said *ride like the wind,* and he recognized, inside her words, like a call to prayer, the daily knell of dark chimes that rang in his blood. He'd thought it was too late for him; there was no time, no hope, no way but to travel forward alone, desirous, unanswered.

She had said *stand in the rooms,* and then stood so close he might have crushed her to him.

Catherine would not know; she would not care. He'd always employed a housekeeper, but five years ago had engaged a nurse-companion, his groomsman's wife, Mary. The couple lived on the property and their children were grown. Mary's only duties were to watch over Catherine, sleeping or waking, cook her food and entice her to eat, bathe and dress her and never frighten her, take her for walks in the garden, sit with her by the pond, read to her. Catherine had loved her piano; she had played for him. Now she only sat, touching one key and another. He wished that Mary might play for Catherine, but a locksmith's daughter did not receive that sort of education. He was fortunate though, very fortunate; Mary was kindly, energetic, Catherine's constant: Catherine's sister some days, her mother other days, or her unnamed friend. He thought of them now as almost one entity — Mary and Catherine — and was at peace in separate moments, when he did not think of the future, about what would happen when Catherine got worse. He believed Mary's presence slowed the progress of the disease; he comforted himself that his wife was not in pain; she was not anxious; she was not distressed.

She did not remember him, or their history or their concerns, for she did not remember herself. Her room was her sanctuary; Mary put her to bed there at 9:00 P.M., like a child, and wakened her at seven. He'd moved a bed and armoire to the upstairs library, a comfortable room, and used the bath across the hall. He had entered his own forgetfulness, by design. Now he must think of Catherine and himself, for he must describe his life to Emily Thornhill. He must justify the change about to happen, with Emily and through her.

He'd met Catherine in Chicago, where he was then living, establishing First National with investors who were longtime business associates. A society benefit for Catholic Charities. She played Bach, and was assured, lovely, sophisticated, an engaged, intellectual Catholic. They toured Italy and the Vatican on their wedding trip. She had let him believe she was his age, a "fact" confided by a friend, but confessed on their first anniversary that she was actually thirty-five, five years his senior — a ruse for which she did not apologize. He might have changed his mind, when they were so perfectly suited! She knew he wanted children, as did she, very much. And they would have them. But they did not. They had dinner parties those first years, musical evenings with her friends, memberships in Chicago museums and clubs; they traveled. She continued to study music, played for a time with a violinist and cellist, offering concerts in support of charitable causes. He invested in real estate, a game of sorts, worked tirelessly to establish the Park Ridge branch, now the primary branch, of First National, and rode, weekends then, his own roan stallion, for he'd purchased the Park Ridge house and acreage for the fine stable and paddock, the fenced pasture.

Catherine was afraid of horses, a fear she had not stated. She consented, surely ten years ago now, to take his arm and walk to the stable, to meet Traveller, the first thoroughbred he purchased at Saratoga, not to race but to ride. To adore, Catherine said. The horse, less than a year old, was stalled and quiet, and William placed her hand on the beautiful arched neck. He remembered the large, depthless eye turned toward them, like a sphere that knew all, and the lush black eyelashes. Catherine cried out and fainted. She made light of it that evening, when he asked for god's sake that she tell him of any anxiety, and not agree to anything, no matter how trivial, about which she had any reservation at all. She said she was tired, had perhaps forgotten to eat. The embarrassed housekeeper admitted that Mrs. Malone often ate little. Though her plate might be empty, she hid the food, wrapped carefully in napkins, behind the canned goods in the pantry, or in the laundry, even in the piano bench. And she was very much disturbed by insects. She heard a wasp, lately, touching against the window glass, the shade, the wall, but there was no wasp.

In time she asked that they not go to theaters, concerts, restaurants. She did not like crowds. She preferred to eat at home with him, and then in her own room, alone, and now, with Mary, for Mary must feed her, like a child. Even five years ago, she was afraid to go outside, particularly afraid of the stable, of the walk to the stable across the grounds, yet she talked to him of Traveller repeatedly, nearly daily; he had saved Traveller from the confusion and danger and bitter contests of the track, the races, from the bells and the guns fired in the air. How good and peaceful here, with him. He kept his horses as they aged, pastured them, named every horse Traveller, so as not to confuse her, ostensibly, but he grew to love the name, and the fact that two and then three horses answered to it, like a good group of brothers. He rode nearly daily now, early mornings, afternoons on weekends, aware that the horse galloping under him shared the name of the favored mount of a defeated Civil War general, a man who'd fought a long, losing campaign out of loyalty, betraying, to a degree, his own ideals. William Malone had not believed in half-lived lives, restricted efforts, repressed desires. He understood them now.

Of course he'd taken Catherine to doctor after doctor, and these ventures, the travel, examinations, interviews, terrified her. He knew now that he should not have insisted, but he was desperate to restore her to herself, to him. Diagnoses varied: neurasthenia, anxious exhaustion, progressive nervous dementia. There was no treatment; the symptoms were psychological in expression but physical in nature. The condition would progress. She must have constant supervision. Institutionalization was indicated if she became violent toward herself or others, and was probably inevitable in any case. This he did not accept. He would hire the care she needed as her needs increased.

Her priest, Father Flynn, came to her every Sunday, to minister to her and hear her confession, and then he met with William, a scotch in the study, a Sunday evening ritual. He called William "Malone," and William called him "Flynn." He was William's contemporary, the only one with whom he could discuss Catherine's condition and welfare. For some years, Catherine had repeated only the preface to confession, *Forgive me, Father, for I have sinned;* she no longer remembered her sins, or the rest of the ritual. Father Flynn sought only to comfort her, and repeated the absolution in Latin. He wished he could offer William some comfort. William, educated by Jesuits, was not Catholic. By now, they were friends. They had their glass of scotch and discussed St. Thomas Aquinas.

Catherine could not sin, and her needs were met.

What of his needs? He was healthy, he worked long hours; he read Saint Augustine and C. S. Lewis, Aristotle and Herodotus, Newman's *Apologia;* he acquired profit; he rode, he discussed matters with his grooms-man. He had never invested in stocks, for himself or others, and kept the bank solvent while other banks failed; he was quite occupied and knew to avoid solace not infrequently offered him: the veiled advances of bank customers or employees would only end in scandal. He did not dwell on his needs. He'd turned away from such thoughts, not to hope or be distracted.

It was changed. He needed to tell Emily Thornhill about the children, to say that certain images returned to him distinctly, like questions.

He saw just now, so clearly, Heinrich Eicher, that Sunday in the snowstorm, days before his death, leading the pony whose name William could not recall, despite their ritual of greeting one another with their horse's names. The boy, Hart, looked miserable, slumped in his heavy clothes. William reined Traveller in, so as not to frighten the pony, and get past them. Then he rode hard, galloping full out, exhilarated, transported, into the wind and the driving fleecy snow. How glorious it was, riding in the deserted park as the snow fell more heavily!

But the child. He closed his eyes to stop the image.

Emily Thornhill's résumé stated her birth date. She was thirty-five. He was thirty when he'd married, well established in his career, planning to start a family. How odd to think it was so long ago, and how disastrous, time's disappearance, a disaster made all the more obvious by Emily's focused concentration and discernment, the angle of her head, her lovely thick hair, barely suppressed with combs and pins, honey brown, glinting with shine, for sunlight from the window fell upon her as she sat in the chair. A light had opened inside him without his realization or permission; he felt intensely his own deep regret, his powerlessness and mistakes in this matter of the children. His life these last years had required his acquiescence, his acceptance of conditions he could not control. He'd continued to behave deliberately in his profession, with every confidence, but cultivated an emotional distance between himself and others. He peered through that distance now as though through mist or cloud; he intuited one face and form distinctly.

Over an hour had passed.

Soon she would arrive to give him the key. He heard the bell at that moment, and rose to open the door.

EMILY FINDS A CONFEDERATE

Abernathy gave Emily the house key in the kitchen, and by way of farewell, Abernathy nodded at Duty in his pillowed basket. "You should take that basket; it's the dog's bed. I didn't, only because I couldn't manage in the cab, with my bag, and the dog in the carrier."

"I will, Mrs. Abernathy, at your suggestion." They walked to the hallway; Emily stepped carefully around the obstructive hat rack. "Bad enough that Duty has lost so much else."

Abernathy didn't dignify the remark. "And you'll need the leash, and the carrier to restrain him." She turned on the porch, her purse on her arm. "Good-bye, Miss Thornhill."

"Good-bye, Mrs. Abernathy, and thank you." She shut the door behind the woman, and immediately heard the fast patter of the dog's nails across the bare dining room floor, into the living room, and there Duty stood, looking at her.

"You are safe now, Duty. She's gone." Emily leaned down, and the dog jumped into her arms. It was a comfort to hold him, and he smelled very clean. Had Abernathy bathed him? Emily looked up the carpeted staircase. "We won't go back up there," she said, and felt suddenly tearful, as though the dog communicated grief, but could not cry. Fantastical thought. She respected animals precisely because they were not prone to human emotions, while human beings must earn her respect. She stood at a journalist's distance, even in the few love affairs she'd allowed herself. She did not know what to make of William Malone.

Duty. What a name. She supposed it was like naming a child Constance, or Faith.

Animals did sustain loss, in the moment. Of course they did. They understood the ravaged or stillborn young near their bodies, but they did not understand disappearance. A dog like this would continue to search.

She walked back through the hallway to the kitchen. The dog nosed beside the icebox, knocking a small glass bowl forward. "Is that your water bowl?" Emily washed it at the sink and filled it. "There. Then we will take a walk around the back." She would buy lean meat and bones from the butcher. And she would pay the doorman to walk Duty — Reynolds liked her, and liked dogs, she was certain. She saw the door to the pantry, a heavy door with a brass push plate. Odd that a dog that size could push it open, even in protective frenzy.

"You finished?" she asked.

Emily unlocked the back door and they crossed through. The lush grass was high and overgrown. There were outbuildings, a large barn in back, very run-down, and at least an acre of ground. Show me everything, she thought, and the dog set off.

He trotted first to the small playhouse, and Emily opened the door. All of the buildings had been painted to match the house, dark green doors, pale yellow wooden siding, muted, dark red trim. The playhouse might have been a storage shed except for the big square window in front. The loose glass was pocked and broken. Emily stood inside amongst the toys and dolls' clothes, cut-up Sears catalogs, broken tennis rackets. A captivating mural, floor-to-ceiling paintings affixed on three panels, adorned half the interior. The colors were faded, but weathering made them more interesting. They were a whimsical mix of geographies: Chinese coolie hats, Japanese kimonos and mountains, South Seas grass-roofed houses and palm trees, a golden road, winding down from distant snowy peaks. To go to such trouble for a playhouse, and then neglect it utterly.

She felt compelled to open the window and swing it wide. Carefully, she turned the latch, imagining upon it a smaller hand. That would be Annabel, the youngest girl, who would have loved this place and not cared that it was run-down, for she would not have remembered days of plenty. Her drawings, projects, the scissors and cut-up papers, implied an air of busyness, little-girl confidence. The fairies. Was she religious? Emily thought she remembered halos or glows around the figures' heads. The family was Lutheran, like most of the neighbors — and the church was just down the block. But Emily hadn't time. She looked up at the house.

Duty jumped past her, out the open window. He'd something in his mouth, a rag or paper. "Duty!" Emily called. He dropped his find and ran to the pond, a fishpond, it must have been at one time. Emily shut the window, latched it securely. Someone should rescue that mural. She set off, quickly, for the barn, which must be the workshop space William Malone had mentioned. William Malone, waiting for her at the bank.

The barn had a haymow window to one side of the peaked roof, and an old winch. Farm to workshop to abandoned building, breaking down naturally as a felled tree. Emily let herself in. It was five years or so deserted, but the light was lovely. Long workbenches on either side, constructed in the space, were solid, monolithic, and the beams of the barn roof were massive. Constructed space registered human intent and endeavor, Emily thought, far beyond the time allotted human lives.

She heard Duty outside, barking his chuffing sound. "Yes," she called, and went out, pulling the door firmly shut. "Let's go, Duty. We must make one stop. Then I'll introduce you to Reynolds, who will become your good friend. I know dogs don't like uniforms, but you must not judge him by his very professional appearance." She paused at a clump of high weeds, for the rag Duty had carried was there on the grass. She saw then the piled rocks and the cardboard sign, still legible, bent upon its stick: *Graveyard for Animals.*

She grasped the rag, for it was rag watercolor paper, rolled into a scroll, tied with a dirty ribbon. It was one of Annabel's drawings, a fairy figure, dressed like the others, in pastel leaves and petals, with legs that dwindled off to nothing, like a wasp in flight. The figure, drawn in ink and delicately painted, then washed with pale blue and yellow, hovered between two clouds. One glowed yellow above; the other, below, darker, streamed slants of rain on an unseen land, but the rain was tinged the palest flush of pink. The wand was there, and yes, the faint glow or halo, here extended wholly around the figure.

This child, Annabel, was not yet ten years old. Emily did not know many children; in fact, she rather avoided them out of some self-protective instinct. She could not judge the art itself except by its intent and effect, but of one thing she was certain: the child was extraordinary. She wondered if anyone had known, and decided she would not speak of it. It was immaterial and would not be understood.

She drove the several blocks to downtown, found the entrance to the lot behind the bank, and parked, rolling the windows a third down. "Now you'll wait here for me, Duty. I won't be long." She put the drawing in her bag. *Sad,* she remembered telling William Malone, and locked the car, determined the word would not apply to them. Walking quickly, she took the Eichers' house key from her bag.

She rang the bell and the door opened. The room seemed dim after the bright sunlight through which she'd entered; she felt the door shut behind her and turned to him, the key in her hand. He took her in his arms so naturally and held her, his hand cradling the back of her head. Instantly, she felt the dark weight within her lift. Abernathy and her deathly look, the half-empty, violated house, the journey before her, all released her, and she turned with him, holding him, or perhaps the room was turning. She closed her eyes and sought his mouth, his full, beautiful mouth that tasted so deeply of him, and felt his hair in her fingers, for she had reached up to pull him closer, and he'd lifted her off her feet.

"Emily, Emily," he said.

"Yes, I know. It will be all right." She felt effortless tears fill her eyes **and saw tears** in his.

They sat opposite one **another** at the round table where she'd taken **notes,** holding hands tightly, intensely silent. He **touched** her hand to his face and mouth; the **simple gesture** was as stirring and intimate as his caress.

"The house," she said quietly, "have you been inside?"

"Never."

"And the playhouse, in the yard, painted to match the house —"

"There's a playhouse?"

"Run-down, with a lovely mural inside. Annabel's redoubt, I think. What do you know about her?"

He touched a fingertip to Emily's forehead. "Brows, naturally perfect and distinct, like yours, amazingly so. Personable child, very lively. A bit stocky, still, with lovely cheekbones, long lashes. Brown hair. Resolute, I thought. 'Fanciful' her mother called her."

"Where's my bag?" Emily reached for it, on the floor. "This is one of her drawings." She pulled off the dirty ribbon and unrolled the paper. "I didn't take this, William, the dog found it in the playhouse, in the mess." She'd nearly forgotten: Duty. "Oh, William, I have the dog, in the car. Abernathy's had the Eicher dog, all this time. And gave him to me."

"To you."

"I had to take him. No one else would. Small dog, a Boston terrier. I think Pierson kicked it hard enough to kill it. The dog knows him, of course. It may rattle him, if I can get the dog close to him. William, you must go there, to the house. He's already rolled up the downstairs carpets, taken things from the walls." She took William's hand, across the table. "Soon there'll be no way to sense them in the rooms."

He enclosed her hand in his. "I knew them, Emily. I can't fill my mind with them all the more. It's difficult enough, and now you are leaving to look for them." He took a business card from his pocket. "Phone me at this number, here at the bank, and at the number on the back, after hours. No one else will answer. You must phone me as soon as you've arrived. Have you booked a room?"

"No." She looked at her watch. She had to get to the apartment, drop off the dog, go to the newsroom, phone O'Boyle. She would show him the drawing; perhaps he would remember it.

"I hope you don't mind. In the interest of time, and your safety, I booked you rooms at the Gore Hotel, in Clarksburg. The address and phone are on the card."

"Thank you. I must go." She held his hand in hers. "I live alone, William, and now, with a small dog. My doorman is eminently discreet. I don't know what is in the way, but I do not require a picket fence." She leaned toward him, and nearly whispered, "I want you, just you."

"And I want you," he said.

She arrived at the *Tribune* office at 4:00 P.M., having settled Duty at her apartment, dog bed by the stove, butcher bones wrapped in the icebox, leash and carrier by the front door; Reynolds was scheduled to walk him at seven, and proffer the bones. A note at her desk informed her that Eric Lindstrom would also be embarking for West Virginia. She supposed she might have expected as much, now that Pierson's arrest was likely. A story like this could preoccupy the *Tribune* for months; typically, a team was assigned to such cases.

Regardless, she was irritated, and surveyed the newsroom. *Trib* reporters were boorish and beefy and smelled of tobacco or bourbon, and speculated amongst themselves about her private life. There, at his desk, was Eric Lindstrom, hired last year from *The New York Times,* source of resentment amongst his older colleagues, beat reporters who'd made him an anonymous gift of a baby's silver spoon the week he arrived. He was a Princeton man who'd lived in Europe and came from money. He certainly looked like money, Emily thought. His well-kept, perfect nails made hers appear naked and ragged. He wore his blond hair swept back, and the girls in the steno pool often followed him to lunch; they said he was more than once mistaken on the street for Douglas Fairbanks. "No, but I'm Fairbanks' cousin," he would say, "and an autograph will cost you a fiver." Then he'd wink, and take the girls along with him, and pay for their sandwiches. They fought to run his errands.

Emily went to his desk. All his papers were neatly stacked in trays. "I hear you're off to West Virginia, Mr. Lindstrom, though I was promised this exclusive before Pierson was arrested."

"It's too big for one reporter now. They've found the victims' possessions in some garage, and they'll be digging for bodies. I'm going tonight with my cameras to Clarksburg, wherever that is. Every newspaper in the country will be there. The press will be falling all over each other."

"And then there's Quiet Dell," she said. "Population one hundred. It's where they'll be looking for bodies. Woods and forest. Mountains. Unpaved roads."

He indicated the chair by his desk, and she sat. "And how do you know, Miss Thornhill? Are you familiar with Quiet Dell?"

"I will be," she said, "very familiar."

"Why not operate as a tag team? I do the photographs and stiff upper lip, the just-the-facts dispatches. You provide features of imaginative detail, and the soulful moral lessons, acknowledged — in the human heart, at least — as the hardest news of all." He balanced a pencil on his knuckles, then turned his hand to weigh it on his palm, looking inquisitive. "Don't know how they'll take to a girl reporter down there, in such grisly circumstances."

"And there's your silver spoon to consider," Emily said quietly. "Bound to serve you well there in the country. What's the nature of the family business, if you don't mind my asking?"

He was going through desk files, packing his briefcase. "Manufacturing."

"Manufacturing what?"

"Pistons." He regarded her. "Know more than you did before?"

Emily raised her brows. "Big? Small?"

"Very big, and very small, Miss Thornhill."

She reflected that the banter was camouflage; his mention of the human heart, though couched in irony, was more telling. "I've just come from the home and playhouse of the missing children," she said. "This story will be dark and deep."

"Yes," he said, "and you are clearly the one to tell it." He met her eyes. "The journey promises to be demanding; you may come to appreciate a skillful accomplice."

"I take your point," Emily said, "but look, a train is too slow. We must have a car, a good one, an impressive one, to smooth our way with hoteliers and sheriffs. We could partner on the drive and share it on-site. A train to the middle of nowhere will take forever."

"I can get a car," he said, "a friend's car."

"I'm sure you have lots of friends."

"I do. A great many friends, who love me to exercise their cars."

She marked the word *love* and realized he was offering a subtle confidence; women did not own cars to lend; his friends were men. "The *Tribune* will pay for the gasoline," she said. "You like to drive, don't you?"

"I do, but I don't like wasting time."

"I'll bet you don't. And you smoke?"

"Now and then, for relaxation. I seldom smoke tobacco, though I confess to a preference for milder herbs that professional journalists do not transport across state lines."

She laughed. "You a jazz enthusiast?"

He regarded her. "Do I look like a jazz enthusiast?"

She leaned toward him and said, in a stage whisper, "Possibly." She'd marked him out as attractive and simply not noticed the rest. He was smart, masculine, homosexual, and careful, not at all obvious. He kept his own counsel, playing innocent with the secretaries and smirking with the men when appropriate. She folded her arms. "Mr. Lindstrom," she said.

He lifted his chin, displaying the chiseled cut of his jaw, and inclined his head toward her. "Miss . . . Thornhill," he said.

He liked women generally, Emily thought, though she could probably count on him to hate the women she hated. He wouldn't judge her or get in her way, yet they could provide one another finely tuned camouflage.

So much could go unsaid. They would be confederates.

He reached for her hand and she gave it. He held the back of her wrist, lightly massaging her palm with his thumb, touching the first knuckle of her index finger with a circular pressure.

"Reflexology," he said. "Ancient Chinese hokum."

"Do I pass?" she asked.

"You're perceptive," he said. "Curious, to a fault. And you're not alone."

"Yes, there's that," Emily said. "Do you mind dogs?"

"You mean, of the canine variety?" He cast a glance at the newsroom's glass partition. Globs of dark color moved behind it in suits. Typewriters sounded in the steno pool, and a haze of cigarette smoke hung suspended, wafting out against the ceiling.

"Yes, strictly canine. I have a small dog I must take with me, for research purposes. It was the Eichers' dog, and doesn't bark."

"Does it talk?"

"Not yet. But it might."

"Separate bylines," he said, "separate hotels. I like my own space."

"I believe you're my man."

"I believe I am."

She handed him her card. "My address, on the back. Pick me up there, in an hour. I have an interview on Dearborn, at five. An eyewitness, of sorts."

"Who's the interview?"

"Charles O'Boyle, the roomer, the one who fingered Pierson, though too late."

"It's so often that way," Lindstrom said. "And we must clean up after, explaining what it means."

"We'll drive all night," Emily said. "If you're not an insomniac, I'll teach you."

He stood, pulling on his suit jacket. "Agreed then. We shall burn the midnight oil. I very much look forward to not sleeping with you, Miss Thornhill."

Emily waited for Lindstrom on the street, under the awning of her apartment house. They would interview O'Boyle, then come back for her luggage, and for Duty. Emily planned to sneak the dog into the Gore Hotel if necessary. He was small enough to fit in a valise and couldn't bark to reveal his presence. In her experience, maids were easily bribed. Where was Lindstrom? She walked to the curb and looked to the right.

Suddenly, he was taking her arm. The car was running, for he'd pulled up just behind her. "Madam," he said, "your chariot awaits."

"My goodness, Lindstrom. I do like your style."

"It's brand-new a week ago," he said, "but thoroughly test-driven. '32 Chevrolet coupe. I like a classic car, don't you?"

She stepped inside, and he closed the passenger door with exaggerated care. The interior smelled deliciously new. "So it's next year's model?" Emily asked.

"We inhabit the future, Miss Thornhill." He'd rolled the front windows down and now took his seat behind the wheel.

She laughed. "Lindstrom, this is so absurd. I feel as though we're off on a first date."

"And so we are, an intricate and demanding date. You must call me Eric, though, when appropriate, and Mr. Lindstrom otherwise. I'm happy to be taken for your lover, your professional partner, your superior, or your *brother* —" He grinned at her, speeding smoothly through the Loop, "but I do not wish to be taken for your chauffeur."

"Fine. And I'm happy to share the driving."

"Afraid not. Part of my deal with our benefactor. Don't take it personally. No one, male or female, can drive this car but me, until I return it, sparkling, to my friend."

"I see, Eric." She folded her arms, and looked at him. "And is he your special friend, of long duration?"

He smiled as though thinking of something delightful. "My friend's duration is excellent, thank you." He glanced over at her. "I like that wide-eyed laugh of yours. I hope to inspire it regularly. And you, Miss Thornhill? Are you planning to tell me all about your special friends?"

"In good time, Eric. And you may call me Emily. Here's Dearborn. It's 1400 Dearborn. Now then: Charles O'Boyle. Engineer of some sort. He knew the family, and put the police onto what they might have investigated much sooner."

O'Boyle lived in a doorman building. The elevator attendant, a petite older woman, managed the wire gate and the levers.

"Seventh floor, please," Emily said.

"Seventh floor, ma'am."

Eric tipped his hat to her, and indicated the long empty corridor when the elevator doors opened. Plush carpet of a busy floral pattern stretched before them. "War of the Roses," he said. And then, "What's the number?"

She was walking briskly, checking doors. "Just down here." Emily knocked. "He's expecting us. Travels a lot on business. Going off somewhere tonight, apparently."

"Fellow traveler," Eric said, and stood behind her. "This is your show."

O'Boyle opened the door. He looked at Eric, and then at Emily. "Miss Thornhill?" he said.

"Yes, Mr. O'Boyle. And this is Eric Lindstrom, my colleague at the *Tribune*. Thank you for agreeing to speak with us. May we come in?"

"Yes, of course." He opened the door wide, inclining his head as though performing an official duty.

Duty, Emily thought. She must remember to tell him she had the dog.

"Please, sit," O'Boyle said.

The furniture was modern; leather chesterfield and two matching armchairs, large coffee table, wall of bookshelves. Emily could see a dining table beyond, and a sideboard, and large, unadorned windows facing the street. The view would be very nice. Emily sat in one armchair, Eric in the other, and O'Boyle on the sofa.

O'Boyle wore a dark suit, smartly cut. He was a bit older than Lindstrom, perhaps, but the neatly trimmed mustache seemed calculated to offset his youthful appearance. Attractive, Emily thought, conservative, a company man. He took a silver cigarette case from his vest pocket and flipped it open, extending it to Eric Lindstrom. "Do you smoke?"

"Not at the moment," Eric said shortly, "but thank you." He looked at Emily as though to signal O'Boyle, who then included her in the gesture.

She demurred. Was he prone to ignoring women, in a professional capacity? She supposed he simply didn't encounter them, traveling for the Dunnegan Company.

"I'm afraid I smoke far too much these days." He flipped the case shut. "I'll wait."

"Mr. O'Boyle," Emily began.

"See here," O'Boyle said, producing a sealed envelope. He placed it on the table, next to the cigarette case. "It's all in this letter, addressed to Chief Duckworth, whom I understand is police chief in Clarksburg." He paused. "I entrust it to you, Miss Thornhill, to deliver to Duckworth personally, and then to publish, to whatever purpose is helpful, to keep the record straight."

"We may publish the contents, Mr. O'Boyle? Exclusively, in the *Tribune*? At such time as the authorities deem it permissible?"

"Yes, well, that is Chief Duckworth's decision. But I would like it published, in the *Tribune* and elsewhere. I want the record straight."

"Of course." Emily took the letter and affixed it to her notebook with a paper clip. "May we speak now, though, more informally? I'm sure the letter will clarify a great deal, but I always find that talking, one-on-

one, can be so beneficial, in helping to recall details. We give you our word that the letter will be published, unedited, just as you wrote it."

O'Boyle glanced at Eric, as though seeking his corroboration.

The two men looked at one another across the table and Emily was struck by some frisson between them. Did they know one another? Schools? Clubs? Surely Eric would have told her, unless he was just now recollecting. They did look cut of the same cloth, strong profiles, both of them: Eric very blond, in a beige summer-weight jacket, his blue-green eyes carefully devoid of their usual knowing expression, and O'Boyle dark-haired, blue-eyed, Irish, no doubt. Catholic, of course. Practicing? Somehow, Emily thought not. She judged him to have come from good family, but not wealth. He was self-made, Emily guessed, had not inherited money or privilege, but was educated among those who took both for granted. He wore the suit, the haircut, the expensive, nicely polished shoes, but did not possess Eric's easy confidence. He was guarded, but why? He was under no suspicion whatever; in fact, he was the hero of the tale.

"Mr. O'Boyle," Emily said, "I'm interested, not just in the hard news of this case, but in the family, in who they were, and what was lost." Emily fell silent. She must let him set the tone.

"They were not lost," O'Boyle said. "They were cruelly deceived, and taken."

She realized he was quite grief-stricken. There was anguish in his slightly aggressive demeanor, some sense of guilt deeper and more complex, perhaps, than what William had described: Grethe at the teller's window.

O'Boyle clasped his hands. "I have it on good authority that Pierson is under arrest, as we speak."

"We are driving there tonight," Eric said.

"Soon we should know more," Emily volunteered, "and Mr. Lindstrom and I will keep you informed, if you so desire. I've spoken to William Malone, the Eichers' banker, and with Mrs. Elizabeth Abernathy, the children's nurse, but you knew the family more intimately, having lived in the household. Pierson's methods will come to light, but you are perhaps somewhat aware of Mrs. Eicher's motives, her frame of mind."

"Abernathy is hardly a children's nurse," he said flatly.

"Agreed," Emily said. "She asked me to take the Eichers' dog, and I did."

He looked at her, incredulous. "You have Duty? I assumed he'd gone with the children. I telephoned Abernathy to ask for the key. She never mentioned —" He shook his head. "I couldn't have taken him, so I'm glad I didn't know. Well. Duty."

"Why the odd name?" Emily asked.

"There is a story about Duty." O'Boyle lit a cigarette. "He arrived a month or so after Heinrich died, a present for Hart from a nursemaid, back when they still employed one. The Eichers were Duty's second family. The first was killed by a tornado, west of Chicago, in the plains. Now he's an only survivor, again."

Eric shot Emily an unreadable glance. "I think I'll have a cigarette, Mr. O'Boyle, if you don't mind."

"Charles," O'Boyle said, extending the open cigarette case. "That's it, then. If they didn't try to reclaim the dog, in all those weeks —" He'd gone pale and spoke with clipped, painful effort. "The monster has killed them."

"Probably right away," Eric said.

O'Boyle stared before him, stunned. "Sorry, I used my last match."

Eric stood and leaned over the table, touching the cigarette in his mouth to O'Boyle's, drawing in the flame. It was easily accomplished, nonchalant, intimate.

Nicely done, Emily thought. "Charles," she said carefully. "Could we start at the beginning? You roomed with the Eichers, for how long?"

"I moved in just after my mother's death, nearly five years ago. She was my only relative, and maintained a household, where I stayed when I wasn't traveling. Her illness imposed . . . financial burdens. Dunnegan transferred me to Park Ridge. Rooming was the obvious solution."

Emily was writing. "You answered an ad?"

"Yes, in the Park Ridge paper. Heinrich had died, perhaps six months before. They wanted local gentlemen, with references."

"Which you provided."

"Certainly." He looked at Eric, and back at Emily. "I spoke first with Lavinia, Heinrich's mother, the children's grandmother."

"Mr. Malone mentioned her. Was Lavinia . . . difficult? Controlling, perhaps?"

"Difficult? No, she was quite wonderful. Wonderful to me, from the moment she opened the door. The children adored her."

"Had they rented rooms previously?"

"There had been roomers before me, gentlemen, supposedly, who didn't work out to Anna's satisfaction."

"Anna?"

"Asta's pet name was Anna, but that's personal, not for publication. The letter is for publication. Do you understand?"

"Of course," Emily said. "You are speaking off the record. You need only say so, and I will hold that part of our conversation in confidence."

"Yes, just so," he said, and then added, "I can't believe she was so rash. It isn't like her, not at all. Anna was my very good friend."

"More than a landlady, you mean. Can you elaborate, Mr. O'Boyle?"

O'Boyle stood up suddenly, explosively, and shouted, "Good god! Is this really relevant? What do you think I mean?"

"I, don't know, Mr. O'Boyle." Emily looked at Eric, who raised his brows subtly, then looked down at his notebook, writing. "I'm just trying to get a sense of the family," Emily went on, "to understand —"

O'Boyle faced her. "They were like family, to me. I was, for three years, the only lodger; I paid to have both rooms, and moved out two years ago. I was working in Chicago and my circumstances had much improved. Still, I spent holidays with them, visited every few weeks. I was there when Lavinia died, and a week afterward. I was there Christmas past, and stayed on into the new year. All this might never have happened, if she had listened to me. If I had convinced her —" He looked away, shaken.

"Of what, Mr. O'Boyle?"

"She told me she was going to sell the house, mentioned changes about to happen. I was alarmed and completely surprised. I'd assumed Lavinia's death would result in an inheritance, but realized my mistake. I determined to take the situation in hand."

Emily fixed her gaze, patiently, on O'Boyle. He wanted to say more, but required her assistance. "In hand," she repeated quietly.

"You didn't know her!" he said abruptly. "You've no idea who she was, nor does Malone, nor, most certainly, does Abernathy —" He walked quickly to the dining room, and took, from the center of the table, a silver tray and tea service, which he placed before Emily. "She was an artist. This is her work."

The gleaming tray was octagonal, and the subtly matching pieces, sugar bowl, creamer, a tall, generous carafe, were sleek, forceful, with squarish handles. The work was eminently formal, each piece finely etched with a monogram, a large *A,* or *E,* in graceful double lines.

"Beautiful," Emily said.

Eric stood to look more closely, the three of them gathered together as though over a cool, reflective fire. "Exceptional Danish design," he said. "Timeless."

"The Eichers were Danish. This is her mark." O'Boyle turned the creamer over to reveal the circular, raised EAE, touched it, replaced the creamer on the tray.

"Do you have other work of Anna's?" Eric asked.

He said her name very naturally. Emily reflected that she could not have done so. Asta Eicher's mark, glimpsed quickly, disturbed her: the bold *A* completely encircled by the linked, facing *E*s, with their sharp feet, and the pronged midline joining all. The *A* was pinioned, encased. Emily had helped her grandfather brand horses and cattle. He maintained there was an art to burning the hide just enough; it was not a wound, but a mark. This woman was marked, bound. She had said as much in this emblematic symbol of the work that so defined her. How much did O'Boyle know?

"I'm trying to find other pieces," he was telling Eric. "Not easily done. She stopped designing or producing soon after she was widowed. I bought this from her, one of the few pieces she'd kept. I wish now I'd bought more, but I wasn't in a position to do so then. Later, she concealed her circumstances, until last December." He bent to remove the tray.

Emily stayed his arm. "Please, leave it. It's beautiful. May I?" She acknowledged his nod of assent and pushed the tray to the center of the table. It's as though she's here with us, Emily wanted to say, but refrained. "It snowed a great deal last Christmas," she said.

"Yes, a huge storm, several feet of snow. I arrived early on Christmas Eve, before it

238

started, and I'd bought the children a Canadian toboggan, big enough to fit us all. We went sledding on Christmas, after dinner and Annabel's play, and the children had opened their presents. I have a snapshot." He brought out a small envelope. "I took these photos. I'm having the negatives enlarged."

The snapshot showed the three children, arranged on the sled youngest to oldest, bundled in coats, scarves, matching blouson hats, in heavily falling snow. None looked at the camera. Annabel looked forward and to the side, snow on her hat and shoulders; Hart looked down; only Grethe looked up, squinting into the storm.

"Those hats are quite smart," Emily said.

"Canadian, as well. I was there some weeks, for Dunnegan." O'Boyle offered another small photo. "I took this on the front porch, a week after Thanksgiving and Lavinia's funeral, just before I left. It's probably the last photo of the four of them, together."

Asta Eicher stood behind the children, a half-smile, somewhat wistful, on her face, her dark hair waved at the front and pulled back. Grethe, nearly her mother's height, very thin, looked girlish, her long hair tucked behind her ears. Hart and Annabel stood with their shoulders back, as though poised for some adversity, Hart very sober, in shirt and tie, sweater, short trousers, hands at his sides. Annabel wore a dark dress with white cuffs and collar, like a pilgrim; she looked wary and devastated, Emily thought, quite different from the child in the sledding photo, only a month later.

"Was Annabel close with the grandmother?"

"Very, and very like her," O'Boyle said. "Lavinia encouraged her tableaus and plays and dioramas, made up fanciful games with her."

"Fanciful," Emily said. That word again.

"It was a source of tension, a bit, between Anna and Lavinia. Annabel was so imaginative. Anna was concerned that she . . . accept her grandmother's death, not idealize her or pretend to communicate with her."

"She pretended that kind of thing?" Emily was writing.

O'Boyle made a dismissive gesture. "Lavinia was the sort who would have said, I'm always with you, or something similar, to comfort the child. I don't know that, but I surmise it. The Christmas play — Annabel wrote pageants for every occasion, starring Hart and Grethe, and even the dog — had a Grandmother character, in the person of Annabel's very old rag doll, Mrs. Pomeroy. She took that doll with her everywhere." He laughed, and for a moment his face relaxed.

"She sounds delightful," Emily said.

"Yes," said O'Boyle, and fell silent.

Emily glanced quickly at Eric, who

prompted her with a back-to-the-point expression.

But O'Boyle came to the point. He offered Emily a third photo, a copy of a studio photograph, it seemed. "I didn't take this, of course: Anna, as a young woman, before her marriage. Lovely gray eyes and though you don't see it here, a smile of such warmth and welcome."

Emily, silent, reflected that yes, she might have been lovely, but looked almost fearful, or too knowing. The times, perhaps, in Europe; the shadow of the Great War. She seemed happier in the later photograph, despite her age and struggles, and Lavinia's recent death — pleased with her children, protective, fondly at ease with the photographer. "Charles," Emily said, placing the photographs on the table between them, "you mentioned her situation, that Christmas, and a determination, on your part . . ."

"She was dear to me. We were very close. I could not let her lose her home, for it was my home, in my heart, as Anna was —" He spoke to Emily alone now, his eyes naked. "I asked her to marry me, I begged her to accept —" he looked away — "my fidelity, my means, my life."

There it was. Emily realized she was holding her breath.

"She promised to consider my proposal, not to come to any decision, about her finances, the house, without consulting me. She was under enormous stress. Emotional issues, self-blame about her husband's sudden death, came to light."

"Self-blame?" Emily tried to breathe the words so lightly that O'Boyle might hear them as his own questioning thought.

"Completely unwarranted, arising somehow from the history of the marriage — they were both artists, supported by family money to a point, but he was the breadwinner. All that was years past. I told her I awaited her answer; I looked forward to a future together. I would be patient, and stay in frequent touch. I knew nothing about any letters, or Pierson, until I phoned in late June. Abernathy said she was away. Had they heard from her? Only postcards. I had to phone a neighbor, Mrs. Verberg, to get his name."

"I'm sorry," Emily said. "This has been much, much more difficult for you than I could have realized."

"She deceived herself," said O'Boyle in a dead tone. "That man used her every disappointment and hope against her."

Emily took the rolled drawing from her bag. "Mr. O'Boyle, Charles — perhaps you'd like to have this, as a keepsake." She smoothed the paper before him.

"One of Annabel's drawings," he said, "from her room."

"Duty found it in the playhouse, actually,

on the floor. It's a bit bedraggled —"

O'Boyle touched the textured surface. "It's so like Annabel. No, you keep it, Miss Thornhill. She made me several presents of her drawings. And keep the snapshots, as well, for publication. The family should be seen as I saw them, in happy times. I can do that for them, at least." He stood then. "I'm afraid I must ask you to go. My cab will be here quite soon."

"Of course," Emily said. "We thank you. You mentioned leaving; we didn't mean to keep you. Work can be diverting at difficult times; I hope you find it so."

"I suppose," he said absently, "but I am going to Mexico. I don't want to be here, as all of this comes out in the newspapers. It's another world there."

"It is," Eric said. "Where do you go?"

They were moving to the door.

"A small village." O'Boyle didn't look at him. "I'm sure you wouldn't know it."

Eric offered Emily his arm, as before. It was dusk. They were in the car before they spoke

"My god," Eric said. "And this is only the preamble."

"I have coffee at my place," Emily said. "And food packed for the car."

"Black coffee," he said, "lots of it."

Duty, fed, watered, walked in Chicago, was

asleep in his basket; the rest of the backseat was taken up with their typewriters, brief-cases, bags of food, a thermos, suitcases. It was full dark, two hours into the trip, and raining lightly. The wipers kept time: *swik, swak.*

Swak, thought Emily, was a legend people wrote on valentines. She had fallen asleep, almost. "Eric?" she murmured.

"Emily?"

"What do you make of him?"

Eric only looked, dejectedly, into the wind-screen of the coupe, the wipers crossing in tandem, the wash of rain flowing off.

"Eric, we have formed an alliance for a common purpose. You must tell me, always, what you think."

"I think you might not know how danger-ous it is, Emily, how wearing, to deny one's deepest impulses, one's birthright, to live with the constant threat of exposure and calamity. Not murder, necessarily, though yes, that too, in certain quarters, but loss of home, family, respect, work, the ability to make a living — the difficulty in forming any lasting intimacy, ever, with another human being."

"Understand me, Eric. His letter, only his letter, will be published. I will not refer to him, publicly or privately, in any other light. Nor will I discuss him with anyone but you. This we promise, between us. Lives depend on these secrets. Yes?"

Eric nodded. "Yes." Rain misted around the car. "Lapsed Catholic," he said quietly, "always worst. Mother's son. Never married. Travels frequently. Vital, repressed. Angry at himself. Covert. Tries to stop, can't. And so takes enormous risks with strangers. I've known so many men like him. I can recognize them across a room."

"So you knew immediately?"

"The moment he looked at me, over your head. It's a look others literally don't see. I was watching you, as well, to see when you'd realize."

"It wasn't the first thing that occurred to me."

"And when did you know?"

"When you lit the cigarette."

"I was making sure you knew. Just as between us, earlier today, I let you realize, when I might have deflected you. You were thrilled with your powers of deduction, but I decided I liked you, could trust you, wanted to work with you, and I walked you in. I'm a faultless judge of these things — survival instinct."

"The thing with the cigarette," Emily said. "You did it beautifully, like a kiss. I thought you were comforting him."

"Perhaps I was. It was just after the drop moment, wasn't it. But I would never have made that gesture in mixed company."

Emily looked into the dark, which parted quickly before them, pierced by the head-lamps. The drop moment. She'd not heard the expression. But yes, O'Boyle had just said, *The monster has killed them,* acknowledging what he feared. She went on, testing her thoughts. "Still, he proposed to her, Eric, and feels desperately guilty that he didn't know about Pierson, didn't save them. O'Boyle loved her, and the children."

"Yes, I think he did." Eric turned to her. "I could love you. It wouldn't change who I am. He believed he could ignore what he needed, and they were a way out for him. He might have saved them; they might have been his life. But she knew better."

"Oh, no, not better."

"I mean that she recognized the truth between them. Perhaps they were even open with one another. And he's right. She was, for reasons of her own, cruelly deluded by this Pierson, who may seem entirely commonplace, but will prove to be very skillful. But also deluded, for he's gotten caught. We don't know yet what he did, but we will soon be much occupied with it."

"And what of Charles O'Boyle? Why can't he be more like you, Eric?"

"Because he's not like me. He lives bereft of any community. Not having a double life, he has almost no life, except in dark forays that he knows to be dangerous."

"It seemed you were moved by him."

"As were you. We are, I'm sure, the only people in whom he's confided, and we are now sworn to a pact, to protect his experience and his guilt."

"But I can't help him. Could you?"

"Christ, Emily, I don't know."

"But didn't someone help you, at some point? Show you how to manage — well, a life inside a life?"

"Is that what it is? No, it's my life, all of it."

▪ ▪ ▪ ▪

VII.

▪ ▪ ▪ ▪

ROOMER WAS SUSPICIOUS
    OF STRANGER

O'BOYLE CALLED POLICE
        WHEN ACTIONS OF MUL-
        TIPLE SLAYER
        CAUSED HIM ALARM

O'BOYLE, IN HIS AMAZING LETTER,
GIVES DETAILS OF THE STRANGE DIS-
APPEARANCE OF THE PARK RIDGE
WIDOW AND HER CHILDREN; OF THE
INVESTIGATION HE PERSONALLY MADE
THAT LED TO THE ARREST OF POWERS
BY THE PARK RIDGE POLICE; AND OF

THE RELEASE OF THE MASS SLAYER
BY THE POLICE IN THE ILLINOIS CITY. IT
IS TOUCHING AND PATHETIC IN ITS DE-
TAILS.

— Special to *The Clarksburg Telegram*,
September 5, 1931

A Chicago man . . . has volunteered to sup-
ply the state of West Virginia with a rope
with which to hang Harry F. Powers (alias
Cornelius Pierson), mass slayer. He is
Charles O'Boyle, former roomer in the
Eicher home. . . . He writes: "Herewith is
my statement of my connection with the
'Bluebeard' Powers case . . .

"Five or six years ago I came to Park Ridge
as a foreman for the J. H. Dunnegan Company . . . I had difficulty in locating a place
to room. . . . My own home having been
broken up by the death of my mother, Mrs.
Eicher consented to provide me board and
room. . . . She had three young children,
Grethe, Hart, and Annabel, and on account
of their being such well-bred children, I
became greatly attached to them.

"On June 29th, 1931, I called Mrs. Eicher's
home from Chicago to . . . learn that Mrs.
Eicher had gone to Clarksburg, W.Va., on
business, with a Mr. Pierson. It was so
extremely unusual for Mrs. Eicher to leave

her children that I was very greatly surprised. . . . Neighbors said they could throw no light on her whereabouts. . . . I felt that something was wrong. . . .

"On or about July 15th . . . Mrs. Eicher's neighbor informed me by telephone that Pierson was on Mrs. Eicher's property and I left at once for Park Ridge. . . . I found that he had entered the garage, locking the door behind him. . . . I noticed a car with a West Virginia license, a Chevrolet coupe. . . . Mrs. Eicher's radio was lashed on to the back of this car with a half-inch rope about sixty feet long, which I had intended to use to make a swing for the children. . . .

"I knew that Mrs. Eicher would not give anyone authority to open my tool box and Pierson or Powers had to enter my luggage to procure this rope. . . . I locked the garage from the outside and proceeded to the police station. . . . I had promised the police that Pierson or Powers was locked in the garage and we were greatly surprised not to find him. . . . Events prove he was probably there all the time. . . . We returned to the station and a detail of police officers was sent to keep watch. . . .

"I had been gone five minutes when Pierson appeared and was arrested. . . . I arrived at the Park Ridge police station the next day and was very greatly disappointed to find that Pierson or Powers had been released. . . . I went to the Eicher home and after reading a bundle of letters which he had dropped in his haste I urged the Chief of Police to get in touch with the West Virginia authorities. . . .

"The rope, which belonged to me and which he [Powers] took with him, I will make a present to the state of West Virginia for hanging purposes, if he is convicted, which no doubt he will be. Am enclosing snaps of the family. If you need me wire."

Asta and children, Thanksgiving '30

Eicher children, Annabel, Hart, Grethe,
Christmas Day '30

■ ■ ■ ■

VIII.

■ ■ ■ ■

Quiet Dell No Longer Quiet — Quiet Dell
was the noisiest and busiest place in West
Virginia yesterday. Thousands of automobiles were parked for miles along the
Clarksburg–Buckhannon highway. No accurate estimate can be made of the numbers who have visited the "Murder farm."
State policemen say they were too busy
handling traffic to attempt to count the
automobiles but there must have been
50,000 at least, yesterday and Saturday
night.

— *The Clarksburg Telegram,*
August 30, 1931

Late August,
Early September 1931
Clarksburg and Quiet Dell,
West Virginia

DISCOVERY

The Gore Hotel was an imposing yellow-brick edifice on the corner of West Pike and Second Streets. Eric pulled up in front of the red-and-white-striped awning.

"Let me get the other bags in and then come back for Duty," Emily said. "He fits in my valise, in case there's a no pets policy." She turned to the backseat and moved the dog's pillow from the open basket to the floor. "Now, you've been walked and fed. Wait quietly, and don't jump about."

"He understands your every word," Eric said dryly, but Duty settled on the pillow. "Isn't it a problem, in and out with the dog?"

"I'll speak with the manager. I must explain that he is not a pet. He's an extremely important material witness."

"Next you'll have his paw on a Bible."

"Animals don't require oaths, Mr. Lindstrom; they are already God's creatures and do not engage in deception. Now, let us proceed. I'm sure you want to be rid of us."

"I'll come in with you, and say we're related. Make sure you're settled."

"Can't we just be colleagues?"

"Best to be both." Eric was out of the car, motioning a porter who appeared at the broad revolving door. The porter's dark red jacket matched the awning, and his sleeves were cuffed with gold braid. A Negro gentleman, he seemed the epitome of genteel Chicago.

Emily, carrying briefcase, handbag, grip, went ahead into the hotel. The lobby was posh, comfortable, sedately furnished with dark green leather-upholstered settees and armchairs. An ornate phone booth stood in one corner near a rack of newspapers on rods; their pages hung down like newsprint flags. Emily perused them: morning editions from Clarksburg, Huntington, Pittsburgh, even *The Washington Post.*

Eric, at the desk, made a point of reading the clerk's name tag. "Good day, Mr. Parrish. I am Eric Lindstrom, and this is my cousin and colleague, Miss Emily Thornhill. We are journalists from the *Chicago Tribune.* I am staying down the street at the Waldo, but Miss Thornhill, I believe, has a reservation here."

"Yes, Mr. Lindstrom. You'll find the Waldo just down the street, corner of West Pike and Fourth. Miss Thornhill has Room 127 here at the Gore, private bath, and 126, as well; there's a door through. Reserved by a Mr. Malone, for the *Chicago Tribune.*"

"Indeed." Eric shot Emily a glance. "That is correct."

Emily stepped over to the clerk, smiling, and noticed a stack of bound newspapers on the long mahogany desk. The word *Widow* jumped out at her. *Decomposed Body Uncovered near Quiet Dell Garage* read the headline. She took a copy as the room seemed to darken around her, and held it out to Eric.

Eric snapped it open. "Sir, this is the evening paper?"

"Just delivered." The clerk scowled. "A bad business, a very bad business."

"Mr. Parrish, I would be obliged if you would direct us to Quiet Dell. It's nearby?"

"Very near, four miles or so. Take Second to Main, which becomes the Buckhannon Turnpike, and drive straight along. You'll see the crowd."

"The crowd?"

"Oh, yes, I'm afraid so."

Eric nodded his thanks and was out the door. Emily looked for the porter and extended fifty cents. "Mr. — your name, sir?"

"Woods, ma'am."

"Mr. Woods, please deliver these to my room? I will be back presently." She heard his "Yes, ma'am," behind her as she pushed her way through the revolving door. The car was running. It was nearly six in the evening of a beautiful summer night. They had two hours of waning daylight.

Emily looked at the words: *Body Uncovered.* So he had buried them, all of them, surely. Eric drove along nearly deserted, brick-paved streets. The sidewalks presented occasional passersby and the Victorian architecture seemed almost a stage set; there was money here, a vaguely Southern sensibility more akin to Baltimore or Cincinnati than Atlanta. Yet it was like nowhere else; she had never been to such a place, with such verdant, encroaching hills and small, brilliant skies.

"It seems a rather nice little town," Emily said.

"Oh yes, very nice. Do you have the paper there?"

On the highway, he drove faster. Hills rose steeply on the right; small, fenced fields to the left, a creek, a few cows raising their woolly heads at the sound of the car. Beyond the rolling land and meandering creek, as far as the horizon, forested mountains rose in line after heightened line.

"Emily," Eric said, "read it to me."

"They found Mrs. Eicher — they're calling her Ada — at three-forty-five yesterday, and then all three children, within a half hour, ten feet from her. Shallow grave. A ditch near a garage, in Quiet Dell." Emily looked up, her eyes swimming.

"Go on," Eric said.

"Cornelius O. Pierson, alias Harry F. Powers . . . held in the city jail. He's been charged. Probable murder warrants, so he hasn't confessed. It gives his address, somewhere called Broad Oaks. Must be a section of Clarksburg. It says he's forty-five."

"Clever how Main Street becomes a turnpike," Eric mused. "Look in the glove box, will you, and get the press card for the windscreen. A garage. I must drive straight up. If it's a mob scene, I can't leave the car to be vandalized, with all the cameras in back. Not to mention the car itself."

"Eric, these are farmers, not hoodlums."

"These are bootleggers, Emily."

"A few are, as in Chicago and everywhere."

"I like it. You're in town ten minutes and ready to join the booster club."

"Well, you can't assume." She flipped her own credential to the outside of her bag and put the press card on the dash. She took the dog's leash from her bag and attached it to Duty's collar.

"You're bringing the dog?"

"You don't seem to understand what a help this dog will be, Mr. Lindstrom."

"There," Eric said. It was a left turn, a narrow, dusty track. The tops of cars shone black above overgrown banks of flowering weeds and brush. Automobiles were parked to both sides for several hundred yards.

Emily turned to see Duty struggling for perilous balance on the edge of the backseat and took him into her lap. She breathed in the crushed green smells of earth, wild mustard, honeysuckle, and then a darker scent. Eric pulled carefully onto an open dirt swath before the garage, which was rude and small, square, flat roofed, with wooden doors in front. The crowd — perhaps two hundred or more, men, mostly adults, a few women — stood quietly. All looked toward the back of the building.

Emily got out quickly, looping the dog's leash around her wrist. She heard then the pounding of pickaxes and the slough of dirt, shoveled and thrown. The smell was the sewer ditch, uncovered. They are gone now, she told herself, they are not here, not even their bodies, but the men were still digging and the crowd was waiting. Eric photographed the throng pressed up to the sides of the building, constantly clicking the shutter as he framed the gathering.

The crowd seemed country people, in overalls, their sleeves rolled up; a few women in housedresses. A quiet restlessness moved among them; few spoke, and only in lowered voices. She followed Eric around to the back. The ditch, a deep gash perhaps four feet deep and three feet across, ran straight some forty or fifty feet from the garage to the back of the lot. A narrow sewer pipe showed along the bottom, and a sort of winch had been rigged near the exposed foundation of the building, for pulling up the bodies with ropes.

Duty struggled forward on the leash, dragging her to the very edge of the ditch. It seemed he might jump in, and the thought horrified her.

The ditch was muddy and wet, for it opened into a little creek whose dark green water lay nearly still, barely visible through the towering, weedy growth along its banks. Scrub trees, purple weeds, stalky blooms taller than the men who stood near them. Was that Queen Anne's lace, grown to such a height? The white flowers were the size of parasols. A smaller ditch, the uncovered gas line, bisected the large one. The two indentions formed a shape very like a cross that emptied into the water. Now she saw men in suits and fedoras, and uniformed police, near the building, watching the work. A ladder lay propped against the back of the garage, and a solid row of spectators, some just boys, had seated themselves along the back of the roof and hung their legs over casually. One or two wore shirt and tie, as though they'd come from jobs in banks or drugstores back in Clarksburg.

There was Eric, standing on the roof behind the seated men, shooting the entire view of the ditch to the creek, and the still, empty field beyond the narrow band of water. She turned, pulling the dog with her, peering past the disturbed ground as far as the horizon. The creek looked no more than fifteen feet across, and she could see the water move, a glowing lip against the opposite shore and gently ascending meadow. The sun was low in the sky and the angle of light burnished the ground. Heavy-limbed trees stood silhouetted in the field, gravid, sentinel, their canopies subtly stirring. The sky was still pale blue against the darker earth, and the creek seemed to mark a line between one world and another. She imagined walking across the water, leading Duty on the leash to that other, empty meadow that lay bathed in the softest pearlized light, but could not bring herself to approach. None of them, on this side, were worthy of that place.

Annabel can dream when she's awake, and waken in her sleep, or she is never asleep, but always dreaming. She moves above or through the urgency of people moving and doing; she turns away at will and bridges great distances in the breadth of a thought. She is here, in the place Grandmother called *below.* Narrow dirt roads thread through the mountains. Drawn closer, she sees throngs of people crowded near the hunched garage. Lines of metal glint in angled curves: the tops of many black cars. The glass of the windscreens sparkles and catches the sun.

She sees the long bright car that pulls up last. A tall blond man exits, heading straight for the crowd, flashing his silent camera, and a woman gets out, with Duty on the leash. Annabel hears the click of the leash moving, and smells the trampled grass, dung, and earth, and so many shoes and boots and mingled bodies. She knows she smells what Duty smells. She cannot feel the weight of him, or the warmth, but senses him intensely, for nothing separates her now from those for whom she longs so deeply. Duty turns his head, confused. His long mournful search is over; he has found them.

Emily stands beside the dark slash in the ground. Duty drags at the leash. He smells some remnant mixed in the earth and pulls Emily to the dirt edge of the gash; he would leap into the dark, roll in it and taste it, as with dead things at home: a squashed bird, a rabbit torn by cats.

Annabel waits in the meadow across the creek. There is no death here, no danger. Birds take wing like glimmers, rising up; rabbits wear their closed wounds like flowers. She knows the gash across the creek is dense and black, deepening, tugging at the crouched garage. The people standing near are quiet, as though gathered for a meeting of great import. She sees Charles O'Boyle walking up out of the ditch, carrying Grandmother's last meal up the stairs on the silver tray. His steps are measured, just as at home on Thanksgiving. He had turned on the landing, the tray perfectly balanced, and caught her eye, for she stood above him waiting, just as now. Then she sees her mother in his arms, for Mother grew faint on Christmas and he carried her into the kitchen. Annabel hears water leap out of the spigot, splattering in the tin sink, but Charles is standing at Grandmother's window, looking at the playhouse through the snow. It is the humid end of summer here, but Charles is putting the warm blouson hats on their heads at Christmas, the Canadian hats for the Canadian toboggan, and hers is banded and jeweled. How odd to think of it, and the light his camera made when he snapped their picture, with the snow falling so heavily.

Across the way, a light flashes from the roof of the garage, like an eye that opens while the ground is sifted and pulled. Deep in the gash, a glow begins. They have found something; they murmur that something is found. Annabel hears Duty barking as he used to bark at home; the crowd is shifting and moving, and she sees Duty pull Emily toward her, straining at the leash.

The dog seemed beset, and no wonder. Emily must work; she must get close to those in authority. She tore her gaze from the meadow opposite and addressed a policeman at the

266

foot of the excavation. "Excuse me, Officer. Can you tell me who is in charge here?"

"That would be Chief Duckworth and Sheriff Grimm. Just there." He nodded toward the front of the crowd. A knot of men concealed the winch. Emily could hear it turning, and the grunts of the men working it. The men standing aside with their hands clean would be her men, and she saw them now, though no telling who was who. "Could you tell me, Officer, which is Chief Duckworth?"

"The tallest one, madam, with the broad-brim hat."

She nodded her thanks and began working her way toward them. She could see Eric on the roof, crouching to shoot the length of the ditch and the meadow beyond. She watched Duckworth, who was tall and quite thin, like a wraith; he wore a beige suit and low boots, and his broad, high-crowned hat was almost laughable. The other man, who must be Grimm, looked to have stepped off a fashionable Chicago street. Perhaps he was counting on being photographed; his smart Panama hat was perfectly creased. She stood at Duckworth's elbow now, averting her eyes from the ditch. The two men were back of it just enough, standing to the side of the turning winch.

Emily began. "Chief Duckworth, I'm Emily Thornhill, from the *Chicago Tribune*."

He looked down at her warily. "You're here late, Missy. The press has been and gone, with the bodies."

"Sir, we have driven all night from Chicago. I bring you greetings from Chief Harold Johnson, police chief of Park Ridge, Illinois, from Mayor William McKee, from William H. Malone, president of Park Ridge First National Bank."

Sheriff Grimm tipped his hat, as though amused. "In other words, Clarence, treat the lady with a little respect."

Emily pressed on, addressing them both. "I very recently interviewed Mrs. Elizabeth Abernathy, the children's nurse, the last person to see them at home, and Mr. Charles O'Boyle, former roomer and friend of the Eicher family, who first notified Park Ridge police of his suspicions concerning Pierson, or Powers, as he calls himself here."

"I see." Grimm looked into the field opposite. "Powers is not homegrown. Married a woman from town a few years ago. He's a cipher. Smooth talker. No accent."

"You've talked with Powers, then?"

"Oh yes. We know how to interrogate a suspect. Your Park Ridge men were quite practiced in that regard as well."

"You interrogated the suspect together?"

"I didn't say that."

"No, you did not."

"The interrogation is ongoing." Grimm

turned to her, lifting his head as though to fully impress her with his persona. He seemed a film star on location, in his three-piece suit, his banded straw fedora. "Powers likes names that begin with *P* — Pierson, Powers — clearly American names. *Cornelius* brings Vanderbilt to mind, wealth, prestige, while *Harry* could be just about anybody. He's not Powers, or Pierson. We'll find out who he is. He'll have a record, under one name or another."

"You said he's 'not homegrown.' You mean that such things don't happen here —"

"Oh, one man kills another in a bar. Rarely, a husband kills a wife, or vice versa. But never a multiple murder." He looked around them, at the crowd. "You can see they're fascinated, stunned. It's as though a rocket full of horrors has buried itself in the ground. A disaster from outside is visited upon them."

"Them?" Emily questioned. "What of the victims?"

He regarded her frankly, as though conceding a point. "It's not *of* them, of us, so there's not the element of mourning, or responsibility or shame, to make it more than bizarre spectacle. It's not that small towns or rural people lack compassion. Surely that's obvious, to a big-city reporter like you."

She looked at him, surprised at his astute description. He displayed a compact, wrestler's physique; she could almost feel his muscles tense under his clothes as he met her gaze. Duckworth had handed her off to him and stood silent, staring into the ditch.

"I believe you're at the Gore, Miss Thornhill?" Grimm kept his tone smoothly noncommittal.

She merely raised her brows and said nothing.

"I did advise Mr. Malone on where to locate you. Regardless, I like to know who comes and goes in this town, though keeping tabs on strangers is about to get much more difficult. I'll send over the police log for the past couple of months. Give you a sense of the community."

"Thank you. That's useful." Emily sensed the shift of the crowd, but Grimm had planted himself squarely in front of the ditch, as though shielding her view. "Are you from here, Sheriff Grimm?"

He looked down the line of the ditch. "Raised in Charleston, capital of our fair state. Dropped out of law school in Baltimore to become a gentleman farmer, but ran for sheriff ten years ago. At this point, I seem to be indispensable."

"I'm sure you are." Duty was jumping at Emily's legs. She picked him up and he strained toward Grimm, barking his whispery bark. "This is the Eichers' dog," she told Grimm. "He knows Powers; I believe Powers injured him, savagely kicked him, just before taking the children away. Might I have an opportunity, in your presence of course, to confront Powers with the dog, at the jail?"

"I'm afraid a dog's ID won't hold up in court, Miss Thornhill." He smiled. "I suppose, at the right moment, it might get his attention. We'll see. But I'll lay my cards on the table, here at the start — the press will be a huge problem in this case. If you can work with me, I might work with you. I suggest we talk privately, soon, in whatever circumstances you prefer."

"There it is," someone called.

"Move back from here, now." Grimm turned from Emily to shout instructions. "Officers, clear the way!"

"What's happening?" Emily asked, but the smell assailed her. Directly across the ditch, she saw Eric, shooting the turning winch, which labored and creaked, dragging a burlap-encased mass through the moist earth. Workmen turning the winch heaved and sweated; Emily could see their wet shirts clinging to their backs. The Eicher family was discovered and gone, as Duckworth had so condescendingly informed her; what was this? She walked quickly to the foot of the ditch as the crowd moved toward the front. Eric, standing his ground, tall enough to focus over the shoulders of the police, had a close view of the bundled mass. Duckworth, tossing his head like a spooked horse, called for a

271

stretcher, and then they were hauling it out, a human corpse wrapped in cloth and banding, the feet dark with crumbling earth. They were a woman's feet, covered in hosiery, Emily could see, even at this distance. Something within her threatened collapse; it was the hosiery, in this dirt, buried so long.

She walked quickly toward Eric. He would want to follow the police van, to know where they'd taken the Eichers. She'd nearly reached him when Grimm stepped between them. "The tearoom at the Gore," Emily told him quickly. "Nine o'clock."

He nodded as Eric took her arm and rushed her toward the car.

"We're a day late here," Eric said, "but that, at least, was luck." He'd maneuvered expertly into line behind the police van and was speeding along as though an official part of the procession.

Bracing herself against the dash, Emily held the panting dog tightly and looked back to view the cars behind them. Duckworth and Grimm had stayed in Quiet Dell with most of their officers; news of another body would draw more crowds. And there would be more digging. The two sedans behind them appeared to be unmarked police cars, and looked no match for Eric's roadster. "Eric," she told him, "you could slow down a bit.

No one is going to try to pass us on this road."

"Emily, yesterday they let reporters in the garage itself, to photograph the Eicher trunks, all the possessions and family pictures, clothing he'd strewn about. We need our own pictures. Do you suppose your pal could get us in for a private look?"

"You mean Grimm?"

"Is that really his name? The natty dresser?"

Emily nodded. "One favor at a time. First I must get Duty in to see Powers at the jail."

"And I must come with you, to protect you, as you are my girl cousin, engaged in investigating a serial murder."

"It appears so." Emily felt Duty relax against her. The dog lay absolutely still, asleep on her lap so suddenly he seemed unconscious. She touched Duty's hard round head and velvety jowls. Yes, asleep. She wanted to sleep herself. Eric was not in this as deeply as she. Part of it, she'd not realized, was the dog.

Eric glanced at her. "You all right?"

"Of course. I could sleep, suddenly."

"It's that dog," he said, as though reading her mind. "Raging around or fallen down in a trance."

"Eric, don't be dramatic. Next you'll be warning me about trolls in the woods."

He smiled. "There *are* trolls in the woods, and he must wear his vest and watch chain at a crime scene. Don't let his attire fool you. Never married, I hear. Predatory womanizer, and never wants for volunteers."

"As though all that isn't obvious. And to my advantage." Noisily, she opened the newspaper beside her, scanning the pages. "Listen to this: the AP has picked up my interview with McKee. Uncredited, of course. *'Mayor William A. McKee, friend and confidant'* — hardly, but that was what he said — *'of the slain widow, Asta Buick Eicher, said today he believed that solicitude of a mother with dwindling funds for the welfare and education of her children, led the widow and her three children to their deaths.'* "

"What's the headline?"

" *'Widow Fearing Penniless Future Sought Wealthy Lover to Safeguard Tots.'* Typical. It's why they call newspapers rags." She dropped it, unfurled, into the backseat.

Eric grabbed the press credential from the windscreen. "Put this away. It can't be far. I'll pull in right behind the van. The car is still clean, thanks to the rain last night, and we look official. We can file from the telegraph office in the Gore, but the film must be flown, as many times a day as I can arrange." He glanced in the rearview mirror at the car trailing them. "That's Chief Deputy Bond just behind us."

"You don't think they're going to let us in,

to the actual viewing."

"It's all in the driving," he said, "and the stepping out of the car. They just might. Grimm sent us, after all, to safeguard the van from spectators, coming and going. See?" He nodded at the opposite lane of the narrowing road. A line of cars sped past them, back toward Quiet Dell.

"There, Eric. The sign up ahead. Romine Funeral Home." Emily turned to put the insensate dog into his open conveyance in the backseat. "It's warm. We must crack the windows."

"The blasted dog," Eric said. He parked gently, adjacent to the police van. "Give me the camera bag. Don't get out until I open the door for you."

Emily ignored him and stepped out of the Chevrolet, holding only her notebook and purse, as police threw open the back doors of the van and reached in for the stretcher.

The Romine Funeral Home loomed, two dark stories of mitered stone. The shutters had been removed from the big windows, and brick columns buttressed the broad stone porch. They'd no trouble gaining access, for Chief Deputy Bond and Dr. Goff, county coroner, seemed to accept them as approved by Grimm. Goff and the mortician were at this moment laying out the remains in the basement. One officer walking the stretcher down the steps had stumbled, eliciting a brief curse from the other. Chief Deputy Bond, an older gentleman in a bow tie, wore his white hair cropped short and held his hat in his hand. Dr. Goff, as thin as Bond but taller, in a dark suit, wore pince-nez and coughed into a silk handkerchief. Bond had startling black eyebrows and cold blue eyes. *Thin lipped* did not describe him; he kept his mouth clamped so firmly shut that his lips weren't visible. He stepped toward the basement door and called, "Halluu?" as though pitching his voice down a well.

"Yes, Deputy Bond." Heavy steps approached, and the mortician, in black rubber apron, shirt and tie, dark trousers, appeared. Here was a man, big, fleshy if not portly, who shook the steps he trod. His broad shoulders hinted at the physical strength required by his profession; he had the hulking, comfortable demeanor of a pleasant, round-faced Santa. Would have to, Emily supposed: consolation, all those grieving families. In small towns, especially, a mortician, akin to a minister or preacher, possessed secret knowledge. His dominion, his access to the body, nude and abandoned on a slab, was total.

"You set down there?" asked Bond. The phrase was toneless.

The mortician nodded. "Dr. Goff is ready. Ma'am? Gentlemen? This way."

Downstairs, Emily heard Goff cough. The

sweet, sickly smell of formaldehyde drew them into what seemed a vast cavern. The stone walls were three times a man's height, and the concrete floor gently sloped to a central, massive drain. Emily had expected a series of metal tables, but the Eichers lay next to one wall on several wooden shelves, layers of sheeting drawn up like bunting around each form. She saw a skull gleam out, with two dark splintered holes at the back of the head, and looked away. The room itself was an underworld as broad and long as a ballroom. No wonder this place doubled as the city morgue; it could receive a lost battalion. The exposed beams of the ceiling were fitted with lamps hung from the rafters; powerful as searchlights, they were completely blinding. One could not look at them directly, but only at what lay bathed in their hot white light.

Emily heard Eric's camera flash, though the small bursts were mere sparks. They stood, all of them, in a semicircle at the foot of the wooden bier, for that was what it seemed. The policemen had removed their hats, and the mortician spoke in gentle cadence. He might have been reciting a rosary.

"I judge the Eichers to have been underground almost two months, and we had rain, a lot of rain, in July, and a hot, dry August. The remains were almost completely decomposed, whereas the recent subject, underground two to three weeks, is relatively well preserved, being a larger personage, and given the clement conditions. I have bathed only the head and hands . . ." He was subtly turning the group to view the brilliantly lit, low table, and the startling form upon it.

The stunned assemblage stood silent. There was no intake of breath, no murmur, but absolute stillness, shared even by the police, who now viewed what they'd carried as folded, terrible weight.

She lay facedown on a dark cloth, her hands still tied behind her. The head was completely bald. It gleamed, round as a globe, and the flesh was deathly white, like alabaster. Her voluminous garments lay about her, layer on layer caked with black dirt. The great bald head, frightening, otherworldly, dwarfed the small, downward sloping features. Her garments shrouded her to midcalf, and her legs, ankles, feet, seemed of deliberate weight, banded in dark swaths of earth. Hosiery, unbroken, encased her heels and arches; nowhere, below the hem of her garment, did flesh protrude. She looked like a powerful, trussed god, sacrificed and cast into preserved form, an object of veneration to be admired or feared.

Still, no one spoke.

Dr. Goff stepped forward, his pince-nez removed to his front breast pocket. He nodded to the mortician, and continued. "The subject lies facedown in order that the manner of binding be photographed . . ."

Eric moved to take a series of close shots. His blond hair looked greenish in the harsh light. Cold moved upward through the stone floor while the lights directed bars of heat at what could not feel or know or turn away.

Dr. Goff conveyed the narrative seamlessly. ". . . though the victim lay faceup in the trench, completely clothed but for her shoes. Note the two straps of webbing, as from a trunk's straps, buckled around the neck. Indentions in the dermis, even weeks later, indicate cause of death was strangulation. A great quantity of jet-black hair" — he paused to cough behind his hand — "once fastened with combs and pins, was found of a piece in the folds of the clothes and saved as evidence. Very rarely, the hair can turn white or gray in a matter of hours, due to severe fright or trauma. In this case, the hair came away completely, a reaction induced before death but perhaps hastened if the victim was dragged by the hair. This seems likely, as the hair lay loose about her."

In the car, Eric took Emily's hand. She returned his level gaze, and he embraced her. She breathed in the fragrance of aftershave and warm dust.

"Miss Thornhill," he said softly, "I'm reconsidering not sleeping with you."

"Ah well," she said, "you're only human."

He pulled gently away. "And some merely take human form."

Powers, thought Emily. She'd seen his photograph, taken from Asta Eicher's correspondence. He appeared average but was maimed, born wrong, an alien smart and brutal enough to be enraged, to plan and do. Surely these acts were revenge. Car doors slammed. The police were taking their leave. "Let's go," Emily said. "They can see us."

"You're my cousin," he said. "I've every right to comfort you."

"Then do. Let's drive — away from here." She had not taken a note. No notes were necessary. It was nearly 8:00 P.M. Dusk leavened the cooling air. Eric headed toward the country. They rolled the windows down and he sped faster, past fields and lone barns.

"Let's yell," he said, and leaned into the rushing air. "Ahhhhhhh . . ."

The noise disappeared behind them. She drank in the clean smell of clover and alfalfa, and shouted until she was breathless.

Eric dropped her at the Gore and drove directly to the airport, to get his film on the evening plane to Chicago. He would come by later for a stiff brandy. The storefront telegraph office next to the Gore was open to the hotel lobby. She herself must file tonight, after her interview with Grimm. He would want ground rules observed in exchange for information. She had walked the dog behind the hotel and secreted him within her valise, and now she lay on the bed in Room 127, arms and legs flung wide like a child. Duty curled beside her. What strange universe was this? Sheriff Grimm. Mild-mannered Parrish, manning the desk at the Gore Hotel. Children, perished. Pierson was now Powers, in homage to himself: cunning, unpunished. That body today, the limbs bound. Deputy Bond. One's word is one's bond. Dr. Goff, coughing. Grethe, like Gretel, bread crumbs in the woods. Lavinia. Laver: to wash. Clean, washed vines. Annabel. Belle: beauty. A banker named Malone. Perhaps only loaned to me, she thought. One of her lovers, years ago, had jokingly called her a thorn on a hill. She must get up and wash and dress. She must be alert and on her game to meet with Grimm, but she gazed at the ceiling fan turning above her and closed her eyes, only for a moment.

Annabel is with her mother. She does not know how or where, but there are broad green lawns and a wading pool with four fountains; a white statue of a girl and her dolphins holds aloft a pitcher and garland. That is Athena, her mother tells her without speaking. One does not need to speak here and everyone is present, inside the turn of the air. The light is soft and full, like twilight, though it will never be twilight and the light will never go. Her mother encloses her, is everywhere about her, and says there is no darkness anymore, or sleep or hunger, or striving toward one thing and another. A dapper young man approaches, holding a baby. He has a mustache and his reddish, ginger-colored hair is neatly trimmed. He wears dark trousers and a fine button-down cotton shirt, spotlessly white, the sleeves rolled up and banded. He is so at ease and familiar, his collar open at his throat, and rocks the round-faced, barefoot baby in his arms. She's a year old today, the man gives Annabel to understand, and she knows the baby is herself: her father stands before her in the midst of numerous guests. A pony whickers nearby and Hart is riding him; Betty, their nurse-maid, holds him in the saddle. Annabel smells Betty's nutmeg and vanilla scent, smells it too on her father's shirt, for Betty does the laundry; perhaps the fragrance of the soap powder Grandmother prefers is the barely discernible perfume investing all. Hart is laughing, and the sound, for he is very young, four, perhaps, tinkles lightly above Betty's soft encouragements. Someone calls for Heinrich, and he looks at Annabel, warmly and proudly, knowing all so completely. She reflects that his hair is not black and only looks so in photographs, yet the memory of his hair in her fingers, long and coarsely thick, is true. She feels Hart beside her now, very near, just as in the car that day stopped at the gas station, with Pierson inside buying ice creams. Hart fixes with her on their father's face and they rise above him; Heinrich looks up at them with happy certainty. Hart wears their father's white shirt like a cloak, and Charles' long white scarf; Annabel clasps both his hands as the air billows under them, blowing the scarf out and filling the shirt with wind. Borne up, flying or gently falling, warm, suspended, they pull one another closer; she looks into her brother's delighted eyes. Duty stands on a white bed below them, barking excitedly, but they cannot reach for him. He knows them but is not with them.

Emily has slipped through the fence; she is small enough to fit herself between the rough wood slats and run ahead of her grandfather to see the new calves. She runs into the field, the morning sun glancing down in shafts, and the field under her still dewy, thick and tufted, deeper than the tops of her boots. She sees the cow with her two calves, the young calves barely standing, trembling at the force of their mother's tongue. They blink their doelike eyes and Emily slows, not to scare them. She hears behind her a breathy roar of exhale, like a rumble in a bellows, and sees the bull. He's huge and smells of dung and heat and the white mud caked to him. A small bird sits upon one flank. The bull's rheumy nostrils quiver; he lifts his big head. She goes hot all over and her head buzzes. The bull lowers his ringed nose and stomps the ground, throwing up clods of dirt. Emily sees the little bird rise straight into the air and turns to run. She can't hear for the dense noise in her ears but feels the pounding of the animal stun the ground. She sees her grandfather standing on the fence, braced on the upper rung, reaching for her, shouting. Somehow he grasps her wrists and swings her high, an endless arc, while the bull thunders past, pivoting his immense weight and rumbling like an engine. Emily cannot catch her breath, and her grandfather is holding her, gasping with relief. We must all embrace Duty, she hears him say, but no one says it; she is only thinking the words as the dog runs back and forth across the bed in the Gore Hotel, jumping frantically at the turning fan above them.

She sat up, her hand on her forehead, to find her brow was moist. She felt in the grip of some panic and saw the time: Grimm would be waiting. Let him wait: she must have ten minutes. She grabbed the frantic dog and went to the bathroom, where she ran a puddle into the tub and put Duty at water's edge. She bathed her face and smoothed her hair while the dog drank as though parched. "There now," she said. "Whatever it was, it's gone now."

Emily focused her thoughts in the elevator, emptying her mind of all but what lay immediately ahead. She'd thought the tearoom would be full, a warm night like this, but Grimm sat alone at a table by the wall. She nodded as he looked up, grateful the chairs were upholstered, that there was a pot of tea.

"Miss Thornhill." He poured her a cup.

"Sheriff Grimm." How smooth he was. Eric was no doubt right about him. He hadn't changed his clothes, had come direct from Quiet Dell. She could smell that green, dusty smell that was so redolently everywhere.

"I've ordered supper. I hope you don't mind that I've asked them to serve us here. Crowded in the restaurant, in the lobby, everywhere. Noisy, with reporters and the curious. The hotels are doing quite a business. Crime pays for some, eh?" He raised one brow. "Pays us, I suppose, though we're not often taxed with this order of thing. Once in a lifetime, probably. For you, as well."

"Let us hope." She preferred not to joust with him, and drank her tea.

"I understand you were at the morgue today."

"We were. Mr. Lindstrom will of course

285

provide the police with copies of the photographs, courtesy of the *Tribune*." She noticed Grimm's hands and his even, well-tended nails.

"He will, and the negatives as well. Those photographs are police property. I spoke with him. He's not so receptive, your Mr. Lindstrom. Concerned about journalistic independence."

"Of course. Aren't you?"

"I'm concerned with lawfully executing a serial murderer against whom all evidence is likely to remain circumstantial." He nodded at the waiter. "I ordered steak, and fish for you. Acceptable?"

"Perfectly. Separate checks, please; my editors require it. Now, you were saying . . . But hasn't Powers confessed?"

"He has, after interrogation, but he's hired a lawyer, ex–prosecuting attorney, who's insisting Powers' bruises — sustained in resistance, you might say — be photographed, to render the confession inadmissible. We tried to stave it off, but he's gone to another county to get the order."

"The lawyer's name?"

"Law."

Had she heard him correctly? "The DA's name is Law?"

"Law. J. Ed Law. A real milquetoast, gaunt and righteous, but he's on his game. He'll claim duress, but if the circumstantial evidence is overwhelming enough, an inadmissible confession won't matter."

"Duress," said Emily. "So they beat it out of him."

"Expertly," Grimm said. "Does that concern you?"

"I don't condone police brutality, and I assume it's not your regular practice, but I can't pretend to sympathy for Powers. His guilt seems certain."

Grimm nodded. "He would not have admitted to a thing. He specializes in brainless, childlike, continual denial, touring his own crime scene with mild, objective interest. He will do well in court: he's oblivious to verbal badgering. During the other, though, he cried out once or twice. Words, like curses. I'm sure he's not American."

"You couldn't discern . . . which language?" Emily leaned toward him in unconscious response to the nature of the information.

"It was an instant's utterance. Guttural. A Germanic language perhaps. He's adapted like a native, but his picture will be everywhere. Someone will know him."

"And now, this fifth victim. Who is she?"

Grimm looked into the empty room, shaking his head. "Powers is sloppy, arrogant, hurried. He burned trash at the garage to destroy evidence, but we found a bankbook and address book, half burnt, in the ashes. She's from Northborough, Massachusetts. Dorothy

Lemke. We've notified the family. A married sister and an aunt."

Emily opened her notebook and began to write. "Yes?"

"Maiden name, Pressler. Married name, L-e-m-k-e. She's divorced, fiftyish. Childless. Family will be here tomorrow, the aunt, the sister, and her husband, to identify the body. They'll be staying at the Gore. You'll have an exclusive."

Emily was writing. *Divorced when? Why?* She raised her eyes to his. "The access is appreciated, but I need to know now, Sheriff Grimm, if there are expectations I'm obliged to meet, in return for any privileges you might offer."

"There are expectations." He lowered his voice and leaned in. "I want the facts straight, at least in the top-tier coverage, which the *Tribune* will provide. Nothing I can do about the rest. And there will be . . . facts, documents inadmissible in court, that must find their way to public knowledge, for the good of the case."

"I see." Emily realized he'd signaled the waiter to stay away. Now he raised his square, well-cut chin, and the waiter moved soundlessly to her side, balancing a huge silver tray on his shoulder. Food, placed before them on gold-edged china, was everywhere; the waiter removed the salver lids with flourish.

"I thank you, sir," Grimm was saying.

"Steak here is very good, and the rainbow trout are local, caught today. Your best entrees, possibly. Agreed?" He smiled at the waiter, man to man.

"Yes, sir. The potato croquettes, the scallion gravy, the fried green tomatoes, all specialties of the house. Anything else, sir? Wine? Cocktails?"

"I believe we're fine." Grimm watched the waiter retreat. "Are we fine, Miss Thornhill?" Surprisingly, he tucked his napkin into his shirt collar like a workingman. He could not have planned a gesture more appealing to her.

She took a breath, and spoke clearly. "I am happy to publicize any information you deem important, within the context I choose, as long as its veracity is unassailable. You must assure me of this, personally. My sources, should you become one, are sacrosanct; I was once jailed for protecting one."

"I know. Forty-eight hours, wasn't it? The settlement house story, year or so ago, according to my friend at Chicago City Hall." He answered her small shrug with his own. "The food here, honestly, is decent."

The fish was mild, lemony, delicious. She loved the feel of it in her mouth and felt herself enter a rarefied zone, despite her fatigue. All that she swallowed, smelled, saw, simply fed her intensity and accuracy. The food was a means to an end, as was the empty tearoom and the privacy between them. The difficult moment was achieved, and the reserve with which they now proceeded was professional rather than guarded.

Sheriff Grimm ran a hand through his hair; he might be forty, forty-five, one of those very dark-haired men who go prematurely gray, and his nearly silver hair was thick, lustrous, stylishly barbered. Even now, at the end of this long day, the pale blue pocket square in his breast pocket was perfectly folded. The impression of bearded shadow on his jawline only heightened the sense of an animal virility couched in faultless social perception. Not a usual combination, and all working to a purpose. His eyes were bright blue, and his black lashes and brows made their color noticeable from across a room.

"Sheriff Grimm," she said. "Are you related to Deputy Bond?"

"My uncle," Grimm said, "on my mother's side."

She nodded. The blue eyes, the brows. His father's mouth, perhaps, and perfect teeth. "So," she said, "Dorothy Lemke. Born in Northborough?"

"Maybe. Address book notes contacts in St. Paul. Ex-husband from there, possibly. Some money, not clear how much."

"And when you spoke to the family, did someone mention that she was childless?"

"The aunt told me Lemke had a son, died young of an illness, some years ago. Lemke lived with the aunt, but visited the sister's house with Pierson, as they were going off to be married, late July. Two of the trunks in the garage at Quiet Dell are Lemke's."

Emily wanted to see those trunks and remembered Eric's request. "I know local press have been to the garage to photograph the victims' possessions, but the *Tribune* wants us to compile our own documentation. Might we go there tomorrow?"

Grimm ate with finesse, spearing his food neatly, but pulled a piece of bread apart with his hands and touched it to the bloody juices on his plate. "Early tomorrow. Nine A.M. Bond will call for you here. We can only spare a half hour to catch you up."

"That's very generous. Thank you."

"The Lemke family should be here by noon. I suggest you interview them in my presence, upstairs, after we escort them from the morgue. I'll bring them to your room. No photographer." He paused as she nodded agreement. "An officer will take all of you to the station, where the relatives will identify certain articles. Deputy Bond will bring Powers out. Stand close to the sister; appear to be one of the family. Then produce the dog quickly. Lindstrom should be there, and pick his shot, but the dog is not in the picture."

She allowed herself a restrained, admiring smile.

"I only wish I could see it, but Powers'

lawyer is a stickler. Deputy Bond can pretend happenstance if the timing works." He wiped his mouth, put his napkin aside, and regarded her.

The waiter had cleared, deftly serving coffee and berry pie.

She opened her notebook. "Can we establish the time line, for my notes? You arrested him on the twenty-seventh?"

"Yes, on the basis of letters found in the Eicher home, brought here by Park Ridge officers — twenty-seven letters, from a Cornelius Pierson to Eicher — Powers maintains a P.O. box, 127, in Clarksburg under the name of Pierson."

"There were twenty-seven letters," Emily said, "he was arrested on the twenty-seventh, and his P.O. box number was 127?"

Grimm nodded. "He married Luella Strother in 1927, on June twenty-seventh. He likes that number, perhaps. The date of arrest was coincidence."

Powers was married. Emily wondered what wife would marry him. "Was the wife surprised, upset? Did he resist?"

"Park Ridge and Clarksburg officers were watching the Quincy Street house, in Broad Oaks. Powers drove up around noon and went inside. Two went to the front, others to the back. She answered the door and we identified ourselves, asked to see Harry Powers. She didn't blink an eye, only called to him."

"What did she say?"

" 'Harry, someone to see you' — or something similar. We rushed the house as he tried to get out the back. He asked about a warrant, then came quietly, to 'clear up the confusion.' He said he was Mrs. Eicher's financial adviser, friend of the family. We got a tip about the garage that night. Numerous trunks ransacked, some of it the Eichers' possessions, according to the Park Ridge officers. And the smell, the setup. Blood on the floor. Soundproof board in the basement cells. We went back the next morning, searched the well, uncovered the ditch back of the house. Found her that afternoon, and the children soon after. Eicher was likely dead and buried before he went back to Park Ridge. The burials seemed separate events — she was in the middle of the ditch, at the deepest point. The children were piled together, close to the creek. We interrogated him all last night. Today, we dug more. You were there." He seemed to consider. "Lemke was buried very near the garage, as though in haste."

"Quiet Dell," Emily said. "Sheriff Grimm, were the women, the girls, violated?"

"No. That would have been mentioned in the initial coverage, as it plays directly to motive. He bound and starved and beat them.

The boy probably resisted. He died of two blows to the head, skull fractures. The females were not sexually attacked, but the boy — and this must not come out until the trial, perhaps not even then, are we clear?" He waited for her assent, and continued. "The boy was emasculated."

"After death?"

He didn't waver. "Almost certainly. Yes. After death."

She chose to believe him. Hart was not there; the boy had flown. The bird had flown, was the phrase, and the soul was often imagined as a bird.

The moment pressed down on them.

Emily was still. It was all changed. Her vision had gone dark for a moment, but she felt calm and her blood quieted. Yes, it was after death, for this shambling, brutal creature, so filled with violent shame, would have done that in secret, in a privacy that was absolute, all of them dead around him. He did not require the boy's fear, only his person, still warm, and no one must see. The act was the antithesis of the criminal persona Powers cultivated: gentleman Romeo engaged in murder for profit, moving one state and alias to another. She imagined him, an adolescent never given his due, prevented from success for reasons he couldn't fathom. He'd stood aside, angry, watchful. Empathy puzzled him: he could not feel it. A means of agency presented itself: one scam led to countless others. His well-chosen subjects were so willing, so open to seduction.

"Miss Thornhill?" Grimm was watching her.

"Yes, I was only thinking." Hart. Brave boy, fighting impossible odds. Annabel, it suddenly came to her, had run. That's why the straps of her shoes were broken. Emily saw the shoes, with the straps torn.

"Sheriff Grimm," she said. "I thank you, for all you've done. These children are quite real to me." She reached into her bag for O'Boyle's letter, and gave Grimm the snapshots of the family. "Charles O'Boyle took these pictures of Asta and her children. He asked that I give them to you, with the proviso that we agree on the best use of them. The letter, perhaps, should be saved for the trial — but the *Tribune* would like to publish the photos immediately, and the AP will undoubtedly run them."

Grimm looked at the snapshots. "The pictures in her trunks were formal, and not recent." He rubbed away a smear on the image of the children in the snow. "You take the snapshots, and publish them. For now, I'll enter the letter into evidence."

They gathered their things and moved toward the lobby. Grimm had taken her arm as they walked to the elevator.

"Oh," Emily said. "Duty. I must get some

leftovers. Meat, I suppose. For the dog. His name is Duty. That's what the Eichers called him, or it was his name when he came to them." Hopelessly, she stopped speaking.

"Go to your rooms. I'll have them send something up."

She washed her face and took the pins from her hair, and wondered what had become of Eric; she must let him know about the morning visit to the garage. She called the Waldo and left a message, suggesting breakfast at eight at the Gore. She must hope that room service, this late, would respond to Grimm's request. Duty lay on the bed, composed, appearing noble and neglected.

"I do apologize," she said to him. "I know I promised. And I suppose you must be walked. I've taken down my hair before I thought of it."

Someone knocked on the door, quietly.

She opened the door full on, and was shocked to see Grimm himself. "Oh," she said.

"Room service is closed." He'd removed his hat, as though on a social call, but stood back from the door to hand her a small parcel, tied in wax paper and string. "For the dog. And you needn't hide it anymore. I spoke to the management."

She saw that he was quite serious. "Thank you," she told him. She felt him notice her scrubbed face, her hair, an unruly mane cascading over her shoulders and breasts. He turned away with a pained expression. She heard him walk off to the left, toward the elevator, then peered out to be sure. Eric stood to the right, at the corner of the hallway, and mimed turning a key in a lock. She gave him an exasperated look and motioned him closer. Quickly, she grabbed Duty's leash and latched it to his collar, and met Eric in the doorway.

"You're joking," Eric said.

"I'm not, please. Walk the dog. Then come back, and if we are not too exhausted to speak, we must plan."

"Must we?" He took the leash and gave her a small bottle of brandy from his suit coat pocket. "Can you find some glasses at least?"

She closed the door after him. The front window of Room 127 looked out on West Pike Street. She opened the window wide to let in the night air. There was not a car in sight. She thought again of the dinner napkin tucked at Grimm's throat. Her grandfather had sat down to supper just so, all those summer evenings of her childhood. She leaned on the windowsill, clinging to the image of his clasped hands, bowed head, the short prayer he said at meals, and had a sudden impression of him close to her, kneeling down and speaking urgently.

She saw Eric then, with Duty, walking from

Second Street to the corner. He leaned on the street sign, just beyond the hotel's red-and-white awning, and gazed back at the hotel, scanning the facade. He saw Emily and grinned. On impulse, she leaned out and threw her hair over her head, like Rapunzel. She heard his soft laughter but felt a sudden, choking shame and turned from the window in tears. She felt her way to the bed and lay shaking.

Someone must pull her from this well, for she was pressed close in a deep, narrow place. She knew unspeakable things that she must acknowledge. These things happened, or so people said. Mothers must protect their children. She was not a mother, but she spoke, she wrote, for mothers, for men and women and the children they had been. They must know how to recognize a surface that was form and camouflage, how to read through to what was real, to read horror, even. One must mount a defense, to save what could not save itself.

How did it begin, such deep self-hatred, shame that turned to fury? Emily felt him there, among his kill, wild with power he did not possess but took when he controlled the means. It was a first time, unplanned, the still-warm child exposed before him. He was not known to have preyed on boys; Hart Eicher was an accidental opportunity, a revelation, perhaps.

She opened her mouth to breathe.

That instant, she heard Eric's knock at the unlocked door.

He pushed it open. "What is it? I could feel you fall to pieces, from outside." He lifted Duty onto the bed. "There, dog, revive her." Duty nudged the curve of her shoulder, licking her face. "I take it you had a grim conversation," Eric said carefully. He sat beside her. "All right, then. Emily, you must talk to me."

She lay motionless. "Not yet. Just, stay here."

Hair was dead cells, Emily's hairdresser was fond of saying, but strong, lustrous hair that grew to great length was a sure sign of health, like the teeth and the inside of the mouth. And so: Lemke's hair: vitality, strength, no matter her age or heft. The coroner's phrases: *severe fright or trauma . . . the hair came away completely, a reaction induced before death.*

The letters between them would say what Emily knew, for Powers' every correspondent revealed her crucible. Lemke had no doubt written of losing her son, of his goodness, his illness and death, the pain she'd fled only to carry it with her, how *she sometimes saw him before her* — the phrase flew into Emily's mind — but her family had saved her, saying succor would come, she must be patient, and now Cornelius was her own heart's companion; a new chapter was before them.

Emily would never tell it, never write it, for there was no way to prove it, but she knew what Powers had said and done. Bound, Dorothy broke the noose and dropped to the basement floor. Roused to fury, Powers showed her his secret. Emily saw his hand, with the thing curled there.

She sat bolt upright, flinging her hand against the washbasin and pitcher. The rooms had this old-fashioned touch; the maid filled the large pitchers each afternoon. This one was heavy white ironstone, filled nearly to the brim. Emily stood to grasp it at the base, and could lift the spout only as high as her forehead. The water crashed over her in a cold, furious rush; she wanted to throw the pitcher onto the tiled bathroom floor and smash it to pieces, but Eric took it from her.

"Drink this," he said, and took her in his arms, pouring brandy into her open mouth. "Now, again." He watched her drink and held her on her feet as he pulled the bedspread from the bed to drape around her. "You're shivering." He picked her up and sat with her in the armchair, rubbing her back, her wrists, as though he'd pulled her from the sea. "All right, then?"

"Eric," Emily said, "I'm so indebted to you."

"Likewise," he murmured.

In a moment, she sat back to look at him. "The Eicher boy was emasculated. It's not to be known . . . until the trial."

He met her eyes. "That is what Grimm told you."

"Among other things." She could not mention the rest. "But that is the thing I had not expected. It has set my mind going. I must get out of these wet clothes. Can you wait?"

"Yes, Emily. I shall wait right here. Might I have, though, the glasses you promised me?"

"Of course." She gave them to him, from the small cupboard by the table, and went to the bathroom to strip off her clothes and throw the damp bedspread to the floor. She pulled on her robe, a Japanese silk in a pattern not unlike the style of illustration in the Eicher playhouse. Duty jumped at her and stood, paws on the rim of the tub. His water bowl was full, but she lifted him in, placed the stopper, and ran him the puddle he required. Perhaps the water was colder thus, perhaps he felt safe in the tub. She put her hand on him. "He was your boy. I know, Duty. Your boy." She waited while the dog drank and found herself weeping effortlessly, as if these were not her tears. Whose, then? She took her hand from the dog's muscular back and wiped her eyes. "Come on, then," she said, but Duty jumped from the tub and ran before her.

Eric had arranged the brandy and glasses on the table by the sofa, and poured the tumblers an inch full. "Ah, you see?" he said.

"Civilization."

"Or its appearance." She took up her glass. "To survival, and truth."

He touched his glass to hers. "To health, Emily. And home."

"I'm glad O'Boyle is in Mexico."

"I wish I were with him."

"Do you, Eric?"

"No, no," he said, licking brandy from his lips. "Better to be here with you." He took her hand and looked at her quite seriously. They laughed at the same moment. "Tension," Eric said. "You've tears in your eyes, but it's tension."

"Release of tension," Emily said.

He swirled the dark brandy in his glass. "But it's odd, about O'Boyle. When we were in that cave of a morgue, I was focused on the images as evidence. I stood right under the lights for the close shots; they were white hot on the back of my head, like tropical sun. I had a sense of O'Boyle looking at me, as though I were far below him in some bright, lit space. Like a public square or a beach. Each day here, I feel as though I'm seeing what he does not."

"To know this, about Hart Eicher," Emily said, "would shatter O'Boyle."

"It exposes the narrative Powers constructed. A lady killer, yes, but purely for profit and sadistic control, or a myth he perhaps believes."

"Attack, mutilation, elevates him. Does he want men then? Why mutilate the boy, and not the women?"

"Perhaps something was done to him when he was a boy that age. Perhaps he's heterosexual and impotent. Impotent because he wants men? Seems awfully simple. If he wanted men, he could find them; men do, every day. Does he want a woman he can't have, mother, sister, so it's all taboo? And they owe him? He wants them to suffer; he wants to watch."

"He has them, that way."

"The point is," Eric said, "he can't have anyone, until he kills them. That's why he kills. The rest is empty form and fakery, and control, to keep some sense of order."

Yes, Emily thought. "Is that bottle finished?" she asked softly.

"Afraid so. I shall go now."

"Tomorrow then. We will go to the garage at Quiet Dell with Bond."

"I'll be at breakfast, here, at eight."

Emily nodded. "I will interview Lemke's relatives, who arrive tomorrow to identify her. Bond will take us to the jail and produce Powers, but you must simply appear there, to photograph the confrontation."

"Powers and the relatives?"

"Yes, for the *Tribune.* Duty is not to be recorded."

He gave her a look. The dog was sound

asleep at her feet. "Don't get up. And go to sleep, please. The door will lock as I leave."

Emily heard him try the door, to be sure, from the hallway. She turned off the light and thought of William, and home, when she could leave here. He had said to telephone, and she must. She reached to stroke the sleeping dog. Duty barely stirred. She could not sleep: she planned. She would close off this room tomorrow, set up the adjacent room for the interview. It had the smaller bed, a table for dining, a settee. It would be the aunt and the sister, and likely the sister's husband. Emily would order tea and sandwiches, in case they had not stopped for food.

The night was close. Emily lay in bed, her damp hair cool along the pillow. She was not afraid or distressed. Her thoughts were clear.

In affect, Powers was gentlemanly, courtly. The threat was never sexual, one reason he succeeded with these women in midlife, women likely already ravaged by men or by fortune; they wanted care and protection. They were not heiresses; they hadn't great riches. They wouldn't imagine someone murdering and swindling for their savings, going to such trouble, when he'd convinced them he had his own means. And they would not find him out by demanding potency: women of any age were discouraged from making such demands. These women were not young. Youth wanted penetration; young love wanted pierced to the quick. The brain, the heart, the body, wanted sex and love, wanted trust, the equivalent of mother love in one's lover: unconditional love, passionate, true, at least in the instant.

Asleep, Emily saw and felt it.

Dorothy lay in the earth, trussed in burlap. Her hair was loose about her, fallen from Powers' hands, for the noose had snapped immediately, not killing her. Roaring at her stunned, bound form, pleasured, he took the secret, small, soft, like a mouse of flesh, from its place. The scream that rent him open was her scream and his own; he used the strap then, pulling it tight around her neck until she died, and then dragged her to the ditch by the long rope of her thick dark hair. Dead, she frightened him when her hair came away in his hands. A moment, an instant: he was terrified. He threw it down upon her quickly, all of a piece.

Emily woke early to type a first dispatch and found the morning edition of *The Clarksburg Exponent* slipped under her door. A banner headline proclaimed the known details: *Fifth Love-Farm Victim Found, Webbing Strips Lashed Tightly About Her Neck.*

An old photo of Lemke graced the front page below the fold, with a caption stating only that police identified the victim as Mrs.

Dorothy P. Lemke, of Northborough, Massachusetts. Lemke had not been pretty in her youth, like Asta Eicher, but her eyes were wide-set and her open, indirect gaze almost wistful. Her hair was beautifully done, thick and dark. Emily guessed the portrait was taken on the occasion of Lemke's marriage to Pressler, whoever he was, and that Grimm had released it surreptitiously, through a contact at the *Exponent,* just after finding the body. She skipped to the end of the article: *The new body had not been buried as long as the first four. A considerable quantity of her jet-black hair was saved as an aid to positive identification.* The coroner was quoted indirectly, but no one would mark the word *saved,* or know what it meant.

She threw down the paper and dressed quickly in a dark suit and sensible low shoes. She trusted Grimm's pronouncement that the hotel would accommodate Duty, but leashed the dog in her valise regardless, tucking in the finger bowl she'd brought from home. She felt the door lock behind them and stepped to the elevator, which revealed Coley Woods, the Negro porter, elegantly turned out in his braided jacket.

"Mr. Woods, good morning."

"Miss Thornhill." He nodded and stepped back to allow her entrance. "I'll take you directly down, or we'll be delayed on second and first."

"Thank you, Mr. Woods. You must be pressed with arrivals. You saw the paper?"

"Oh yes. That woman stayed in your room, night he brought her here. Middle of the night too, not usual."

Emily turned to him. "Dorothy Lemke? She stayed here, with Powers?"

"No, ma'am. She was alone. Drove up before the hotel, one thirty in the morning, end of July sometime. I went out to get her bags, couldn't see who was driving. Brought her up here to Room 127."

"To my room," Emily said.

"Yes,'m. She only stayed a few hours, left before seven A.M. that same day."

"Mr. Woods, you're saying she slept, most likely the last night of her life, in 127? Did someone reserve Room 127 for her, or was it coincidence?"

Woods slid his gaze toward her. "Ma'am? Mr. Parrish can advise on reservations. But you know, it don't matter. The devil walks abroad. Churches around here? They're full up."

The elevator opened on the lobby. She gave him her card. "Mr. Woods, may I speak with you further? Something more may come to mind." He only nodded as she stepped past him. She saw Eric in the tearoom; he stood to receive the weighty valise, which he placed gently on the floor under their table. "Eric," she said.

She had wanted to phone William. She was too late.

"My dear cousin," he replied, taking his seat. "You look as though you've seen a ghost. If so, don't tell me."

She busied herself cutting slices of country ham and bits of egg into small pieces. Duty was sitting up in the valise, his head protruding slightly. She filled his bowl, positioning it within.

Eric ate, ignoring her ministrations. "I have the photographs from yesterday, just in on the plane. My assistant stayed up all night, printing them, and released the garage pictures to run with the Quiet Dell story in the *Trib.* They ran your piece about the Eicher house, the animal graveyard, Annabel's drawings, yesterday, with O'Boyle's snapshots. The house is attracting crowds. McKee has posted guards."

"And the morgue photos?"

"I have them. Not for publication, as Grimm asked. I gave him copies, and the negatives, an hour ago." He flung open one of a pile of newspapers. "I've been to the kiosk and bought them all. They're compiling a legend for him. *Murder Farm Romance. Lady Killer Romeo.*"

"Lady killer," Emily said. "That term again, an homage of sorts to an attractive man successful with women."

Eric signaled for more coffee. "But successful in a predatory way, purely for his own gratification. It's an apt word." He picked up one of the papers, open to an image of Powers in horn-rim glasses, salesman for the Eureka Vacuum Company. "But to look at this short, dull-seeming pod of a man, one knows he was never confident with women until he worked out writing to them. He needn't even troll for women; they presented themselves and he knew to choose the most vulnerable."

"They've released the letters to the press," Emily said. "More fodder for the Romeo myth."

"I have it on good authority," Eric was saying, "that Powers tracked the progress of a correspondence with an elaborate system of phrases he took from love columns and romance magazines, and articles ascribed to Valentino. He filed letters from women according to a code. Everything having to do with Eicher or Lemke was filed under P-15. It will all be in my story tomorrow."

Emily felt nauseous.

"It's so childish," Eric went on, "the busy-work of a boy accountant. He is subnormal, an outcast who couldn't hold a job. Eureka fired him for stealing vacuum cleaners. Why P-15? *P* for Powers? Fifteenth time?"

"He liked numbers, and repeating numbers," Emily said.

"Emily, do eat. And when you can, you

should telephone William Malone. I hear he's trying to make arrangements for the Eichers."

"What do you mean?"

"To bring them home, Emily."

Bond's police car assured them swift passage. They sat in the backseat, which was high and stuffed with horsehair. Eric's camera bag, their valises, and Duty's carrier were arranged in the deep floor. The car bounced along, raising a great deal of blond dust, very close, on Emily's side, to the split-rail fences of the fields. Negotiating the turn onto the dirt road to Quiet Dell proved challenging. Bond required his bullhorn; farm trucks, smart roadsters, even carriages, jostled for space.

"Of what is Quiet Dell composed?" she asked. "Are there businesses, a store or gas station further on? Where does the road go?"

Bond neglected to answer, but his detective called back to her. "It's just farms one after t'other, set far apart mostly, to Mount Clare, 'bout four miles distant. Road just goes deeper in, following Elk Creek, and there's a right pretty waterfall at the end."

"The end?" Emily asked, but they had arrived, and she was surprised to see that a fence of tall white pickets stood between the road and the garage property. Cars were parked as far as the eye could see. Onlookers stood in long lines perhaps four across, proceeding first to the front of the garage and then around behind it, to view the long T-shaped ditches and the winch. Entrepreneurs were selling lemonade and sandwiches from carts; one man hawked broadsheets hastily printed with the legend "Bluebeard of Quiet Dell."

"Deputy Bond," said Emily, struggling from the car with her notebook and valise, and Duty on his leash, "who has authorized the fence, the salesmen? Does Sheriff Grimm know of all this?"

"Private property," Bond replied.

"But it's Powers' property, isn't it?"

The garage doors were half open to allow light to penetrate, but police directed onlookers past while Emily and Eric went inside with Bond. The interior was big enough for three or four cars. Brick tile walls, concrete floor, and a basement formed by the foundation walls. A large trapdoor to the rear lay flung open. Rough stairs led below; a broken rope still hung from a rafter above them. Several trunks sat to one side, thrown open. Emily looked only at the objects there, for the idea of the basement made her dizzy. Duty walked back and forth, back and forth, until she pulled the dog to her on the leash. Eric was shooting close-ups of various possessions police had taken from the trunks: Emily recognized photographs of Heinrich Eicher, holding baby Annabel, and formal portraits of the children. Silver buckles and spoons and a graceful ladle lay tumbled amongst children's clothing and a baby bonnet — clothes the children had obviously outgrown. Asta Eicher must have brought them along as objects of sentimental importance. There were no toys; she'd thought they were going back for the children and their things. According to O'Boyle, Annabel would have brought the rag doll to which she was so attached. But it was not here. Powers' property seemed mixed in indiscriminately: small, cardboard-framed photos of various women, such as portrait studios send their customers for display proofs. There had to be fifty. The letters themselves had been removed and held in evidence, but Emily wrote down the names on the signed photographs: "your Bessie," "from Virginia, for 'Connie' only," "fondly, Your Edith."

The suitcase Coley Woods had carried for Lemke was at the police station; film taken from her box camera was being processed. Emily had imagined a framed photograph of Lemke's child, in a silver frame such as ladies kept on pianos or mantels, but no. It was too long ago. Any image would be a small one; she would keep a treasured likeness in her handkerchief box or jewelry box, protected. Oh, confused, panicked, had she somehow thought he'd got to her darling boy? Unbound by ropes and straps, she would have lunged for Powers' throat. Right now, Dorothy's relatives were journeying to the Romine Funeral Home morgue. They would have driven fifteen hours, scarcely stopping. Emily wanted, suddenly, to be back in her room at the Gore. She looked for Eric, who was packing his camera, and Deputy Bond, who stood at the garage doors, forbidding entrance.

Emily closed herself in. She could see the lobby of the Gore beyond the carved oak panels and etched glass of the phone booth. Mr. Parrish was at Reception, awarding keys; Coley Woods passed by toward the elevator, laden with baggage. Emily searched her billfold for William's card. She felt she was in a religious enclosure, like a confessional, and fixed her attention on the heavy black telephone. She held his card, with the numbers. Which was his direct line at the bank? She dialed a number and the line engaged. It rang, a low, neutral signal.

If she were there, left behind, and he were here, she would have paced the cage of their separation, marking out the hours. Don't be a woman, she told herself. Urgent matters required his attention, including this case. He was trusted, respected. She thought: He is good. What was goodness? Valued, well educated, privileged, did not make goodness. Some trial the soul met, that required surrender and nurture: his wife, her illness, ac-

313

ceptance that her condition defined his, and going on, without bitterness.

She hung up, and tried the second number.

Her grandfather would have said William Malone had "character." Character did not take advantage, but used power for good. The concept aroused her suspicion. People did not speak of women or laborers as having "character," though they might be seen as "noble" in their purity of being, like the animals in the fields.

He picked up. "Hello?"

She saw his desk and the phone in his hand. "William?"

"Emily. God. At last. Are you all right?"

"Yes, yes. William, I'm sorry —"

"Of course you're all right. Forgive me. I have just . . . longed to —"

"— to call you only now. It has been —"

"I know. I can only imagine. I so regret that I'm not there with you. I've read all your coverage, of course, and his —"

Eric, he meant. Could he be concerned?

The line buzzed unreliably, but the connection held.

"William," she said. "I have been so occupied."

"We're speaking now, Emily. It's not important —"

But she went on, in a rush of words. "I felt, hearing your voice at such a distance, that I might be distracted, lose focus." She was astonished at what she'd said and knew it was true. Separated from him in these horrors, she had put him away from her in order to perceive clearly and quickly.

He said, more softly, "I think of you in every breath. I fight the impulse to fly there on some pretext, but I must not interfere."

"William, it's chaos," she said. "The crowds, the police and press —"

He waited, listening.

"The family are taken from him," she said. She saw them, each one shrouded and separate.

"Emily," he said, "we must bring them home. I've spoken to police and morgue officials there. Pittsburgh has the closest crematorium. I've arranged for Romine to transfer the remains tomorrow by hearse, and a mortuary there will ship the caskets by train to Park Ridge, according to my instructions: Annabel with her mother, and Hart with Grethe." He breathed. "I would have asked your —"

"I know," she said, "it's right that they not be separate any longer." She closed her eyes and thought, Even in darkness, there is goodness.

"Emily," he asked, "will you come with them?"

"Of course," she said. They should not be alone; she would go with them.

"Emily, I must ask your counsel, about

something else."

"Yes, William."

"It is known here, through the *Tribune* and small-town papers farther west, that I am involved in the case. I've received inquiries from persons who think they recognize Powers. A Henry Kamp, from Belmond, Iowa, and a Mr. Aukes, from Ackley." He paused. "Is that near your grandparents' farm?"

"It's a few counties west." Iowa. How could it be?

"They are both Iowa farmers, these men, and don't seem to be in communication. They want to speak with you before talking to police or reporters."

"If you could let them know, William, that I will be home in two days' time, and will contact them immediately."

"I will, Emily. Soon, then."

"Soon."

She stepped into the lobby, leaving their mingled voices in the phone booth.

"Miss Thornhill?" It was Parrish, at Reception. "There's a telegram for you. I was just sending it up."

She took the telegram. He would have signed it, "William Malone." He was with her; he would meet her in Chicago. She looked across the desk at the clerk. "Mr. Parrish," she said. "I understand that Dorothy Lemke stayed here at the Gore, in Room 127,

316

probably the last night of her life, back in July."

"Yes," said Parrish, "the police have taken that night's register into evidence. I was on night duty, and signed her in." He added, "I didn't mark it, really, except that she was alone and it was late, past midnight. I didn't see her check out — not my shift — but no one spoke with her. She gave the porter her key."

"Mr. Woods, you mean," Emily said, to elicit Parrish's affirmation. "An excellent porter, Mr. Woods. Very professional."

"Yes, Miss Thornhill."

Emily arranged Room 126 for the interview and sat waiting, aware that Dorothy Lemke had slept in 127, Emily's adjoining room, for a few hours at least, alone, in happy anticipation. Powers had gone home to Quincy Street, to Luella Strother, his wife. What excuse had he given Lemke, to fetch her so early, before breakfast, before anyone but the porter and night clerk saw her or spoke to her?

Grimm knocked and stood aside, and the Lemke family was in the room, a heavy, grieving presence. "This is Mrs. Charles Fleming, Mrs. Lemke's sister, and her husband, Charles Fleming. This is Mrs. Rose Pressler, the sisters' aunt." Grimm introduced them rapidly, and sat in the straight chair to the left, as if to hurry the proceedings along.

The women were big women, while Charles Fleming seemed their overgrown son, thin and jagged in his brown suit. He was wide-eyed, intense.

Having just seen her, Emily thought. They had all just seen her.

"I'm Dorothy's aunt Rose," the older woman said to Emily, and reached for her hand.

"This must be so difficult for you," Emily said.

They shook hands all around.

"Please, call me Gretchen," Lemke's sister said.

Gretchen had been the pretty one; her round green eyes and fine features were a bit lost now in her plump face. Pleasingly plump, as they said; Emily could imagine her engaged in tinkling conversation, for she had a breathy, little girl's voice. Gretchen looked the younger sister, by at least ten years.

"Please," Emily said, "sit down. I'm so sorry for your loss. May I offer you some hot tea? There are sandwiches, as well. I know you drove a long way." She sat in the straight chair opposite Grimm, the Lemke relatives between them, and opened her notebook. The tea tray was on the low table. Emily leaned forward to pour two cups, and offer the spoons and sugar. The women seated themselves on the settee, looked at the hot tea, didn't touch it.

Charles Fleming settled into the armchair and crossed his long arms over his chest. "That your dog there?" He jerked his head at Duty, who lay beside Emily's chair.

"That is the Eichers' dog, Duty. He was orphaned when the family were killed, so, yes, now he is my dog."

"Killed all of them," Charles Fleming said.

"Yes." Emily supposed she must tell them, as the plan required their permission. "I think the dog ran after Powers, as he was taking the children away, and he kicked it, injured it badly."

"The jail after this —" Charles Fleming looked at Grimm for confirmation. "Bring the dog."

"What a good idea. Thank you, Mr. Fleming. Now, can you tell me, from the beginning, about Dorothy and Powers, what you yourselves witnessed." Emily addressed them all. "Try to keep the facts very clear. You will be called as witnesses, no doubt, and opinion or supposition weakens your testimony. This interview is for the *Tribune,* but it will be widely circulated. Perhaps we can work together to clarify important points."

"He called himself Pierson." Charles Fleming sat forward, turning his hat in his hands, pressing the felt brim so hard that his knuckles were white.

"He was at our house," Gretchen Fleming

319

said, "on a Monday afternoon, the twenty-seventh of July it was. Arrived at two or so and sat down with us at the kitchen table, with Dorothy, to talk of their plans. Said he was a civil engineer and gave us to know he had property, a big ranch in Iowa his overseer ran. Valuable land, he said, as well as parcels in West Virginia, where he was working presently. Do you recall, Aunt Rose?"

Aunt Rose put her hand upon her niece's generous thigh, and gave her a cup of tea, nodding at her to drink it. "He told us he was advising on a bridge, across a gorge in West Virginia. Very high cliffs, he told the boys, when they were home from school. And they must come to his ranch to visit Dorothy and him. Seventy-five cows and as many hogs, and he raised all the corn to feed them, he said."

"How old are the boys?" asked Emily.

"Eight and ten," Charles Fleming said.

Gretchen held the tea before her and spoke over it, expressionless. "She was all aglow, like the Dorothy of years ago. They would marry in an office, Dorothy said; at her age it should be modest. Well, you'll need witnesses, I said. That should be Charles and me. Stay the week and marry here. You were home from work by then, weren't you, Charles, when I said that?"

"I heard you say that." He looked down, gripping the hat, his jaw tight.

"But no," Aunt Rose said, "he was in a rush, to check on the bridge project down South and then get back to his ranch, to relieve his overseer. It would be a road trip for them, a sort of honeymoon. Dorothy said she would take photos to send us."

"And here they are!" said Gretchen Fleming. "He has them!" She turned to Grimm.

Grimm took the photographs from his pocket and put them on the table. These were enlarged from the box camera snapshots. Emily remembered Grimm's comment: Powers was sloppy. He kept the camera but didn't bother to dispose of the film. There were three snapshots of Dorothy, three of him, obviously taken at the same picturesque views along mountain roads. Powers wore his glasses, white shirt, suit trousers, smiled. Dorothy outweighed him by thirty or forty pounds. Dressed elegantly in black, she stood, arms at her sides, looking askance in the sun, with a pleased, happy expression. Aglow — yes. The word described her.

Gretchen went on bitterly. "To think he talked to my boys, telling them all his stories. They were full of questions. How did he light up the farm and the house at the ranch? Why, he had his own electric works! He impressed them so, lying."

"He talked big," Charles Fleming said.

"Some tell tales to children," Aunt Rose said. "But I said to myself, if even half was true, Dorothy would have no worries. He said they'd be back in two weeks. We all sat down over supper."

"I'd sent the boys to bed." Gretchen put down her untouched tea. "It was just the adults. He took Dorothy's hands before us, like a pledge, said he was going to give her everything she would wish for, that he wanted her to be happy. She said he was her change of fortune. And he said, 'My dear.' "

"That part fooled us," said Charles Fleming.

Aunt Rose said, "I asked her in private, was she sure? She said she could weep with happiness. No one was so fine, so respectful, as Mr. Pierson. How could I ask her not to go?"

"Did you hear from her in the month she was missing?"

"We had three letters, that wasn't her writing," Gretchen Fleming said.

"No need to describe those," said Grimm. "They will come out at the trial."

But Gretchen went on. "She said she wasn't marrying after all, because 'she told things that wasn't true and was found out.' Can you imagine, saying such about herself?" Gretchen addressed Emily in disbelief. "And she was going on a long cruise with a rich lady that hired her as companion! Glad she would never marry now; she would have missed all this!"

"Dorothy had been married before, in St.

Paul?" Emily was writing, but they said nothing. She tried again. "She appreciated another chance."

"St. Paul was never her home," Aunt Rose said carefully. "After her boy died, she had a hard time. It was polio, and she nursed him one whole summer. He wasn't but four years old."

Emily followed an instinct. "Was Dorothy herself ill, then, from the strain, and came home to you?"

"She was much preoccupied." Aunt Rose took an envelope from her purse and gave it to Emily. "She wrote her will. That is her true voice, that we want people to know."

"The will must be quoted exactly," Grimm said.

"Of course," said Emily.

"What it doesn't say," Aunt Rose added, "is that everything reminded her . . . of her boy. She used to say she saw him before her, just as real, and knew not to move, or he would disappear. Oh, it was terrible."

"But she got better," Charles Fleming said. He looked at his wife.

"Of course she did," Gretchen Fleming agreed. "That was only at first. She worked at the library, she did companion nursing — not because she had to, for she had her own funds, and a home with Aunt Rose, but she liked to. She was a good companion, capable and steady. She might have gone on as such."

"I knew." Aunt Rose looked before her. "I had a fever and saw Dorothy, looking up through a narrow opening and begging for her life. But I told myself I was ill, and worried for her."

"She wanted to leave," Charles Fleming reminded them. "She went off happily, thinking the best."

"She knew she'd always have a home with me," said Aunt Rose. "Dorothy was like my own daughter."

"She didn't deserve this," Charles Fleming said.

Gretchen Fleming accepted the handkerchief her aunt offered. "Oh, I hope she is with her boy?" It was a question, and she wept.

The jail was a series of warrens in the first floor of a large Victorian building. Outside, mounds of earth were thrown up; construction of the new courthouse had just begun. Townspeople milled around the one large tree, all of them men in work clothes, clearly aware that Powers was inside. Bond drove the group to a sheltered area, out of sight of the crowd. They entered through a hallway and found themselves in a front office. One of Dorothy's trunks, brought from Quiet Dell, lay on the table behind the desk. Chief Duckworth held the lid open. The trunk, Emily saw, was lined in calico print paper.

"Do you recognize these articles?" Duckworth asked.

Behind him, Emily saw Eric, and beckoned him forward to stand with her, out of the jumble of officers and press. Duty was in her open valise, moving restlessly.

"Those are her slippers and underclothes," said Aunt Rose.

"Those are her dresses. Her jewelry box is not here." Gretchen Fleming stood with her aunt, and the two women began going through a pile taken from the trunk.

Then Bond brought Powers from his cell. Bond, who was not a tall man, was a head taller than Powers, who was unshaven, pudgy, soft.

Gretchen Fleming rushed forward. "I know you! You stayed at my house. Say you know me!"

Powers, silent, bit his lip.

Bond placed himself squarely between Powers and the assembled group and demanded, "Do you know these people?"

The women, with Charles Fleming behind them, advanced on Powers. "You killed my sister," Gretchen Fleming screamed. "Why did you do it? Have you got a heart?" She pointed at him, ignoring the flash of Eric's camera, and reached across once to hit his chest with her fist.

"No," said Aunt Rose. "He is a beast."

Powers blinked and turned stiffly to Bond. "Is that all?" he said.

"No, that is not all," Bond answered sharply.

"What did you do with her money?" asked Aunt Rose.

"I have nothing to say," Powers replied.

"She would have given you her money," Charles Fleming shouted, "to spare her life."

More people had suddenly poured in, and there were shouts of "Keep 'em back!" as though a mob had gathered. The group around Powers loosened, opening the way. Emily unleashed Duty and lowered the valise to the ground. The dog leapt the distance in two bounds and fastened his teeth in Powers' ankle, snarling.

Powers jumped and began kicking out wildly. He was handcuffed and dragged Bond with him; Duty was latched on. The snarling was like the seizing of a small, efficient engine.

Emily stepped forward and addressed Powers in a loud voice. "This is the Eichers' dog. I believe he knows you."

The detectives and Lemke's relatives stared; Eric put down his camera and shouted at Powers, "Hold still." He grasped Duty's jaws from behind as Emily held the dog, and the terrier released his grip. Someone was coming up from behind in the hallway, yelling, "See here! See here!"

"That's Law," said Bond.

Powers was sputtering, "I don't wish to be

made a public spectacle. Take me back to my cell."

Emily faced him, a foot away, holding the lunging dog. "This is Duty, Hart Eicher's dog, and Annabel's, and Grethe's. You killed them. The dog knows you."

"Who is this woman?" Powers said, backing away.

A tall white-haired gentleman with a small mustache was pushing toward them, calling over the heads of the detectives crowding his path. He addressed his client from a distance. "If you have nothing to say, keep quiet!"

"That is an unusually smart dog," Aunt Rose remarked loudly.

Bond was marching Powers to his cell. "Tell Dr. Goff to bring some antiseptic," he shouted to an officer.

"If only the dog had got his throat!" Gretchen Fleming called after them.

Emily was about to file her story in the Gore Hotel telegraph office when Grimm signaled her from the window that faced the lobby. She went to the tearoom to find him at the back table; it seemed now a kind of private office space devoted to their conversations, but she hadn't long. She must file.

Grimm smiled as she approached. "Where's your accomplice?"

"Do you mean Eric?"

"No, the one with the teeth."

"Oh. Duty is asleep upstairs. The whole thing exhausted him."

"I don't wonder. I would say the identification was positive."

"It was positive for me," Emily said. "I hope it wasn't a problem."

"Lots of confusion, luckily. Law was preoccupied with the crowd in front of the jail, and once he could hear the shouting, Powers was not so concerned with the bandaging and antiseptic Goff administered. The city jail is too accessible; we're moving the prisoner to the county jail tonight after dark."

"You expect a lynch mob?"

He signaled the waiter, who approached with a loaded tray. Grimm had ordered lunch for them. "Relax, will you, Miss Thornhill? We are having lunch." He looked at her, amused, until the waiter departed. "The fact we're moving Powers is privileged information. If I wanted him lynched, I'd tell you to announce his departure, but that's not my intent."

"I see," said Emily. "But you are concerned."

"There's growing outrage. Luella Strother leased the garage property at Quiet Dell, the murder scene, to some concern that tried to fence it off and charge admission. The farmers have torn the fence down twice, outraged that she's trying to make a profit." He'd ordered soup and sandwiches, and moved a plate toward her.

"Thank you," she said. She saw that he enjoyed working with her, looking at her, and felt what she knew was a ridiculous impulse to protect him by distancing herself.

"I suppose it's silly to be so pleased the dog tore into him." Grimm smiled.

"I must file soon," she told him. "Of course I won't mention the dog at the jail today, nor will Eric. I don't think other press even saw it; they were caught up in the mob at the front."

"The relatives arranged for Lemke's cremation, and went home. They'll be back for the trial, of course. As will you, Miss Thornhill."

"Of course." She put one of the small sandwiches in her mouth in two bites, and saw Grimm watching her. She realized that his pained look the other night had been self-restraint.

"Look," Grimm said. "Concerning the forged letters from Lemke — Powers may not have forged them; it may have been Luella. We brought her in for questioning. She spent the night in jail but we had to release her this morning. She provided a handwriting sample, and we have others, from Powers' papers. An analyst is coming in from Washington, D.C., tomorrow."

"Luella. I must get to her today, this afternoon."

"That shouldn't be hard. The sisters were

stonewalling the press about Powers, but now they're mounting a bit of a campaign. Public sympathy, lest they be run out of town. Or we arrest Luella, if we can prove anything." Grimm loosened his tie and collar.

"What can you tell me about them? They run a grocery store?"

"Matching spinsters. Luella, born in 'eighty-eight. Eva, born in 'eighty-six, the older sister."

"But Luella is married to Powers."

"Doubt it was ever consummated." He paused.

"Go on."

"They met through a matrimonial agency; we have the letters. Powers was living in Ohio, and came here. It's my bet Luella knows the same lies about him everyone else knows, but that doesn't mean she's innocent. The sisters dress poor and the grocery is modest, a neighborhood place, 111 Quincy, in Broad Oaks, but the mother owned property."

"The mother's dead?" She was eating the soup Grimm had slid toward her. Vegetable soup it was, with barley.

"Died, oh, four years ago, soon after Powers married Luella, within a month or two. The sisters inherited everything. Neighbors think he was involved."

"How?"

"Vague. She was fine, a busybody, began to

fail over a matter of weeks. Her hands were numb, she said. Collapsed on the sidewalk. Powers hosted the funeral like a grandee."

"So — arsenic poisoning?"

"She was cremated, and no one filed any complaint. We have, from Powers' seized papers, a 1928 will in which he leaves everything to Luella, and a power of attorney that would have given him rights to all his wife's property, both dated the same day. But neither was ever recorded or signed."

"Someone wouldn't sign," Emily said.

"Law has the right to review all evidence, and Powers authorized him to slip these to the press, to create sympathy for the wife. Banner headlines this afternoon." He gave her a tightly folded copy.

"What do the sisters know of the garage?" Emily put the paper in her valise for later perusal. She must file, she was thinking, she must file.

"Not all the victims' possessions were in the garage. We found clothes and linens strewn around at the Quincy Street house where they live, back of the grocery on the first floor."

"You think they knew about the women, the letters?"

He shrugged. "They knew he didn't work, that he traveled all the time. He must have been contributing money, and they didn't mind how he got it. We're tracing the letters he was caught with. And there's the matter of the checks, from Lemke's funds. Powers cashed them under an alias in Pennsylvania, put the cash in his account, then wrote checks to Luella. We intercepted this letter from Powers last night. I want you to release it, tomorrow, quoted word for word."

She felt his hand at her knee, under the table, and realized he was passing her the letter. "To agree, I must read it now, before you."

He folded his hands and nodded. "It's your scoop, Miss Thornhill."

It was a typescript copy of the original, and went on at some length. She read, quickly:

My beloved dears,
We are facing a bitter fight and should we fight together, we will win . . .

They will say that the check I gave you the other day was part of the estate of Mrs. Lemke. . . . testify that you gave me $4,000 for the purpose of building a house at Quiet Dell. You gave me $2000 one day and $2000 a few days later.

The check that I gave you was merely the return of your money as I had been unable to proceed with any plans due to this trouble. I paid you back the biggest share by check and partly by cash.

If you will testify to this, they will have no case against us and then we will keep the money. . . .

Testify to this, dear. Do not say a word to anyone previous to the trial, but testify to it at the time. . . . The second development is about the alleged clothing they got at the house. Listen dear, it is useless for you to get them to believe that you did not know the clothes were in the house —

Here is what you must do. Now Dear, when they question you again, let on that you are strong against me, and hate me for what I have done, and then tell them I brought the clothes from Quiet Dell, that they were from a friend, who said he would call for them.

This is all you absolutely know. This will clear us and will be in keeping with my present plans. . . . I ask you to write back three words to assure me you are with me.

Do not be fooled by officers' easy talk. We must work together, remember dear. I will defend you at the cost of my own life.

Don't worry and be advised.

Love and kisses, from Harry

Emily felt ill, as though the taste of something bad had gone clear through her. She raised her eyes to Grimm's.

"Well?" Grimm said.

"What a clever letter. He admits to nothing specific and directs them in every detail:

they're to say a nameless someone would call for the clothes."

"Yes. He's deluded, and sly."

"Has Luella read this?"

"She will read it in the newspaper. The *Exponent* and the *Telegram* will reprint it from the *Tribune.*"

"And you hope to cast guilt on them with this?"

"Most certainly, or at least counter their claim they knew nothing. If they say that they gave Powers cash, we may not be able to prove it's the Lemke money. There is also the court of public opinion. They may, in fact, keep the money, but they will be shunned in this town. They can't pretend to be Powers' innocent victims."

" 'Present plans,' " Emily mused. "And odd that he begins the letter to them both, and ends by addressing only one."

"Yes. See what you make of them. Guilty or not, they don't know who he is. But we must, Miss Thornhill, to make further progress."

She stood and collected her things. "Yes, and I must file, Sheriff Grimm, and say goodbye. I will be in touch, of course, but I will be leaving Clarksburg tomorrow, with the Eichers' bodies, to Pittsburgh, and then by train, to Park Ridge."

He stood. "I know. I wish you a safe journey. You've represented them admirably, and

I look forward to working with you through the trial." He dropped his eyes, sincerely, it seemed. "I hope you don't judge us too harshly for what has happened here."

She drove with Eric to Broad Oaks, to join press no doubt flocking to the storefront. "It should be this way," she said, consulting the map Parrish had provided.

The town unscrolled like a newsreel as they passed. She reflected on the very intuitive Grimm. He knew of William Malone, had spoken to him in the matter of sending detectives from Park Ridge at the start, and in arranging for the Eichers' removal. He'd advised William on reserving her rooms at the Gore. Perhaps he'd assumed Emily was some chippy, and revised his opinion on observation. Nevertheless, she would make her own reservations in future, before departing, in fact. She wanted, for the trial, the exact two rooms she now occupied; Parrish would hold them for her, regardless of the trial date, which was yet to be determined. It would be late autumn, even winter, and she would be here some weeks. William would visit her, discreetly; he must see this place, and know what she knew. He could book at the Gore. They would be together, on this and many trips.

"And here it is," Eric said. "Broad Oaks.

You with us, Emily?" He slowed to read street signs.

"With you," Emily said. She fell into a reverie, a dream to oppose darkness, though the day was very bright. This travail would end with William, her hands in his. William would travel to her; her home would be their home. His property would be his wife's home. His stables were there, his job. That was perfectly fine. They would have a life. She would love him. She loved him now, before he was even fully known to her.

"So," Eric said, "Luella Powers."

"Luella Strother —" Emily began.

"Powers," Eric reminded her.

"If you insist," Emily said, "but, I'm certain, not married in the usual sense. She was his front or his accessory, and benefited from his larceny. She knew more, but we don't know how much."

"She made few demands," Eric quipped. "It's the necessary attitude if one is married to Bluebeard. At any rate, go on."

"Luella Strother Powers, forty-three, and her sister, Eva Belle Strother, forty-five, run a neighborhood grocery store at Quincy Street; it should be ten blocks or so, that way. They live off several inherited rental properties, left them by their mother, who died soon after Powers turned up."

"Convenient," mused Eric. "You seem well informed, cousin. Read this fairy tale, printed in the local rag the day after Powers was charged in the Eicher murders. Read it aloud, will you?"

"Date of August 29, *Clarksburg Telegram. 'Powers' wife . . . still expresses her faith in her husband and believes he is innocent. She caressed him and called him Honey when she talked with him last night.'* So," Emily interjected, "she did visit him at the jail. Not such a shut-in. It goes on, brilliantly written — *'She is a rather large woman with red hair. She calls her husband Harry and insists his name is Harry F. Powers. Mrs. Powers absolutely denies she knew about her husband's alleged love racket. Even when shown love letters in her husband's own handwriting to women all over the country she still insisted she loved him intensely and intended to stand by him until the last.'* "

"You see? Loyal. A martyr to helpless love."

"Today's *Exponent* tells a different tale." Emily took the folded paper from her notebook. "Grimm said Powers' attorney leaked this to the press. Ready? The banner headline: *'Believe Powers Tried to Obtain Property Rights.'* And the copy: *'Found yesterday among the belongings of Harry F. Powers was a copy of a document that would have given him power of attorney to sell or otherwise dispose of the property of his wife and her sister, had it been recorded.'* " Emily looked over at Eric and read, with dramatic emphasis. " *'The paper was not recorded, however. Why, has not been revealed —'* "

Eric gasped. "And what are we to make of this?"

Emily read aloud, as though delivering an onstage monologue:

"It is believed that Powers had both papers drawn up, possibly without his wife's knowledge. . . . They had been married at that time less than a year. Possibly he showed his wife the will as an inducement to get her to sign the power of attorney, and possibly she refused to sign. . . . These papers and other evidence . . . indicate that Powers may have had it in mind at various times to 'do away' with his wife and her sister. They are said to have told neighbors that they were going to sell out and 'go on a long trip west.' "

"No need to go west," Eric said. "They are among the brute's victims."

"Victims that lived with him for four years," Emily scoffed, "providing suitable cover as he came and went, with large sums of cash purloined from some mysterious source —"

The streets grew narrower, hilly, still cleanly brick-paved. Well-kept, working-class Clarksburg, upstanding enough. Concrete steps, four or five, ascended the grassy banks to the sidewalks; more steps led to the houses themselves, simple wood-frame structures built into the upper or lower sides of the hills.

"Here," Emily said, "Quincy Street."

Beside her, Duty began growling. Eric pulled the car over and put a calming hand on the dog. "There now, old man. You have found it: the Powers' Grocery."

"Shhh, Duty. You must wait for us. Eric is quite capable." She put the dog in his carrier, out of sight on the floor of the backseat, and cracked the windows.

It had to be the grocery. Crowds stood in front, in both side yards, and along the sloping sidewalks, talking in small groups. A house turned storefront, the building was weathered, unpainted wood. Concrete steps led to a high front stoop and black screen door. No sign identified it as a place of business, but a wooden marquee, silvered the color of barn board, rose above it. The entire structure was impressively blank, the frontage just large enough for a door and two household windows. The house broadened in back, with wings to both sides. The peaked roof indicated a second floor.

"Can it be people buy groceries in that building? Give me the small camera." Eric lowered the window and took several shots in natural light.

"Eric, we must go in. I've something to say to them."

"Emily, I ask you to humor me. Stand well back from these women. Agreed?" They got out of the roadster, Emily with her notebook and a copy of the *Tribune,* Eric with his camera.

A sunburned, sweaty boy, his chambray shirt hanging open, his dark hair in his eyes, stood squinting at the roadster. "That your car, mister?"

Eric locked the car and addressed the boy. "It is my car, sir, and I shall pay you a quarter to watch it for me, standing just there."

"I'll watch it, mister," the boy said.

Eric took Emily's arm, and crossed the street with her. They ascended steps to the sidewalk and began walking to the entrance.

Emily half expected Eric to open the door with his handkerchief, but it wasn't necessary. Another reporter, exiting, held it open for them.

The inside was dim, for there were no windows but the two in front. The room, with its three rows of partially stocked shelves, smelled of sawdust, and the counter was to the right. A few reporters stood interviewing the sisters. The cash register, once ornate, was tarnished black. A tall thin woman, evidently Eva Belle Strother, stood behind the bare wooden counter and smoothed a newspaper that lay open before her. She was sallow, rigidly upright, her gray hair pulled back in a tight knot. Her long apron seemed an accessory.

"All I know is that we are thankful we are here," she was saying. She looked down at the newsprint, posing for photographs while reading the story of her narrow escape.

"Miss Strother," a reporter called out, "there's a rumor, now that your sister has been held and questioned, that you are leaving town. Any truth to that story?"

Eva Belle shrugged and looked up. "Why should we leave?" she said, defiant. "We own this property, not Powers."

She was colorless, ironfisted. She had not signed Powers' document, or even considered doing so.

Luella Powers sat in a chair to her sister's

341

right, partially hidden behind the counter. Her hair was reddish, badly dyed; she wore rimless glasses, had a weak chin, and pursed her lips like a mole peering at daylight.

Reporters, one after the other, directed questions at her.

"Mrs. Powers, you first told the *Exponent* that you have known Harry Powers for decades, that your mother and his father were friends years ago. In fact, you met him through a matrimonial bureau, didn't you, and married him in 1927, in Oakland, Maryland."

"We have nothing to say," Eva Belle Strother remarked.

That number again, Emily thought. Had Powers hypnotized Luella? He'd affected bedraggled captivity at the jail, but his blue eyes could seem almost mesmerizing. Their focus was searing.

"You told police he had visited Chicago three different times," a reporter said, "and then that Chicago was merely halfway to his former home in Cedar Rapids. What is the address of his former home?"

"What about his frequent trips from home, Mrs. Powers? Did you never question his long absences?"

Luella sat upright for a moment and declared, "I was never afraid to trust him. He's just as good as any other man. One's just as ornery as the other."

"Ornery?" Emily stepped forward to address her, moving to Eric's left. "He is accused of brutally murdering women and children. Do you call such behavior 'ornery'? Mrs. Powers, have you anything to say about the crimes of which Harry Powers is accused?"

Eva Belle Strother cast her steely gaze across the room as Eric stepped in front of Emily. "All I know," she repeated tonelessly, like a taunt, "is that we are thankful we are here."

"Powers was fired from the Eureka Vacuum Company three years ago." Eric glared at her. "What is his source of income? How might he repay you a loan of nearly four thousand dollars?"

"My sister has been ill for two years. She knows nothing of all this." Eva Belle turned to Luella, directing her.

"Did you write letters, Mrs. Powers," Emily said, "pretending to be Dorothy Lemke? Did you write what Powers told you to write, and not ask why? You will be found out. Your handwriting will prove you an accomplice."

"You heard me! We have nothing to say!" Eva Belle shouted, bracing both hands on the newspaper before her.

"You have a newspaper there," Emily said. "I have a newspaper here." She held a copy of the *Tribune* before her, open to a three-column picture of Asta Eicher and her children. She walked forward as Eric kept pace beside her. "This is Asta Eicher, widowed mother," Emily said clearly, forcefully. "This is Grethe Eicher, fourteen years old. This is Hart Eicher, twelve years old, who fought to protect his family. This is Annabel Eicher, nine years old. They are all free of you, and the animal you sheltered here." Emily snapped the paper shut.

They turned as one, walking out through the crowd. More neighbors and townspeople had crowded inside, or gathered on the stoop, attracted by the sound of raised voices. Emily felt Eric behind her, and then his hand on her shoulder, and at her arm.

"So," Eric said in the car, "that is that." He'd given the boy his quarter before driving now, headlong, back toward the Gore. "I think it likely you will be the story tomorrow, cousin."

"I don't know what came over me," Emily said darkly.

"Avenging angel," Eric murmured.

"And the way you kept shielding me, as though they're witches! And what protects you, if they are really necromancers?"

"My sword and my shield," he said. "Emily, we are going home tomorrow. I will pick you up at the Gore, and deliver you to Romine. Are you sure about riding with them to Pittsburgh?"

"Yes. Duty and I will sit in the back, alone

with our thoughts, and our burdens just behind us. I will stay at the crematorium, be sure William's directions are followed, and those Pennsylvania folk will get us to the train. Someone must stay with the Eichers. They can't be shipped — like freight."

"Well," he said, "I shall miss you and Duty, driving back."

"Even Duty?"

"Oh yes. In my opinion, he has earned his passage."

"Tonight I shall file a last story from the Gore, concerning Dorothy Lemke. Clarksburg could be a pretty town, in these lovely mountains, if one stumbled into it from a different dream."

Emily, her packed bags beside her, scanned her copy. She'd written the headline and subhead — *LEMKE REMEMBERS HER OWN LOST CHILD; Divorcee's Excursion to Bucolic West Virginia Ends in Tragedy, Reporter Writes from Hotel Room Where Lemke Spent Last Hours* — and ended with the will, a simple document dated July 22, 1927. Dorothy was alive in the words.

To Whom It May Concern: I, Dorothy Pressler Lemke, make my will and testament. Whatever money there is left after I am cremated, and my ashes strewn in the wind, I don't want them kept or buried by anybody. Whatever money is left, I leave five hundred $500.00 dollars to my sister in Northboro, River Street, Mrs. Gretchen Pressler Fleming. And if I should need someone to take care of me before I die I leave that party two hundred $200.00 dollars, besides their wages, will have to be taken from the bulk of my money. And the rest I leave in memorie for my little boy, who died in 1923, to the children's crippled hospital to make some little boy or little girl well and strong. I do not want that anybody should do otherwise, as any luck they shall not have out of it, if anybody tries to do otherwise as I have here dictated, I like to see my wishes fulfilled and everybody concerned about it, will be happier for it, these is my last will.

■ ■ ■ ■

IX.

■ ■ ■ ■

Banker's Charity Provides Funeral for
Mother, Tots . . . With the estate of Mrs. Asta
Buick Eicher wiped out entirely by mortgages on her Park Ridge home . . .
William H. Malone, Park Ridge banker,
today agreed to pay all funeral expenses
for the family of four, murdered by Harry F.
Powers. . . . It was funds furnished by Mr.
Malone that helped greatly in solving the
mystery of the disappearance of the Eicher
family . . . and today he drew an additional
check for $1,500 . . . to pay the funeral
expenses.

— *The Clarksburg Exponent,*
September 1, 1931

August 31–September 2, 1931
Park Ridge, Illinois
Clarksburg, West Virginia–Chicago, Illinois

WILLIAM MALONE: GOING HOME

She has not phoned him, and he cannot reach her except by telegram. He could phone the Gore, of course, but he must observe propriety, and not presume or make demands. He reads her every dispatch, the words going to the heart of him as he tries to breathe above them.

He is in no position to assert his will or his desires. She is an independent woman not bound by convention. His life now appears to him as barren convention, nothing but convention, for she has stood close to him, like a fire.

They declared themselves here, in his office.

It bound him more deeply than the marriage vows he's respected until now, though his marriage is one of fact rather than experience, love, even habit. He only provided, and was alone.

She was alone, like a flame burning in a

dark field. He walked through the field, toward the glow; he entered a heat that drew him deeper into the roar of his own pulse.

His dreams taunt him. He must speak with her.

He must bring the Eichers home, and he values Emily's counsel most. Cremation is the only recourse, in Pittsburgh, and transport by rail back to Chicago and Park Ridge. The Broadway Limited stops in Pittsburgh en route from New York to Chicago. Their final burial in St. Luke's cemetery, across the park from his home, does not concern him; the Lutheran minister is planning the service, involving the children's Sunday School class, and the neighborhood taken up with the tragedy.

The cremation is the true ceremony, in William's mind, a purification to take them away from the earth that enclosed them past all help, past his help. He wants to be present, with Emily, in the small chapel he imagines.

The bodies are taken from that ground, where the children lay together, ten feet from their mother. Had she realized, for some moments or instants? He cannot think of such suffering, and only hopes it was true she died a week before them, else why forge her name on a note?

Sitting at his desk, he feels, like a blow to the chest, a certainty that Powers had asked for the note and she had gently refused. She knew her accounts did not contain a thousand dollars; perhaps she tearfully confessed her true circumstance and the confession immediately preceded her death. They'd agreed to marry in their letters, apparently, before ever meeting; Powers had planned to kill the family all along, and built the garage for that purpose. She died, at least, not knowing that he would take the children, that no one would stop him.

He sees Grethe Eicher before him; she's her mother's height, and Hart is nearly as tall. They are not "tots" or "infant children," as the newspapers daily proclaim.

He is certain the boy struggled.

Hart Eicher, in line at the teller's window, looks at William Malone, watchful, suspicious. He is not intimidated by a bank president who claims friendship with his mother. If the man is such a friend, why doesn't he pay off the Cedar Street mortgage, before Anna Eicher begins corresponding with suitors through the American Friendship Society? His personal funds might have saved their lives rather than paid for their burial.

You did not know, Emily tells him.

He imagines the Lutheran church, with four caskets lined up in a row, a devastating thought. It is some comfort, to mingle their ashes in two caskets — the mother with her youngest child and brother with sister. It is the only comfort.

He must speak with Emily. Phones ring in the outer office; he has said to hold his calls. His direct line is open.

Last evening his wife's confessor, Father Flynn, had stopped by unannounced, to thank William on behalf of the community; this thing preoccupied everyone. Perhaps that was God's plan, Flynn said, for in life we are in death.

He is fifty-one. His father died young in a hunting accident, or that was the story the family told. William was three. An only child, he was carefully instructed in the use of firearms, and hunted from the age of twelve with his grandfathers. Close friends, they had married their son and daughter and helped raise their grandson; William and his mother lived on one estate or the other. She decided not to remarry after the accident; it would have complicated a clear legacy, for his grandfathers loved him as a son. One of them, each summer, took William and his mother to the Continent; they schooled him in business, art, ethics. Both lived into vibrant old age.

He might have twenty years with Emily, thirty years: a lifetime, for some. Or his wife could outlive them both, he thinks ruefully. His grandmothers had died in their forties, and neither husband had remarried. He'd married late, the object of his mother's nurture and intelligent interest. She'd not approved of Catherine, but supported his choice, and died within five years of the marriage, before Catherine's disease took hold.

Accident, illness, happenstance. He cannot lose Emily. Her profession imposes risk, surely. Mayor McKee, in frequent conference with editors at the *Tribune,* showed William the morgue photographs entered as evidence in the case.

The morgue looked like a cave; Emily had entered it with Asta Eicher, with the children. She'd stood near them with a *Tribune* photographer, one Eric Lindstrom. A gentleman, William was told, a respected journalist. She's not alone, he tells himself, and that is good.

His telegram will have arrived hours ago.

Extraordinary, all that has happened.

He thinks, I must speak with her.

His line rings, and he picks up immediately. "William?" she says.

EMILY THORNHILL: TRAIN RIDE

It was ten o'clock of a beautiful morning. Emily waited in Eric's car with her suitcases, her grip, her valise, and the dog. Eric was driving back to Chicago with their typewriters and files of case coverage. Clarksburg's fulsome ash and maple trees cast moving shadows on the yellow-brick pavement, the sidewalks, the stone outbuilding to the back of Romine Funeral Home. The house itself towered above. To the left, three blocks across, Emily could see the rear wing of the Gore Hotel. Though it was early, an assemblage had gathered to witness the beginning of the journey: the mortician, in business attire and a formal, cutaway jacket; boys in suits, short pants, and knickers, men simply looking on; photographers, waiting. All of them, men. Women did not gather to witness such events.

"Emily," Eric was saying. "You're sure you don't want me to take Duty, so that you don't have the dog, in addition to all else?"

She wanted to say that the dog was the only family left the Eichers, and Duty must stay with them, but she only looked at Eric fondly. "I've just walked him. He will be fine, three hours to Pittsburgh."

"And on the train?"

"Surely there are stops along the way. We shall dash off, and dash back." She reached over to smooth Eric's collar. "Eric," she said, "there is Iowa. I must go there for some days, immediately after the service for the family. To find where he came from, who he is. I have a lead who contacted William, after it was published that he is funding —"

"This," Eric finished. "He is funding this." He took her hand. "I will come with you. The *Tribune* will send us both, and rent a good, unfashionable car the farmers will recognize

354

as sensible. I'm along as photographer, exclusively."

"Have you been to Iowa, Eric?"

"Never. I hear it's flat in every way, and terrible, I'm sure."

"No, Iowa is beautiful. My grandparents' farm was near Fairbank. It is still there. We shall stop by. Farm people understand those sorts of visits."

They sat without speaking. The group on the sidewalk milled slowly about. The sky was bright blue. Tall trees stirred, their frothy shadows moving on the brick street.

The mortician stepped forward to open the back doors of the hearse.

"Ah, look," said Emily. "Here they are."

They got out of the car and stood beside the hearse. Eric took photographs but Emily only waited, with Duty. Two men came bearing each pine coffin, for they were not heavy. And what was inside? Delicate, unimaginable forms, wrapped in white muslin.

The men moved deliberately, sliding the boxes carefully in; they fit, just, for they were measured to order.

She stood near the coffins, to say good-bye. Lightly, she touched the wood of each, and saw the small brass labels, each held with a single rivet, on which words were inked: Asta Eicher/Annabel Eicher. Grethe Eicher/Hart Eicher.

No one standing here had ever seen them,

yet she felt she knew them. Would the feeling fade in time, or was she bound to them, as to her family who were gone?

Eric took her arm and she stepped back. The mortician fastened the doors of the hearse.

Eric had transferred her luggage, and Emily shook hands with the mortician. The men bearing the coffins would drive. She was in the hearse as though transported, and Eric was leaning in, talking to her, but she did not catch the words. Duty was leaping back and forth, from the deep floor to the narrow seat, and she caught him up, for the hearse was in motion, driving away. She could see the resting coffins in the back, through the long glass panel behind her, and the drivers in front, through a smaller window. The hearse windows were darkly tinted and the world outside was tinctured and fluid, like a photograph developing in solution. It seemed the world she'd come from, walked through, survived, for a time. She felt death sitting next to her, invisible, pleasantly self-involved, like a companion traveler on any public journey.

The Beinhauer Crematorium was a stone structure with the arched doorway of a church. Deep in the apselike entrance, the walkway echoed with footfalls. The staff appeared the moment the Romine hearse arrived. Four men in dark suits carried the caskets inside. Another approached Emily, helping her from the car as she bade good-bye to the Romine employees. The man escorting her was clearly in charge.

He introduced himself as "owner of the Beinhauer establishment" and took her hand. "Miss Thornhill, I thank you for accompanying the family. This has been a tragedy. Please let me show you to my office, and then to the chapel and garden. Many of our clients wait there as their loved ones receive services."

Emily nodded, and took his arm, allowing Duty to follow with them on the leash. They must stop in the office. She, the responsible party, must sign forms. A decision was necessary, the man was saying; William Malone had not specified directions on a matter of some import. The man stayed near her, speaking softly; he smelled of oranges, as though he'd just torn one apart with his fingers.

She sat in an overstuffed chair drawn up before his desk. To both sides of its ample Victorian surface, crystal bowls brimmed with orange potpourri: cloves, dried orange peel and rose petals, bits of cinnamon stick.

"Miss Thornhill, Mr. Malone specified that the remains leave Beinhauer, as they are now contained: mother and daughter in one casket, and brother and sister in the other, after cremation."

"Yes," Emily agreed.

"But I must ask, in the matter of the cremation itself, shall each body be cremated separately, and enclosed in a box" — he placed upon the desk a small hinged box of dark wood — "or an urn, of which there are many designs" — he indicated a shelf behind him. "Or shall the bodies be cremated together, two by two, if the ashes are to be mingled for burial?" He waited.

"I see what you are asking," Emily said.

"I telephoned Mr. Malone earlier today with the question. He said to follow your instructions. Forms directing the procedure must be signed before we proceed."

"I think the bodies must be cremated in pairs, Mrs. Eicher with Annabel, and Hart with Grethe." Emily reached for Duty and settled him in her lap. "The thinking is that the family be united and no longer alone. They were separated — by force. A mother and her children. You understand."

"I do, Miss Thornhill. I have the necessary forms prepared." He took a small stack of papers from his desk and moved them toward her. "Then there is the matter of the receptacle, for each pair of remains." The small hinged box sat before him.

"You have only this one box, then?"

"This box is usual, and most economical. My concern is whether it will hold two, or both . . . the young lady was fourteen, and the young man, twelve years of age —"

Emily held Duty in check. He had put his paws on the desk and seemed prepared to leap onto it. "Of course, I see. Do you have a larger box?"

"We have this model." He turned to open a cabinet behind him. "It is meant to resemble a ship's box and is often used for military funerals." The box was walnut, and twice as large, the top fashioned in the carved lines of a sailing schooner. The sails were embedded mother-of-pearl.

It was the size of her own jewelry box at home, Emily reflected. "May I . . . hold it a moment?" she asked. She opened the proffered box, and Duty nosed inside. "May we use this box, in particular? Forgive me, but this dog was Hart Eicher's dog, and I think this box . . . is rather masculine and appropriate, if any such object is ever appropriate." Grethe would not mind, thought Emily.

"It will be that box, then, for Hart and Grethe Eicher. And for Mrs. Eicher and Annabel?" He moved slightly aside in his wheeled desk chair, allowing Emily to see the shelf of displayed urns.

"Yes, an urn. Could you . . . move them to the desk, please, so that I can compare them more easily?" She put the box to the side of the desk and waited as he arranged several metal urns in front of her. Some were engraved with flowers or scrolls. Duty jumped down from her lap as Emily studied them.

She'd taken one up to see it more closely, and turned to see Duty lying before a low shelf that displayed a white urn; it was the size of an apothecary jar. "Oh," Emily said, "that is a lovely one."

"It is, yes. It's not for sale, I'm afraid. It has been in the family since Beinhauer opened in this location, in 1910. It is alabaster, with a lovely relief sculpted into the front. Let me show you." He rose to retrieve the object and placed it carefully on the desk.

The alabaster was translucent, like marble lit from within. The small relief described a standing angel whose wings flared to the double handles of the oval receptacle. Emily removed the lid, which fit quite securely, and locked into place once turned. "How ingenious," Emily said. She looked up at the gentleman opposite. "Your name, sir?"

"I do apologize. I'm Louis Beinhauer. This is my family establishment, begun by my grandfather."

"And taken up by your son, perhaps?"

"Perhaps," he said. "Or my daughter, who has displayed more interest."

"You are a modern man, Mr. Beinhauer. Is the family of German origin?"

"German on my father's side. My mother was Danish."

"Like Asta Eicher. She and the children were Danish, and spoke Danish a bit, I understand, at home, but the children were all born here, and thoroughly American."

He smiled. "I'm afraid I would not recognize Danish, except for the songs my mother sang."

"One does not forget those songs," Emily said, "even if the words are only melodies." She touched the alabaster urn lightly. "Mr. Beinhauer, the Eichers were done a great wrong. We are only receiving them now, back from a dark place. This urn before me should hold the ashes of Annabel Eicher and her mother, whose family name was Anna. Anna, I'm sure you know, means 'favored of God, given of God.' " She paused. "Mr. Beinhauer, I know I am asking far more than is required, but I ask you to let me purchase this urn, at any price you suggest, for Anna Eicher and her daughter Annabel."

He was silent for a moment. "Miss Thornhill, my daughter's name is Annabel. Please allow me to provide this urn for Annabel Eicher and her mother."

Emily nodded, for she could not speak.

"Will the urn be seen," he asked, "or buried in the casket?"

"I wish it might be seen — at the memorial service — but then it will be buried, in the cemetery near the Lutheran church the children attended, near their father's grave, and their grandmother's."

"So be it." He stood. "I'm pleased to accompany you while you wait, if you wish."

"Not at all, Mr. Beinhauer. I thank you on their behalf for such a generous gift, and I am pleased to wait alone."

He showed her through the small chapel to the garden back of the building. It was a courtyard with a fountain, and plantings of rose trees set off by boxwood hedges.

Emily sat on a white iron bench. She saw a long stone structure to the far rear of the property, with small Romanesque windows of leaded glass. A smokestack rose above it and smoke poured constantly forth. Duty walked up and down the stone paths. She took the leash off his collar so that it wouldn't drag behind him.

She waited on the platform of Pittsburgh's Pennsylvania Station with her luggage, and Duty suitably enclosed in his carrier. Louis Beinhauer himself accompanied her in order to present special permits to the Pennsylvania Railroad conductor. The caskets, draped in dark blue satin, would be loaded onto the baggage car. Emily walked behind the wheeled biers, holding Duty in her arms, while a porter followed with her luggage. Passersby stopped respectfully; many of the gentlemen removed their hats.

The train came on, shuddering the platform, blowing steam straight up in shots of plume. "It's the Broadway Limited," Mr. Beinhauer was saying. "Just on schedule. You will make Chicago by nine tomorrow."

The maw of the baggage car opened; Beinhauer's employees loaded the caskets. He introduced Emily as a representative of the family, and a valued *Chicago Tribune* journalist. "This gentleman will show you to your compartment," he said.

"Mr. Beinhauer, I can't thank you properly, on their behalf, and for showing me . . . such consideration." She felt tears fill her eyes, though she'd determined not to weep. She'd not done so, even when he'd opened the two simple mahogany caskets in the viewing room. Fold upon fold of white satin lay within, fixing, in one casket, the box with its sailing schooner, firmly within an ocean of satin waves. In the other, the alabaster urn lay enfolded as though in shining cloud.

Beinhauer tipped his hat to her now as the conductor helped her onto the train. Her private compartment, the conductor explained, was courtesy of the railroad. "The observation car at the far rear has an enclosed outdoor deck," said the conductor, "very popular with those wishing to observe Kittanning Gap, summit of the Alleghenies."

"The train itself is so lovely." Emily followed him through the generous vestibule. The way narrowed; they passed an open compartment and the conductor showed her to the next. Each seated four persons comfortably on facing upholstered seats for day travel, but made into sleeping accommodation of one full-size bed. The conductor pointed out her compact private lavatory, whose tanks the porter filled on a schedule.

"Thank you, sir. We so appreciate the privacy."

"Enjoy the train, ma'am. You should have a quiet ride. The dog, leashed, is allowed anywhere but the dining car, but you may pass through to the observation car or lounge."

"The *Tribune* so appreciates the flexibility shown us. I know it's quite unusual."

She sat, facing forward, and unleashed Duty, grateful the compartment allowed him freedom of movement. She took off her hat, gloves, jacket, for she had dressed somewhat formally this day, and lay her head back on the cushioned seat to gaze at the blur of the large window. She'd left Clarksburg only that morning, aware of the caskets behind her as they shifted slightly on the winding mountain roads. Dorothy Lemke, Asta Eicher, the children in their headlong travel, had likely seen the same hairpin turns and picturesque observation points.

She thought of Eric, driving to Chicago, then of William, and wanted him with her. "Duty, you must be thirsty," she said, for the dog pawed excitedly at the window, licking the glass. She took his small bowl from her valise and filled it at the lavatory; Duty drank noisily, then stared fixedly outside.

She must look over the armful of newspapers she'd purchased at a sidewalk kiosk just outside the station. Stories she'd hurriedly filed yesterday appeared in the *Tribune*. She opened the paper to below the fold, to see her article on Grimm's intercepted missive. *"Let On You Hate Me," He Writes Wife* headlined Powers' letter to Luella. Emily checked to see that the text was quoted exactly, and read her own careful words:

> . . . said to have been written shortly after Powers' arrest. . . . How it was translated is a mystery, but Chief C. A. Duckworth . . . admitted its contents were familiar to him. "Yes, I have seen that letter. I am sorry that it is out." . . . He would not give further information . . . other than to say, "It is the Powers letter!"

Papers from New York, St. Louis, Washington, D.C., Charleston, Pittsburgh, featured Powers, front page, item after item gleaned from local reporters or the AP. Powers' published directive, *Say You Are Against Me,* undermined the sisters' claims, one column over, just as Grimm intended. The train had reached full speed. They were going home, all of them; Emily could not cross the distance fast enough. She pulled Duty to her for comfort and thought of the baggage car she'd glimpsed from the platform. The Eichers were there. She felt them profoundly, moving with her, as though the cremation had distilled the power of their vanished lives and released them from any confines.

She closed her eyes a moment and allowed herself to remember the open caskets. The yards of white satin brought to mind the wedding gowns the girls would never wear, the bride Hart Eicher would never touch. An upper-class, European family, transformed to striving, penniless Illinois householders, was ended; if there were any relatives, Emily would not be here, thinking of weddings that could not happen. She wished to hear quiet, trilling laughter from the identical compartment behind her: children and fond parents would so enjoy such a train ride, sleeping all night in a bed that gently moved with the roar of passage. She lay across the seat, pulling up her knees like a drowsy child.

She must sleep, even for a few minutes. Duty lay in his carrier, insensate. She pillowed her head with one arm and felt herself rocked in the intense forward motion. It was as though she flew forward and fell backward, back and back, into warm enfolded safety she could not remember.

Annabel is above the train, borne up gloriously on the ruffling air, for the cloud of the steam engine's heat is like a rolling wave. It is nearly twilight below. The train gleams along its length, roiling the gathering dusk.

She is with her mother; Grethe is with Hart. Some trace of them is here, secreted together in the dim baggage car. She sees into the lounge with its facing sofas and armchairs: the manicurist polishing tiny scissors, the barber folding towels. Tables in the dining car, menus in place on the white tablecloths. Small lamps at each table cast illumined half-moons.

She sees within; she flies above. Charles' long white scarf streams from her, winter silk that something tugs and wants. She follows it down, passing her hand through the stream of the train, and sees Duty at the window. She can fly along with him this way, one moment to another; she hears his ragged, excited breathing. He has found her again, a sense only. She would throw her scarf through to him, to smell, but it is only air, the air of her.

She sees Emily sleeping and must tell her that Duty needs some remnant, some scent still real and left behind. Mrs. Pomeroy, hidden, has the golden cord about her. Duty must have it, and Mrs. Pomeroy's soft face, her fabric skirt. Annabel can see through Duty's eyes, a sideways veil, and smell intensely, following a scent that disappears.

Annabel flies faster now, higher in the blooming air above the train, and beyond. She sees her street, her house, skips away as

St. Luke's opens its broad doors for the service. She knows the pale blue robes the children wear, and the songs they sing: Jesus loves them. The words follow her to broad, flat fields flung open to the sky, and a deep barn filling with hay. Annabel wants to see but hears the train, louder and louder, everywhere about her. Their compartment is quite comfortable and Grethe is playing jacks, laughing as she never did, scooping up the metal jacks between bounces of a small red ball. Their mother smiles, her hair done up fashionably, her eyes young. Duty cannot smell or see them, but knows them and waits to hear his name. Mother will take them to the observation deck; the view is grand and disappears like a film before one's eyes.

Annabel flies before them. The train shines into the dark, lighting the rain in Quiet Dell, lighting the slippery road. Mr. Pierson's car is there in the ditch and Mrs. Pomeroy has fallen in the wet mud. Annabel takes her up quite easily, only thinking of touch, until Mrs. Pomeroy is in the car, hidden deep in the crease of the backseat. The doll is cotton batting; she can crush quite small. Annabel tells Emily: the world is air and the heavy train moves through it.

Emily is swimming in her sleep, for the heavy rain buoys her up like a river and she floats within it. To one shore the sun is shining brightly: that is Mexico. Charles O'Boyle stands on a balcony with Annabel, who clutches her faceless rag doll and puts out one hand that a bright parakeet might land upon her finger. To the opposite shore a snowstorm rages. Emily finds herself with Charles and the children; the long toboggan is quite large enough for five and she is on the sled. He takes their picture as snowflakes drift and fly, catching on the children's eyelashes and their blouson hats. Duty barks from the porch, snapping at the snow. How odd to hear the dog bark, a deep and welcome sound, for Duty has never been injured and Powers has not arrived. Powers will never arrive if Emily stays on the sled. She holds on to Grethe tightly, a head taller than the slender girl, and feels Charles pressed close behind her. He has got them to the top of the hill in the park and shouts, over the wind and whirling snow, to hold on; they must hold on to one another. They are flying down, too fast it seems, from day to night, and the snow all about them turns to heavy rain.

It is a pounding, clattering storm on a humid summer evening; a car is stuck in a ditch, sitting lopsided so that its headlights shine askew. Emily hears a train, far off behind the trees. She must get the children onto the train, for it is Powers' car in the ditch, his empty car. The back passenger door flies open. She sees a glow within, shining up through the backseat — a small, weak glow, like a firefly trapped in the palm. Something is there. Emily hears Duty barking his raspy, broken sound, very near her face. The dog barks, furious to be heard, for someone is knocking, knocking. Emily hears the train roar up about her.

"Ma'am? Ma'am?"

The sound is lost in the noise of the train, which drops away suddenly. She is awake.

"Ma'am? Porter, ma'am."

She was on the train, of course, and stood so suddenly she had to catch herself. She opened her door to the porter, a Negro gentleman in spotless white, bearing a silver pitcher in a pleated cloth napkin. "Good evening," she offered. "I do apologize, I must have fallen asleep. Do you have the time?"

"Why, ma'am, it is just dinner time, seven P.M. What time would you like your reservation? And may I refresh the water in your server?"

"Of course. And, might I have dinner at seven-thirty?"

"For one, ma'am?"

"Yes. You could make up the bed as well, please. And would you wake me tomorrow at eight A.M.? A knock on the door will suffice." She returned his assenting nod. "I'll go to the observation deck now, I believe."

"Oh yes, ma'am. We are climbing the Alleghenies and it's not full dark."

■ ■ ■ ■

She was alone on the observation deck but for the small red signal lights to either side of the awning above her. The deck seemed the prow of a roaring ship, climbing an ocean of rushing air, racing forward as the heights of the mountains dropped below. She could barely keep her feet, the sight was so dizzying, and she sank onto one of the fixed benches, her valise upon her lap. Duty was in it; she leashed his collar and lifted him out. It was a walk of sorts, she supposed; he sniffed his way along the edge of the platform, safely, it seemed, as the rails were too tightly spaced to allow even a small dog to slip through. He lifted his leg at the corner and urinated into the air like a sailor on a vessel, and then stood, ears blown back, eyes nearly shut, scenting the darkening air.

What a peculiar character, for he was certainly not a mere dog! Many, she supposed, entertained such notions about their pets. She'd grown terribly fond of him. She'd never had a pet, other than the dogs and cats on her grandparents' farm, who never truly belonged to her. As though summoned, Duty came to her and nuzzled her hand, then lay at her feet. She watched lines of track disappearing into the dark, only to continue, back and back and back. The family was on the train, at last.

She thought suddenly of the muddy shoes lined up as evidence in Grimm's office, of Dr. Goff, the coroner, coughing in the morgue, saying August was hot and dry and July was wet. Raining, yes, it was raining that night. Powers had made them walk through the mud, or he dragged them, feet sliding, for it was late and they were asleep, or he had drugged them. Why not drive the car into the garage? Some fact evaded her, some image.

She kept Annabel's one bedraggled drawing, that Duty had rescued from the playhouse, at her *Tribune* office. Emily saw the sprite or fairy creature as an aspect of Annabel herself; the glow that extended around the figure, so insubstantial and delicately wrought, seemed the essence of the child.

Emily closed her eyes to hear the train, to feel the vibration, and saw, in the slanted rain of Annabel's drawing, Powers' tilted, empty car, and the left rear passenger door standing open.

Where, in fact, was Powers' automobile? Grimm must have impounded it. Surely they had searched the car, but perhaps not deeply enough. Something was there, in the fold of the backseat. She would tell Grimm to pull out the seat and look properly; she knew he would do as she asked.

Duty was at her knees, and then in her lap, jumping up excitedly to lick her face. She felt a weight lift from her. The train raced forward. All was left behind, escaped. The dining car had seemed a narrow palace: the waiters in white jackets, the curves of the recessed ceiling set with faux medallions. She would have dinner, carry a plate back for Duty, and sleep deeply for the first time in many nights. Tomorrow she would arrive in Chicago. Arrangements were made: a Park Ridge mortician would receive the caskets.

William would meet her. The train sped her closer and closer.

She disembarked at Union Station onto a crowded platform. The porter followed with her luggage. They proceeded to the baggage car, and a gentleman stepped forward.

"Park Ridge Mortuary Services. Are you Miss Thornhill?"

"I am." The baggage car doors were not yet open, but the man seemed to have brought a small delegation. She saw the wheeled metal biers behind him.

"We shall handle all details from here, Miss Thornhill. Please meet your party outside at arrivals, front of the station. Town car number twelve." He gave her a card.

Emily turned away. Of course William would not be here, on the platform. He was protecting her reputation. The porter, still beside her, took the card she offered, and her suitcases; they walked toward the station. She followed the porter blindly into the vast terminal, through its entrances and exits, onto the street. A long line of cars was drawn up. The porter turned to her, smiling, indicating car number twelve. She took his gratuity from her purse, balancing her valise and the dog in the carrier.

Instantly a driver was beside her. "Miss Thornhill, let me assist you." He led the way with her suitcases, then paused at the car to take the dog's carrier and opened the passenger door of the Model A town car. It was dim and quiet within, for the tinted windows darkened the brilliant light. The driver put down a block for her to step up, onto the running board.

William was in the far corner, not to crowd her, she knew, and reached for her. She was in the car, his hand grasping her forearm, supporting her and pulling her gently toward him.

The driver put her valise and carrier inside and closed the door. She was beside William. They were enclosed; no one could see them. "The cremation was done . . . with every consideration," she said in a near whisper. She felt tears on her face, and was in his arms.

He held her tightly to him. "My love, I am so sorry I wasn't there with you. Can you forgive me, ever —"

She pressed her brow to his lips to answer the words and offered him her mouth. Kissing him, she said, "Come home with me now."

"Anywhere," he said. "Home, if that is what you want."

"Yes," she said, weeping, "yes."

"Tell me the address. Just say the address."

She told him and he half stood, leaning forward to repeat the address and slide shut the small panel of the driver's partition, closing the curtain. She had opened her jacket and blouse, and lifted her breasts free of her chemise and undergarments, for she wanted his hands on her, and his mouth. The drive from the station was twenty minutes, along the lake. She would have what she could of him now, and then they would be together in her bed. It was miraculous. She said his name in a kind of desperate happiness, again and again, as though asking something of him, but she was kneeling in front of him, stroking his thighs, unfastening his trousers.

Later they would have a routine, and safeguards; William would arrive in a cab and come up the back staircase to use his key, unless Reynolds, so protective of Emily, was at the desk. William would rent a room at the Drake, be seen checking in, and go to her place at once, calling the hotel for messages until he returned to check out. He stayed at weekends, and two nights or so a week. They did not go to restaurants, or the theater; they did not walk together through the lobby of her apartment building, but only in the park across the street, late at night. He kept clothes in a closet she cleared for him, and brought his books when they could read in one another's presence, lying close together, and not feel so urgently the press of time.

That first day, William paid the driver while Emily took Duty inside to stay with Reynolds. She would be occupied, she said, the entire day; she was on deadline and must not be disturbed; she would ring down later for her suitcases; would he walk and care for Duty until this evening? She stood at the elevator then, holding her valise, with William. They rode the elevator to her fifth-floor corner apartment. Emily unlocked the door, shaking, and William bolted it; he picked her up and carried her in the direction she indicated, to her bed. And so they began, in the morning, with sunlight streaming through the windows, and the blinds half drawn. They could not have imagined the feel of being naked together so quickly, so easily. Their knowledge of each other was surely intuitive, for they were blindly inside one another and did not look, did not see, until some time later when he asked her to stand, slicked with sweat, beside the bed. She came to him but waited, breathing, holding herself above him, touching his eyes, shoulders, the swell of rib and pelvic bone, the dark thick hair of his sex, wet with her, before she drew him barely within her, looking at him, until he was fully inside and they were blind again, rocking one another to slow the race forward, inward, to prolong their union, for here was the meaning of that word, in their bodies and pounding hearts.

She slept for a moment in his arms and woke up afraid. "You must never die," she said. "Or die without me."

The light had changed; it was afternoon. They had opened the windows. Sounds drifted up from the street.

"You are strong and healthy," she whispered. "Tell me if it isn't true."

"If what isn't true, my girl."

"There's not some hidden weakness in your heart, in that broad chest, or in your head."

"I have a very competent physician who wonders aloud at my constitution. I extol riding, but he says it's genetic, that I descend from a strain of healthy, English, working animals that found their way to privilege, and so grew even stronger."

"You will stay with me always."

"I shall be here, as long as you allow me near you. I cannot be without you, ever again."

She touched his face. "How can it be that we've found one another, in this sadness? Am I wrong to rejoice in you so?"

"We feel guilty because we have our lives

and hopes. But we are not guilty."

"Will you stay with me?"

"I will live with you, here, in these rooms, or anywhere I can find you. I will allow you whatever separation you need; I will never compromise your reputation, but I must have you, and know I can have you."

"You will stay with me, William. And I shall stay with you."

They kissed one another, several times, lightly on the lips, like children.

"The service is tomorrow. William, tell me what is planned. Will you speak?"

"Only briefly, to say why there are two caskets. It begins at eleven; there is lunch for the neighborhood children afterward, in the courtyard of St. Luke's, while many of the adults walk to the cemetery, a block away, for the graveside rites."

"It will be crowded, I suppose, but I must bring Duty. Will the press be allowed in, or must they wait outside?"

"Press may attend, but not with cameras or notebooks, or to question anyone present. St. Luke's has organized ushers, to seat everyone. Those from Chicago or elsewhere will be on one side of the church, and those from Park Ridge on the other, with the neighborhood children together in the choir. They will sing three songs. It will be short. I will speak, then the pastor, with the songs between, and it will end."

"I will not be near you."

"No, my darling. I shall be on one side of the church, and you on the other, as at a wedding. I begin with a quote from St. Augustine. Shall I tell it to you?"

"Yes, tell me."

"St. Augustine said, 'The law detects; grace alone conquers sin.' "

"My grandfather used to say that grace is God's mystery, and the mystery of grace is that it can never come too late." She rested her head on his chest, for something dark had dropped within her. "But what is grace, William? How is sin conquered, when it has tortured and killed?"

"Grace is an element of the divine, within the realm of the natural world, in which time passes. Or that is what I believe." He gathered her hair in his hands. "You are grace, or we approach grace, for this is surely goodness between us, and this gift, so unexpected, does not end, for if I never touched you again or saw you near me, you are with me. That is what we have, possibly all we have. It is so much. I have no conception of a god or gods, but we have this."

She pressed her ear close against his chest. "I hear your heart, William."

"Emily, don't be afraid." He kissed her eyes. "You are strong on their behalf. There have been, and will be, men like Powers. The difference is only details."

"Evil does not consider," Emily said. "Surely Powers is evil."

"He is a man who bent things to his will, to have what he wanted, to feel arousal and climax in the only way possible for him."

"Yes, it's that simple, on that level."

"It comforts us to think that those who commit horrors are a species apart. Men and women sin, while animals act on instinct." He pulled her close and laced her fingers in his. "Yes, humans are animals, thank god. But we are aware of time. We contemplate sin and goodness. What is most horrifying and reasonless, we must simply accept and mourn. I think this is the truth."

"Will you say so, at the service?"

"No. I will try to say how Anna Eicher fought to keep her children in their home, that Annabel was, in a sense, the celebrant, with her plays and drawings. And I must speak of Grethe and Hart, together at the bank. That will be difficult."

"You could not have saved them, William."

"You have said that, in trying to comfort me. But I could have saved them. Many in the town might have saved them, and I must say so, for everyone must acknowledge it. We cannot blame Anna Eicher for her hopefulness, for to find such a creature as she found is surely as rare a catastrophe as being struck by lightning."

They lay together, listening, for rain had begun, gently, in the sunlight.

■ ■ ■ ■

X.

■ ■ ■ ■

Advertisements in cheap, pornographic ("love" and "art") magazines . . . are packed with announcements of "red hot" photographs, vigor tablets ("Glow of Life"), bust developers, sex secrets, aphrodisiacs ("Essence of Ecstasy"), contraceptives. Plentiful also are the advertisements of so-called matrimonial bureaus. . . . Stressed in the advertisements, prominent on the lists are Wealthy Widows:

"LONELY HEARTS — Join the world's greatest social extension club, meet nice people who, like yourself, are lonely (many wealthy). . . . We have made thousands

happy. Why not you?"
— "We Make Thousands Happy,"
Time magazine, September 14, 1931

SEPTEMBER 4, 1931
CHICAGO, ILLINOIS–WAVERLY, ORAN, AND FAIRBANK, IOWA

EMILY THORNHILL: IOWA, OH, IOWA

She was in the sanctuary at St. Luke's, and Duty had got loose from his leash. The dog was sitting by the altar; Emily must retrieve him without disturbing the service. The children, dressed in white, were singing "Jesus Loves Me" in a jaunty round, and the words of another rhyme bled through as they joined hands and formed a circle before the pews of mourners: *Ashes, ashes, we all fall down!* The stained-glass window behind them was intensely blue, and the lamps above the congregation swung wildly on their long chains. The children began to pull one another to and fro; Emily looked through their flashing legs for Duty. She could not see the dog and rose from her seat. The reverend had gone but William stood naked behind the pulpit, visible from his chest upward, his broad shoulders achingly beautiful. No one seemed to notice his nudity. She saw herself, through his eyes, standing in the congregation, calling attention to her own distress in the packed church. He signaled her to leave, and motioned more urgently, speaking to her across the distance between them, but she could not hear him, or the children, for the shrill ringing in her ears.

She opened her eyes, in her own bed, relieved, troubled, for the phone was ringing. It was not yet six in the morning. Good news did not come at such an hour. She got to the phone and took up the receiver, the straps of her nightgown fallen off her shoulders.

"Emily, I'm sure I woke you, but I must fetch you in half an hour. We are going to Iowa. We must leave by seven." It was Eric, calling from a booth on the street, for she heard a streetcar turning, clanging its bell.

"We're driving? I must pack —"

"We are not driving, Emily. There isn't time. We are flying and will be back before dark, to make the evening edition."

"Have you got an airplane, Eric?"

"Yes, and a pilot. The *Tribune* has hired the plane. We fly to an airstrip in Waverly, which will put us —"

"Fifteen miles from Sumner, and twenty from Fairbank. I know those towns, and can direct you. You've found a car there?"

"Afraid not. We'll see what we find in Waverly."

"You mean you have no car?"

"Emily, let me surprise you. Warning: the

386

flying itself can be dodgy, but the air is still today. It's a beautiful plane, a Tin Goose. I like it so much that I want one for myself."

"On your salary?"

"No, cousin. A trust fund purchase, perhaps, drawn from the capitalist profits generated by large and small pistons." His voice dropped; he seemed to turn away from the phone, as though checking his watch. "Wash your face, and dress for walking in fields. I have a thermos of coffee and your typewriter, and will be there in twenty minutes."

They rang off. Iowa. She'd not been back since her grandparents' deaths, and selling the farm. Duty seemed to study her woefully from his pillowed basket. She raced past him to throw on her clothes. There would be dirt roads and paths, fields to barns. She wore thin cotton socks under her leather boots, which laced to the ankle. She had never flown and preferred trains, which were so civilized. Eric must have been up all night, arranging this. She pinned her hair tightly, hastily, and was at the elevator, then downstairs, where she gave instructions to Reynolds, to walk and feed Duty. Reynolds had installed a basket for the dog under the reception desk; Duty often sat with him during the day, when no one was about.

Emily stood on the sidewalk in front of her building. She was nearly chilly; rain had cooled Chicago overnight and autumn would be upon them. Already, the tips of the foliage were reddened; the big oak opposite, in the park, flared with yellow.

A cab drew up to the curb before her.

"Emily. Join me." Eric leaned across to open the passenger door.

They walked from the terminal to the edge of the paved runway. The plane sat alone; it seemed a thing of myth, Emily thought, a shiny tin creature with a snout, the gleaming wings a single span over the cabin. The front wheels splayed far out on their struts, tilting the plane's nose and fierce propeller skyward. The runway glistened, still wet.

Eric was at her elbow, pulling her forward.

The steps folded down magically, and a man disembarked to help them in. Bags of mail took up much of the passenger cabin. The pilot and copilot were outfitted in caps and goggles as though to conceal their identities, and directed their two passengers to sit just behind them on child-size jump seats. The roar of the engines dwarfed all sound and the propellers turned faster, invisibly; the aircraft bounced along straight down the runway, flying forward on the bigger front tires like an elongated car with fins. There was a whoosh of sound and they were airborne. The ground dropped away dizzyingly fast.

"How high can we go?" Eric shouted.

"She'll make six thousand feet, but no need today. It's clear, almost no wind. We can cruise at half that, and keep the passenger windows open." The pilot checked his instruments.

They looked to Emily like an assortment of toy dials. The floor pedals reminded her of treadle sewing machine paddles. They were climbing, pillowed in air, dropping and ascending by turns. She would have been ill in the enclosed passenger cabin, but here she felt almost as if she participated in flying the plane. Suddenly the ride was smoother, and the roar dulled.

In minutes, Chicago was behind them. Eric leaned over the copilot's seat. "My god, the flat Midwest. Everything but Chicago is Iowa."

"It's not Iowa yet," Emily said. "Iowa will seem a grid from the air. The fields, this time of year, are wheat or corn. Pale yellow or bright green, like a checkerboard."

"Perfect for flying over," he said.

The airstrip in Waverly looked ridiculously short, but the pilot circled, dipping lower and lower, until he set the tapping wheels on the dirt. Braking sharply, the plane stopped just a few feet from the edge of the runway and made a tight turn; the wings ruffled the tops of the corn and the force of the glinting propeller shivered the field. They coasted slowly back toward a small outbuilding. A parked car and farm truck sat to the side, and a man stood, arms folded, watching the plane.

"Leave the typewriter," Eric said. "We'll use it on the way back." He waited for the sound of the propellers to cease, then stood as the copilot let down the steps. Emily followed Eric. "Eric, who is that man, standing by the field?"

"That is Mr. Jacob Aukes. I sent him a telegram from you, in the interest of time. He's driven here from Ackley and very much looks forward to a ride in the plane."

Emily walked briskly toward Mr. Aukes. Her boots did nicely on the dirt of the airstrip. "Mr. Aukes, how good of you to come." She grasped his hand.

"That's quite a contraption," he said, looking at the plane. He was dressed in overalls and a straw hat of some age. "You said in the telegram that you need to drive to Oran. I have business in Waverly. My grandson drove our truck over, followed me. You can borrow it, exchange for a plane ride, if you can be back by five or so. I reckon this airplane will be waiting for you."

"It certainly will, Mr. Aukes," Eric said, "and we shall be back long before evening, depending on the accuracy of your information. Can we buy some refreshment here? We're pleased to swap a plane ride for the loan of the truck, but we'll need directions to Oran." He indicated a small building just ahead that seemed to serve as a terminal.

Inside, the luncheon counter was un-manned. Bottles of root beer sat in rows beside the cash register. They left generous payment and opened three bottles. Emily sat down with Mr. Aukes and Eric, to take notes. "Mr. Aukes, you contacted William Malone of Park Ridge to say you recognized news-paper photographs of Harry Powers."

"His name is Harm Drenth. His mother was my wife's cousin. My parents were born in Amsterdam, but my wife and her family were from Beerta, little town in a farming region called Drenthe. We married here, after her family came over to settle near Kanawha." He looked at Eric. "Kanawha is other side of Belmond. Lot of Dutch settled there. Farm-ers, or those wanted land to farm."

Drenthe, region of Netherlands, Emily wrote, *Beerta, Kanawha.* "Did you know of this, Harm Drenth, as a child? Did you know the mother? The father? Was there a sister? Pow-ers told a minister, in jail, that he had a sister named Greta, but said his parents were dead."

Aukes was looking out the window at the airplane. His grandson stood talking to the pilot. "My grandson is sure excited about this plane ride."

"I'm sorry to keep you, Mr. Aukes," Eric

said. "We are extremely interested in your answers, however, and in finding —"

Aukes interrupted. "You'll want Drenth's father, Wilko Drenth, who lives near Oran now, 'bout two mile from Sumner, with his son-in-law, Evert Schroder. Harm Drenth's mother was Jane Druker, same surname as my late wife. They were cousins. It was known in the family that Wilko sent the son, Harm — you might say Herman, here — to America when he was eighteen, to work on a farm. The Drenths had a small store in Beerta; Harm would not go to school, he drank, got into trouble. He broke into his parents' store once through the roof tiles, to steal money. Harm was given free rein as a boy, and was too spoiled to do as he was told, or that was the story in the family."

"Spoiled?" Emily asked.

"Or maybe he just did as he liked, and no one could stop him."

"When did you last see him?"

"About nineteen year ago, make it about 1912. He came to visit his sister. Showed up in a new Model T Ford town car, said it was borrowed from a well-off employer. Drove my wife and me, with Greta and her husband, back to Greta's to see his parents, on a Sunday afternoon. They were staying with Greta, near Geneva, visiting from Wisconsin. The parents were renting their farm, up in Cumberland, and trying to buy another in

Crookston, Minnesota."

"A car like that must have been quite unusual here. Did the parents ride in it?"

"Wilko wouldn't get in the car. I do remember that. Greta was quite pleased to."

"He was on good terms with his parents, though, as you remember that visit?"

"The mother hoped for the best, as mothers will. It seemed he was doing well. They gave him their savings, to go and pay the balance on the Crookston land. He gave notes instead, which proved false, and skipped out with the money. The family never saw him again."

"Did the family look for him?" Emily asked. "Look for the money?"

Aukes shook his head. "Not to my knowledge. Says something, I'd guess."

"Did they report the theft?"

"Wilko is not a man who reports his son to police, even for stealing a life's savings. It would shame the family. Harm did enough of that — soon they heard he was jailed, up in Wisconsin — state penitentiary at Waupun, almost two year. The parents left the state, then. They'd lost the Crookston farm, and came back to Iowa."

"Harm Drenth was jailed? For what, Mr. Aukes?" Emily was writing.

Aukes folded his hands. "Not certain. Harm's mother wrote to him at the prison, but they returned the letters unopened after his release. She died not two years later. The family always told that she pointed to her son's picture, within arm's length of her deathbed, and said, 'He is alive. He will come back someday.' That was the story."

"They thought Harm was dead?" Emily wrote, *Shame. Didn't look for him. Afraid? Not sister. Rode in front with Harm.*

"Maybe," Aukes said, "or there was a story he went to South America. Wilko Drenth moved in with his daughter's family, after he was widowed. Evert Schroder is sensible, respected; Wilko got on with him. There are two grandsons, namesakes, Wilko and Evert. Young men by now, I'd say — fourteen, fifteen. All of them farming. Hard work."

Two generations, same names. Emily paused, looked up. "And Greta?"

"Died about four years ago. Remember her funeral. My own wife was ill at the time."

"Ah. I'm sorry, Mr. Aukes." Powers did not know his sister, his mother, were dead. He told women, in his letters, that he had a large property near Cedar Rapids, and mentioned the Midwest in his personal ads. What was the wording? *As my properties are located through the Middle West, I believe I will settle there when married.* Yes, those were the words. She had the ad itself, taped to the cover of her notebook, cut out from the American Friendship Society circular.

Eric leaned across her, and put his hand on Mr. Aukes arm. "We should go. Your plane ride must be fifteen minutes, so that we have fuel to get back."

Aukes nodded. "We got plenty of chores in town, after the plane ride. Meet you here. No rush."

"The plane is a beauty," Eric said. "I shall return your truck within four hours, and you shall return my airplane." They shook hands.

The truck was a Chevy, with a rattling bed in back. A farm truck, Emily knew, for hauling seed and supplies. "He has a record, just as Grimm thought; I must telegraph Grimm. Eric, we have found him. Harm Drenth. That his name is Harm —"

"Yes, I know. Don't say it." Eric was starting the engine, turning a wide circle onto the road. "Now, if the truck works. It's straight over on Route 3. Oran Savings Bank was one of the few banks in the state that did not close last year, or at all since the Crash."

"Their money here is in their land," Emily said. "My grandfather used to say that land is real, and money is not."

"I know you are fond of your grandfather's words, but one must have money to buy land. No one knows better than Wilko Drenth." He looked over at her. "Does it look familiar?"

"Oh yes," she said. "It is home." She fell

silent as Eric drove, smelling the dark soil through the open windows, and the sweet grassy smell: fields, both sides of the road, flared into distance, vibrantly green, sunlit. Acres of growing corn. The sky was a palette of shifting color and clouds. Rain here blew up like biblical storm; clouds boiled forward and rain slanted down in sheets. And the Drenths had come from Holland, where the sea was always near, to these inland, endless plains, where they could farm their own land and every householder had five or six cattle, a henhouse, fresh eggs. Or that was so until the last decade. Now times were hard, very hard for some.

"How long since you've been here, Emily?"

"Almost ten years." She'd not been back since selling the farm at Fairbank in '22, after the last funeral. Her solicitor put the funds in gold; she'd not lost it in the Crash. Even now, she dreamed of buying back the farm, but for what?

"We will find Drenth's father," Eric said, "get a corroborating photo, and go by your grandparents' farm. Where is Fairbank?"

"Fairbank is quite near. We can file there. It's larger than Oran. Do you see, Eric? How beautiful? The fields, the black earth. Acres of corn lit up in bright patches or shaded in miles of cloud. Nothing stands up but windmills, silos. Do you see those trees, off in the distance? They are cottonwoods. They can grow a hundred feet tall, but only live seventy years or so. They're prone to decay."

"They are not pistons, which live forever." Eric smiled. "Cottonwood. I'm ignorant of cottonwoods."

"There are male and female trees; the male trees flower in April, and wind scatters the pollen. The female trees bear fruit, a seed encased in a fibrous pod that bursts open. The white fluff flies everywhere, like wisps of spring snow."

"Like cotton," Eric said.

Nothing so beautiful, she was thinking. Every year, after her father's death, she'd arrive in May, alone, on the train from Chicago. Her grandparents met her in the wagon, at the station. The old mill was just behind, and the stream; the cottonwoods, a grove of them, knotted the ground with their roots. She could see, from the train windows, miles away, the white fluff drifting past, whirling in the blare of the steam engine. When she was young, in the first years after her father died, her mother would send a trusted maid along on the journey. The train windows were open despite the dust and cinders. Emily would lean out as far as she could in the noise and clamor; the maid clasped her legs tightly, lest she lose the child. Emily no longer remembered the maid's name or face, but the feel of someone pressed close, a clinched face hard against the backs of her thighs, arms pulling down on her as she arched away into loud, rushing air, was a first erotic memory. The smoke of the engine curled behind as the train rounded the curve to Fairbank, and she saw the station ahead, in the snow of the cottonwoods. Women walked the wooden sidewalks with parasols, to keep the floating wisps from their bonnets.

"How will we find them?" Eric asked.

"We shall ask at the post office in Oran," Emily said, "for the Schroder farm."

Oran's one broad street was paved with gravel and featured a dry goods store, a blacksmith and garage with gas pumps, a fire station with a steam-engine pumper, a restaurant and drugstore. The post office was a small building with a storefront window and hitching post.

Inside, a tall woman whose light hair had gone gray distributed mail into post office boxes. The glass doors were numbered, on two of the four walls, from the floor nearly to the ceiling. The postmistress wore a U.S. Mail apron, and rubber thimbles on her fingers; she sorted mail from a deep canvas bag held open on a wooden frame.

"Good day," Emily said. "I am looking for Evert Schroder. I'm told that he lives near Oran. Can you direct me, please?"

"Why would you be looking for Evert Schroder?" The woman didn't look up, but went on sorting mail.

"Why, I used to live near Fairbank," Emily said, "on the old Thornhill place. I believe he knew my grandfather, Frank Thornhill. I'm here visiting."

The woman turned to look at her over bifocal glasses. "Frank Thornhill, you say? He was one of the biggest landowners around here. That was quite a farm."

"Yes, I know. I spent every summer there, and sold the place when they were gone. I'm Emily Thornhill. I live in Chicago now."

"Why, come in. I'm ill accustomed to strangers, but you are not a stranger. Frank Thornhill. My older brothers grew up with his boy, spent more time at John Thornhill's place than they did at home, my mother always said."

"Yes, John was my father."

"Course he would have been. I'm remembering now, they had the one boy, and we had such a crowd, the boys slept three to a room. My mother liked your grandmother. She used to say, 'Take some of mine.' And your grandmother would tell her, 'I can't do it, Marta, you know you would want them back. Just lend me them for afternoons and dinner, after their chores this summer.' She didn't want her boy growing up an only child."

"She nearly died in childbirth, and couldn't have more children." Emily walked close to the counter and looked into the woman's weathered face. She was sixty-five, perhaps, but strong, her gaze direct.

"Baertman was our surname. I'm Marta Baertman, like my mother; I never married. Did your father ever mention the Baertman boys?"

"He died when I was seven. But my grandmother was fond of them, I know."

The woman had pushed up her glasses, and regarded Emily kindly. "And your father? He must have died young."

Emily only nodded. "You know the Schroders, then? They are Dutch, as well, I think."

"Oh yes, Oran is a small place. Evert and Wilko are just moving from their farm to a bigger one. I saw them drive by in the wagons not an hour ago. Keep going, past the church. Take the dirt road on the left, a mile or so. You will know the place by the faded yellow barn."

"I thank you, and I'm very glad to meet you."

The woman grasped Emily's hand in hers. The pliable thimbles on her fingers felt cool and nearly silken, they were worn so thin.

Later, in the truck, Emily found her wrist marked with dark smudge, and was suddenly aware of the grave news she was bringing. The hurried nature of the search had preoccupied her, but the truth about Powers cast long shadows. The prodigal son they feared had come home; now he could not remain a mystery. To know one's son a murderer, abnormal, perverse, violent, a man who talked his swindler's game and had his twisted way, was mournful, deathly knowledge. What sort of man was Wilko Drenth? And Schroder, the son-in-law? What had they to do with any of this?

Eric stopped the truck. The farmhouse, across the pasture, was a two-story frame structure with a broad front porch; the barn, more distinctive, was dark yellow, faded to a gold tinge. The high peaked roof promised a deep interior; above it, the copper weather vane, gone blue-green, was still.

They walked up the dirt path to the barn. A wagon with a wide, flat bed stood empty, angled into the open double doors of the barn. Two men were putting in the hay. They'd ripped open the roped bales, and pulled the hay apart with pitchforks. One man stood hip deep in loose hay, forking hay to the other, who pulled it into the mow.

The older man must be Drenth.

Both men, dressed in overalls, work shirts, utilitarian wide-brim hats, were short of stature, like Powers, but they were muscular, fit; Drenth was stocky, his white hair and Vandyke beard neatly trimmed. Darker in coloring, Schroder wore wire-rim glasses that magnified his brown eyes.

Emily approached and smiled at Drenth gravely; he turned an open gaze to her, and a look of surprise. His eyes were bright blue, like Powers' eyes; he glanced quickly at Schroder. The two men were working partners in a successful enterprise; even now, in difficult times, they were moving to a bigger farm. Twenty years in America, among Dutch friends and acquaintances: they had worked hard, despite setbacks. This was not the fantasy farm near Cedar Rapids, the easy life Powers advertised, but they had prospered.

She must begin. "Mr. Schroder? Mr. Drenth? I am Emily Thornhill, from the *Chicago Tribune,* and this is Mr. Eric Lindstrom, also from the *Tribune.* We're sorry to interrupt, but we are here on a matter of importance. It concerns the Harry F. Powers case in Clarksburg, West Virginia, and Harm Drenth. We want to interview you for the *Tribune.*"

The men exchanged a phrase in Dutch. Wilko Drenth continued working with the pitchfork, moving great forkfuls of hay to Schroder, who turned them in midair, into the mow. The work was practiced and powerful, rapid. Drenth looked to be in his midsixties, but he matched Schroder in strength and speed.

"May we show you a photograph?" Emily asked. The hay whirled past her, smelling of grass and dust.

Eric stepped closer. "Have you heard of the Powers case? Do you see the Chicago papers, the Cedar Rapids papers, perhaps?"

"No," Schroder said. "We are moving stock, machinery. We must move this hay into the mow, and go back for the stock."

"Mr. Schroder, we don't mean to interrupt. May we talk to you as you work? What a beautiful barn. How many acres have you?" She didn't wait for his answer. "I grew up in Fairbank, in summers, on my grandparents' farm. Not far from Oran."

"We had a hundred and sixty acres other side of Oran. This farm is over three hundred." Schroder kept working. Then he asked, "How did you find us?"

"Powers, who is arrested in West Virginia, told his minister that he has a sister called Greta Schroder."

Schroder looked away from her. "There are many Greta Schroders. Why have you come here?"

They know, Emily thought. "One of your late wife's relatives by marriage, a Mr. Aukes, recognized photos from the newspapers. Another farmer from Kanawha, a Mr. Kamp, said he employed Harm Drenth on a farm, some years back. Your family originally settled in Kanawha, from Holland. Is that right?"

"In Kanawha, Ackley, Oran. Up to Wisconsin and Minnesota," Schroder said. "Twenty years. Hard work."

"Yes, on good land, it is still hard work." Emily turned to Wilko Drenth, who looked at her through the hay as it turned between them. "We must ask you, Mr. Drenth, as Harm Drenth's father, to identify the photo."

Drenth spoke to Schroder in Dutch.

"Mr. Drenth," Schroder said, "does not speak much English. He does not read English. And better he knows nothing of this. My wife's brother took money from the family and disappeared, years ago."

"I know, Mr. Schroder. No one asks anything of you, but that you identify the picture. I believe the man is his son. He has hidden his identity for many years. The family is not responsible in any way, but the police must identify him, and that is why we are here, from Chicago."

Wilko Drenth continued looking at her through the falling hay, as Schroder translated. He spoke, finally, in a booming voice, as though he was hard of hearing. "He has . . . other name?"

"Yes," Emily said. "He is arrested, in West Virginia, under the name Harry Powers. He is accused of murder —"

"Murder?" Drenth stabbed the pitchfork into baled hay that was shoulder high beside him. He stood quietly for a moment, looking down into the layered hay, then motioned to Schroder. "Let us see this picture."

"Emily," Eric said, "come to the door of

the barn. Let Mr. Drenth sit down."

There was a milking stool at the barn door. Wilko Drenth sat and Schroder came to stand beside him. Emily gave them the *Tribune,* folded to show photographs of Powers. *Murder Farm Romeo Confesses* ran the headline. Just below was the Quiet Dell garage photo Eric had taken, with the police lined up in front, Duckworth in his white hat, and Grimm in suit and tie: *Garage Where Five Lives Were Taken.* The caption under the photo said all:

This is the garage near Quiet Dell, West Virginia, where Harry F. Powers, operator of a mail-order matrimonial bureau, strangled to death two women and three children, according to his confession . . . locked them in dungeon chambers . . . then taking their lives.

Eric quickly took photographs, but Emily stood watching the men, noting every nuance, for these were reticent farmers whose faces showed little. Schroder looked fifty but might be younger; he was clearly protective of Drenth; the men, widowers, were raising the grandsons, running their farm without help, without women.

Schroder seemed almost angry. "It looks like him, but until it is proven Powers is

Harm Drenth, no one can call him a murderer."

Drenth stared at the picture. He looked up as though puzzled. "Where is this Virginia?"

Emily felt she could not answer.

Eric asked about Aukes' stories: the robbery of the family store in Holland, the mother's words about her son's return.

Drenth and Schroder spoke rapidly in Dutch, and Schroder responded. "None of that is true. Harm left the family in Cumberland, Wisconsin. We heard he went to New York, then to South America. He learned the English language very fast, he spoke very well . . . better than any of us."

A wishful version of events, Emily thought. Another Harm in a faraway country, who had not done these things. "He was jailed, years ago, at the state prison in Waupun, Wisconsin. Do you know why?"

Drenth didn't answer directly. He spoke in phrases, which Schroder repeated in English. "Harm was smart but wouldn't go to school . . . he was never married when we knew him . . . he was cruel."

"What do you mean, cruel?" Emily asked.

But the men went on, Drenth speaking in quick Dutch, Schroder translating. "There must have been about four thousand dollars left to pay on the farm in Minnesota, but Harm took the money and we lost the farm." They were Drenth's words, but Schroder added, "He wanted nothing to do with work, and once tried to kill his father."

Drenth studied the pictures. Powers' studio portraits, five years ago, and more recently, as a heavier man, in suit coat, bow tie, portrayed him as a successful businessman. He looked unkempt and battered in the cell photograph. Drenth could not read the caption under the garage photo; Schroder would need to tell him later, about the children.

Schroder, reading over Drenth's shoulder, blinked rapidly behind his glasses and gripped the rough door of the barn. Dutch words burst from him. *Kinderen* was among the rush of sounds. Schroder had said part, if not all.

Wilko Drenth said quietly, "He was not a good boy. He has been gone so long — I believed him dead. It were better so." He stood and gave the newspaper to Emily. "If he did this, killed all these . . . why feed him? Hang him."

The silent barn, the piled hay, seemed to witness the words. Apology or condolence seemed too small a response. She could at least warn them.

"There will be more reporters," Emily said, "over the next weeks. If you have a gate to close, at the road, you might —"

They were turning back to the work, taking up the pitchforks. "We have no gate," Schroder said. "We needed no gate."

"Schaamte, schaamte, schaamte," Drenth

was murmuring, "God help me," he said to Schroder in English.

"What was that?" asked Emily.

"Het meer, het meer —" Drenth said, piercing the sharp tines of the fork deep into the hay. *"Ik wist het toen."*

"He saved Harm from drowning when the boy was twelve," Schroder said. Hay was flying at him, for Drenth was throwing great forkfuls so quickly that Schroder had only to touch their whirling projection to direct them into the mow.

"Thank you, gentlemen," Eric said, and took Emily firmly by the arm.

They walked back to the truck. "The town will close ranks around them," Emily said.

"Tell me you will not send Grimm word of Powers' record in Wisconsin until I get this film back to the *Tribune,*" Eric demanded. "We must break this story, not Grimm." He was behind the wheel, looking at her, waiting for her response.

"It is nearly noon. Drive, Eric, please. If Grimm had the news right now, it would take some time to contact Wisconsin, exchange fingerprint evidence, and ascertain certainty. The news itself would not appear until tomorrow's local editions, and in any case, we have the photo. In fact, we cannot claim that Powers is Drenth, without evidence based on fingerprints, which only police can

408

request. Aukes' story is hearsay."

"We shall quote his story as hearsay, and let the police corroborate it, following our lead. What difference does another day make: Pierson is Powers is Drenth. We did not come all this way to hand Grimm a notch in his belt. Let police in Park Ridge make the ID. It is where Asta Eicher and her children lived."

"It is also where no one stopped Powers or questioned him. West Virginia has the case and must prove the case. Let us not delay justice, Eric, or take credit from where credit is due."

He drove, silent. "Do you have a deal with Grimm?"

"I make no deals, Eric. I am surprised you ask. I do what I feel is called for, according to my own ethics and the demands of the situation."

"I assume you are in frequent touch with him?"

"I phone him if I have reason. I told you at the service, that I asked him to search Powers' car, to pull out the backseat."

"And?"

"He called back that evening, to say they had found Annabel's doll. He is sending photographs, to be identified by Charles O'Boyle, but he prefers that O'Boyle come to the trial, and identify the doll on the stand. O'Boyle mentioned the doll in our interview: Mrs. Pomeroy. The name is in my notes."

"But isn't it true, Emily, that we have no story to file at this moment? We will compose that story on the flight back to Chicago, and publish it in tomorrow's edition with the photograph. Isn't it true that Grimm made you his confidante, because he knew you were in position to aid him in the case, and because he likes looking at you?"

"Eric, do pull over. I said, pull over. We must agree on a direction before going further." She braced herself against the bouncing dash of the truck and turned to him. "I am more than a passenger on this drive."

He did not pull over, for they were the only vehicle on the road, and oncoming traffic in either direction was visible for miles. Eric merely slowed the truck to a stop, cut off the ignition, and turned to her. "Cousin, I'm listening."

"Grimm likes looking at me, yes of course, and I do not consider it unethical to use his attentions to my advantage, especially as he is quite aware that I am doing so. You do the same with the girls at the office who do you favors, and with women you interview. And men would rather speak to a tall well-built blond gentleman who can reveal a superior education or not, depending on the need, than a fat cigar-smoking pundit. Do you agree?"

Eric regarded her. "I agree."

"As to the story, we shall file a teaser, to make the afternoon edition, under both bylines: an Iowa farmer has identified Harry Powers as his son. Full story follows. If I telegraph Grimm, and we are back in two hours, we can phone him to corroborate the Wisconsin identification made through his office, and state the ID as fact. Our stories will then accompany the photograph in the evening edition, which the AP will pick up by tomorrow. As to the Wisconsin angle, I agree; we say in the teaser that farmer Jacob Aukes of Kanawha, Iowa, alleges, et cetera."

Eric looked at her with a quizzical smile. He was angry, or admiring, and had a high color. "You have a bit of dust, here, on your cheek, cousin." He held her chin in one hand and touched a moistened forefinger to the corner of her mouth. "There," he said.

"Are you practicing seduction techniques on me, Eric? You test my patience."

"Do I? You have straw in your hair, as well." He combed her hair with his fingers, loosening the pins, touching the bits of straw as tousled strands of her hair fell from its chignon. "We are both covered with hay dust," he said quietly. "If you were a man of my preferences, with whom I had experienced this journey, I would be tasting you now. As it is, I keep seeing you pour that jug of water over your head at the Gore, so suddenly that you wrenched my heart open."

"Eric, don't play with me."

"Emily, I think you know I am not playing. I find myself very sympathetic to Charles O'Boyle, in consideration of one matter."

Emily felt her hair come down around her. "And which matter is that, Eric?"

His eyes were a lovely blue-green, and serious now, if not as grave and angry as before. "On the matter of marrying a woman, when the woman is superior in every way to any sexual partner with whom one is currently engaged, or whom one employs for pleasure or safety."

Beyond the dash of the truck, a small cloud of grasshoppers whirred along the road, alighting and arising in hopscotch motion. She made herself attend his words; her feelings for him were layered beyond clarity. "My dear Eric," she said, and drew back to look at him. "Perhaps you are speaking to the wrong party. Perhaps you should discuss this with Charles O'Boyle."

"Don't be daft." Eric pulled away from her and turned to face the road. He watched the grasshoppers rise and fall and flow into the field opposite, swallowed by the corn.

"I know you think of him. Have you contacted him at all?" These were questions, and statements to acknowledge. "He did not attend the Eichers' service at St. Luke's. He did not send word. No one, to my knowledge, has heard from him."

"No. He does not answer his Chicago exchange, and careful inquiries of his firm reveal that he has not come back."

"I wonder what has happened to him."

"I don't know, Emily. Perhaps someone has killed him in Mexico; that happens. Perhaps he is in love with some Mexican youth. Perhaps he cannot face coming back. His letter to the police has appeared everywhere, now that Powers is arrested and the bodies found."

"His firm has no address for him in Mexico?"

"Certainly not. That would be very stupid of him. He has probably been in touch with them to say that he is avoiding reporters due to his involvement in the Eicher matter, and of course they would be very sympathetic, as it gives them a direct link to the story of the hour."

She felt, suddenly, the heavy day. The truck on the flat road would appear a small dot from the sky into which they would soon ascend; the leaves of the corn all around them would be invisible; the grasshoppers would live for some days, then litter the ground.

"Eric, shall we file at Fairbank?"

He was starting the truck. "Yes. Your grandparents' farm is there." He looked at her, driving. "We will file the teaser, you will send the telegram. In Chicago, I will make the call to Grimm."

"Yes, you make the call. There is the turn to Fairbank. The farm is two miles this side of the town." Eric was her intimate, she thought, her partner in these depths, like William, but differently. She felt her breath come fast as they neared the turn, and only pointed the way.

From fifty yards, the house came into view. The tall line of cottonwoods was fully in leaf, and their canopies almost touched, rising even above the peaked roof of the house. The modest gingerbread trim was still painted yellow, and the house, dark green. Someone had fenced the yard, and built an outbuilding far back, painted to match the house. The front porch and steps, and the side porch that let onto a circular gazebo, were in good repair, and empty of any furniture.

"This is the farmhouse? It's a small mansion." Eric stopped the truck, shouldered his camera, and came around to assist Emily. He lifted her onto the road and set her on her feet. "You aren't faint, are you?"

"Perhaps a bit. It is only . . . so strange to see this house."

"How large was the farm? Where were your father's people born?"

"They were English and came from East Anglia, nearly two hundred years ago, to a land grant of some three thousand acres. They gave the land, in the 1850s, for Fairbank Township, the Presbyterian church, and the Dutch Reformed, as well, to build the community, and of course the railroad took the land they wanted, for the route and the station." They were walking up the front steps, where they knocked at the door and received no answer.

"No one is home," Eric said.

"I feel as though my grandparents should be here, that I have arrived at the wrong time, and missed them."

"Where was your room?"

"At the far end of the house, just over the gazebo," Emily said. "I loved to wait there at night, for fireflies in the fields."

"Stand just there, so I see the whole house behind you." Eric was photographing the house, the view from the gazebo, all of it. "Your father left here. Did he ever return?"

They sat on the bare board floor, facing one another. "He went away to college in the East, and did return, twice a year, but my mother didn't like the farm. He brought me, when I was very young. Even at two or three, I stayed for weeks. My grandmother . . . adored me, and was good with children."

"Your mother wasn't. Good with children."

"No. She'd grown up in boarding schools and thought I would do the same. She wanted something for herself, some vocation, but was never sure what it was, and women didn't explore such options, at the time."

"How did your father die, Emily?"

415

"He died of pneumonia in Chicago, unexpectedly, in 1903. They couldn't save him, though he was only thirty-three. He never knew about so much — the Great War, Lindbergh's flight, nothing of my life. But when I was here, I felt him close to me, and of course my grandparents spoke of him. They let me know, every day, that I was miraculous, his gift to them."

Eric looked up into the circular roof above them, which was hung with intricate spiderwebs. "Yes, they helped give you that — perceptive confidence. You are seldom daunted."

"My grandmother always told me, 'He is with you, very pleased, very proud.' It's not so different from what Annabel Eicher's grandmother said to her."

"It's quite different, Emily, really," Eric said gently. "According to O'Boyle, Annabel was told to listen for messages from the beyond. But I know you feel a sympathy for her, that is not simply childlike —"

"I suppose I feel a sympathy for who she might have been, and I don't patronize an idea of her, simply because she was a child. Children are themselves, after all."

"Are they?" Eric leaned back against the railing. "Was Harm Drenth 'himself'?"

"I don't know, Eric. How did you read the father?"

"Tireless Dutch farmer. Germanic, typical

of his undemonstrative culture; sons should work, be good. Powers seems to have been uncontrollable early on. I do believe those stories Aukes told us." He stood to help Emily up. "We must find Fairbank, and file."

"I thought I might know when I saw Wilko Drenth, whether he'd done something to his son, or felt responsible — but I wasn't sure."

"I know a bit of Dutch." Eric kept a hand at her waist as they crossed the yard. "Drenth repeated 'shame' as though to himself, but we already knew the boy shamed the family, from Aukes."

"His own shame, perhaps. Interesting how the revelation always comes in the last moments of an interview, just as one nearly turns away." They were in the truck. Emily looked back at the house, thankful for Eric's voice. "What Drenth muttered was like a bitter prayer, or a curse. And what was that phrase he repeated?"

Eric pulled onto the road, throwing up an arc of dust. "I'm not sure, but *meer* means 'lake,' and I think the rest means 'I knew,' or 'I knew then,' as in, 'even then, I knew' . . . something, with certainty, but didn't act on his knowledge."

"Saving the boy, in a lake, when he knew," Emily said. "That is what he meant. His responsibility in these murders is that he saved the child who would commit them. He saved the child, yet he already knew something was wrong. Something a beating, a mother's love, chores, getting older, couldn't fix." She looked about them, for they had reached the town.

"This is Fairbank, then," Eric said.

"Yes. Farther on is the town hall, the school. The train depot is beyond the curve. The telegraph office is here."

Inside, they composed and filed. Emily sent Grimm a telegram:

Sheriff W. B. Grimm Stop Clarksburg West Virginia Stop Powers Served Time Stop Name Of Harm Herman Drenth Stop Waupun State Prison Stop Wisconsin Stop Dutch Immigrant Stop Emily Thornhill.

They would make the airfield in fifteen minutes. Eric drove straight on. The landing strip shimmered to the right. The fields were flung out around them; miles of grain and corn lay open to the cloudless sky. It was pitiless and beautiful. She did not believe in evil, but in mistakes and conditions, in cause and effect across arcs so long that history might seem reasonless, but never was.

She saw the father, in another country, hesitate an instant, and plunge toward the boy in the lake. Not far from shore, but far enough.

And the boy, flailing, saw him, felt the

hesitation, the recognition: Harm would do bad things. He was unknowable, even as a child, to himself, to others. Born different, cunning. Manipulative, unloving, remorseless. Curious. Covert. Taking things apart to see inside them. A clock. A dead bird. A living bird. Blood on his fingers. Washing his hands before they saw. Secret things, a secret life. Stealing small toys for his sister, but hiding her dolls. Cutting up the dolls, tearing off the heads. Pounding, smashing. Bury the pieces. Here, and there, where no one will look.

····

XI.

····

"Where Is This Virginia?"

Wilko Drenth, pious immigrant farmer of near Fairbank, Iowa, recognizes the picture of Harry F. Powers in a newspaper as his son, Harm Drenth. Looking on is Drenth's son-in-law, Evert Schroder . . .

— *Ames Daily Tribune,*
September 5, 1931

A curious trait shown by Drenth was remembered by H. H. Delthouse, who said that Drenth had once borrowed a watch from his brother and had taken it apart and put it back together again before returning it.

— *Mason City Globe-Gazette,*
September 11, 1931

Middle-aged Women Were Favorites: Officers point to the fact that Powers picked middle-aged women as his "prospects" because they were susceptible to his amours. Most of the women with whom he corresponded and who later became his murder victims had passed or were nearing the "fat and forty" age women dread.

— *The Clarksburg Telegram,*
September 12, 1931

Starving: "There are more people starving for love and companionship than there are starving for bread," red-inked the American Friendship Society of Detroit, which offered "ABSOLUTELY FREE" lists of wealthy widows to anybody who had the price of a two-cent stamp. In four years the "society" had collected more than $10,000 in "dues."

— "We Make Thousands Happy,"
Time magazine, September 14, 1931

Discovery of another alias for Powers: Joe Gildaw. Found on a photo of him inscribed in his hand, "Taken Aug. 14, 1924." . . . At the time he was writing to a girl, Anna, at Vanderbilt PA. . . . An acknowledgment of the photo was also found, addressed to Joe Gildaw, Miller SD. Found in the trunk also was a photo of an Illinois woman who had left her home two years ago to marry a man in Iowa and who has not been heard of since.

— *The Clarksburg Telegram,*
September 15, 1931

■ ■ ■ ■

XII.

■ ■ ■ ■

SEPTEMBER 1931
CHICAGO AND
PARK RIDGE, ILLINOIS
CLARKSBURG, WEST VIRGINIA

CHARLES O'BOYLE: CEREMONY
September 4, 1931

He'd stood on a balcony in Mexico, looking down into the square, and made himself acknowledge that he would never see them again. There would be no long table decorated with thistles and pasteboard turkeys at Thanksgiving, no candles at Christmas, or the miniature Yuletide village the girls so adored. He would not bring the children here, to this coastal town of beaches and sun-drenched plazas, after his marriage to Anna.

She'd told him nothing; she knew he would never have allowed her to enter into such folly. He could not blame himself for anything but too much absence. She'd pretended to consider, had agreed to discuss their plans in mid-July, when he was back in Chicago. In that alternate world, they announced their engagement in September, married at Thanksgiving, embarked on a family wedding trip to Mexico during the children's

Christmas holiday. Annabel stood beside him on the balcony, flying a small kite shaped like a bird; Anna kept Grethe close beside her in the crowded square below, shopping for the lace mantillas young girls wore to church. Hart stood near, at the next stall, where boys sold painted maracas made of gourds.

He knew, of course, where men found men, which small tequila bars to frequent, where to have dinner in outdoor cafés after dark, drinking sweet, bitter coffee by the fountains. He avoided what he knew and went, day by day, to the many small churches near the hotel. He lit candles for the children, for Anna, reciting their names like a rosary. The sound of the coins in the offering boxes, the little flames leaping up on the small white candles, were his only ceremony.

He arrived home, unknowingly, the day of the memorial service, and read the notice in the *Tribune.* He would not, could not attend, and was unprepared for the complete desolation he felt on entering his apartment. He could not sleep. He decided to ask Dunnegan for a transfer and leave Chicago. New York, perhaps, somewhere they had never been, where no one would speak of them. His service had taken numerous messages from reporters who wanted to exploit his connection to the case. He'd returned one call, to Eric Lindstrom, late last night.

"Lindstrom? It's Charles O'Boyle."

"You're back then. May I see you?"

"I'm just back. On the day of the service, actually. I could not . . . attend."

"Of course not. I'm just back myself, tonight, from Iowa. We found Powers' father; we know who Powers is. I have a great deal to tell you." He paused. "The Eicher estate is to be sold tomorrow. The contents of the house. Allow me to drive you there, to retrieve your things."

"All of it sold, tomorrow?"

"I know William Malone would like to speak with you, about anything you want withheld from sale, that you might want to purchase. The Eicher possessions belong to the bank now. Do you want his exchange?"

Charles took down the number. "It seems late to phone him. I would like one of her paintings, and, her desk. It should not go to a stranger."

"You need only leave a message, on his service. And may I come by for you tomorrow? You'll need transport, for those things you've stored."

"You're certain you don't mind?"

"Quite certain. I'll be at your building at seven, parked by the curb." He paused, as though to say more. "Good night, then."

Charles found himself listening, after the click of disconnection, to the air on the line.

EMILY THORNHILL: ESTATE SALE

September 4, 1931

Emily wanted to arrive early at the Eicher house, though she'd barely slept. She rode the 7:00 A.M. streetcar from the Loop, the very line Heinrich Eicher had undoubtedly taken daily from Park Ridge to Chicago. It was a mere half hour. Duty sat quietly in her valise, which she held on her lap; she kept her hand upon him, and watched the glint of the rails race past. Trees overhanging the streetcar line had begun to turn yellow and orange, halfway up their branches. She welcomed autumn, and winter's advance; this summer must pass. There must be storms to blow away the images she could not outdistance, and the memory of Iowa's unrelenting sunlight.

Eric agreed not to include for publication the revelation of Drenth's near drowning as a boy, or Wilko Drenth's words, sworn or prayed in Dutch. They were not public statements, for he'd no idea Eric understood. The boy was dangerous. His name did not mean "harm" in the father's tongue, but the father knew: the child liked to hurt things, watch them hurt, he felt no loyalty or guilt. He did not love his father, or anyone.

Many believed drowning an easy death, a fast, rushed cessation: enclosure, drifting down.

Animals left their damaged young on the

ground, in the open, intuiting difference, danger to the herd not visible to the eye. She remembered Annabel's sign: *Graveyard for Animals.* Perhaps it was still there. The bird buried below was bones and dust.

She unfolded her copy of the *Tribune,* delivered to her door each day by six. Eric had filed the follow-up on Powers' Wisconsin imprisonment:

Early Crime of Drenth Result of Spurned Love
Stole Woman's Bridal Outfit in Anger
AP, Waupun, Wisconsin, September 7

Harry Powers, identified today as Herman Drenth, a former Wisconsin resident, served 15 months in state prison here on charges of burglarizing the home of a woman he courted. In 1921, Drenth, residing on a farm near Cumberland, WI, was sentenced for ransacking the house of Mrs. Thomas Early and stealing several articles, including part of her bridal outfit. Mrs. Early has identified a newspaper picture of Drenth; he became angry after her marriage to Early and the burglary followed.

The facts were peculiar. Eric had contacted the husband, who would not allow access to his wife ("she don't want this brought up again") but maintained Drenth had tried to set the house on fire, though no one could prove it. Drenth had thrown all her clothes on the floor ("pawed through them") and stolen personal items, including her wedding garter and bridal veil. The veil. Rip, slash, tear the lace and tulle. More, perhaps. Then burn it, fire the house. Save a scrap.

Powers' world was not this world, though he'd found himself within it, and driven a car, last June, to the house she now approached. His prey was there, waiting.

The Eicher house was a few blocks from the station. She wanted to walk through the rooms once more, with Duty, when there were no crowds; she pictured an auction held in the large parlor, conducted in respectful tones, and rows of folding chairs. Eric was driving out; she would ask him to photograph the children's rooms. Powers had moved things in the downstairs, but she hoped the children's rooms were still untouched; surely the bedroom sets would sell in lots, and be left in the rooms to show to best advantage.

Duty thought he was going home and trotted along briskly. It was not yet eight in the morning, but the sidewalk was strangely crowded. Emily was shocked to see, a block away, the yard of the Eicher house, swarming with people, as at a school picnic. These were not the neighbors, who stood on their porches, watching the milling crowd. Emily could not at first apprehend the sight. The whole house appeared to have been turned out-of-doors. Armchairs and tables, a kitchen stool, a bed and mattress, sat casually on the lawn. Boxes of toys, board games, doll beds, stacks of books, spilled from crates. A child's playpen, piled full of phonograph records and pots and pans, sagged as though broken by the weight.

She saw Eric's borrowed car, parked by the curb. He stood near it, watching the house with a companion, a man of similar height and build. The man turned to speak to Eric; Emily recognized Charles O'Boyle.

Eric saw her and motioned her forward. "Emily. You're here quite early. You remember Charles. He's returned from Mexico. I offered to drive him, before the crowd arrived."

She greeted O'Boyle. "I'm so glad you're back. I was concerned, not to see you at the memorial service."

"No," he said. "I returned that day, but I would have found any church service very difficult. It is all quite difficult enough." He reached down to stroke the dog as Duty crowded close, then indicated Eric's packed backseat, and the full trunk tied half open to fit its cargo. "My stored things from Anna's garage; I'm very glad for help. Hart was to have my college archery set. I couldn't face keeping the toboggan, though it was offered me, and tried to give it to the neighbors. They didn't want it, superstitious I suppose, and so it is there, in the yard."

"Yes, I see." Emily saw the toboggan, hung on a tree limb by its rope as though to display its length.

"We've been here nearly an hour," Eric said. "The sale is set for nine A.M., but I'm told people always come early." He turned to her. "You look stunned, and very upset."

"I'm certainly upset. I'd no idea the 'estate sale' involved their every possession piled up in the yard, to be pawed through like rummage by any curious bargain hunter. Speculators here, as in Quiet Dell, will pay almost nothing and resell these personal things as murder mementos."

"Yes, well," Eric said. "Speculation of that type may be contemptible, but it's not a crime."

"And where are the good rugs, and Anna Eicher's paintings? I thought it would be an organized auction of some sort." Emily could not mention Annabel's things — her books and drawings, her small notebooks.

"Perhaps the bank will sell any valuables privately, but there would not have been much, given Anna's circumstances," said O'Boyle. "Malone interceded yesterday, so that I could purchase a painting, as well as Anna's desk."

Interceded? What did he mean? Emily pulled Duty closer on the leash; people walked here and there, inspecting boxes of rumpled clothing, and crates full to the brim with kitchen utensils. Furniture, a velvet chaise, chairs and tables, sat on the grass, drawn up as though to an outdoor performance. "But how can the bank allow it?" Emily asked. "Why not give all to charity, and not exploit the origins of the objects?"

Eric exchanged a glance with O'Boyle. "Charity does not pay, Emily. The bank wants all it can get. In these times, payment of the debt is doubtful. No one will pay what the house is worth, and these falling-down outbuildings —"

"Are a liability," O'Boyle finished. "Certainly no one will rebuild them, and tearing down the barn studio will be costly." He looked over the grounds. "Some family will have the place at a very good price, if they are not discouraged by the story."

"It did not happen here," Emily said. "The children lived their entire lives in this house, and they were safe, and mostly happy." She addressed O'Boyle. "Isn't that true, Mr. O'Boyle?"

"It's true, and remains true, whoever lives in the house." He surveyed the scene before them. "And it is the business of banks to sell a liability to the highest bidder. As for the Eicher possessions, the bank wants an empty house to sell, as soon as possible." He looked kindly at Emily. "It's sad for us, of course."

Eric shot her a patient, if direct, glance. "Perhaps you should discuss it with William Malone. He's president of the bank involved, as we know."

"I will do just that," Emily said.

"Walk through now," Eric said. "Perhaps there are things you want to save, as Charles put it, from strangers."

O'Boyle was on his knees, accepting Duty's enthusiastic attentions. He smiled up at Emily. "I thank you, Miss Thornhill, for giving Duty a home." He got to his feet. "May I call you Emily?"

"Of course, Mr. O'Boyle."

"Charles, please. And if you need someone to keep the dog at some point, if you are traveling, whatever, I hope you will contact me. I volunteer my services as dog sitter." He reached to take her hand. "Know that nothing you might have done could be more important to the children: Duty has a home with someone who knew of them, and cared for them."

Eric stepped closer to put one hand on Emily's arm, the other on O'Boyle's shoulder. "You should walk through," he told her. "There must be small things you want to keep in memory of them. This is your last opportunity."

The drawings in Annabel's room. Where might they be? In the house still, no doubt. And the house was locked, clearly, for guards

436

were posted. Pay stations were set up in the front and back yards. And what of the mural in the playhouse, the odd netherworld of Japanese ladies and men in coolie hats? It must be saved. Why had William allowed this?

They'd not spoken since the afternoon of the memorial service, for Emily had gone to Iowa so early yesterday, arrived home late, and was completely occupied with writing the Drenth interview. The story of Powers' true identity was corroborated today in all the papers; fingerprint identification was unassailable. The Midwest was back in the news, and reporters were no doubt coming and going in Oran. She hoped journalists didn't find the grandsons, that their friends did not comment, that their father spoke to them, for Wilko Drenth would not, she was sure. *God help me, I knew it then.*

"Emily." Eric stood near her, and spoke as though in confidence. "I'll come with you."

"No," she said quietly. "Is Charles . . . all right?" She glanced and saw him, standing to the other side of Eric's car, looking away from the house, into the street.

"Yes, I think so. It was best that he left when he did. Are you all right? Yesterday was very long and difficult. And I'm sorry all this catches you by surprise. You knew about the sale, surely."

"Of course, but not that it would be like this," Emily said heatedly. "I must go by the bank." She grasped his sleeve and drew him close. "But Eric, you must speak with Charles, about the doll found in Powers' car. He must plan to attend the trial. He is the only one to identify the doll as Annabel's, and perhaps he has a photo of her holding it. That might be very important. Promise me you will speak with him. Abernathy is the only other possible witness, and she is extremely unsympathetic."

"Emily, let us take you home."

"Will you speak with him?"

"Of course. I'll suggest looking for a photograph."

"Mrs. Pomeroy," Emily said. "That was the name of the doll. Take Charles home. As you say, I am here; I will walk through."

"Shall we meet for supper tonight? You shouldn't be alone."

"Eric, meet with O'Boyle for supper. Let me phone you tomorrow?" She turned, looking back at him, and moved into the crowd. She felt invisible, like the Eichers themselves, and picked Duty up to carry him in her arms. She passed through to the backyard and stood before a table of toys. There was Hart's catcher's mitt, worn soft, and his baseball, nestled in the glove, just as before in his room. Emily took it, and the dog nosed the leather, whining. She put them in her valise. If someone challenged her, she would pay, but these things should not be sold. Lifting her gaze, she saw the children's beds, dismantled in the grass beside her.

"Miss, did you want to purchase that?" A woman stood facing her, wearing a change apron, and a small key around her neck on a string. She was actually collecting money into the children's toy cash register.

"Yes. How much?"

"Let me see. It's good leather. Twenty cents?"

"May I ask — who employs you today?"

"Why, I'm a volunteer, for St. Luke's Ladies Aid. The bank is donating the proceeds of the personals sale to the church." She put the mitt and ball in a bag. "I'm giving you the ice skates that are here. They're boy's skates, so worn they won't sell."

Emily took the parcel. The small graveyard sign was still standing, but some child had scrawled on it, savagely, it seemed to her, crossing out *Animals* and writing, *Grethe, Hart, Annabel.* She walked on, to the playhouse. It was entirely empty. The mural was gone. The push mower, badminton set, old trunks, inner tubes, bicycles, the tea set scattered on the floor, were surely in the yard, in boxes, or thrown in a bin. She walked into the empty space.

She must go to the bank. She passed back through the high grown yard, behind the woman from Ladies Aid, and dimly heard her call out, "Those things are free." Emily saw a pile on the ground, as though the contents of numerous drawers had been dumped in one spot. Hairbrushes, hosiery in satin pouches, school notebooks, a folder held together with brads. She picked up the folder and opened it to the first page. There lay the words, carefully typed.

A Play for Christmas
by Annabel Eicher
December 25, 1930
In honor of Mrs. Heinrich Eicher

She strode through the lobby of the bank and did not knock, but flung open the door to William's office, Duty in her arms, and was startled to see him so suddenly, physically there before her. "Can't you stop this?" she asked loudly. "This public sale, everything they owned out on the street?"

"Miss Thornhill. Please sit down."

Emily watched him nod through the opening to his secretary, as though Emily were an irate customer to be managed, before he gently shut the door. He took her hand and walked with her to the table where they had first talked, long weeks ago, when they'd known nothing of one another. Duty lay at their feet.

William poured the dog a bowl of water, and sat before her. "Emily?" He waited for her to hear him. "It is simply bank policy, a detailed legal process we must follow. Were I to make an exception, every aspect of my personal involvement in the case would be scrutinized, and aspersions cast."

"What do you mean?" She searched his eyes. "No. On you and Anna Eicher?"

"Yellow as the press has been, I'm surprised it hasn't been suggested already."

"Let them try," Emily said. "I'll crucify them, in my own paper. You are beyond reproach."

He smiled at her sadly. "Emily, I am no longer beyond reproach. We are together. We must protect ourselves and be scrupulously careful."

"Yes." She grasped his fingers and brought his open palm to her mouth, and sighed against his skin. "I'm sorry. I was expecting, I suppose, a fine arts auction. My judgment is clouded. And I am very tired."

He took her head in his two large hands, his fingers against the tense muscles of her neck, and leaned closer over the table between them. "Your judgment, about anything, is sound, and very important to me. I have stored her paintings, the few pieces of silverwork, the mural panels from the playhouse, the good rugs. All is set aside, with the dining table and chairs, and Anna Eicher's armoire, to be appraised. I shall purchase them from the bank, following the letter of the law. Charles O'Boyle discussed with me, yesterday, which items should not be sold." He spoke quickly, in a near whisper. "Yes, there are furniture and dishpans, sold for others to buy and use, but you know that those you mourn are beyond harm, beyond hurt. They have no need of dishpans."

Emily nodded wordlessly. She did mourn them, more so as time went on, and she pursued some reason or rhyme to the mystery of how it could have happened. *The devil walks abroad.* Was it that simple, when heaven too, was so at hand?

"Now, then," William said, his hands on her shoulders.

She felt drowsily warm at his touch, and then ached. Her breath quickened; the ache moved through her, but he withdrew his hands, and only looked at her as though something might devour them both. She moved to him and he stood, hands raised almost as though to stop her, but she laced her fingers in his and pulled his palms hard against her. Her eyes widened. She felt slapped awake.

"Not here," he said. "You must go."

"When? What time can I expect you?"

"I have reservations at the Drake. I will check in and come to you by six. Is Reynolds on?"

"You'll stay the whole night? Yes, Reynolds is on."

"Take a breath," he said, smiling. "You

must be your usual, composed self."

"I shall be quite composed," she said, but stepped back. "And I have no reason to come here, to the bank, again."

"I have this for you," he said, and picked up a large manila envelope from the table. "No, don't look at them here. Give me your valise." He slipped it inside. "You must go," he said again, more quietly, and then in response to her questioning look, "They are Annabel's drawings, from her room."

He loved her. He had gone to that house and removed and sleeved the drawings, so carefully, for Emily, for he loved and knew her and understood why it mattered so deeply. They might have lived all their lives and not known one another, in such close proximity; Park Ridge was a streetcar commute from Chicago and her brownstone apartment building, viewed now from the small park across the street. She walked, the dog's leash in one hand, clasping the envelope of Annabel's drawings to her chest. The fulsome canopies of the trees lining the avenue were tipped with gold; the rain beginning to fall was almost mist. All those objects set out in the Eicher yard would be wet and ruined. She did not care; the drawings and mural were safe.

She glimpsed her fifth-floor corner windows through leafy boughs and knew she would embrace William soon in those rooms so known to her, and so changed. The bench just here faced the crosswalk and she sat to catch her breath. The dog turned a kind of circle and leapt up, tangling his leash in her feet.

Annabel smells the trees; their bright leaves glint like dampened fires. Emily is here by the crosswalk in a city park, and these small lawns and banks of garden are Duty's own: he knows the gravel slides and rabbit holes, the tunneled warrens under roots and bushes. Annabel feels herself in Emily's arms, and Duty jumping toward her, but those are only her drawings Emily holds. Annabel herself, so like those figures, needs no wands or wings or scraps of raiment. She knew it might be so; Grandmother had said perhaps one world was another: *you see what is and what will be.* A barn in Iowa fills with hay; a dark aura casts shadows before it, trailed by the powdery scent of Emily's perfume. The grandsons are in school; Drenth like *drenched:* stolid, strong blond boys. The oldest will soon work the farm full-time; he's nearly a man, walking back from the fields on a fall evening two years hence. Smoke curls from his grand-father's window, as though a long wick is extinguished. He runs up the farmhouse stairs, turning on the landing. Annabel turns with him, her white scarf flying out, and sees her own house in Park Ridge. Duty and Emily are in the playhouse and Grethe is in the mural, wearing the Japanese robe Mother painted. Colorful figures move with her: men in sampan hats and vests, ladies with sashed waists and wide sleeves. There is quiet birdsong in the paintings, but the backyard through the playhouse window is noisy with Hart's shouts and whistling. He wields his catcher's mitt from the back stoop, throwing a baseball for Duty. The ball flies, hard as a stone, over the empty grass, and suddenly the yard is full. People stroll about, looking through baskets and open bureau drawers. Her mother's vanity stands awkwardly under a tree. She looks into the mirror and the long glass fogs as though steam pours upon it. The toboggan, hanging from a branch, twists with its own weight. Annabel hears the snow that swirled around it, and the wind on the hill in the park. Charles is pulling the sled and they are trooping after in their blouson hats and gloves and boots, sinking in snow to their knees. The crest of the hill is like a pedestal in a churning cloud. Charles positions the sled and they pile on, shouting and linking arms. Snow lifts around them in wide sprays and their long smooth glide is begun.

WILLIAM MALONE: LIKE ANYONE
September 18–19, 1931
She made dinner for him often, for he spent

every weekend now at her apartment, and drove in midweek as well. He'd inquired, and was buying the apartment next to hers through his lawyer; the large two-bedroom would give them the entire floor. Later, all will be in Emily's name. It was a surprise that he could not keep much longer; the construction of breaking through was involved, and the renovation of an expansive outdoor terrace, private from the street. She would go to West Virginia for the trial, for a full month, she said, to be in the town as preparations began. He'd engaged an architect and planned to begin renovations then, cutting doors and pocket doors, finishing the walls, while she was gone. The interior décor would occupy her when the trial was over, and planning the terrace garden would help her envision a future, their future.

She should be in Clarksburg now, she often said; she would have gone there already, he was sure, but for him. He waited for something else to interest her, some case as important, but he knew there was no such case until the trial was over and the man executed.

She talked at least weekly to Sheriff Grimm, who seemed to be in charge, to Gretchen Fleming, the Lemke woman's sister, and to O'Boyle. Eric phoned her frequently, calls she cut short when William was with her, but the two seemed to enjoy a close platonic friendship. Eric called her "cousin."

Just tonight, Eric had assured William that he watched over Emily carefully. They both knew, Eric said, as though in confidence, that Emily could be impulsive, and was too attractive to behave quite so independently. William made no comment. A dinner party, given by the *Tribune* editorial board, eddied around them; Emily was on the other side of the room. Emily was his, William reflected; he should be her protection and could not publicly offer it. They'd attended the function separately, appearing merely acquainted as they took part in conversations concerning the Powers case, the ongoing controversy around Prohibition, the economic climate, the mayor's well-oiled administration. Every man in this room, Eric included, William knew, was a millionaire, and would double his wealth as the Depression limped on.

Dinner was served at a long table accommodating eighteen or twenty. Emily was seated with Eric at the far end. William noticed that some seemed to view them as a couple. They traveled together and were known to partner in covering a crime that only seemed to snowball in anticipation of the trial, which it was said might take place in an opera house, like an entertainment. William's own dinner conversation preoccupied him; the lawyers opposite were interested in a joint investment that could prove very profitable, but he glanced at Emily to see Eric touch her wrist and gaze at her over their raised glasses. The man seemed at pains to give the impression they were intimate. She was using Eric's attentions to avoid looking at William, to appear engaged. Eric signaled the waiter to refresh her drink, for Prohibition was a mere joke at private parties such as this.

Finally, guests began departing. Eric announced to the host, in everyone's hearing, that he would escort Miss Thornhill home, and helped Emily on with her wrap, touching her hair as though he often did so.

William concluded his conversation, unhurried, setting up a series of meetings in the coming week; commercial real estate was a freshly consuming interest now that he spent so much time in the city. He took his own cab to Emily's apartment and entered by the stairs, walking the five flights up. He was no longer concerned about meeting anyone in the hallway, for he knew the only other apartment on her floor was empty. He unlocked Emily's door with his key, calling out, "Darling?" and she answered, over the sound of the filling bath.

He moved toward her, into the bedroom, aware of the open bathroom door and the moist, steamy air.

"I'm just getting into the bath," she called to him. "Come in if you like. What took you so long at the party?"

"Business. More reason to work in Chicago." He heard the water move as she lay down in it. He wanted to go into the narrow room and look at her, reach for her, but he stood at her dresser and confronted his reflection in her mirror. Water splashed. He thought of Catherine, bathed by Mary like a child, in a plastic seat that kept her upright in the tub.

Catholic marriages could be annulled. It was an arduous process, but Catherine did not know she was married, and he could afford to care for her. But he had taken a vow. And to legally acknowledge Catherine's condition as reason to end their marriage seemed a betrayal that flew in the face of this gift to him, this miracle.

"William?"

He heard Emily in the bath. Water, dripping and pouring. She was soaping her arms, her legs, her beautiful limbs that clung to him and pulled him against her, that he stroked and held in every possible configuration. He felt it was all preamble, the ground of his deepening knowledge, desire, need for her, and was momentarily astounded to find himself standing in her bedroom, a room now so familiar.

He removed his tuxedo jacket, his vest, the studs of his pleated shirt. He put them in the mahogany tray she'd purchased for him.

"Emily," he called in to her, "does your friend Eric know about us?"

She hesitated. "What do you mean?"

"What do I mean? That seems an evasive answer." He waited. He knew she would come to the door of the bath, and look at him gravely; they did not converse from separate rooms.

She stood, her robe unbelted, gazing at him, as though considering entering the bedroom. "I certainly haven't told him about us, and he hasn't asked."

"He gives the impression, in public, that he would not need to ask such a question, because he would already know the answer."

"Are we speaking in riddles?"

William kept the room between them. "He assured me, in a private moment tonight, of your safety in his care, on the Powers case, as though aware of the depth of my concern. He then implied the depth of *his* concern, and his delight in you, to everyone at the party."

She walked toward him, her robe open, smelling of roses. The moisture of the hot bath clung to her hair. She nearly spoke, but hesitated.

"Eric is a very attractive man." William was arranging his shirt studs into an even row, within the tray. "About your age, isn't he? Well off. Family money. And never married."

She stood by the dresser.

"Is he a homosexual, Emily?"

She watched William. "If he were, or people thought he might be, that would be quite dangerous for him, wouldn't it. He would be ruined in every society, but for a small, secret one. I'm sure we can't imagine."

"You care deeply for him, don't you?"

"Of course I do."

"Then we need say no more about it."

She touched her warm hands to his shoulders and chest, following the thin furred line down his belly to the clasp of his trousers.

"I have something for you," he said, "something very important to me." He took the object, a small suede change purse, from his trouser pocket and put it in her hand. "It was my mother's. I don't know why I want you to have it, except that she carried it with her always, and I have kept it in my desk for years, all the years, it seems, that I have waited for you."

She sat, and held the purse, and opened the brass clasp.

"It is empty," William said, "and smells faintly of roses, like you. I sometimes feel that what I can offer you, so deeply felt and meant, has an element of emptiness. It's not the marriage I wish for us. It may never be."

Her eyes shone up at him. He turned off the lights, and went to her.

They slept, so conscious of one another that

they woke together. She opened the drawn curtains near 10:00 A.M. and prepared coffee, fruit, eggs with ham, and thick brown bread. They sat in armchairs opposite one another, at the marble slab of her kitchen table. They ate without speaking much, only smiling. Emily poured his coffee full again, and got up to warm more milk.

William watched her, aware of her inside the robe, of her hands, touching cups and plates. These moments of pause transported him; he wished only to extend them, to control the hands of the clock on her kitchen wall.

She turned to him and reached for his hand. "What are you thinking, looking at me so?"

"Only that I feel a warmth such as children feel, perhaps, completely in the moment. Being here, talking to you."

"Yes. We are talking, like anyone."

"We are going to get better and better at this."

"At talking, William? And breakfast?"

"At everything, Emily."

She touched his throat, his hair. "If we were married, wouldn't we get used to one another, finally, walk about, have breakfast every day, read the paper in our armchairs —"

"Emily, we do walk about and have breakfast, but I will never get used to this. Whether we marry is in God's hands. But having been married, and lived so alone for so long, I can only tell you this is nowhere usual."

She moved to sit beside him, nestled close in the wide upholstered chair. "I'm more like you than you know. Work, my constant, acquaintances rather than friends, and no relatives but my mother, who doesn't know me, as Catherine doesn't know you. I would simply have gone on as I was."

The phone rang, startling them both.

"You needn't answer," William said.

"No one would ring me on the weekend, unless it was important."

The phone rang, and stopped, and began again.

"Forgive me, I must answer." She picked up the receiver, and held it so that William could hear Eric on the other end.

"I've had a phone call from Grimm." Eric was calling from the street, nearly shouting into the phone. "He expects a riot tonight, a lynch mob at the jail. Crowds are gathered. I am flying to Clarksburg."

"Swing by for me," Emily said.

"Half an hour."

She put down the phone. "Don't look that way, William. You know I must go."

"Of course you must. Phone me, and stay with Eric at all times. You must stay in adjoining rooms, at the Gore. I'll take care of it."

"I'll be gone two days at most. Come and help me pack. I must hurry. You'll finish breakfast then, after I leave? I love to think of you here, even if I must go."

"Then think of me here. Reynolds will take the dog?"

"Yes. I'll call to inform him. You need only lock up, and go down by the stairs."

"The secret passage. Go now. Get dressed." He heard her in the bath, in the bedroom, drawers pulled open and shut.

He'd never seen this place that took her from him, but he would attend the trial. His presence was expected, given his part in the drama. He would go to Quiet Dell, and stand with her on that dirt road, and view the spectacle at the opera house. He must witness all, then bring her back with him, forever.

EMILY THORNHILL: SWIFT JUSTICE
September 19–20, 1931

Eric hired a car at the Clarksburg airport and they went directly to the jail. It was heavily guarded. Perhaps three thousand had gathered, filling Third Street for blocks. The instigators were a group of a hundred or so. A great steel bin held boulders and rocks taken from the ground, for the foundation of the new building was dug and roped off, and earth piled to one side. Men climbed upon the mound now, to stand above the crowd and shout epithets. Others lined the borders of the bin itself, taking stones out and stacking them, arming themselves for the expected assault on the police station. "Lynch him!" rang out repeatedly. "Don't waste a rope," someone answered. "Here, rocks and fists!" a female voice responded. Laughter rippled like ricochet. "Swift justice," a man called, setting a more serious tone.

The mob was waiting for dark, and the surging crowd waited for the mob to act. Tense expectation reigned. It was 6:00 P.M., but the sheriff's office had switched on the lights at the construction site.

Eric steered Emily through the crowd. "Excuse me," he repeated, "we have business with the sheriff's office . . . excuse me, please excuse us, we have business —"

They made their way. Two fire trucks were drawn up before the station door; firemen had unrolled the hoses and held them ready, aimed at the crowd. State police stood posted at hundred-yard intervals, formally outfitted in broad-brimmed hats, double-breasted jackets, blouson trousers, and high black boots. They remained at attention, shoulders back, surveying the ragged front edge of the crowd.

Emily addressed an officer. "Excuse me, sir. Might you please get a message to Sheriff W. B. Grimm, that Miss Thornhill and Mr. Lindstrom, of the *Chicago Tribune,* are here to speak with him."

"Get back, both of you." The man didn't

look at them, but stood with his hand on his holstered pistol, glancing at his fellows, stationed to his right and left. "No press interviews now. No one is allowed in the jail, and no one in the crowd can advance from this point."

Emily pretended affront. "Officer, we have information for Sheriff Grimm, pursuant to this demonstration, information he has asked us to convey. You must give us leave to go inside."

Eric showed his press credential. "The sheriff personally alerted us to events. We have come directly from Chicago. Please allow us entrance."

The trooper gave him a withering look and jerked his head. They walked quickly toward a line of city police, who parted almost surreptitiously to allow passage and stood back in formation. Emily heard movement in the crowd, and isolated catcalls, but they were inside.

Numerous uniformed officers stood in groups. Some inspected tables on which rifles and tear gas canisters lay arranged end to end.

Grimm was in the outer office and stood as they entered. "Who let you in here? I was informing you of events, Lindstrom, not inviting you to the jail. And I did not expect you to bring a woman into a lynch mob."

"You remember Miss Thornhill, Sheriff

Grimm. It is our job to cover every aspect of the case —"

"That's not my concern." Grimm turned to Emily. "They are a disorganized mob, inflamed by rumor over the last two days. We are prepared, but they will rush the jail. My men will show you to an upstairs room and you are to stay there. Do you understand?" He pointed at Eric. "She is your responsibility."

"Yes," Eric said.

"Stay clear of the windows," Grimm told Emily, "and shut them if we are forced to gas the crowd. Officers will shutter all windows from the inside if the crowd lobs rocks or explosives."

A machine gun lay on the desk between them.

"Are you prepared to use that gun to defend Powers?" Eric took a camera from his bag.

"I must defend Powers and the rule of law, and everyone in this police station, including the two of you. Put the camera away. Do not, I repeat, do not, take photographs inside the station, or of the prisoner."

"Eric —" Emily cautioned.

"Understood." Eric held up open palms, as though in surrender.

"That way." Grimm pointed to a staircase. "It is called the medical room and adjoins the police chief's residence, to which the door is locked. If I see you down here, Lindstrom, I will lock you up. See how you cover events from a cell."

"Thank you, Sheriff Grimm." Emily pushed Eric toward the stairs and followed him quickly up. The stairs let out into a hallway with two small offices on one side, and a large room on the other. This was obviously the "medical room," bare but for a steel exam table, a sink, and a large, wall-mounted first aid cabinet. A desk in one corner held a typewriter. Two generous windows provided an excellent view of the crowd.

"This is perfect." Eric gazed down. "We couldn't have a better vantage point." The mob pressed against a construction bin of rocks, just beyond the ring of state police. It was twilight. Flood-lights, hung high on poles, beamed down. Isolated small groups lit torches.

"Turn him loose, turn him loose," they began to chant.

"It's an ugly crowd," Emily said. "Grimm was not happy to see us."

"I've had far worse greetings." Eric smiled. "Do stay back from the window. There is even a typewriter, Emily. You need only sit at the desk to write your copy."

"You seem so pleased. This could get quite ugly, if they rush the station."

"I predict Grimm will retain control. He is kingpin of this domain, and the ultimate

458

professional." Eric opened the window, standing to the side, out of view, and began photographing the crowd. "I'm close enough to focus on faces, and I can see the entire front of the station."

"You will provide Grimm with photographs of the ringleaders, if he needs them, and prove your worth."

"I don't think you need prove yours. He's as smitten as Grimm gets." Eric looked over at her.

"That's really enough."

He moved to the other side of the window, shooting the vast throng of spectators that filled Pike and Third Streets. Then he turned and photographed Emily, who stood with the desk chair before her. "I have disobeyed Grimm, but only for posterity." He put down the camera. "I know you are happy. Malone seems completely devoted to you, and I'm not one to believe happy couples are married couples."

"Is it so obvious?"

"Only to me. And I will protect you, always, just as you protect me. In fact, we protect one another, at gatherings like the *Tribune* affair, but my feelings for you run far deeper than appearances. As counsel or help, no matter the need, I am sworn to you."

"And I to you." A roar went up at the window. "Take care. They may notice the flash of your camera, and not want record of themselves." She walked closer behind him to see the crowd sway and begin to push forward.

"Give us the fiend!" a woman screamed. Glass shattered and police poured out of the station, standing two and three deep behind the state troopers. Grimm, at the front, pistol drawn, fired a warning shot. The mob, inflamed, threw a barrage of rocks and bottles, pressing the police, who surged forward against them. Officers lobbed tear gas into the crowd. Two hundred or so men, wielding clubs, rushed the jail from Third Street. The mob had dragged the hose from one fire truck and now strained to overturn it; firemen maintained a constant burst of flaring water from the other. The gas was everywhere, hissing and popping, and the crowd fell back choking. State troopers surrounded a few men and pulled them quickly into the station. The crowd jeered, but the police drew weapons and held them overhead in a show of force.

Grimm addressed the crowd through a bullhorn, standing at the door of the station. "The prisoner inside is charged with a terrible crime, but you have entrusted these officers to uphold the rule of law. They will fight to the last to defend the dignity of the county. Do not endanger their lives or your own." He waited. "If any of you are ever charged with a crime, know that we will go to equal lengths to protect you. We are under oath and sacred obligation."

Eric shut the window; the wind had shifted and the smell of the pungent gas burned. Emily saw, from the darkened room, those not immediately dispersed by the gas begin to move. They faded back like dark patches, out of the light.

There was commotion downstairs, and shouting. Police were strong-arming the mob leaders into cells, slamming cell doors, calling to one another, "Secured." "Secured." "That's the last, eight secured." They must have moved the new prisoners directly past Powers' cell. One called out in a sonorous baritone, "Vengeance is mine, saith the Lord." "Shut your trap," said a voice.

Emily heard quiet weeping. She went to the landing at the top of the stairs.

Grimm appeared at the bottom, glaring at her, his suit spotless, his hat pushed back on his head. "All right?" He barely acknowledged her quick nod. "Shutter the windows." He waited, listening as Eric slammed the wooden shutters closed and slid the iron bars across to bolt them. "No cameras," Grimm said. "We are bringing him up."

She stepped back and felt Eric's hand at her waist, drawing her into the far corner of the room. She stood against him as footsteps began to mount the stairs. Chains clanked, step by step. Eric drew her behind him. A group was upon the stairs, moving slowly as though in concert. Grimm was in the room with four officers; two more held Powers between them, a red blanket over his head and shoulders like a cloak, his hands and feet manacled. He hunched in the blanket, sniveling, holding up his chained hands. She saw his wet blue eyes peering out and wished the mob might have him.

"Gentlemen," he was saying. "I surely thank you for your protection tonight, and for guarding my home. My poor wife. I know you will leave your officers in place. I'm most grateful. That mob would have torn me limb from limb —" He minced forward, encumbered by the short chain fastening his ankles.

No officer addressed him; they only acted in formation, unlocking the door to the police chief's quarters, moving Powers out while the crowd was distracted.

"Where are you taking him?" Eric asked.

"I am going to Moundsville," Powers said, as though pleased. "Gentlemen, I —"

An officer behind him slipped a gag over the blanket, into his mouth, stopping the words. Emily counted fourteen police. One remained to lock the door behind them, and turned to face her.

"May we stay?" she asked the officer.

"You'll stay right where you are until I give you leave."

"May I use the typewriter?"

He shrugged, eyeing Eric.

They could not hear the vehicles moving off, but knew there would be three: one to precede the prisoner, Grimm in the police van, with his guards and the manacled Powers, and a third to guard the caravan from behind. Moundsville was an hour's drive. They were taking him to the state penitentiary, to death row, most likely, which featured the most secure cells in the state. Grimm had gained some sort of special permission, without accepting a change of venue for the trial.

Emily rolled the desk chair into place and began to type, utilizing the paper in the desk drawer. The carriage stuck, but she almost enjoyed slamming it back at certain punctuating moments.

Eric sat down to wait. "May I open the shutters?"

"No." The officer removed his billy club from his belt and stood tapping it lightly against his leg.

Emily began to write her copy:

Saturday Night Melee Surrounds Murderer Powers in West Virginia Town. Clarksburg, West Virginia, September 20, 1931: Special to the Chicago Tribune, by Emily Thornhill. An angry mob of 3000 townsmen surrounded the county jail at dark on Saturday, September 19th, nearly a month after Powers' arrest for the murder of five persons. The crowd demanded Powers' release to "swift justice . . ."

She and Eric were allowed to leave within the hour. Groups still clustered on every corner. The police station was shuttered and guarded, the fire trucks in place. Eric walked her to the Gore and went back to photograph what was left of the crowd. She filed at the telegraph office, rousing the dispatcher, and left a message with William's service, not to wake him.

She did not know the desk clerk on duty, but William had asked for the same rooms as before. Eric, when he came in at 2:00 A.M., insisted on leaving the door through unlocked, as though she might be carried away in the night. Later they would do a feature to accompany his photographs. The actual riot, in the dark, translated as blurs and streaks, but the pre-assault images, taken at twilight, seemed carefully composed. Legions of male faces turned to the camera like bland, inquiring flowers; all were white men in pale shirts or coat and tie, their hats at rakish angles. Some actually stood within the construction bin as though posing among the rocks, and the lights above them glowed out like planets.

■ ■ ■ ■

XIII.

■ ■ ■ ■

DOG TWICE BEREFT
For the second time in his short life, Duty, a Boston terrier, finds himself the only survivor of a family wiped out by death. He belonged to Mrs. Asta Eicher, Park Ridge, Ill., widow, murdered by Harry F. Powers, "Bluebeard" of Quiet Dell. Several years ago Duty was owned by a family which was killed in a tornado.

— *The Clarksburg Exponent,*
November 5, 1931

NOVEMBER 20–21, 1931
CLARKSBURG, WEST VIRGINIA

A SMALL THEFT

The streets of Clarksburg were strung with pine roping and velvet ribbon to herald the holiday season. Emily would celebrate Thanksgiving at the Gore Hotel and return to Chicago soon after the trial. William questioned her resolve in arriving so early; the trial was set to begin December 7. What was there to report, but the trial itself? Everything, she assured him. He would attend the trial and stay at the Gore, near her own suite. Emily, just arrived by train from Chicago, was somewhat amazed to find herself at the Gore reception desk, holding Duty on the leash. Clarksburg and Quiet Dell had seemed, since her flight here two months ago, so sharply resonant and yet so distant.

"Oh, hello — Mr. Parrish, isn't it?" She glanced quickly at his name tag and leaned near to glance at the register; hopefully no other press had yet arrived. "Rooms 126 and 127. I reserved the rooms with the door through. I have the dog, as before."

"Miss Thornhill, we've been expecting you, and we'll make the exception; no one complains about a dog that doesn't bark."

"Ah, yes." Local papers had picked up Chicago coverage: Duty's photograph and history under a heart-wrenching headline.

Parrish peered over the desk. "And I reckon the two of you could sell that second bed at a premium if you'd a mind to, with everything that's going on. Porter!" he called.

"Oh no, I've too great a need of the space, for interviews and an office. I do apologize for all these bags, though." She'd brought all her files, her typewriter, warm clothes, boots, Duty's accoutrements, and in a separate grip, her loveliest nightgowns and sheer lingerie, her own soaps and perfume. She'd grabbed her valise, assuming its weight was more notes, and discovered on the train that it still held Hart's old skates, his catcher's mitt and baseball, from the Eicher estate sale last September. She felt quite stupid, for here they must stay until it was over.

She turned to follow the porter, the Negro gentleman she'd interviewed last summer. They were all here to play their parts, and the production was finally starting.

"Ma'am." The porter was standing back, her luggage piled on the cart, indicating the open elevator.

"Thank you, Mr. . . . Woods."

"Yes, that's right, ma'am." He stepped in behind her, expertly maneuvering the cart.

The doors shut soundlessly. "Will you be testifying?"

"Yes, ma'am, they say so, though it won't take long to say my part."

"I remember." Dorothy Lemke, fiftyish divorcée, arrives very late after motoring from Massachusetts with Cornelius Pierson, checking in to the hotel for a few hours. Lemke checked in alone and checked out alone. They were observing propriety, was undoubtedly his excuse for not touching her except to bind and kill her.

The afternoon was not completely gone. She would unpack later, for she wanted to walk to the jail. She must start off, be inside the story again, quickly.

Snow was forecast and the air was sharply cold. Powers' recent move back to the city jail was known, and the building fully garrisoned with a detachment of state police, city officers, sheriff's deputies. Forty or fifty onlookers huddled near the jailhouse doors, dressed in farmers' overalls or their Sunday best. It was Saturday; working people were at their leisure. Police held the crowd in check, but the gathering registered a wave of disturbance at every entrance or exit from the jail. Reporters and photographers, interviewing Duckworth, Grimm, or Powers' attorney, J.

Ed Law, came and went, seemingly by appointment. Just now, an enterprising photographer incited reaction, setting up a shot; how did the town view Powers, the fiend now returned for the trial of the century? The crowd surged, shouting. Emily, press credential in hand, approached the doors. She felt herself jostled, and looked to see a child ducking down, skirting the throng behind her.

She reached into her coat pocket for William's present and gasped to realize she'd been robbed. Her valuables and money she kept inside her clothes, but his mother's purse, which she liked to touch as she walked, was gone. She set off after the child at a full run, pushing her way free, for she could see him walking nonchalantly along the sidewalk, until he sensed her attention and glanced back. His gaze met hers for an instant before he ran, fleetly dodging passersby. Emily could not bring herself to shout that he be stopped; she attracted curious stares but kept him fixed in her sight as he dodged and weaved. The town was crawling with police, but of course no one noticed a boy running along the street.

She called out to him, "You there! Boy! Stop!"

He did not, but fled into the alley beside the Gore. Emily arrived just behind him, relieved to see a blind alley, bricked off at the end. Lined with trash cans and pallets, it served as garbage pickup and delivery site for the hotel. She saw the boy standing, filthy in his cap and long coat, next to a drainpipe, amidst the cans.

"Do not run," she said, walking up on him, "the police are right behind me." He was young, she saw, nine or ten perhaps, a full head and shoulders shorter than herself, and very thin and dirty. "Step out here, please," she said. "I have told the police I want to speak with you before asking their assistance."

The boy peered up the alley, gauging his chances, no doubt.

"Give me my change purse," Emily said. "I shall call them unless you obey immediately. Return what you took from me."

Carefully, he stepped out, and at her beckoning motion, walked close enough that she could see his face. He was certainly a child. His dark hair fell in his eyes as he reached into his clothes for the change purse, and put it in her gloved hand.

Emily opened the purse and unsnapped the clasp to show him that it was empty. "There. I didn't follow you over money. This purse is very old and belonged to someone dear to a friend of mine. It is precious to me. That is why I chased you."

Frowning, poised to run, he flicked his gaze at her.

"Hardened criminal, are you? What is your name?" She saw him startle, almost imperceptibly. The movement was involuntary. Perhaps he was cold. "I said, what is your name?"

"Randolph Mason Phillips." He glowered, angry to be detained by a woman.

"And where do you live, Randolph?"

He looked about him. "Here."

"Do you mean you haven't anywhere to live?"

He looked straight ahead and said nothing.

"Where are you from, then?"

"Coalton, in Randolph County."

"Where is your father, Randolph?"

"He died in the mines."

"Where is your mother, then?"

She saw his head move, again, almost imperceptibly, and he blinked, as though in response to a feigned blow.

"She died," he said.

"I'm sorry," Emily said. "Whom do you live with, then?"

"I was living with my uncle but he run me off," the boy said. "I ain't going back there."

"If I asked your uncle why he . . . made you leave, what would he say?"

"He's too drunk to 'member that far back."

"I see. Did he hit you?" She waited.

He looked at her as though she was simple. "Course he hit me. He hits ever'body gets in ten feet of 'im."

"How old are you, Randolph?"

"Twelve, almost." He scowled, pursing his mouth.

"Are you hungry?"

Again she saw his head move, and the accompanying blink of his eyes.

"Listen to me, Randolph. You must stop stealing from the crowd. The police will catch you, and put you into the reformatory."

What good were such threats, when he was living on the street? She could not leave him, nor report him. His slight stature moved her to continue. "I'm a reporter, here to write about the trial. You're not going to steal any more because you are going to work for me. I am going to give you a job, if you want it, and I will pay you a wage, as well as room and board."

He pulled his loose coat closer about him.

It was a woman's coat, far too large for him, and old and worn. "Do you want to know what sort of job?" Emily asked him.

He lifted his head, appraising her.

"You will be my assistant and archivist. An archive is a collection of documents. The job involves cutting clippings from various newspapers, and glue and paste, and keeping dates in order. Can you read?"

"I can read."

"Do you have a favorite book?"

"*The Deerslayer,*" he said.

"That's a good book. Did you read it yourself?"

"Someone read it to me," he said. "Then I read it myself."

"Well," Emily said, "I would like you to come with me, Randolph. I have a separate room in the hotel where you can sleep, and you can begin work tomorrow, that is, if you're willing to have a bath and a meal. Are you willing?"

"Yes." His soft voice was barely audible. Perhaps he was apprehensive, but she must be clear.

"One more thing, Randolph." She softened her tone. "If you steal from me, or from anyone while you are in my employ, I will turn you in to the police. I need to hear that you understand, and that you accept my terms."

"I do," he said.

"All right then." She began walking, back toward the hotel. He fell in beside her. She thought he might run. Far simpler if he did; she'd already decided not to pursue him.

But before they turned out of the alley, he stopped her. "I'm not called Randolph, miss. That were my father's name. I'm called Mason."

Duty greeted them, bounding about their feet as Emily stepped inside. She'd thought the dog might be hostile, for Duty was a suspicious guardian and the boy smelled of the street. She felt even more confident that he stole by necessity, and not happily. "This is Duty," Emily said.

The child knelt down, saying, "Hey now," as though comforted, it seemed to Emily, and surprised to find a dog in a hotel room. Perhaps he'd never been in a hotel.

She ordered two meals, steak, mashed potatoes, carrots and peas, and a breakfast steak and soup bone, from room service. The boy was famished. He ate the steak immediately, holding it in his hands up to his mouth, chewing it down until it was gone, watching Duty gulp cut-up meat from a plate.

She handed the boy his napkin, to wipe his hands. "Do you eat vegetables, Mason?"

"Yes, miss."

"Have some then, with your utensils, perhaps."

He began to eat the vegetables, the spoon in his right hand and the fork in his left, shoveling the peas and potatoes onto the spoon. She considered her own meal, and looked up to see that his plate was clean.

"Miss," he said. "I don't like milk. You have mine. I ain't touched it."

"You haven't touched it."

He nodded.

"Mason," she said, "I hope you don't mind if I correct your speech. People think they know all about you when they hear you say 'ain't.' Of course they don't, but they leap to conclusions. If people are going to believe that you're assisting me, you will need to do a few things differently. It will be as though you're an actor, playing a role." She paused, hoping not to offend him.

"Yes, miss."

"Do you mind if we practice something?" She moved his empty plate and place setting across the table, and indicated he sit on the couch beside her. "I can't possibly eat so much steak, so I'm going to ask you to share half. But I want you to use your fork and knife as I do."

He sat beside her and took up the fork in his left hand, and the knife in his right.

"Yes," Emily said. "Keep the utensils in your hands, just so, the whole time you are eating, putting them down only to wipe your mouth with the napkin —" She shook out his napkin and put it across his lap. "Now, ready?"

Together, they ate her supper. Both plates clean, he leaned back from the low table and said stiffly, "Thank you, miss."

"Did you have enough to eat?" She saw him nearly smile. "May I show you your room then, and tell you a bit about the job you'll be doing?"

"Yes, miss."

"Now, one must not work without payment, and I will pay you, but I am also, of course, paying your room and board, so the wage must be adjusted accordingly. Do you agree?"

He nodded. Perhaps he had not eaten a full meal in some time, for he looked sleepy.

"Now, we will need to work every day until the trial is over, but you may manage your own time and stop when you like. If I pay you twenty-five cents a day, is that acceptable?"

He widened his eyes in surprise. Perhaps she'd offered too much. She supposed men dug ditches here, for such a wage. Still, the child must have some money saved, for whatever situation she could arrange for him after the trial. She started then: there were three loud raps at the door, and Duty leapt up.

The boy half stood, clearly frightened.

"Sit down, Mason, it's all right." She went to the door, and opened it to Coley Woods. "Mr. Woods," she said, and stepped into the hallway.

"Is everything all right, Miss Thornhill?" The porter looked down at her, his dark eyes soft and inquiring.

Of course, he had seen her come into the lobby with a ragged-looking person in a bulky coat. Woods was concerned for her. "Yes, Mr. Woods, quite all right, but thank you for asking. My nephew will be assisting me for the duration of the trial. There's surely an extra charge, since the second bedroom is now occupied. Could I settle all this tomorrow? He's had a long journey."

"You can arrange it with the desk. How old is your nephew?"

"He's nearly twelve. We've organized time off from school. He wants to become a journalist someday."

"The charge for minor children is adjusted."

"Thank you, Mr. Woods. I'll put the tray out, as soon as we finish dinner. Good night, then." She stepped inside and latched the door. Tomorrow, she must buy the boy a suit and introduce him to the hotel staff. Best to limit their observations until he was a bit more practiced in certain social graces. "Mason?"

"Miss?" He spoke from the corner of the room. "Do I have to leave?"

"No. Come and sit down." She moved to the couch and indicated the chair opposite. "Why would you need to leave?" She waited for him to sit. "You must be honest with me. Is someone looking for you, Mason? Your uncle, perhaps? Or the police?"

"The police ain't —"

"The police aren't."

"The police aren't looking for me."

She watched his face carefully. "Is your uncle looking for you?"

He frowned and blinked his eyes. The thatch of dark hair, fallen forward, moved on his lashes. Again, the slight wince. "I don't have no, I mean, any uncle, miss."

"So, who ran you off, Mason, as you put it?" Clearly, she thought, someone had.

"My father did, a lot of times. He hit me but I always came back, because my mother, she was sick. He wouldn't help her." The boy looked away, and nearly whispered. "She told me he drank more after he got hurt in the mines. He would go away, leave us be, but then he would come back."

And terrorize them, Emily thought. "Mason," she said gently, "when did your mother . . . pass?" She did not like the expression, but thought people here probably used it.

"Beginning of October. I walked up the hill to get the neighbors, and we said some words over her. I didn't have any way to pay the undertaker, or a minister. We made a funeral for her in the garden. It's the way we do."

"I see." She realized that the old coat he was wearing, now hanging in the closet, must be his mother's. "Your father wasn't there, for the funeral."

"No, miss, but he come back that night, drinking, and I hid in the woods until he was asleep. Then I come back for her coat and some things. She had told me to leave, that I shouldn't stay —" He faltered a moment. "I walked to Coalton and got a ride to Clarksburg with a farmer."

481

"And how did you come to be staying near the Gore?"

"They was always people, and —"

"You stole from them, picked their pockets?"

"Sometimes, miss. But I swept the alley, too, and he — that man" — he nodded at the door — "put food out for me. And he let me shine shoes, and paid me a few cents."

"What man? Do you mean Mr. Woods? The porter?"

"I didn't know 'twer him knocking, miss."

"Of course you didn't. But he is a good man. He listened to my story and didn't give you up, or embarrass me. Look, Mason. From now on, we'll say you're my nephew, just as I told Mr. Woods. I think he will allow us that fabrication. And you'll call me, I suppose, Aunt Emily."

"Do I have to, miss?"

"In general, I do not advocate lying, but people will not believe we're related if you call me miss."

"All right, miss. I mean, all right."

"I'm sure you're tired. You'll have a bath, and a warm bed. How does that sound?"

"I'm glad to have a job, miss. I mean, I'm glad —" He reached down to lay his hand along Duty's back, and the dog yawned.

He was certainly a polite boy. His mother had loved him, it seemed, and tried to teach him. "Mason," she said, "your mother would understand, as I do, that you stole because you were hungry. That is over. I will trust you, Mason, unless you give me reason not to. This must be clear between us."

He sat up straighter and squared his thin shoulders, and shook her hand when she offered it.

"Very well then, this is my room, and here" — Emily led him through to the smaller room — "is your room, and your bathroom. Let me draw you a bath. Please leave your clothes on the chair here, and I'll get a bathrobe for you." She poured some lavender oil into the water, to banish the smell of the alley, and hasten sleep, as well.

On her knees by the tub, she heard the dull thud of Duty's small rubber ball, and Mason praising him in a low voice. William and Eric would think her rash, but they were not here to judge. She fetched the bathrobe and laid out soap and towels. She called him in, and he came, Duty at his heels.

"Knock on my door when you finish. All right, Mason?"

"Yes. Thank you, miss."

She lay down on the sofa in her own room. She must have slept, for his knock roused her. She peered through the dim room as at an apparition. His wet dark hair was swept back from his face, so that his pale complexion and fine brow were obvious, and he looked even younger. She walked him back to his room and pulled open the covers on the high spool bed; he stepped on the foot-stool to get in.

"Good night, then," she said. He looked back at her, nearly asleep, and she put the dog next to him, where the boy would feel him breathing. "You'll see," she said, "Duty is a fine companion."

In the bath, his clothes, folded so carefully, were nearly rags. She washed them in the sink and hung them to dry. Surely he wouldn't object to a haircut. She wondered how well he could read. Certainly he was quick, living by his wits, with a mother to mourn if he ever felt safe enough. She turned off the light and walked back through to her room; Mason was asleep, Duty in his arms. The dog raised his head, and moved his stump of a tail.

Duty woke her, barking his ragged *chuff* from the foot of her bed. "There now," she said, pulling on her robe. She walked through into Mason's room to find him sitting in the armchair, fully dressed in the clothes she'd left to dry last night. "Good morning, Mason. Did you sleep well?"

"Oh yes, miss. I mean, yes."

"I hope Duty didn't wake you."

"He was wanting to go out awful bad. So I took him on the leash, around the hotel. I hope that was all right. I used the key that was on the table."

"Yes, fine. That key is yours." She saw that he had pulled up the covers on the bed. "Let's order breakfast. You must be hungry."

He nodded, and watched her call down to order.

Duty jumped into the armchair and settled beside Mason, gazing back at her. "It will help me a great deal if you take responsibility for Duty, walking and feeding him and keeping him company, while we are here. Much of the time, he's stuck in the room. Luckily he doesn't bark."

"Why doesn't he bark?"

"Well, that's a story. I told you I am here as a reporter, to cover the trial coming up. Do you know anything about the Powers trial?"

"Everyone knows," Mason said.

"As for Duty's bark, or lack of it, I will tell you that Duty was Hart Eicher's dog. Having a dog's good instincts, Duty disliked Powers. Powers demanded the dog be locked up, telling the children they would be back to fetch him, but Duty broke free to race after them. Powers likely kicked him in the throat, and hurt his larynx. That's here, where the voice resides." She touched her own throat and paused; Mason was watching her, spellbound. "Duty is fine now. He loves breakfast steak, or hamburger, cut into small pieces. Room service often sends up leftovers, and doesn't charge."

"They like Duty here," Mason said.

"We are fortunate in that." She heard a knock. "Come. There is our breakfast." Mason brought in the tray and she cut Duty's steak, then took up her coffee. How strange that William, in a sense, had brought Mason here, with the gift of his mother's change purse.

Mason ate eggs and biscuits and put down his bowl of oatmeal, a third full. "Miss, I can't finish. Can Duty lick the plates?"

Emily shrugged. "Yes, no harm. I'm sure Duty has licked many plates." She watched the boy set the bowl down against the wall. "Now, Mason, could you read this aloud? It concerns our friend, Mr. Woods, and the Powers case."

Mason took the newspaper she offered, and read:

"Coley Woods, colored porter, is certain he carried Dorothy Lemke's baggage into the Gore Hotel at 1:30 A.M. on July 31. She arrived in a car driven by a male companion . . ."

"Good, Mason. How did you learn to read so well?"

"My mother used to teach me, with the Bible. She liked me to read it to her."

"That was wise of her; the Bible is not easy to read. As to your work, I must have a record of coverage about the crime and the trial,

486

under the correct date. You will save me time by clipping the articles, and picking up newspapers at the kiosk near the police station. You will charge these to my account; you may also charge meals from room service or the hotel tearoom. Always be professional, for you represent me, and the newspaper for which I write."

Duty sneezed, and jumped into Mason's lap.

"By 'professional,' I mean that you must look well groomed and be generally pleasant. Never dignify rude remarks by responding in kind."

"What if someone tries to hit me, or chase me?"

"Mason, if you present yourself differently, it's unlikely anyone will disrespect you. People are so influenced by appearances." She paused. "That's why I hope you will let me buy you a suit, and a warm coat, for you must look as though you read as well as you do. It was so good of your mother, to teach you to read the Bible. Do you mind if I ask what else she taught you?"

"I know some poems by Sir Walter Scott," he said, "and some by Mr. Robert Burns. My mother used to say them, and she liked me to tell them to her. One is about Scotland. My mother's father come from there, and taught her the words."

"I'd love to hear it," Emily said.

He stood and recited:

"My heart's in the Highlands, my heart is
    not here,
My heart's in the Highlands a-chasing the
    deer;
A-chasing the wild deer, and following the
    roe . . .
My heart's in the Highlands, wherever I go.
Farewell to the mountains high-covered
    with snow;
Farewell to the straths and green valleys
    below;
Farewell to the forests and wild-hanging
    woods . . ."

Emily smiled, but he was not looking at her;
his eyes were trained on a middle distance.
She heard a faint brogue in his voice. "Why,
that's beautiful, Mason, and you say it well."
He waited a moment, but he finished:

"My heart's in the Highlands, my heart is
    not here."

Emily saw the movement of his head, the
near wince, the blink of his eyes, and realized
she should not have asked him to recite; the
words could only remind him of his mother,
who may have died as he sat helplessly beside
her. "These mountains seem like highlands
to me." She hoped to distract him. "I grew

up in Chicago, in the winters, but spent summers on my grandparents' Iowa farm, after my father died. They died as well, but I was grown by then."

"My mam took sick last winter," Mason volunteered, "and he never took her to a doctor. He just let her lay there. He said 'twas no use, she had the same as her sisters."

"And what was that?"

"She just took a'bed and stopped eating, but for the soup she taught me to make. Meat cut small, rabbit or squirrel, some bones for marrow, carrots and spring onion we grew, salt and chicory, 'taters if they wasn't green. And she had me put up, for winter."

"Canning, do you mean? Preserving?" Emily encouraged him, for he seemed to want to speak of her.

"Yes, miss. I hid the jars, or he shot them for targets, when he run out of bottles."

"Did your father teach you to steal, Mason? To pick pockets?"

"Oh, he did, miss. He said it were the one thing I could do."

"Did he? Well, he is mistaken. You will put your quick mind to far better use. Perhaps one day, you will teach others, as your mother taught you."

He looked at her, doubtful, until she mentioned his mother, and his eyes lightened. "She said I was like her." He nodded as though to himself, then cast his eyes down.

"My father said, often enough, that I were no son of his."

"Mason," Emily said, "you will be your own man."

He only glanced at her with questioning eyes.

"We must purchase warm clothes. And a haircut. Do you mind?"

"No, miss. I want to look . . . professional."

"Fine," she said. "I'll dress, and then we'll go, and give Duty a walk, as well."

Emily led him down the stairs to the street; she wanted to go directly to the haberdasher's. "Mason, does anyone else at the hotel, other than Mr. Woods, know you?"

Mason held Duty's leash. "No. I don't think he wanted anyone to see he was giving me food, or letting me shine shoes." He walked head down, his bare hands in the pockets of his mother's coat, the leash looped around his wrist. The loose coat, like a cloak, flared up in the wind.

"I see," Emily said. "Let's go this way, down Pike Street. I believe I saw a sign for a men's and boys' shop." Pine garlands swung above them, between the gas lamps. "They certainly decorate for the holidays," Emily said, "just as in Chicago."

"Clarksburg is the biggest town around," offered Mason.

"It's a lovely town, and the park is so near

our hotel. Here we are." Emily stepped into the store vestibule, out of the wind. Mason stood back doubtfully. "Come in. You must try things on, to know they fit. Yes?"

He followed her in and stood nervously by, removing his hat, as a clerk wearing a tape measure around her neck approached them.

"Good day," Emily said. "We need to outfit my nephew. He's outgrown his things completely. Please show him what you have that works with brown, and he will choose."

The clerk nodded. "Young man, the dressing room is in the back."

Mason came out, finally, in a brown suit that set off his dark hair and eyes. Emily could not help remembering that Hart Eicher was not yet into his first long pants, when Powers took him away. "Splendid," Emily said.

"And now," said the clerk. "Leather brogans for indoors, and warm boots. Snowstorms here go on for days." She looked over at Mason. "The skating pond is frozen already."

Emily remembered Hart's ice skates, still in her valise. Mason was slighter than Hart looked in photographs. "Can one rent skates, at the small park there?"

"Oh, yes, miss, when the kiosk is open." The clerk looked from Emily to Mason. "Young man, I'll call the salesman who deals with men's shoes. And I'll bring several overcoats."

Emily watched her go. "Do you like the clothes, Mason? I think your mother would be very pleased, to see you dressed well."

He sat up a bit straighter.

The shoe salesman came to measure Mason's feet, and Emily stood to peruse a rack of men's scarves. He must choose one himself, and a warm winter cap.

"Ma'am?" The clerk presented Mason, in a winter coat of brown herringbone. He wore a matching cap, with earmuffs that pulled down.

Emily asked, "Which scarf do you like, Mason?"

He looked at them. "The white one," he said.

"Excellent." Emily paid cash. "Please deliver the boxes to the Gore Hotel. Here is my card." She took the clerk's hand. "We thank you so much."

Mason, noting her gesture, shook hands as well. "Thank you, ma'am."

Outside, Emily gave Duty's leash into his gloved hand and straightened the collar on the coat. "There," she said, "you look professional and handsome. More important, are you warm?"

He nodded shyly and walked with her back toward the Gore, to the large newspaper kiosk across from the police station. Construction on the new courthouse progressed despite the weather, and tall stacks of yellow brick, covered in canvas, lay inert as monuments. She glimpsed the town library, and determined to take Mason tomorrow to get a library card. He could go on his own then.

"Mason," she said, turning to the kiosk, "we will learn the proprietor's name; you must always address him formally."

They stood before the large display of magazines in racks, and stacks of newspapers. "Sir?" Emily called up to the man in the stall. "Do you remember me from last summer? Emily Thornhill, journalist from the *Chicago Tribune*? I'm here to cover the Powers trial, and this is my nephew, Mason Phillips, who will be assisting me."

The man put his cigar aside. "Ma'am," he said, "Murphy." He touched her fingers over the distance, and Mason's as well.

"Mr. Murphy, we will need the newspapers on this list, morning and evening editions, starting today." She took the list from her purse. "Mason will be picking them up, morning and afternoon, on my account, and I will need a weekly receipt. I'd like to pay you now for the first week."

"He's your clipping service, is he?" The man peered down.

Emily nodded. "Your enterprise here is impressive, Mr. Murphy. You have everything through the East and Midwest, and even West Coast papers. Do you sell sandwiches, as well?"

"Just hot pretzels, coffee, hot chocolate."

"I'm sure, in this cold. Mason can order whatever he likes. Just put it on my account."

"I recommend the hot chocolate," said a voice behind her.

She turned to see Sheriff Grimm, clad in a long dark overcoat. "Sheriff Grimm. Of course, you're just across the street." She felt her gloved hand enclosed in his, and turned to Mason. "This is Mason Phillips, my nephew. He has time off from school to assist me, and collect the newspapers from Mr. Murphy."

Grimm looked at Mason. "You've brought the dog, and your nephew as well. Good to meet you, Mason."

Mason offered a serious expression, shook Grimm's hand, and said nothing.

Emily was glad they'd gone to the haberdasher's first. She prayed Grimm would not ask Mason the name of his school, or any number of things she could not anticipate.

"Murphy," he called up to the proprietor, by way of greeting. "We'll have three hot chocolates. And I know you'll show these visitors every consideration." Grimm regarded Emily with the inclusive gaze that seemed to take her measure. "You're here well in advance, Miss Thornhill."

"I came down by the station to see you yesterday," Emily answered, "but it was . . . crowded. I'll call for an appointment."

494

He was reaching for the cups of hot chocolate. "Starting tomorrow, no one goes in or out but my officers. Law will conduct press interviews from his office, as will the prosecutor. Powers is back in custody, and all other prisoners are at the county jail. The curious persist in gaping, but if the press is elsewhere, the curious may follow."

"I'm sure," Emily said. "Mason, careful, the chocolate is steaming. Thank you, Sheriff. Just what we needed."

He turned to Emily. "Miss Thornhill, I suggest we meet at the Gore in an hour. I hope you'll allow me to buy you lunch."

"Of course, Sheriff." Emily signed her account and paid Murphy cash. She watched Grimm approach the police station; the group clustered by the door parted at his approach.

"Master Phillips," said Murphy. He handed over a cloth sling bag of newspapers. "My newsboys carry these. Bring it each day and I'll have your papers ready."

Mason slung the bag over his shoulder. "Thank you, Mr. Murphy. And you can call me Mason."

The man would watch out for him, Emily knew.

They walked back to the hotel through hastening snow. "It's good that we ran into Sheriff Grimm," Emily said. "He knows your name now, and has made it clear to Mr. Murphy that he must deal fairly with us. I mentioned that you don't carry cash — I don't want anyone bothering you. But do stay in this general vicinity. I realize you know the area well, but I need to know you're safe."

"All right."

They'd reached the shelter of the Gore Hotel awning, which snapped overhead like a flag, and were inside quickly.

"Miss Thornhill, and Duty." Mr. Parrish greeted her from the desk. "And who is this?"

"Mr. Parrish, good day. This is my nephew, Mason Phillips. He's assisting me through the trial. He'll be in Room 126, adjoining mine. Please bill my account."

"Very well. Your age, Mason?"

"Twelve," Mason said, "on Christmas Eve."

"A Christmas birthday. And not so far off!" Parrish smiled approvingly.

Emily was about to congratulate Mason on his auspicious birthday but caught herself. She would know her nephew's birthday.

"Miss Thornhill, numerous parcels are delivered for you. The porter is here."

Coley Woods was piling the parcels on the cart; they followed him to the elevator and then to the room.

Mason looked shyly up at him.

"Mr. Woods, I was unaware that you were acquainted with my nephew, Mason Phillips. I want to thank you for your kindness to him in the past."

Woods merely inclined his head. "No need to speak of it."

"Mason," Emily said, "would you lay the newspapers out on your table? I'll be right in." She waited a moment. "Mr. Woods, I've hired this boy to help me, and given him a place to sleep. Do you think I've made a mistake?"

Woods' attentive gaze fell over her. "No, ma'am. I think he is a good boy. And better off with you, than in the alley behind the hotel. I hope it works out, ma'am. It don't seem he has anyone, here."

"No. Though I'm . . . not thinking ahead, beyond the trial."

"Course not. No sense crossing a bridge until you feel your feet on the planks. But no one will ever know from me, ma'am, that he was sleeping in the alley."

She moved to press a folded five-dollar bill into his hand. "Please take this, in some thanks for your kindness to him."

He stood back. "No thanks is due for charity, ma'am. I thank you for taking him in. I could not do it myself." He was gone before she could reply.

Emily felt a bit light-headed and went to the window. The child's birthday was Christmas Eve. Where would he be, and with whom? Surely not with his drunken father. She opened the window wide to feel the snow on her face.

"I've got them ready," Mason said behind her.

She turned to him. "I was getting some air. I love snow, don't you?"

"Sometimes. It can be awful cold."

She shut the window. "Let's see what you have."

He led her into his room, where he'd put the newspapers on the long table. Emily gathered scissors, glue, and tape, and stacked the large scrapbooks she'd packed for clippings.

"Pull the armchairs over, Mason. You must be comfortable. Start with the local papers. Harry Powers is Cornelius Pierson; that was a name he claimed, an alias, so you will see both names, and his real name, Harm Drenth, but he is charged as Powers. See?"

Mason lay the open paper flat before them. "He bought them ice cream."

Emily sat beside him. "You needn't read everything, only enough to organize the clippings." She saw him scanning the words, so sat beside him to read the article. What had Powers to do with ice cream?

SLAYER GOT OUT OF CAR IN NORWOOD
Local Barber Identifies Powers from Photographs: A witness . . . saw Harry F. Powers, alias Herman Drenth, mass slayer, in an automobile near Clarksburg, Harrison County, with the three children of Mrs. Asta

Buick Eicher. . . . "Powers drove up to the Norwood confectionery store," said Eugene Averill, barber of Hazelwood Avenue, Norwood. "Powers purchased three ice cream cones. . . . He then drove away with the children in the direction of Clarksburg."

She told herself he would have followed the case regardless, living in the town. "Does it bother you, reading the clippings?"

"No. It's like a detective story. Here is another, with the Powers name."

"Yes, it's about Powers' attorney — his lawyer."

"Look, this one says about Sheriff Grimm." Mason outlined the newsprint borders of the story.

Plea for Powers Uncertain, Third Degree Alleged: J. Ed Law, Clarksburg attorney for Powers . . . said he had obtained a court order . . . for removal of the prisoner from Grimm's custody.

"What is this word? And, *third degree?*" Mason asked.

"*Alleged* means 'unproven,' " Emily said. "Mason, I will get us a dictionary. It's good to look up words and see the meanings. As for *third degree,* Law is saying the police were . . . too forceful."

"Law is the lawyer? Because of his name?"

She saw merriment in his eyes. "I know! It's happenstance, or a coincidence. Law must know Powers is guilty, but . . . Law might say he is defending the law! Do you suppose?"

Mason smiled widely.

"Look," Emily said, "here's one more item in the *Telegram.*"

Trial of Powers, alias Herman Drenth . . . will be held in *Moore's Opera House* on South Fourth Street . . . use of the building is $500 a week. . . . *Moore's Opera House* has a rear entrance back of the stage which can be used in taking the prisoner to and from the scene of the trial. The Opera House has a seating capacity *of at least* 1,250.

"It must be very big!" Mason said.

"Yes. So, they've decided on the opera house, and they plan to hold the trial onstage. That is so completely wrong."

"Why?" Mason asked.

"Because it is a trial about the loss of five lives, not a play or musical review. Do you see?" She sighed. "I condemn them, but I myself will take my place in the audience."

"Will I go?"

"I will take you inside, but not to the trial. Bad enough that you will read about the case. Now, I must go. You have the room service

500

menu. Order if you get hungry. I shall be back in an hour or so. Let's see how long you need for this lot."

Grimm sat at their usual table, at the rear of the tearoom, his hat and folded topcoat on the chair beside him. He stood as she arrived. "Miss Thornhill."

"Sheriff." She took off her own hat and smoothed her hair, taking her notebook from her valise. "Thank you for updating me. I'm sure you're busy. I saw that the opera house is engaged for the trial, and that Law is, shall we say, actively defending Powers."

"Law is sharp and somewhat conniving, and interested in public office. He was state's attorney for a number of years, but wins more attention and income with high-profile cases. He will take a self-righteous tone on behalf of blind justice. The prosecutor, Will Morris, is able, if not as ambitious." He signaled the waiter. "The 'special' is chicken croquettes. Acceptable?"

"Certainly, thank you. Law won't succeed in his charges, I assume."

"Law is setting a tone for the press, to open the trial with a smoke screen of protest, which Judge Southern will acknowledge and dismiss." Grimm stopped speaking, discreetly, to address the waiter. "The special, for both of us, and hot coffee." He looked pleased for a moment, and sat back expansively. His open jacket revealed his vest and watch chain, and his powerful torso.

"So," he said.

The word was a subtle breach. She glimpsed a slim shoulder holster and derringer fit tight to his waist, and steeled her expression to meet his gaze. Grimm was almost professionally discreet, but he would see her with William during the trial, in proximity to William on the street or across a room, and know; he took her temperature with every glance. Regardless, his counsel was essential. Inside the case, they shared a dark ethos. She did not care that Powers was beaten, that Grimm had supervised or skillfully beaten him; she knew what Powers was. And Grimm, despite the slow mechanics of charges and trial, posturing and show, took personal responsibility: he would see the case won.

She remembered Mason, upstairs. "Sheriff Grimm, might you have a dictionary you could lend me? It's useful for Mason to look up words he doesn't understand, in the newspapers."

"You're sure you want him understanding what he reads about Powers?"

"He's a perceptive boy."

"All the more reason he should be doing sums in class, and going ice skating."

"The world is as it is, Sheriff Grimm, and I am here to guide him. If justice ensues, he may feel he played a small part."

"It is your affair, Miss Thornhill. I'll leave a dictionary for you at the reception desk." He paused. "I want to tell you, now that it's certain, that Powers will be charged with five counts of murder, but prosecuted for the murder of Dorothy Lemke."

"Only for Lemke?"

"The evidence against him is circumstantial, and most overwhelming in her case. But the Eicher murders cannot be mentioned in court, except as they pertain to method and motive in Lemke's death."

"The Eichers will not be mentioned?" For a moment, she could not catch her breath.

"They will be mentioned indirectly. Morris will get it in, but the jury will be instructed to disregard any statement concerning them, in coming to a verdict." He leaned toward her. "Powers can only hang once."

"Will he?"

"He will. The state will see him hung."

"The world should know exactly what he did," Emily said.

"There's no need. I must ask you to maintain confidence in that matter." He nodded, unsmiling, over her head at the waiter, who set plates before them. He waited, and continued. "We have numerous inquiries from relatives of missing women who suspect Powers, convinced they recognize his photograph.

Pure supposition. The Lemke case is strongest."

Emily looked at the food, her heart pounding. She thought of Hart Eicher, resisting. "This myth of the deadly ladies' man he no doubt enjoys, the fame he will retain . . ."

"He'll retain nothing; he will be executed and cease to exist. You don't look well. Are you faint?" He took a slim flask from his suit jacket pocket and poured a bit of brandy in her coffee. "Drink it. You're as pale as this tablecloth."

She sipped it, and pushed the food away. "Perhaps there should be a hell, for some offenses."

"Do you want some air?"

"I'm sorry. I'm all right. It's unprofessional to be . . . so angry."

"Is it? I don't think so. You found Drenth, and his record. I knew you would."

"Yes."

"Miss Thornhill, how did you know the doll was in the car, and exactly where?"

"I don't know. One gets hunches that are not always correct. I thank you for acting on what I told you." She must get word to Eric. Charles O'Boyle need not attend the trial.

Grimm took a small parcel from the chair beside him. "I suppose it's a theft of sorts, from the people, but it seems a restoration as well. Only the Lemke case will be tried, and I don't want the child's doll to stay in a box of state's evidence. I consider it personal property, and return it to you."

"That is her doll?"

"Yes."

"It can't be used as evidence?"

"It cannot. Will you take it?"

They stood, and he gave it into her hands.

Emily let herself into her room to see Duty sitting on her bed, and a carefully stacked room service tray on the bureau. "Good. You've had lunch, and a walk, I'm sure." She put her valise beside the dog and went to Mason's room. "How are you getting on?"

"Finished with this morning's clippings."

"Mason, we should go to the park. Do you ice skate?"

"We used to, my mother and me, along the stream, with blades tied to our boots. She taught me to skate a circle."

"Did she? Hart Eicher loved skating, by the worn look of his skates. I brought them with me — I was given some of the children's possessions when the Eicher estate was sold last summer."

"I could try them," Mason said.

"I don't mind renting you skates, Mason. I shall have to rent my own. And Hart was a bit huskier than you —"

"It would be good to use them. We always used what we had."

Of course they did, thought Emily, and took

the skates from her closet.

"They feel right, I think," Mason said, trying them on. He stood, the skates laced. "But I never wore ice skates before, like these."

Emily knelt to feel the hard toes and worn leather. Mason was small for his age. Perhaps he would hit a growth spurt and catch up to his feet, for the skates fit. "Goodness," she said, "they fit nicely. And they can sharpen the blades at the rental kiosk."

"Would he mind, though?" Mason looked up at her. "Mind someone using his skates."

"I'm not sure those who are gone still think of such things. And you are caring for Hart's dog, that he loved so. Surely he'd be pleased if you use his skates. I'll rent a pair, and we'll give it a try, shall we?" She was putting her desk to rights.

"Look, Duty is following you. He thinks you brought him something from lunch." Mason nodded at the dog, who stood by her, holding in his mouth the parcel Grimm had given her.

"Duty! You took that from my valise. It is not a toy!" Of course, she thought, it was a toy, and very familiar to Duty.

"What is it?" Mason asked.

"It's — Well, I'll show you later. Let me know when you're ready and we'll" — she took the parcel from the floor — "go out." Duty followed Mason back to his room. She put the doll into her bureau; she could not

506

bring herself to unwrap the parcel and searched instead among her papers for Annabel Eicher's notebook. The typescript "A Play for Christmas" was here, from the estate sale. She was sure it mentioned the doll. In their first August interview, hadn't Charles O'Boyle said the doll was in the play? Here it was, listed among *The Players: The Grandmother — Mrs. Pomeroy (voiced by Annabel Eicher).*

Emily looked through the pages. The story had to do with baby birds saved in a shoe, and the end was a Christmas carol.

Christmas would come, even to this place.

"I'm ready," Mason said. He stood in the doorway, holding his winter coat, scarf, hat.

Emily looked at him and knew she must take him with her, and fight to do so, if the father objected.

"Are we going?"

She met his pleased gaze. "Yes, only not quite yet."

"Duty, do you smell a treat in there?" Mason put his coat on her bed and leaned over the dog, who sat by her bureau.

"Mason, a rag doll that belonged to Annabel Eicher is in that drawer. It was returned to me today. I don't see how it's possible that Duty knows, or smells a scent, when the doll has been sealed up for so many months."

"Should we give it to him?"

"I don't know, Mason." She stood and moved to the foot of the bed. "But do, please, take it out of the drawer and unwrap it."

Carefully, Mason took the parcel and put it on her bed. He withdrew the shrouded doll, which was wrapped in white cloth tied with twine. Mason slipped the twine aside and opened the cloth.

"So," Emily said, "this is Mrs. Pomeroy."

The small rag doll was seven or eight inches long, with cloth limbs, sewn-on features, yarn hair. The dress was muslin, once a shade of pink, worn very soft. The pinafore had been white. A scrap of round gold braid wrapped the waist, like a belt. Felt sewn to the feet, meant to suggest shoes, was nearly worn away.

Emily smoothed the doll's dress and picked it up. The back, and the cloth hands and feet, were stained dark; it must have fallen or lain on a muddy surface before Annabel pushed it deeply into the crease of the backseat. The face and the front of the dress were only slightly discolored, and looked almost as they must have appeared last July, on the journey to Quiet Dell.

"You said Duty ran after them." Mason knelt to lift Duty and his basket onto the bed. "Dogs remember a long time, in their way."

"I suppose they do." Emily put Mrs. Pomeroy in a corner of the basket, and the dog lay down, smelling the doll as though to be certain, and curled near, one paw upon it.

"Maybe he was still trying to find them,"

Mason said, "and now he thinks he has."

"Let's hope so," Emily said. "Shall we leave him to rest, and walk to the skating pond?" She turned to the window. "It's a lovely, fleecy snow. The wind has picked up but the sun is shining."

Together, they went to look. Snow fell steadily through the bright air, blanketing streets and sidewalks, the hotel awning, the long dark curves of parked cars. Snow layered merchants' signs and the limbs of trees, dusting passersby who, glancing up, wet their eyes and lips, and hurried on.

Annabel likes to dart about after the gentleman with the luggage, in and out of the elevator, and follow him when he pushes the cart to stop at numbered doors. She knocks when he knocks, races to the end of the corridor and back before anyone answers, whirls into the room before him. She might pass through one wall and another, into the air along the windy streets, or see him wheel the rattling cart to the elevator and dash inside, her hand upon the cart. She fancies he knows she's there, for he hums the same hymn every time or whistles it low until the doors open. Duty, their last day home, lunged at the pantry door and wriggled through, racing for their scent and the sharp, silencing boot, but Emily has brought Mrs. Pomeroy to him at last.

Annabel must see. She looks down at the

saved bundle, so small on Emily's big white bed. The boy bends to unwrap the cloth; Annabel puts her hands in his, almost touching, feeling. Mrs. Pomeroy is changed, and muddy on her back, but no one must wash her; the smell Duty wants is on her dress, and the cord must stay round her. Annabel must leave her, for the darkening road at Quiet Dell is cold now, the ruts and puddles frozen dry. Snow has filled the holes and rushes along the highway into town.

Annabel loves the clean cold snow and fierce wind; she pulls the storm with her, circling the hotel, blinding streets and passersby, filling the empty alley. The snow is fugue and counterpoint, a contrapuntal pounding; she plays *pianissimo, staccato, forte, glissando;* the gusting wind is a deep broad phrase, and Grandmother accompanies her right-handed, tossing away the falling pages. *Da capo,* she nods, turning and whirling; she sets the metronome's *tick tick* and whispers, over the hours and days below, *diminuendo.*

■ ■ ■ ■

XIV.

■ ■ ■ ■

"Yes!" said the child. . . . "Home, for good and all. Home, forever and ever. Father is so much kinder than he used to be . . . home's like Heaven! He spoke so gently to me one dear night when I was going to bed, that I was not afraid to ask him once more if you might come home; and he said Yes, you should; and sent me in a coach to bring you. And you're to be a man!"

— Charles Dickens, *A Christmas Carol*

DECEMBER 4–6, 1931
CLARKSBURG, WEST VIRGINIA

EMILY THORNHILL: A PRELUDE

The trial would begin in three days. William and Eric were flying to Clarksburg with Chicago journalists this afternoon. The snows had stopped last week, and runnels of melting ice were heard in the streets, but storms were forecast.

"It's snowing," said Mason, beside her at the window. "But not much."

He was learning to sense her preoccupations. "Yes," Emily said. The glowering skies and errant flakes were mere foreshadowing.

Mason took a conversational tone. "Mr. Malone and Mr. Lindstrom — do they ice skate?"

"Oh yes, and both well, I'd wager. You improve daily, Mason, but they shall have to be patient with me." She rested her hand on his shoulder. "I'm a bit nervous that they arrive. They'll both stay here at the Gore. I told you that Mr. Lindstrom has worked closely with me on this case — we've been to Clarks-

513

burg twice before. He's rather dashing and quite droll. Do you know that word? It means, to be funny in a quick, understated way. Useful for a journalist. Eric grew up privileged, and has every confidence."

"Did he go to a good school?"

"Oh yes, several of them." Emily looked down at him. "Everyone needn't be droll, Mason. You would do well at a good school. You are so clever. Plenty of dull boys go to good schools."

"Then why are they there?"

She laughed. "They have families with money and reputation, or perhaps just money, while the boys with no money, with manners and a connection, are often smartest and work hardest." She could tell he was marking her words. "Some use privilege to do good, Mason."

"I read about Mr. Malone in the clippings," Mason said.

The wind shook the glass in the panes. They both felt it and stepped closer to the window. The snow was heavier so quickly, blown and whirling. The clock in the room chimed three.

Emily clasped her hands. The boy had likely heard country people rail against bankers, as well they should. "Mr. Malone, as you know from the newspapers, does good."

"Is he . . . droll?" Mason asked.

"No, actually," Emily said. She felt nearly blinded with anxiety, and peered into the snow. They should have landed. They should be at the hotel. She turned away from the window and sat, facing the door. "Mason, why not tidy your work? I know Eric will want to read through it, perhaps tomorrow after he's rested."

"You don't want me to wait with you?"

"No. Go along now, and shut your door, so that I won't bother you." She thought of her plane ride to Iowa in perfect summer skies and could not imagine suspension in such furious air. She must simply concentrate on bringing William to her through miles of tumbling cloud. She heard the wind and the silvery ping of sleet. Mason was in his room and then back, his hand on her arm as though rousing her.

"Someone's knocking. At my door."

"Your door?" Of course, William knew she had both rooms. She stood and walked to the adjoining room, Mason beside her like a shadow, and composed herself, hearing the soft repetitive knock. She opened the door wide, stunned with relief.

He'd come directly to her, moisture sparkling on his coat, his bags on the carpet beside him.

"Mr. Malone," she said, and felt herself in his arms. It was in her eyes, she knew.

"Miss Thornhill." He inclined his head, as though to a stranger on the street, and looked at Mason. "And who is this?"

"This is Mason Phillips, my archivist."

"I see. How do you do, Mason?"

"Very well, sir." He shook William's hand firmly, as she'd taught him, then glanced at her and half turned toward his worktable. "Excuse me, sir, I was just doing these here."

He was trying to remove himself, she thought, from what must seem confusing, but they were in his room and he had nowhere to go. He put his hands on an open newspaper as though to turn the pages.

"I don't mean to interrupt," William said. "Miss Thornhill, my room is down the hall. At your convenience, I should appreciate an update on the trial and your coverage."

"In ten minutes' time, should we say?"

"Yes, certainly." He paused. "I would like to see the courthouse and the opera house. I understand it's a short walk?"

"Yes, both are near the Gore."

"In that case, let us meet in the lobby. Dress for the weather — the snow has turned to sleet." He moved his gaze over her, for Mason was back at his table and could not see them.

She offered him an expression of surprise. "Of course, Mr. Malone. I shall join you . . . very soon."

He was waiting near the door, and they were immediately outside. He wore a calf-length wool coat that hung loose from his broad shoulders, and a thick black angora scarf.

Sleet pelted the hotel awning and slicked the sidewalks; he opened a large umbrella over them. No one was in the streets. The sky was the color of pewter and the day was darkening.

"My darling, thank heavens you are here." She took his arm, for the umbrella sheltered them from view. "You have not kissed me. Whatever is the matter? Was it an awful flight?"

"It was a bit turbulent, but nothing is the matter. I need some air, and some sleet, I suppose, after the plane, to . . . acclimate."

"Are you queasy?"

He laughed, and put his gloved hand on hers. "No, love. I am relieved, and thinking very clearly. It was more than turbulent. The plane slid off the runway and would have flipped over, but for a stand of accommodating fir trees, loaded with snow."

"William!" She stopped and turned to him. "You didn't tell me! You weren't hurt? No one was hurt?"

"Oh no. It was . . . a spiritual exercise. Your friend Eric was seated beside me. I believe we have bonded forever."

"One does bond in that fashion, with Eric. Now you must kiss me, so many times. Oh, I knew — Must we keep walking?"

"Yes, to some shelter, outdoors perhaps. Is there anywhere near?" The sound of the sleet abated, but he held the umbrella before them to break the wind.

"I'll take you to the skating pond in the park. The Victorian gazebo will certainly be unoccupied. We turn here. It's just there, two blocks down, gaslit at night, quite pretty. I brought Hart's ice skates with me, don't ask why, and they fit Mason. I rent a pair at the kiosk. We bring Duty and skate almost every afternoon."

"Emily, who in the world is that boy?"

"He was a street urchin, picking pockets, and very well, so I hired him. He's my archivist, and clips all the coverage —"

"I realize. Does it seem, a rather grim pastime for a child?"

She smiled. "Grim, did you say?"

"Yes, I met Grimm, on arriving at the Gore. In any event —"

"It is surely less grim than living on the streets, prey to any manner of person. His father is a drunk and petty thief who beat him; he is an only child, like us, William — who tried to care for his mother, and sat beside her as she died."

They entered the park, sheltered by enormous pines that broke the wind. The gazebo before them, with its dark slate roof and chest-high, white clapboard walls, seemed a circular boat on a lake of snow. A small matching kiosk, the skate rental, closed and padlocked, bordered the pond.

Emily clasped William's arm. "Isn't it

beautiful? I've longed to show you this place."

"Emily," he said.

"William, I know what you will say, but say it."

"The boy's father is a drunk and a thief; the boy is a thief. His background, sadly, is established; you cannot erase it. He is not an infant, whom you might influence early on. How can you trust such a child?"

"How might he trust me, is more to the point. It will take time. He's intelligent, very, I think, though he went intermittently to a country school. His mother taught him at home, from the Bible and her own books; he knows half a volume of Robert Burns by heart, which he used to recite to her. He relishes organization, and learns quickly."

"How old is he?"

"He turns twelve on Christmas Eve, though looks a bit younger."

"He is Hart's age."

"Yes. Many children are Hart's age."

The skating pond lay before them, the ice glistening and dark. The gazebo was empty; the numerous benches were pushed aside. William put his arm around her and led her up the steps. "Here," he said, "out of the wind, with a clear view of the wood."

"Yes, and the mountains beyond. Magnificent, aren't they? And harbor such difficult lives. The miners live out there, up impassable roads, in houses that are not heated or plumbed. They live as the first settlers lived, two hundred years ago."

"Are you cold?" He pulled her close on the bench.

"No one can see us here," she said, and sat on his lap, embracing him, her face in his warm throat. "Oh, I long for you too much. I must put you out of my mind until we are speaking or touching."

He opened his coat to enclose her. "Put me out of your mind? We can't have that. You are on my mind, in my mind, always." He lifted her face, to kiss her, small kisses against her skin. "You are the air I breathe, the air itself."

She pulled off her gloves and put her hands inside his shirt, on his skin. "You have a key for me, to your room?"

"Of course." He buttoned his voluminous coat around her to enclose her completely, and pulled up the generous collar to shield them both. "Emily —"

The wind quieted. Snow fell haphazardly in big errant flakes. "Shall we go back to the hotel?"

"Soon."

"You want to talk to me before you ravish me."

"That is exactly right." He smiled, laughing with her, his face in her hair.

"It's a compliment, I suppose."

"Emily, it's important." He drew back to look at her.

"All right." She felt a tremor of fear but put her hands against his throat, to feel his voice, and met his eyes. She'd seen them well with tears, and startle in ecstasy, and yield to her across a room.

His eyes held hers. "If you want a child, we can have a child. There is no impediment."

She did not speak at once. The wind, gusting across them to the wood, seemed to take her words. She drew closer against him. "William — if we'd met much sooner — I would love to have had a child with you . . . you should have children —"

"Emily, we could have a child. You are young enough. It is not too late, if that is what you want. There is no lack of funds. I told you about the apartment in Paris, that my grandfather purchased years ago. We could have the child there, and you could adopt it —"

"Adopt my own child? So we are talking fairy tales and secrets."

"You speak French. You could work from Paris for a time. I'm talking with associates about a financial venture there. We could live in Paris every summer, completely freely, and continue in Chicago, as before, in a larger apartment, with help for you, so that you could go on working."

They sat without speaking, watching snow come on from behind the mountains, stirring the faraway evergreens and concealing the distant hills. The storm approached like a curtain moving within itself.

"Here is the snow. I'm so glad you're safe." She kissed him slowly, deeply, and said, against his mouth, "So, you have thought about this, before today."

"I have been thinking about it for weeks."

"But you did not mention it until today."

"Emily, it seems the time to mention it."

"Because you feel I am entered into a folly."

"I don't know. Are you? Why did you not mention the boy to me, in any conversation?"

"At first I didn't know that the arrangement would even last until you arrived, and then I thought it better that you get to know him yourself. William, I have simply hired an assistant of sorts, and given a boy a place to sleep and food to eat. But, this child of whom you speak — do you have a burning desire for a child?"

He held her face in his gloved hands. "My desires . . . are completely satisfied."

"Then we are fortunate, because I don't want to share you with an infant, even our infant. As it is, I must share you, and wait for you." She looked at him. "Are you disappointed in me?"

"No. My disappointment does not live in any world you inhabit."

Snow grew thick about them, blowing like cold dust into the gazebo, falling in heavy slants onto the woods and frozen pond. She saw his eyes change and moisten, and reached inside his clothes. "Only turn this way," she whispered, for they were sitting at the end of the bench, and she must get her legs behind him. There was no impediment; she'd inserted her pessary and left her undergarments aside an hour ago, for she'd thought they would go directly to his room. She wore only her garter belt and wool stockings under her skirt. His hands found her bare thighs and hips and were inside her; she pulled up layers of fabric and bent her knees behind him, to brace him against her.

He moved farther to the edge and held her on his thighs, in his hands, just enough away to thrust inside her, and stay. Each time was more intense, and they held themselves from one another, to look and see, as they had looked at one another that first day in his office, and not touched.

The snow was blinding beyond their shelter. They were wholly enclosed, for the gaslights and pond were barely visible. The street and buildings opposite had disappeared. "We are absolutely alone," Emily said, and breathed, "it is our storm." Then language deserted her.

Snow fell into the evening. She stood at the reception desk to ask for her messages. William was having dinner with Morris, the prosecutor in the case. She would hear it all later, and had dined with Mason at the Gore restaurant as he subtly counted the new guests; there were thirty. Only first arrivals, she'd assured him; trains were delayed in the storm. He'd informed her that the Gore telegraph operators had given him leave to hold Emily's place in line, at every break in the trial, so that she could file quickly. He was a wonder. She wished she were teaching him literature or art history rather than newspaper coverage of a heinous crime, but fortune had introduced them here and now. She'd sent him upstairs, for they were just in from walking the dog. How might she help him feel comfortable with William, with Eric, and provide them demonstration of Mason's qualities? She determined to have dinner for the four of them in her rooms.

"Miss Thornhill, you have messages." Parrish put them in her hand.

"Mr. Parrish, I want to order room service dinner for four, tomorrow evening at seven. May I order from the restaurant menu?"

"Of course, ma'am. Simply write your order, and sign it." He produced the menu and a sheet of Gore Hotel stationery.

"It will be my nephew and me, and the two gentlemen from Chicago, Mr. Malone and Mr. Lindstrom. I shall write notes to be delivered to them. Is that all right?"

"I shall see to it, ma'am."

She opened her own messages: a note from Eric: *Survived flight. Must repair psyche. Din-*

ner tomorrow? The second was from Grimm. *I have news. Tearoom, 8 p.m.* It was eight now. "Mr. Parrish," she said across the desk, "I need to meet with an associate. Might I send up hot chocolate for Mason?"

"Of course, ma'am. Mr. Woods will take the order up, and let the boy know you are delayed."

She nodded her thanks, aware that Grimm's news likely concerned Mason. The boy had left home nearly two months ago, but she must know how to contact the father. Last week, in the calm before the trial, she'd taken Grimm into her confidence. He liked Mason and was certainly the one to advise her. She could not leave Mason here, and must seek his father's permission to do otherwise.

Grimm sat at the table in the corner, tea service for two before him. Their meetings here were no longer confidential; numerous tables were occupied.

"You've been out in the weather." He stood to take her coat, then sat, openly appreciative, watching her.

She shook the snow from her hat, a fox hat in the Russian style, and wondered with whom Grimm spent nights such as this. He had a woman, more than one, she was sure. She sipped her tea, and regarded him. "So, Sheriff Grimm? Did you find Mason's house, in that place?"

"Near Coalton, up a hollow from the town. I'll tell you straight out, the father is dead, was dead for some days when we found him. Snow was blown onto his bed. That a child should live in such a hovel, with a drunken father whose filth was piled around him even before he froze to death —"

"You're certain? The man was Mason's father?"

"The county sheriff was with me, and knew him. Neighbors identified him as well."

"Is there anything, to be given Mason?"

"From that shack? I think not. They were tenants, and the father had smashed what they had. There's a marked grave behind the house. The mother, neighbors said, died last fall. We helped a neighbor bury the father beside her, and finished as the snow began." Grimm folded his hands and looked at Emily. "Mason is an orphan. He will likely go to Pruntytown, if you don't take him."

"What is Pruntytown?"

"Industrial School for Boys. They're taught a trade, but it's no orphanage. Young thieves, beggars, grifters."

Emily squared her shoulders and leaned forward. "Of course I will take him. Can you help me? I must be responsible for his care, his schooling."

"If you're certain, a legal guardianship is easiest to arrange. There will be documents to sign. The Randolph County clerk will

526

search files for record of Mason's birth, and I have copies of the parents' death certificates. No siblings, and no known family." He paused. "Will you tell him of his father's death?"

"Yes, I must," Emily said. "It's terrible, though will be a relief to him, surely, but I must have an alternative to offer before giving him such news."

"I'll let you know when the papers are drawn up. Dissuade him from going back there. The state of the place —"

"Of course. I understand." She stood.

"You know, gratitude can be a heavy weight. You might consider that trouble could arise at some point."

She took up her coat and hat. "I consider what Mason endured. Thankfully, he knew a mother's love. I look forward to hearing from you."

"Yes, soon. We must accomplish this before the trial."

"Good night, then. You know . . . how sincerely I thank you."

His frank look was his reply. She felt his gaze as she walked away, and a mild chill as she gained the hotel stairs. Walking the two flights up, she thought of Dorothy Lemke, ascending with Woods in the Gore Hotel elevator, and Asta Eicher, who'd likely not seen Clarksburg at all. Powers, never broaching the physical except in words, had sustained their hopes over months and hundreds of miles. These women were vulnerable, but they were not stupid. One false move would have spooked them. Powers was a chameleon, a consummate actor whose skills merged perfectly with his desires. No one saw, in September's shambling prisoner, the man his victims experienced.

Grimm had spoken early on of Powers' *brainless, childlike, continual denial* and *mild, objective interest* in the crime scene: Emily had noted the phrases. Mild objectivity did not seduce women to his will. Perhaps his present alias was apt. She saw his eyes flash out at her, that day in the jail; his pupils had seemed to constrict sharply and his irises flared. She remembered an illusion of lit pinwheels spinning, pulling her sharply in. Then it was gone.

She stood before the door to her room and turned the key in the lock. No one would glimpse his capabilities, in the courtroom: Powers would make certain. She wondered what guise he would adopt.

Dinner in Room 127 was a small celebration: William and Mason stood beside her as she opened the door for Eric, who grasped her by the shoulders like a brother.

"Eric, come in." William indicated Mason. "This is Mason, Emily's assistant. Or archivist, I should say."

"Emily is assisted? Hello, Mason. William, you've recovered, I hope." They shook hands, and Eric turned to Emily. "Believe me, we are on a first name basis, for we nearly perished together. Cousin, I was on the brink of religious conversion."

"Only the brink, Eric?" Emily affected surprise. "Mr. Malone, can you testify to this?"

"Call me William, please." His gaze took them in, especially Mason, whom he warmly included. "Yes, the plane dropped and tossed, but it was the landing, actually, coming to rest against the trees, that seemed most miraculous."

"Just so," Eric agreed.

"We were anxious about the storm, weren't we, Mason? But you are here, and we've ordered dinner. Come and sit down, both of you. Mr. Malone — William — has brought a wonderful cognac from Chicago."

"Happy to hear it." Eric sat beside Mason on the settee and took a package from his briefcase. "Libation was on our minds. Emily, I've brought your favorite sherry, and something practical as well. Mason, how are you getting on with Duty?"

"Duty is very good," Mason said. The dog jumped up and settled between them. "He knows all kinds of tricks."

"He does indeed. This is for him. Emily?"

"Give it to Mason. He's in charge of Duty."

She stood behind William's armchair, resisting the desire to put her hands on him, for she'd left his bed not two hours before.

Mason, smiling, reached into the sack Eric offered and held up a small red garment, thickly knit and oddly shaped.

"Is it a scarf?" Emily asked.

Eric laughed. "Note the four armholes and generous chest. It's a serious coat, hand-knit for a bulldog type, and the collar rolls up or down, to shield his ears."

"Will he wear it?" Mason asked.

"He might, for you, Mason," Emily said.

"What do you mean? We are marooned in the Arctic, and Duty is no fool." Eric stood to turn the sweater right side round in Mason's grasp, and show the shawl collar to best effect. "It's wool, quite warm and pliable. There's a technique for putting it on. I'll show you later this evening. For now, he's meant to lie upon it, so that it smells of him."

"Why don't you take everyone to your room, Mason, and show them your work desk? Mason's made quite an organized archive." There was a knock at the door. "Our dinner," Emily said. "Go now, while I put everything on the table."

She waved off their offers of help and answered the door. The roast pork smelled deliciously of caramelized apples and parsnips; she'd ordered corn pudding and carrot slaw, and pumpkin pie for dessert. Mr. Woods laid everything out quickly. She was glowing, she knew, for it was going well; masculine voices rose and fell companionably in Mason's room.

"I'll leave the salver covers on the dinners, and the cart, with the pie." Mr. Woods paused to inquire, "Is everything well, Miss Thornhill?"

He was her ally, Emily knew. "Very well, Mr. Woods."

"Ring for the coffee, and the whipped cream for the pie, when you're ready." Discreetly, he shut the door behind him.

Emily walked through to Mason's room to see him seated at his table. William and Eric stood to either side, perusing the scrapbooks of clippings. "Gentlemen," she said.

Eric looked up. "Smells delicious. But I do want to read through all this. Mason has given me leave, after dinner."

"Yes," Mason said quietly, looking up at him. "And you know, I remember you from last summer. I watched your car — while you went into the grocery."

There was a beat of silence.

"In Broad Oaks," said Mason, "on Quincy Street."

Now Emily remembered. The boy with his dark hair in his eyes, long hair, unkempt, but not as long as when she found him in the alley. She was so taken up with confronting Luella Powers, she'd barely glimpsed the child. And Mason was so changed now. Eric did not recognize him.

"Of course," he said, "and you watched it well, I'm sure."

"You gave me a quarter." Mason's voice dropped. "I thank you very much. You drove off fast. I couldn't say it then."

"We were rushed," Eric said easily, "but you're very welcome, Mason, and it's good you said something. I'd never have remembered. You've grown since then and acquired numerous responsibilities, not to mention a haircut and appropriate dress for an archivist."

Mason stood, tugging his vest to straighten it; he'd worn his suit to dinner. "Emily — Miss Thornhill — wanted me to wear professional-looking clothes."

"Yes, he's been such a good sport about it," Emily said quickly. "We've said he's my nephew, to satisfy any queries." She must know, she must ask, or the others would wonder. "Mason, how curious, that we met before. Did you remember me, as well?"

"I do now," he said apologetically. "But it was mostly the car I was looking at, and he was driving it, and he looks just the same. I knew he was with a lady, but you got out on the other side, and I didn't see your face. After, he put you into the car so quick."

"I certainly did," Eric said.

Mason looked at Emily, his eyes alight. "I

can't believe it was you!"

"Yes, Mason, I was there." She felt, unaccountably, bathed in happiness.

"Well, then," William said. "Shall we dine?"

She stood aside as Eric and Mason preceded her.

Mason turned to Eric. "Everyone was following the reporters to Broad Oaks. I thought I might get a ride home. You flicked the quarter right into my hand."

"So I did. And where is home, Mason?"

Emily saw him blink, and the slight, involuntary flinch. "Out to Coalton," Mason said. "I'm helping now, for the trial."

"You're one of us, then," Eric offered.

"And I'm very glad," Emily said. William, close behind her, kissed the back of her neck, and she walked quickly to the dinner table.

"Lovely spread, isn't it, Mason?" Eric was seated beside him. "Puts the restaurant downstairs to shame."

Emily sat by Mason, for he still watched her in company, to be sure of table etiquette. She put Mason's glass of water before him and indicated William's chair. "William, do sit there, by Eric."

"Certainly, Emily. Thank you."

"Salvers," Eric said. "I do like a good salver cover on my plate, don't you, Mason?"

"I do like a good salver, Eric." Mason removed his salver lid and held it over his head like a trophy, beaming as Eric immediately followed suit.

"All right then," Emily said. She stacked lids and trays on the cart.

Eric called for the sherry and cognac. "We must have a toast to celebrate our community."

"You're very droll," said Mason shyly, as though offering great praise.

"I quite agree, Mason." William was pouring. "Emily, sherry? Eric, cognac for you?"

"Most certainly. William, where was this bottle of good cognac while we suffered that infernal airplane ride?"

"In the belly of the plane," William said. "On the way back, I shall have a flask in my pocket."

"Don't let's think of future plane rides," Eric said. "I propose a toast, and everyone must join in."

They looked at one another, all warm glances.

Eric raised his own glass. "To our very fine dinner. To Emily's home away from home, Duty's new coat, Mason's skills, and William's good fortune in all things."

Together, they drank, and ate their dinner, like a family on good terms. They remarked on the continuously drifting snow and agreed it was well the Gore had drawn up the red-and-white summer awnings, for the snow would certainly have broken them.

■ ■ ■ ■

The sky was a brilliant blue. Emily walked with Eric and Mason through streets increasingly crowded for the trial, toward the park. Duty stayed to the cleared sidewalk, for the drifts to either side were waist high.

Eric was taking what he called set shots: buildings, streets, scenes. "One cannot mistake Clarksburg for the South in December," he said. "Chicago will be confused by all the snow."

Emily dropped a little behind. She liked to see them together, and considered Eric's comment. West Virginia was not seen as Southern in the South, nor forgiven for siding with the Union seventy years ago, but had seemed the South to Emily last summer. Clarksburg was nearly snowbound this winter. Snow gleamed by day and shone at night, brighter than the gaslights. Today the town ladies circulated in the crowds, handing out leaflets about their historic downtown district.

"Is that your favorite camera?" Mason asked, and drew Duty closer on the leash.

Eric paused. "Best for stills in daylight, and certain trick shots. One may appear to photograph a small frame but actually include a wider view."

"Why?"

Eric showed him. "To look closely at a

535

wider context, or include a reluctant subject. There will be plenty during the trial. You've a bustling little town here, Mason." He waited for Emily to fall in beside them. "I'm sure you know the whole story, Emily."

"Named for a general in the seventeen eighties. Railroad money, mining boom. A river, for shipping goods. The usual tale, I suppose." Immigrants and the children of struggling farmers worked in the glass factories by the river; established modest enclaves, including Broad Oaks, where Luella Powers and Eva Belle Strother ran their storefront grocery. These weeks, reporters and the curious bought their products as souvenirs; the sisters charged inflated prices for small tins of mustard and baking powder.

Last summer and fall, veritable motorcades of cars had proceeded to Broad Oaks, then out Main Street to Buckhannon Turnpike and the dirt road that led to Quiet Dell. Entrepreneurs had looted the premises of anything they could carry.

The three of them approached the park. A man on a bench near the entrance displayed a scrawled sign: *Powers Murder Relics.* "Here," he called out to passersby. "Only here."

He thrust something at Emily.

The thing was in her gloved hand: a plain white envelope. She drew from within a paper scrap inscribed in pencil script, *Piece of soundproof board, used by Harry Powers during his notorious Murdering, Aug. 1931.* The board itself, a small dense square about as thick as the sole of a man's shoe, was marked *Harry Powers* in purple ink. The number 3 was legible on the surface.

"How did you come by this?" Emily asked the man.

He wore his hat pulled low, and his soiled dark scarf was around his mouth. Only his dark eyes gleamed out. "That's not for you to know, missus."

Emily asked the man, furious, "Why is it marked with a 3?"

"Because each is numbered. They is only two hundred, and this one here is number 3." The man looked around her at Eric. "Do ye want it or not?"

"I do not," Emily said, "and you should not be selling it. Who gave you leave to tear apart a scene of terrible suffering?"

"I got to make a dime," he said.

"Then perhaps you might seek honest labor." She turned to move away.

The man addressed Eric. "You want it?"

"No," Eric said. "But I will give you fifty cents to photograph it, there, on the bench beside you."

Emily pulled Mason on, but he looked back to watch Eric lay out his white handkerchief, and position the object for the shot. "Why is he taking a picture?" Mason asked.

"To prove that men can be so low. That man may need to make a dime, but he does not care how." They passed through the gates of the park. "He is a thief, for taking the object, and worse than a thief for selling it to others like himself."

"Eric is not a thief," Mason said decisively.

"No, he is doing his job, and journalists must sometimes pay an unsavory source for the greater good of documenting what is happening or has happened. And Eric will photograph the man" — she turned to glance behind her — "and report him to police for profiteering."

"What about the ones that sell photographs? Are they wrong too?"

They were in sight of the pond. "Let's stop there, at the bench just beside the gazebo, to put on our skates." Emily took Mason's arm and sat close beside him. "You're right to ask. It's a difference of degree, in a way — people who sell photographs of the victims, of Powers, benefit by the curiosity and fascination we feel at news of a terrible thing. Images make the story real, so that we understand and question it." She took their skates from her grip.

"The boy tried to help his sisters," Mason said.

"You read that in the newspapers you are filing." She looked into the air, which danced with snowflakes. "Yes, Hart Eicher was a brave boy."

"Where is he?"

"I don't know. Here, perhaps, in the snow that's falling, happy you're using his skates. He can fly along above the ice without them, or that is what I imagine."

Mason knelt to pull his laces tight. "Will Eric skate? Or William?"

"Eric is going by the Gore, to leave off his cameras. He'll rejoin us soon. And William is already here, skating far out there somewhere. I'll put Duty's coat on him and lace my skates, but you go ahead. You're a lovely skater; I love to watch you."

"You'll come out later." He was walking the short distance to the pond, sinking in hard snow to his ankles.

"I will, Mason. Go along." The boy needed to move in the cold air, get out of the hotel, away from cutting and pasting such words. Was it an education? Not a good one, but a real one, she supposed. And the adults near him now, to guide and help him, were some compensation.

Tomorrow, on the eve of the trial, she had an appointment at Grimm's office. The forms were prepared. She must speak with William today, and secure his permission if not his blessing. If Mason were her ward, he would know the nature of her commitment to William. She would tell Mason of his father's death and offer her protection, her home, away from this place. "Duty," she told the dog softly, "you must make it all right for him."

Mason, skating, turned to wave. He executed a small circle, then doubled back and sailed past her, once and again, his long white muffler streaming.

She applauded. The sound echoed over the ice, cracking in the air. Farther out she glimpsed William, a lone figure skating in a racer's powerful stride.

WILLIAM MALONE: OPEN ICE

The pond is solid as granite, frozen to its depths. William leans in, gliding, and skates for the open ice. Clarksburg is a near carnival of reporters and press. Curious throngs tromp the snowy streets. No vacancies at the Gore Hotel, named for a respected Southern family, he knows, but, as Emily says, the Gore Hotel.

Tomorrow the trial begins. William will see Powers in the flesh, onstage: a repellent entertainment. William's box seat will overlook Emily's; the first dozen rows of the orchestra are reserved for press. He skates full out, leaving the town behind.

Emily has told William details the public will not know. That Powers mutilated the boy, and her deduction that the murderer displayed his trophy to the last victim, pleasured himself before killing Dorothy Lemke, is too abhorrent to imagine. William clasps his arms behind him and leans in low against the wind. The pond is perhaps a half mile across, large enough that the far side is open ice. He turns sharply to cut his blades against the surface and skates backward in a sweeping curve, the snowbound edge of the land an undulating line.

Alone on the ice, he lets himself acknowledge that Emily's acute perception of these horrors frightens and amazes him. That she is not unaffected by what she knows makes her seem all the stronger. She is stubborn, sometimes disconcertingly impulsive, for she is so sure of her instincts, and healthy, sound, yet in moments of deepest intimacy, sometimes in the rippling paroxysm of climax, she sobs as though reaching some bottomless grief and pouring it from her.

She says she cannot escape this labyrinth without him, that together they are living opposition to Powers' cruelty, that such goodness — she uses the word repeatedly — flies in the face of darkness. William cannot define goodness and bids her not speak in absolutes, but she references an understanding to which he's long ascribed, that the appearance of a thing is a mere hint or indication of its reality. Superficial judgment of their situation, certainly the judgment of the state, would label them wanton adulterers, engaged in betrayal of his unknowing, invalid wife, but superficial judgment is meaningless.

He looks up at the gazebo across the pond and starts back across in the falling snow. He knows he will recognize Emily from some distance, her long coat that draws in at the waist and flares nearly to her ankles, the fur hat that frames her face, her way of moving.

How ironic that Powers will hang for the last murder, as though the Eichers never existed. William skates faster, gaining the center of the pond. The Eichers did exist. Hart's look, that day in the bank, reproves William daily. What must he do, now that it's too late? Unbidden, Mason's eyes and expression, the image of his face, fills William's mind. The Eicher boy was fair. Mason is darker, and watchful, with the look of the hurt child who survives on wit and speed rather than charm, but they both have square faces, regular features, the straight backs and broadening shoulders of natural athletes, though he's certain Emily's orphan has never engaged in sport. William skates faster, turning to approach the gazebo. The snow is thick, the flakes big as popcorn, though the sun is shining. He looks to see Emily gliding toward him across the ice, holding Mason by the hand, both of them skating and stepping by turns, and Duty in his knitted coat, gamely keeping pace.

The arc of the ornamental gas lamp cast a mild light in the fleecy snow. Eric arrived as they were leaving the ice, and William retrieved their possessions as the rental kiosk locked up.

"William," Emily asked, "might you walk by the pond with me? Eric and Mason must go back, for poor Duty has ice in his paws." She turned to Mason. "You and I will have supper in the room tonight, warm and cozy. I'll be back very soon."

"I shall look after them," Eric said. "Mason, I'll take the skates, and you the dog, and we'll walk back double time."

She watched them go, pulling her scarf close around her, and turned to William. "Do you mind? Are you cold?"

"Never, this close to you. Was that a wholly transparent excuse? Are we headed for the gazebo?"

"No, darling. The element of surprise is lost." She laughed and took his hand as they walked along the path skirting the pond. "I must talk to you, and Duty is not my concern." She stopped, and embraced him. "William, I've been wanting to speak to you about Mason."

"Have you? You've known the boy scarcely a month."

"And he is the same boy, day to day. He is not educated, but he's bright, and learns quickly. And he is still young, not twelve until Christmas Eve. His mother died in October, and his father will not claim him."

"How do you know this, Emily?"

"Because I asked Sheriff Grimm to go to the boy's home, as Mason described it, to find the father, and the mother's grave."

"And did he?"

"The mother's grave is there, marked. And the father was in his bed, frozen to death, with his jugs of whiskey near him. The sheriff, there in Randolph County, was with Grimm and identified the man. Neighbors were relieved to hear that Mason is in Clarksburg and has a place to sleep."

He stopped and turned to her. "When did this happen?"

"Just yesterday. I asked Grimm last week for his help, in finding the facts about Mason's situation."

"Does he know his father is dead?"

"No. I haven't told him yet, until I knew what else to say. What shall I say, William? What shall we do? For whatever we do, we must do together." She turned to face him. "Understand I am not asking you to commit your resources; he is my responsibility. I want to become his legal guardian; his home would be with me."

"What does he make of me, I wonder."

"I believe he looks up to you, and finds you a very different sort of man than he has known before. You are kind to him. Eric is kind, as well. He knows you are both . . . my friends."

"Eric will not be making love to you in the same apartment, and drinking coffee with you at breakfast, in Chicago."

She smiled. "There is always the Drake, and taxicabs. And he may spend school terms away at some point. I suppose I will need a bigger apartment."

"I suppose you will."

"And Mason will need to learn discretion. He is a private sort of boy, an only child, like us. Eric will be a kind of uncle to him, I think. We must trust one another." She turned to face him. "Come with me, William. Come with me in this, for I cannot turn from my responsibility, or give you up, or allow anyone to come between us."

"Come with you, Emily? Nothing can keep me from you. If he is your ward, your family, he is mine. We shall widen our circle, and do what we can for the boy. Are you crying? No need."

"Oh," she said, "there is need. I love you so and believe in you, and now I love you more, which I did not think possible —"

"Don't cry, Emily. The tears will freeze on your lashes."

She took the handkerchief he offered and held closely to his arm.

■■ ■■

XV.

■■ ■■

Photos Trace "Powers" from Iowa Farm to
Slayer's Cell: As Harm Drenth, son of a
Dutch immigrant farmer, in Iowa, in 1910.
As Joe Gildaw, of Miller, S.D., in 1924. He
was then a matchmaker, writing love notes.
As Harry F. Powers. Photo taken after his
arrest here on August 27, 1931. As Cor-

nelius O. Pierson, he wore glasses.

— The Clarksburg Telegram,
December 5, 1931

Stage Set, Powers Trial Begins: An advance delegation of special newspaper writers and photographers arrived here yesterday to "cover" the Harry F. Powers murder trial beginning tomorrow. . . . It is believed that 70 seats reserved in Moore's Opera House for the press will be occupied during the trial. . . . Several out-of-town telegraphers arrived yesterday and transmitted the first stories over the 29 special wires.

— The Clarksburg Exponent,
December 7, 1931

December 7–9, 1931
Clarksburg, West Virginia

THE TRIAL

December 7, 1931

Emily made her way to the opera house over streets of hard-packed snow. She went early to avoid a scene, but the scene prevailed, for the truly intent had queued up at dawn on South Fourth Street. State troopers patrolled the sidewalks, attempting to move the crowd along. The police intended orderly first-come, first-served general admittance, but a mad surge would ensue when they opened the doors. Overflow was allowed in throughout the day, one person admitted for each "audience member" departing. Regardless, box seats, reserved seats, the press rows in the orchestra were off-limits to the merely curious. The town fathers would bring their opera glasses, and the town wives their furs, for the businessmen leasing the opera house had turned the heat on only this morning.

Emily could see her breath in the lobby. Eric was across the street, photographing the crowd. She clutched her valise and stenographer's notebook, intending to take down actual testimony rather than wait for its release by the court reporter. She downplayed her knowledge of such mundane skills, but her transcription was so fluid that it served to anchor her perceptions. The words were but the spoken lines; the story wove between them, and the meaning lay deeper still.

Aisles carpeted in crimson separated three broad sections of seats, while the balcony, box seats, and second-floor gallery were set off as though held aloft in sculpted gold seashells. It was charming and odd, for acres of deep snow were the only ocean afforded these inland mountains. Journalists' seats were assigned, as though to a performance. Emily stepped over ropes marking off the press section to her center seat, second row from the stage. Excellent seats. Grimm had taken a hand, she suspected. She heard a rumbling all about her, and felt it in the floor, for the throng was filling the hall.

Reporters filed in. Some of the men wore press cards in their hatbands. Emily looked for Eric and saw Grimm, standing far left, first row aisle, checking his pocket watch as though timing the start of a performance. He wore a light brown suit — creamy it was, nearly beige — a white dress shirt buttoned to the starched collar, and a light satin necktie. He was a gentleman sworn to the forces of light, should anyone need reminding, while Law, walking onto the stage now in his pinched black suit and overcoat, tall and wraith thin, with his yellowish white hair and sparse mustache, defended the very devil.

Emily sat back, momentarily blinded by the flash of Eric's camera, for he stood just at the edge of the proscenium, shooting the house itself. Suddenly the lights dimmed, a signal it seemed. Eric gave her his camera and stepped nimbly over an empty front-row seat to his place. She trained her unbroken gaze before her.

Judge Southern took his seat on a platform in the center. The jury, all men in dark suits, walked in together. The paneled jury box, swinging door and plush theater seating intact, had been moved from the courthouse and reassembled here. The jurors sat as one group, as though rehearsed; most retained their overcoats, pulling their collars up for warmth.

Emily had stood upon the stage. She'd promised Mason he would see the opera house, and so Grimm had brought them last week to see the cavernous empty theater. Mason stood peering into the balconies, enchanted, while Duty plumped to his haunches and looked off toward the wings. Grimm had switched on the overhead "border lights." Dozens of red, white, and blue lamps, unseen by the audience, hung from the ceiling, bathing the stage in tones that duplicated daylight. She remembered panels of scenery, covered in draping. Amazingly, these were now revealed, and the border lights shown down upon them.

Tall canvases depicting forest trees were arrayed behind the assemblage, concealing the wings of the stage. The branches, daubed with pastel leaves, glittered as though dusted with mica. Directly behind Judge Southern was a rendering of a small-town street; the church was just to his right. The "town" seemed nearly lost in trees. How might the branches sparkle so? The illusion of depth was startling. Prosecutor Will E. Morris and defense lawyer J. Ed Law now walked on from opposite wings and seated themselves at counsel tables downstage.

Every seat in the opera house was occupied, yet the house fell silent. Emily heard boots marching. The audience subtly shifted to view stage right. A detachment of state troopers led Powers in. His wrists were handcuffed, his feet manacled. He walked stiff-legged, looking narrowly ahead. The metal dog collar around his neck was attached to a long chain, and the chain hung down his back, for the trooper in charge had just unlocked it from the metal cuff on his own forearm. Powers looked dumpy and unremarkable, despite the armature restraining him. His light brown hair, carefully combed, billowed up to one side. Full, ruddy cheeks, a small bow of a mouth, thin, compressed lips: he was a bit less florid after three months in custody, his short, powerful arms concealed in a standard-issue black suit. White shirt, tie; shoes newly shined. He looked almost bored, like a clerk wandered into the wrong hall, forced to observe mundane proceedings. He sat in a swivel chair near his counsel, his back to the audience, turning only once to survey the hundreds of faces watching him.

Law stood and began declaiming, filing a motion for a change of venue: the community "was strong against" his client; a gang had "mobbed the jail and tried to lynch him." Powers didn't flinch. Judge Southern denied the motion. Law demanded the defendant be removed from Sheriff W. B. Grimm's custody due to "the shameful way he and his deputies treated my client." Denied. Morris rose to review the case.

Emily leaned forward to capture his exact words. He recited the facts: investigation of Powers' matrimonial racket, the subterranean death chambers at the Quiet Dell garage, removal of five bodies from a drainage ditch behind the building, all due to "information received from Park Ridge, Illinois, that Mrs. Asta Eicher and her children had vanished with a Clarksburg man."

Law was on his feet. "Exception! We are not trying the Eicher case!"

Powers yawned audibly, eliciting chuckles far back in the balcony gallery, and gazed at the ceiling.

"Bastard," Eric whispered.

Southern trained his withering gaze high over the footlights, reproving the spectators farthest removed from his influence.

Morris stood center stage, stating that Powers was charged with all five murders but indicted and tried for only one: that of Mrs. Dorothy Pressler Lemke, a crime for which the state "demanded the execution of the accused, that he hang by the neck until dead." Morris glared at the gallery, requiring silence, then called Chief of Police Clarence Duckworth to the stand.

Morris addressed him. "When you went into the Quiet Dell garage of the accused, what did you discover, if anything?"

Law, seated, raised his fist. "Question objected to!"

Southern banged his gavel. "The objection is overruled."

"Exception!" Law replied.

Duckworth spoke so laconically that his account seemed indisputable. "I noticed some of the books had Mrs. Eicher's name on them, and some of the children's names."

Law stood, gesticulating. "I move to strike testimony referring to the Eichers' names."

"The motion may be overruled," Southern said.

Morris stepped to the edge of the stage and turned to Duckworth. "Did you have to go outside of the garage to get down to the under compartment?"

"No, go down from the inside, right hand corner." Duckworth spoke as though directing himself at the scene. "A trapdoor that would let down, but it was open. . . . I entered into the basement with a flashlight, and it was about four rooms . . . over one of the doors I found blood had run down . . . for a distance, very distinctly . . . and we tore off . . . some of the soundproof wallboard, and blood had come through on that in large clots."

The rustle and general movement of the audience went still.

"I came back upstairs to the garage there and moved a trunk, and on the floor was a large clot of blood. It was a foot and a half square that the floor was very bloody . . ."

Emily gripped her pen, writing. Powers brought Hart upstairs, before he killed him. Why? To make him watch — Grethe's death, or Annabel's. She started, for a baby began wailing in the gallery. So much blood, from his head, and then, when he was still —

"We closed the door and nailed it up," Duckworth was saying, "at about eleven o'clock that night. . . . The next morning we went back with the state police and I directed the sheriff to open up the ditch that led from the garage to the creek."

Morris never glanced up. "Chief Duckworth, I will ask you to state whether or not you then, or later, asked the defendant anything about the goods . . . as to where he got them, or whose they were."

Duckworth raised his noncommittal voice, as though to project to the galleries. "He said . . . the things found there belonged to Mrs. Eicher of Park Ridge, Illinois."

Law bounded to his feet. "I move to strike that out, Your Honor."

"The motion is overruled," Southern said.

"Ex-cep-tion," Law returned.

Morris spoke over him. "Chief Duckworth, you stated that he said he had been to the Eicher family at Park Ridge. Did he tell you when he had been there, or how often?"

Law stood and raised his long arms in supplication. "Objection! I repeat: we are not trying the Eicher cases!"

Morris, his patience exhausted, turned on Law as though instructing him. "These cases are inseparable in the finding of these goods and investigation leading to the discovery of the body for which he is being charged; and it is a part of the *res gestae.*"

Southern was unperturbed. "It may go in."

"Exception!" Law raised a pointed finger in punctuation.

Res gestae: "things done." Secondhand statements could be admitted as evidence only if spontaneously repeated by a witness. Emily knew the case against Powers depended on such evidence; all was circumstantial. The witness must have participated directly in the witnessed event, and speak with no premeditation. Duckworth had certainly participated.

Morris moved on, questioning Duckworth about the removal of the bodies from the ditch, four bodies, a woman and three children, and "one more body found, up nearer the garage, that was brought to the Romine undertaking establishment."

Morris faced the audience. "I will ask you to state whether or not you are acquainted with Mrs. Charles Fleming of Northborough, Massachusetts, and her husband."

"I am." Duckworth spoke into a hush.

Morris looked at the jury. "I will ask you to state whether they . . . identified the body last taken out of the ditch, at the Romine undertaking establishment."

Law stood. "Question objected to as suggestive and leading."

"He may answer." Judge Southern scowled.

Duckworth's answer was specific. "Mrs. Fleming did." His words evoked the body and the slab: one sister viewing another.

Morris asked about the search of Powers' property at Broad Oaks, Clarksburg, and stood unmoving as Duckworth described a large trunk in the Quincy Street garage, "filled with women's and children's clothing . . . on top was a Kodak. We . . . turned it over to Dr. Goff, and he had the film in it developed."

Morris asked Duckworth to identify the here produced photographs. When and where did Duckworth show Powers the photographs, and what did Powers state about them?

"He said he could not deny it," Duckworth answered. "One was his own picture, and the other . . . Mrs. Lemke, of Northborough, Massachusetts. And the Kodak . . . was Mrs. Lemke's Kodak."

And what about the living quarters, above and behind the Quincy Street grocery? How did Duckworth gain entry?

There was no warrant, Duckworth explained, because Mrs. Powers, the defendant's wife, and her sister, Miss Strother, "own the property and gave me permit to go in it."

Morris asked, "What goods, if any, did you find there?"

Duckworth was deliberate. "There were two women's coats, heavy winter coats, a large number of dresses, all kinds of women's wear, bedspreads, linens, tablecloths, pillow slips, a large number of them."

Pillow slips. Emily felt a dull pain in her head. Dorothy intended to keep house, and the bedrooms of her new husband's several properties must be done up in her own family linens.

Duckworth said the piano bench was piled full. Another back room "had been used more for plunder . . . and then there was a dress or two that was found in wardrobes of the house . . ."

Luella and Eva Belle, helping themselves to what they wanted. Dorothy's clothes in their closets. And the police would not arrest these women; they were "borrowing" what Powers "stored for a friend." At least it was known. The town would ostracize them, Emily thought, the grocery would fail. They would live, peering from their windows, on their modest rental income.

Morris paused. "I will ask you to state, Mr. Duckworth . . . if there was part of a charred or burned bankbook found in a brush pile near the Quiet Dell garage."

Law leapt to his feet. "Objected to, suggestive and leading . . ."

". . . overruled," Judge Southern finished.

"Exception!" Law tossed his head as Powers looked into the wings, where a stagehand was adjusting an electrical box.

"Describe the bankbook," Morris commanded.

"Part of it had been burned, and it was very distinctly 'Dorothy Pressler,' the name on the book, and 'Worcester, Massachusetts.' "

And what had the defendant said, in jailhouse interviews that followed, concerning any association with Dorothy Lemke?

Duckworth explained that Powers had signed a confession to all the murders on the night of the twenty-ninth, the day "the Lemke body" was found in the ditch.

Forced to shout over the loud murmur of the crowd, Law thundered, "Objection! That confession is inadmissible as coerced and will not be introduced here!"

"Sustained." Judge Southern banged his gavel once. "Order!"

Morris walked center stage and shouted to be heard. "I will ask you to state, Mr. Duckworth, whether the fifth body found in this ditch, buried there, was clothed in a dress when you saw it at the morgue of the Romine undertaking establishment."

"It was. I have it in my custody."

"Do you have it here, today?"

"I do not." But he had clothing taken from the exhumed body, and stood to open an evidence bag, pouring it out onto the table adjacent to the witness stand: her torn undergarments, stained with blood.

The general murmur resounded. Photographers in the press section stood on their seats, jostling for view. Flashbulbs popped in concert. It was a moment played for effect, but nothing compared to the sight of Dorothy Lemke's bound, engorged corpse, her domelike bald head shining in the underground morgue, bathed in hot white light. Eric's photographs were police evidence, but perhaps the jury would see them. Emily sat watching Powers, who glanced vaguely at the bloody clothes and seemed much distracted by the swaying of the ropes offstage.

Law would have his day: he charged on cross-exam that Powers was "the victim of third-degree techniques. . . . You were there on the night of Friday, August twenty-ninth," Law stated, "at the jail, or about the jail?"

"I was," Duckworth said, "to ask if he had any statement to make."

"What kind of statement did you want?"

"What he knew about these five people being murdered."

"And you were insisting on that, weren't you, Duckworth?"

"No, not exactly," Duckworth said. "He made a statement."

"Who else was there?" Law demanded.

"There was state police there; I don't recall their names."

Law peered across the footlights into the front row. "Could not recall their names, now, at all? Do your best now and see if you can. . . . Did you see Sheriff Grimm there, in and out?"

"I don't recall," said Duckworth, obliging, contemplative.

Law referred to September's lynch mob. "You were present, Mr. Duckworth, on the

561

night of September nineteenth, at the county jail?"

"I was."

"You state there was no demonstration with an object to enter the jail, is that right?"

"No, there was no one came anyways near the jail."

"They came near enough for the sheriff to seize them?"

"They was seized on disorderly conduct more than anything."

Law paced the stage. "You say you have not learned of any threats of violence against said Powers . . . that he ought to be hung, drawn, and quartered . . . did not deserve trial . . . haven't these expressions been common, and you have heard them frequently?"

"No, I cannot say that I have." Duckworth gazed before him, sharing patient consideration with twelve hundred spectators. It was a masterful performance.

Emily glanced at a newspaper that had slipped to the floor by her feet. A legend a column wide, bordered in black, leapt out at her.

REMEMBER:
The Hundred Neediest Cases

She stared, reading the words in present context. Grimm had spoken of dozens of inquiries from relatives of missing women.

How many more had inspired no search? Might Powers have killed a hundred women? How many, then? She had to remind herself the words were a Christmas plea.

Judge Southern called for the noon recess. The hall moved and shifted; floorboards groaned overhead. Emily closed her notebook. Police took little notice of willing disappearance. If Powers picked the right victim and bade her come to him, he might leave no trail at all. He traveled constantly, and must have done so for over a decade previous to the four years he'd lived in Clarksburg. The Eichers had no money; Powers was caught because he went back to Park Ridge for radios and rugs, determined to realize a profit.

Law and Powers were nearly alone on the stage. Emily watched them, transfixed. Heads low, they conversed in earnest. She saw Powers nod, and once he smiled broadly.

She hurried to the telegraph office to file. Mason was already at the front of the line. Emily joined him now, resting her arm on his shoulder for a moment, and leaning down to stroke Duty's short, alert ears.

The proprietor remembered Emily and leaned over the counter to greet them, ignoring the lengthening line. "Money can't buy the education you're getting, young man," he told Mason. "You see: in the right hands, the law of the land is sufficient to redress wrong."

Emily disagreed. She handed over her copy, a feature on the opera house typed up before the trial began. She would turn in her substantive feature this evening, including the afternoon's revelations, building on the theme of justice as macabre performance. "Thank you, sir," she said, and to Mason, "You look very well today. Have you had lunch?"

"Yes, in the tearoom with Mr. Malone. He sent you this." Mason gave her a small warm parcel.

"Ah." She followed his gaze to see William in a lobby armchair, nodding at them over his newspaper. They'd agreed he would leave the trial early to meet Mason. The parcel would be a sandwich for her lunch. "Sorry I wasn't able to join you, Mason."

"There's ever so many clippings now, with the trial," Mason said, "but we're going to the park first."

"Good. It's a lovely clear day. Go along then." William would walk with him, see him to the room, and come back to hear testimony. She watched them exit the hotel and knew she couldn't eat, her mind was so occupied, but the sight of them was nourishment. Tonight she would have supper with Mason in their rooms, and describe a future she hoped he would accept. Early that morning, she'd met Grimm at the courthouse and signed the forms, volunteering herself as Mason's legal guardian. It would take some time, and she could stop the process if Mason refused, but arrangements must be made.

"I'd like to know how he gets on," Grimm had said.

She'd nodded. "I shall let you know. What would you have done, if I hadn't taken him?"

"I'd have taken him myself, provided you left us the dog." He'd smiled and reached to shake her hand. "Much better that he go with you, of course. Congratulations, Miss Thornhill. I believe you've gained a ward." He'd accepted her heartfelt thanks.

Now she looked for Eric in the crowded telegraph office and went to stand near him. "Have this sandwich." She put the bag in his pocket.

Reporters poured in, lighting cigars and cigarettes, joking and laughing. "Mr. Exception," they called Law. "Do Not Recall" Duckworth was the object of new respect.

Eric was filing his feature on matrimonial agencies. "Fascinating reading, cousin. I lead with Powers' own personal ad and finish with another just come to light. You might like to read it. Direct from 'Cupid's Columns,' St. Paul, Minnesota. Date of December 30, 1927."

Emily read:

517 — Clarksburg, W. Va. Refined American

lady of the highest class, desires correspondence for matrimony only. Age 44;
Ht. 5–4; Wt. 110; brown hair, blue eyes, very
intelligent, good cook and housekeeper and
a good businesswoman. Have a piano and
considerable means. Will marry as soon as
suited. Bachelor preferred from ages 44 to
52.

"Luella's ad? But she and Powers were married in June of 'twenty-seven."

"No. It is Eva Belle Strother's ad. Like
Luella before her, she joined numerous
clubs."

"I'm going outside to breathe," Emily said,
"and back to the opera house."

She stepped out, shielding her eyes. The
snow was bright as knives. Powers would have
watched the Midwest lists, and cities distant
but reachable by car. Asta Eicher had placed
a single ad with a Detroit agency. Emily
walked quickly; the trial would soon continue.
Scores stood in line at the opera house, under
the marquee and out into the street, hoping
for entrance to the afternoon session.

Emily nodded to the officer in charge and
stood by the marquee advertisement panels.
The "N.R.A.T." (No Room A' Tall) signs
were slid into the four large panels, and
propped on a straight chair by the curb.
"Sandwich men," so called because they wore
signs fixed over their shoulders, back and

front, chest to knees, walked about like a perverse deck of cards emblazoned with headlines; they publicized songs, phonograph records, pamphlets about the "West Virginia Bluebeard." Mature women in fashionable clothing, their reserved seats secure, came and went, dressed in dark colors but festooned with brooches, jet necklaces, fringed satin scarves. Perhaps they imagined themselves decked out for a show business funeral. "Isn't he horrid looking?" said one, passing Emily. "Those blue eyes," said another. "They say he's a hypnotist." A third shrugged. "He's fairly good looking — no wonder all those women fell for him." Emily wished for a cigarette, that she might blow smoke in their faces.

Eric was beside her. "Come in. Goff is the next witness."

The painted scenery had been moved closer during the recess, as though to focus the view. It looked as if the painted trees, stirred by a sudden wind, might fall on the heads of those onstage, and ropes dangling in the wings were more obvious. Emily thought of Charles O'Boyle's widely published letter, offering West Virginia the gift of his rope.

"Eric," she said, "have you spoken to O'Boyle?"

"Every day. He's reading the coverage."

"Every day?" Emily said. "I'm glad, Eric."

"Yes." He looked at her, pensive, as though he too pondered bounty arisen from devastation.

Judge Southern rapped his gavel. "Court is in session."

Morris began. "You are Dr. Leroy C. Goff?"

Goff sat upright in a fine dark suit, his shoulders squared, light reflecting off the lenses of his gold-rimmed glasses.

Did he, on the twenty-eighth day of August, view the bodies of a woman and three children at the Romine undertaking establishment?

Law stood. "We object to that for the reason that we are not trying the Eicher cases."

"Overruled." Southern glanced at him.

"Exception!" Law sat, glaring as though insulted.

Morris persisted. "Dr. Goff, I will ask you to state . . . examination of the woman found on that occasion, and what you ascertained as to the condition of the body."

Goff consulted his notes. "The body of the woman was badly decomposed, the odor was very offensive . . . bruises could not be identified positively . . . there was a constriction about the neck . . . the lungs were in collapse . . . no contents in the stomach, small intestines, or upper part of large bowel."

She'd not eaten for several days before she died. Emily heard her, gasping for water in the dark.

"The hyoid bone was fractured and down to the cornu," Goff said.

"What is the hyoid bone?" Morris asked. "The cornu?"

"It is a small bone . . . between the larynx and base of the tongue. The cornu is a horn on one end of the hyoid bone . . . there had been considerable violence exerted . . . in order to fracture this bone . . . the bruised tissues of the neck and this fractured bone led to conclusion that death was caused by strangulation." Goff produced the handkerchief, and coughed.

At Morris' request, Goff read from the report concerning the girls: "The first girl was sixty-two inches tall. The second girl . . . fifty-three inches tall . . . much too decomposed to determine the color of her eyes."

Her eyes were hazel, Emily wrote in the margin of her notes.

"Her hands were tied together behind her back with a sash weight cord . . . death caused by strangulation." Goff looked up from his notes.

The bodies had no names.

Now they spoke of Hart.

"The skull had been crushed . . . right on top . . . two holes, like he had been hit in the head with a hammer, or some instrument of that kind." Goff touched his head, indicating the site of the wound. "The hammer just cut out a hole . . . and the other wound, the hammer did not hit square . . . crushing through the skull." There was general murmuring and movement in the audience. Goff paused. "There was discoloration and constriction around his neck, very marked. He had a gag . . . something stuffed in his mouth, and the cloth looped or tied around his neck, a strangle cloth . . . and fracture to the bone, hyoid bone —"

Morris questioned him: "That is the same bone you were talking about in the others?"

Goff asserted, "Yes, sir, and the injuries to his head would have caused death, but he was certainly strangled in addition."

Someone in the gallery retched.

Emily waited, her breath shallow. They must say what Powers had done, his violation of the boy's body. It should be known, but she could not prove it, for it was hearsay from a confidential source. She looked up at William, in the gallery above and to her right, and saw him lean into the railing before him, as though to move toward her.

Law sprang to his feet. "I move to strike out the witness's testimony with regard to the examination of the boy's body just completed." It was theater, with Law shouting, drawing attention to himself when details were most grotesque.

Judge Southern declared the motion overruled as Law shouted, "Exception!" and shook his fist in the air. Southern ignored him and leaned back to attend Morris' question to Goff, "regarding a woman purported to be the last woman taken from the ditch at Quiet Dell."

No, they were not going to say, for they were on to Lemke.

Eric, beside her, pressed a small vial into her hand. "Emily, take this."

It was smelling salts. She resisted the impulse to throw the glass vial at the stage.

Goff was testifying, reading his notes. "Her hands tied behind her back with a window sash cord . . . a webbing band strap was twisted around her neck and her body tied up in feed sacks. She was dressed with stockings and dress and underclothes; her hair was, had been, long and black and done up with pins . . ."

And gone from her head, fallen from her round bald skull. Emily prompted him to say it. He did not.

". . . an operation scar over her lower right body or abdomen, three and a half inches long . . . like a drainage tube had been in the wound. . . . The lungs were completely collapsed . . . fracture of the hyoid bone, contusion and discoloration . . ."

The redirect began, but Emily could not continue writing. She heard Law propose, "Isn't it true that . . . collapse of the lungs follows immediately after death, in any case?"

Goff coughed. "I don't know that it is."

Law adopted a professorial tone. "You don't know that it is not?"

"No, sir." Goff answered with an air of patience.

"That's all, Your Honor." Law pretended to satisfaction.

Southern banged his gavel and announced court adjourned until tomorrow, December 8, at 9:00 A.M. Emily looked numbly before her. Audience members in the orchestra section and galleries began to stand and shift, moving to the lobby.

She had typed her notes into a cogent account. "Here you are, sir. Special to the *Chicago Tribune.*" Emily waited as he transmitted her words. The first day of the trial was finished. Mason stood beside her.

"This is the entire transmission, Miss Thornhill?"

"Yes, thank you. Date of today, December seventh. I shall be sending more tomorrow morning."

Mason looked up at her. "Was it terrible?"

She knew she must look exhausted, and didn't want to worry him. "It's going exactly as it should. All right, Mason?" He picked up the dog, for Duty was jumping at his knees; she bent down to embrace them both and usher them before her to the elevator.

Her concluding graph had to do with the lights, and stagecraft itself: *Tall scenic panels of glittering papier-mâché trees and a "back-drop" of a typical small-town street, a church at the judge's back, set the stage for a living drama of life or death, and love.*

Love, of course, was her angle, not the moral tedium concerning knaves and "love criminals." News coverage, legitimate or yellow, constantly pressed the notion that a bad end awaited women who responded to invitation, who wished for romance and the only self-determination available to most: a respectable, financially solvent man. Woe to the buxom woman over forty who imagined sincere interest in her exhausted charms. Powers and the case itself were excuses to shame women and keep them in their places. She could not entertain the deeper questions for the *Tribune;* her dispatches must be entertaining and factually accurate, but her bias underscored every line.

Mason turned to smile at her. They ascended, ensconced in the soothing machine hum of the elevator, blessedly alone.

The crowd was on trial, to Emily's mind, this crowd and every crowd drawn by grim spectacle, by fascination with each new detail; she was herself on trial, pointing out storybook elements in a case in which the murderer's given name, Harm Drenth, duly matched the sobriquet of Sheriff W. B. Grimm. Grimm was looking extremely handsome, his hundred-watt smile grown brighter at each interview, on each transport of the accused from the jail to the opera house. Powers followed him, manacled, in tow between armed guards like a shambling accountant trailing a movie star.

Mason was opening his door with the hotel key. Bless Grimm, he had helped them; and William, waiting to hear Mason's answer, would stand by them.

"Let's go through into my room," she said, turning on lights, "and sit here, on the settee." She watched him order on the hotel phone and thought to put off her news, to be sure he ate his meal, but found she could not.

"Mason," she said, and he turned to her. "I must tell you something that is important and difficult." His face paled. She went on hurriedly; unconsciously, she extended her open hands toward him, and he took them, pressing her fingers in his smaller ones as though to hold on through the moment at which they'd arrived.

"Sheriff Grimm has made inquiries; he told me that your father passed away some days ago." She must say it all at once. "He was drinking, as you've said he does, and fell asleep in his bed, and did not wake up. It was very cold — it is, very cold —"

"He froze, then."

"Yes, he froze, and felt no pain, for he was asleep."

Mason nodded. Duty was in his lap. "I

don't have to be afraid, then —" His voice broke and his eyes filled.

"No, never." Emily clasped him to her gently, tearful herself, and was silent until he looked up at her, as though for reassurance. "If you want to stay here after the trial, I shall help you find a situation. If you have no reason to stay, you might consider coming back to Chicago with Duty and me, where you would make your home with us, and when you are ready, attend a good school, perhaps a boarding school such as I attended myself, where you would receive an education and have friends your own age. But your home would be with me." She paused, trying to gauge his reaction. "It would be a big change for you."

"Yes —" His eyes widened and he blinked, cringing ever so slightly in that old, involuntary movement. "I mean, yes, I want to come with you. I will . . . help you, and take care of Duty —"

"Of course, but you needn't help . . . at home, with clippings and filing newspapers. You will just be at home, studying, getting ready for school, seeing a new place, a big city, Chicago —"

"Oh, yes," he said, "and I will go to school, like other people."

"Yes, and I could become your legal guardian. Your home with me would be protected. Might you agree, Mason?"

He nodded, his eyes still brimmed with tears. "And does it mean, no one can take me away from you? My mother used to worry, that if anyone saw where we lived and knew she was sick, they would take me away from her, and her not strong enough to get me back."

"Ah, Mason." His head on her shoulder released a weariness that seemed to fall down all around them. "My boy," she said, and knew it was true for the first time. "You have a home always. I will honor your mother, just as you do, and try to guide you."

"She would be so glad." He closed his eyes for a moment, his long lashes brushing his cheeks.

Emily held him close beside her. "I'll engage a tutor to help you, and perhaps in spring you can apply to schools, nearby I hope, so that you can come home easily to see Duty and me, and Eric and William, on weekends and holidays. For we would all miss you a great deal, if we don't see you often."

"And I would miss you," Mason said. He looked wistful, uncertain.

"But we will be together." She smiled softly. "What is it, Mason?"

"Sometimes" — he faltered — "I think about stealing, to know I still can. I'm afraid to forget."

"Afraid to forget — you put it so well." She sat a moment, then took up her purse and opened it to him. "Steal from me then, Mason, only from me, and tell me about it if you like. To know you're protected, after so long, will take time."

He reached inside and brought out a small pearl button, and clasped it in his hand. "I'll keep it to remind me."

Emily blessed the anonymous glove whose button had come loose months ago, no doubt. His eyes were full, and hers as well. She touched her mouth to his forehead, and sat back. "Are you hungry? I'm starved."

He nodded, for they could smell the food arriving, and heard the knock at the door.

Mason went to the door and opened it wide. Mr. Woods wheeled in the cart and looked at them over the table as he set it, for they were both gazing at him so happily.

"Can I tell him?"

"You may tell him, Mason, and tell whomever you like. It is not a secret."

Mason said, with shy pride, "Mr. Woods, Miss Thornhill will be my legal guardian, and I will be going home with her to Chicago when the trial is over."

"Well, my stars. That is good news for both of you." He shook Mason's hand, and then Emily's.

They ate as though famished, and then Emily insisted Mason take a warm bath and go to bed, where he might read his library books as late as he liked. He was asleep in twenty minutes, and she put on her hat and coat, and took Duty out on the leash. It was frigid. The night sky above her was clear and pierced with lights, the line of the horizon curving above dark hills.

The hotel was quiet. She passed her room and went to William's, and knocked softly.

He opened the door, his robe pulled loosely on, and led her near the window to see her face in moonlight. "What's your news, Emily?"

"It's cold out, very cold," she whispered. "I must get into bed with you this second, and Duty too. Take off my boots."

"Only your boots?"

"For now." She'd shed her coat and hat, and leaned back as he held one ankle, then the other, to his naked thigh, and caressed her feet inside her heavy stockings. She pulled his robe away and followed him into bed. They lay embraced, the dog near them. "William, he said yes. He's so happy, to know he's safe."

"He's far more than safe, but safety may be what he can comprehend just now."

"So much to do. I must find a tutor, a larger apartment, yet I must be near the *Tribune,* and in my same neighborhood."

He was taking the pins from her hair and lifting it free. "Emily, you have a larger apartment." He waited to meet her eyes. "I've bought the apartment next door, which is twice the size of yours, and has a deep broad terrace, with planted beds. The construction of breaking through is finished. The small details must be completed to your taste."

"What? Do you mean, we have the entire floor?"

"It was meant to be a surprise, a luxurious love nest. Now it shall be more. There are two additional bedrooms, one for Mason, each with a bath. A library, a living room with a fireplace, a kitchen to be fitted out, a small conservatory by the terrace —" He stroked her face. "Emily, you look stunned."

"You must have been engaged . . . for months —"

"In the purchase and planning, yes. The breaking through was not difficult. It was one apartment, years ago; there's still some fine architectural detail. It all occurred to me because I needed to dodge neighbors on your floor. Safety concerns me, sadly, just as it concerns Mason." He searched her eyes. "I hope you're not unhappy, that I took your life in hand without permission."

"My life is in your hands. I gave permission long ago."

He held her face and kissed her deeply.

"The taste of you," she said, "like heaven. Oh, I must go. The trial begins in a few hours. I must sleep."

"You will." He pulled her before him to the

edge of the bed and pushed her clothes up between them. "Don't you need this now? Time is short, for we met so late." He stopped her voice, his fingers on her teeth. "It will take a moment, and let you sleep soundly, so soundly, to face tomorrow."

THE WORD OF "LOVE"

December 8, 1931

Stage left featured a single row of chairs for witnesses. Gretchen Fleming held her purse on her lap; Emily could see her press and release the clasp. Coley Woods and Truman Parrish sat to her right, with two men unknown to Emily.

Eric leaned close to her. "Bank tellers."

Yes, Lemke's checks. The tellers, their fitted suit jackets buttoned, their pocket squares neatly obvious, were here from Uniontown.

Dr. Goff was on the stand to "produce and identify" the band tied around the neck of "the last woman found in the ditch," Dorothy P. Lemke. "This is a webbing band," Goff said, holding it up. "It looks like it might have been a buggy strap, and it was placed around her neck like that."

Morris interrupted him. "And tied there?"

"No, sir, it was not tied there. There was a buckle or something on the end, and when we took it off it dropped to the floor, a metal fastener or buckle, and we did not pick it up then, and it became lost."

"For want of a nail . . ." Eric said under his breath.

The buckle was part of the murder weapon; why else, but to tighten it and watch her struggle, would Powers have attached it? Emily imagined it falling away, trampled by Goff or the police.

Exhibit "Band" was filed; Morris asked Goff to produce what tied or wrapped the body in its burlap sack.

"Yes, sir. This is part of . . . what I understand to be a liner for an inner tube on an automobile tire . . . placed on to protect the inner tube."

Exhibit "Inner Tubes," tattered pieces, was marked and filed. And yes, Goff had accompanied police and Powers to the morgue, to view the victims. "Heavens, isn't that horrible" was Powers' placid remark. Emily glanced up to find William in his box-row seat, staring ashen faced at the players on the stage.

Morris called, first a bank teller and then a cashier, from the Second National Bank of Uniontown, Pennsylvania. Both identified Powers as the man who came to the bank on August 1, 1931, demanding payment on two checks written on the bank — by Dorothy Pressler Lemke, and by Dorothy A. Pressler. One A. R. Weaver had endorsed both, and the combined amount was in excess of four thousand dollars. Weaver returned, they said, on August 7, and got the funds. Asked to identify the man who obtained the money, both witnesses, in turn, pointed dramatically at Powers.

Coley Woods confirmed that he was employed at the Gore Hotel as night porter on the night of July 30, 1931. Yes, he remembered a white woman who registered that night, Dorothy A. Lemke. "Around one-thirty in the night . . . I responded for the baggage."

"What do you mean?" Morris asked.

Emily leaned toward Eric. "He thinks the answer too well phrased to be understood by the rabble."

"I went out," said Coley Woods.

"That should be clear enough," Eric said quietly.

Truman Parrish followed Woods on the stand. Morris asked that he produce and identify the Gore Hotel registry sheet showing the name of Mrs. Dorothy A. Lemke. Parrish offered the broad white sheet. "It is registered, 'Mrs. D. A. Lemke.' "

Law objected. "There is no definite proof that this is the same party. . . . Mrs. D. A. Lemke . . . is not the name or initials of the party claimed to have been killed —"

Gretchen Fleming stood in her seat, flames of color in her cheeks, but Morris quickly asked for a short recess. Witnesses were shown offstage to the left, the jury to the right. By turns, counsel, judge, and defendant, dog-collar-chained once more to his minder's steel cuff, left the stage. Four state troopers' boots resounded in perfect time until the general clamor eclipsed all.

She stood in the lobby with Eric.

"Take this water, Emily. Are you all right?"

She drank. "Are you, Eric?"

"It helps to know there is life beyond the opera house. We will go back to Chicago, Emily, to lead changed lives." He leaned with her against the wall, out of the milling crowd.

"Your life is changed, Eric? By Charles O'Boyle?"

"Yes, changed. We are seeking adjacent accommodations. A stairway closed off, easily restored, a door built through; we shall be neighbors and business associates."

"That is how it's done," Emily agreed, smiling.

"Have you something to tell me, Emily?"

"I think someone else might like to tell you."

"He did. Mason joined William and me at breakfast, and told us both. Not a secret, he said."

"No, when so much is, and must remain so."

"It's curious, isn't it? Social convention restricts and threatens, yet class and convention protect us if we behave within certain parameters."

"Not everyone is so fortunate."

"No, but we are all quite capable of being happy."

She wanted to embrace him. "Yes, and Mason will come with us. You will be Uncle Eric."

"Far too bourgeois. But I will be his family, with you. He must be allowed false steps, Emily. He will surely make them."

"As will I, Eric. What do I know of children? Only to respect him and try to help him. William says my family is his. I still feel as though eggshells may crack."

"Emily, they will, or not, despite your vigilance. Dare to hope. What's destroyed is in the past, and we are attending to it."

Chimes rang; an intermission was over.

So much to say. Morris had needed to prompt other witnesses, but he would have drilled Gretchen Fleming to answer only what was asked. He must direct her intense desire to lash out at Powers. Her sister, but for the Eichers' deaths, would have remained anonymous darkness in a ditch. Now one victim might avenge another.

Gretchen Fleming took the stand; her testimony was practice for Law's cross. Emily could almost hear Morris: don't let him bait you, confuse you. Don't look at Powers, look at me.

Morris approached her. "Please state your name."

"Mrs. Gretchen P. Fleming." She clutched the purse hidden on her lap.

"Mrs. Fleming, did you know Dorothy Lemke, or Pressler, in her lifetime?"

"Yes, she is my sister."

Present tense, Emily noted.

"What was her maiden name?"

"Dorothy Pressler."

"Did she marry?"

"Yes, sir, she married Lemke, from St. Paul, Minnesota."

"Did she continue to be the wife of Lemke?"

Emily silently counseled her: no comment on the scandal or reason for divorce.

"She separated from him in 1924. Divorced."

Quickly, smoothly, back and forth.

"How did your sister write her name, or do her banking, if you know?"

"When she left her husband in 1924, she sold her home in St. Paul, Minnesota, for about four thousand dollars, and so they settled the money, and she brought the money on to Worcester, Massachusetts. She had hard feelings with her husband."

"Now, Mrs. Fleming, just answer the question," Morris cautioned.

"Well, she had accounts in . . . her maiden name, and in the name of Lemke, Dorothy P.

Lemke, her married name."

Morris led her to the point. "And did she sometimes write her name as D. A. Lemke?"

"Yes," Gretchen said. "Her given name was Dorothy Ann."

All this to ascertain that Lemke's signature on the Gore Hotel register, D. A. Lemke, was in fact the Dorothy Lemke who returned to New England in 1924 to live with her aunt and work as a lady's companion.

Gretchen Fleming blinked in the lights. Emily continued writing testimony in shorthand, for there was no way of knowing what she might need to quote. She drew a tight, automatic script and closely observed the witness, and Powers, and the performance of one for the other.

"When did you first find out that your sister was corresponding with this defendant?"

"June, the twenty-fifth, or twenty-seventh it was . . . she told me about how she was going to be married to a man out in Clarksburg, West Virginia."

Law attended Gretchen's testimony; she was mistaken about dates and kept correcting herself. "I will ask you to state whether you received notice that your sister was dead in Clarksburg."

"Yes, sir, I received notice."

"Did you come here, and did anyone come with you?"

"I did, with Mr. Fleming, and my aunt,

Mrs. Rose Pressler."

"Did you see your sister here, then?" Morris spoke as though Dorothy might have been crossing the street.

"Yes, sir, in the undertaker's room, in the morgue."

"Tell the jury, Mrs. Fleming, whether or not you identified your sister there at the undertaking establishment."

"Yes."

"And how could you do that?"

The spectators in the opera house grew hushed.

"By the shape of her body, and . . . she had the same round face I have . . . and very even teeth . . . I could tell that it was her."

"Was there any mark upon her body or her abdomen?"

"Yes, sir, she had an operation in 1927. She was in hospital two months, and stayed with me two more . . . she had quite a scar . . . her appendix removed, and her right ovary." Gretchen spoke clearly. "It was a very bad sore, and I had to treat that sore . . . some four or five weeks . . . it discharged . . . it left a particular scar."

Ugly, Emily imagined, puckered, the shape of the drainage tube. So Gretchen had nursed Dorothy, who might have died of infection if not for her sister's care. But she survived.

The questions continued, and the scenery began to sway, almost imperceptibly, and then in a subtle rippling, as though someone had brushed against it from behind. Powers looked away, and put a hand to the side of his face, as though to shield his eyes.

Could Gretchen identify the clothing her sister wore at the morgue?

"Yes . . . same dress she left my house in . . . that jewelry, a brooch, was on her dress right up here . . ."

Morris kept his questions short and clear. "The coat I hold in my hand now, marked 'Exhibit Lady's Fur Coat' . . . Whose coat is this?"

Gretchen seemed subtly agitated. Emily wondered if she felt ill, or just exhausted.

"That is my sister Dorothy's coat . . . she bought that in New York . . . last Christmas." Gretchen touched a hand to her hair, as though to steady herself. She identified her sister's handwritten endorsement on "Exhibit Lemke check, sum of $2,754.22, Worcester County Institution for Savings," and on "Exhibit Pressler check, sum of $1,533.01, Worcester Mechanics Savings Bank." Both were dated July 28, 1931. It was obvious from the exact numbers that Dorothy had withdrawn the entire contents of the accounts.

The scenery panels of forest trees were noticeably swaying, and Emily heard laughter in the press corps. "Breath of the angels," someone whispered, chuckling, and "Try his manacles, a backstage door is open." Perhaps.

The opera house was drafty. Powers alone seemed inured to the cold, but he hunched now, brought his arms to his head, and covered his ears.

Morris gave Gretchen Fleming the sheet from the Gore Hotel register. "Is that signature of 'D. A. Lemke' your sister's writing?"

Of course it was.

Law, on cross-examination, asked only "At the time you saw the bodies at the morgue, the body of what you believe to be Mrs. Lemke, the remains were in a very badly decayed condition, were they not?"

Gretchen Fleming answered, "Yes, sir, they were."

"And much swollen," Law said.

"Why, I did not notice the swollen so much." She glared at him.

Emily wanted to cheer.

Annabel finds herself upon a stage she knows. The production is well along. Women in the box seats cover their faces with the gauzy veils of their hats, to see and not be seen. Annabel smells the perfumed hankies they touch to their eyes and noses, but the spider that scuttled over her sits just here in his swivel chair, reeking of the ditch. She moves amongst the painted trees, a swaying waltz to show the limbs in motion, and turns in measured time, trembling the ropes that dangle in the wings.

Slumped in his chair, Powers feels the air upon him. She spins the wheels on his chair so fast that he feels a buzzing under him, and she follows when he stands and swears, his hand upon the book. Women are weeping now, but she is drawn away. The footlights cast their blinding gleam onto sunlit fields, a flat sea of waving grass. Seasons have blinked by and the blond grandsons are riding the smoky tractor in spirals, each with a foot braced on a fender. Annabel sees the farmhouse far off, and their grandfather at an upstairs window. His share of the land will go to the boys in equal parts, to keep them on the farm; they are good workers and good boys, and land is the only protection.

The old man pulls a chair, a straight wooden chair made on his own lathe, to the window. All that winter, words he couldn't read in the newspapers, and photographs.

The boy was off, a broken clock, a complicated works. He jabbered and mimicked, cunning, watchful, hoarding things and then creatures, concealing all until the father found pieces on the rubbish lot behind the store: birds, young kittens, his wife's small dog. The boy was twelve. The father beat him. Forced him to bury it all by lantern light, keep it secret.

Secret. Afraid in his sleep. A weapon near his bed, but the boy wasn't interested in guns or fighting; he wouldn't make a soldier. He liked soft things like himself, and now the father knew why. The father knew, and saved him in the lake. Beat him, at fifteen, sixteen, for stealing. Beat him for drinking. One summer, Gypsies camped near town: a child, old enough to walk, missing and never found. Send Harm to America.

America, so vast he hoped the boy would disappear, but all those years, he traveled, a welter in a caravan. Took names, threw them down like parts on a heap. The tractor turns round, back toward the barn and the house.

He looks at his land and wishes for a cold wild storm.

Law stood at the lip of the stage as though to present the main attraction. "Mr. Powers, you are the defendant in this case?"

"Yes, sir."

"I will ask you to state what is your name, and where you were born."

"My true name is Herman Drenth."

"Now he tells us," said Eric, not bothering to speak quietly.

"How do you spell the last name?" Law asked.

Powers wore an expression of affable satisfaction. "D-r-e-n-t-h."

Law went on to elicit short facts: born in the Netherlands, 1892; came to this country in 1910 at age eighteen, to West Virginia in 1927, married and settled in Clarksburg.

"He's thirty-nine," Emily murmured to Eric, "not forty-five. Another lie."

Law looked pleased. "Been a resident of Clarksburg ever since?"

"I have."

"Mr. Powers, I will ask you to state if you knew, in her lifetime, Dorothy Pressler Lemke?"

"Yes, sir."

"Under what name were you known to her?"

"Well, I was first introduced to her . . . by the name of Harry F. Powers."

"Where and when?" Law stood by, listening.

Powers obliged. "In this city . . . either late in the summer or in the early fall of 1930. I just don't remember . . . I forget just what place. . . . I happened to be walking along and met her."

"Who introduced you?" Law asked.

"Charles S. Rogers," answered Powers.

This same Rogers, Powers now told all assembled, put Asta Eicher on a train for Denver. Emily glanced at Eric, who shrugged.

Law drew Powers out. "I had known Mr. Rogers since the winter of 1925. . . . I was on my way to Canton, Ohio, and he was walking along the highway, and I just gave him a lift."

Emily marked the phrasing. A journey, joined.

"About when did you last see him?" asked Law.

"The last time I saw Mr. Rogers was June of this year . . . at Park Ridge, Illinois."

Law went smoothly on. Had Powers "entered into any correspondence or developed your acquaintance further" with Mrs. Lemke, after their introduction in Clarksburg?

Powers looked mildly puzzled. "Well, I don't hardly know how to explain that without causing misunderstandings in the court."

His tenor voice was completely without accent, Emily noted. "Don't hardly know" was an affectation; his English was that of an American with a few generations of established family behind him.

Asked how he "came to write" to Mrs. Lemke, Powers again described Rogers. "Mr. Rogers was the man who . . . showed me a list of names, and . . . called my attention to Mrs. Lemke's name, and says, 'This is the lady you met some time ago, last fall' . . . but I did not recall that . . . the meeting had only been for a few seconds. . . . I had to go to the bank and the bank was about to close, and so I did not talk to them much that afternoon."

"Rogers," Eric said quietly. "Grim cupid, traveling around with Dorothy Lemke."

"Well, by the way, let us go back to Rogers," Law said, as though merely wondering. "Where was his home; where did he live?"

"I can only tell you what he told me . . .

that his home was in Pittsburgh . . . but he was mostly . . . here in this state, in Fairmont, West Virginia; that is, he made his home there, according to what I understood."

All thirdhand knowledge for which Powers was not responsible. Skillfully false, Emily thought, and so practiced.

He told a version of his history with Dorothy Lemke: first trip to see her July 9 or so, for three days, but "not much of a feeling . . . just like acquaintances."

Powers, not a suitor constricted by employment, described coming "home from the first trip" on the seventeenth or eighteenth and finding two letters from Lemke, inviting him "to take a vacation with her." He left July 20, to arrive in Uxbridge, Massachusetts, on the twenty-third, where "she was employed," and stayed five days.

Driving here and there, Emily noted, three or four days at a time, on what funds and for what purpose, and bread lines in the streets.

"You were known to her at that time under what name?" Law prompted, as though to be helpful.

"C. O. Pierson, or Cornelius O. Pierson, or whatever it might be," Powers said mildly, as though names were of no consequence.

No law against deceiving lists of women, was the implication, or renting a post office box to manage one's replies. Emily gazed at the jury, whose faces betrayed no expression.

Law asked if Powers had met or visited any of Mrs. Lemke's relatives.

"I met Mr. and Mrs. Fleming and their family . . . Northborough, I believe the name of the town is." Yes, they'd remained overnight. At no time did he refer to Dorothy by a first name; they'd stopped because "she had two trunks over at her sister's house that she wished to ship to Fairmont, West Virginia . . ."

"And who lives in Fairmont?" Eric asked sotto voce. "Why, Charlie Rogers lives in Fairmont."

As did Cornelius Pierson, Emily thought; he'd likely told Dorothy, as he told Asta Eicher, that he lived at the Fairmont Hotel, the best in the area. As for the post office box in Clarksburg, he was often in Clarksburg on business, and came and went at the hotel frequently; he could not expect a reception desk to handle his mail.

"Now," Law said, "to whom were these trunks addressed?"

"To myself."

"Under what name?"

"C. O. Pierson."

Of course, for that's who he was at the time. Emily sighed.

During his visit to Mrs. Lemke, Powers stayed at the Uxbridge Inn, where "every day . . . she would come there to see me." Mrs. Lemke wanted to visit friends in Fairmont, West Virginia, and in Paris, Illinois.

"She expressed her desire for me to go with her there for a sort of vacation, and for the purpose of becoming better acquainted."

He then explained a "misunderstanding" during the ensuing "vacation" that rendered him the wronged party. "We had taken a room apiece and each . . . had retired." It was a summer evening and still daylight. "I decided to go and talk to Mrs. Lemke awhile . . . her door was halfway open. . . . I could see Mrs. Lemke with her back toward the door. I walked in on my tiptoes like, thinking to play a little joke on her, not letting her know I was near."

Emily glanced up at William and found him looking directly at her. Powers on tiptoes. A little joke.

"She was reading a letter . . . and grabbed that letter which she was reading, quickly, and tried to tear it." Powers sat forward as though to create suspense. "I could tell there was something secret about that letter . . . a letter and a picture in a little frame. . . . I recognized this picture as a man I had met. . . . I noticed the postmark off of the letter and it was mailed from Clarksburg." Powers said he withdrew the letter against her will and read it. "This man was to meet her in Uniontown, Pennsylvania, . . . at the appointed place, and it ended with the word of 'Love.' It was signed, 'Cecil,' " Powers emphasized. "This picture is the man I

596

recognized as . . . Cecil Johnson."

Might the fog roll in more heavily? Not at all, for the Lemke checks were cashed in Uniontown, and this rambling story was why.

"We drove to Uniontown," Powers said.

"That would be the morning of the thirtieth of July?" pandered Law.

Powers took up the tale. "Well I did not say to Mrs. Lemke, during the trip . . . that I intended to leave her there. . . . I thought that she would realize that much without me telling her. . . . I parked the car along the curb." He got out to look for a suitable place for lunch, came back, and Mrs. Lemke had disappeared! As there "were no hard feelings of any kind," he started to look for her, "not wanting to leave her there without someone helping her along." He found her in a restaurant with Cecil Johnson, who invited Powers to join them. The gentlemen, both in town on "private business," shook hands. Johnson asked Powers to cash two checks for Mrs. Lemke.

Asked to elaborate, Powers explained. "I had cashed checks before for this Mr. Johnson, and so I considered him an acquaintance, and then of course I wanted to accommodate him if I could. I says, 'How big is your check?' 'Oh,' he says, 'Mrs. Lemke has a check' — in fact, he says, 'she has two checks . . . they are both cashier's checks . . . you needn't be afraid of them.' " Powers gazed into a middle distance, wearing a look of slight concern. "I objected to cashing those checks. . . . I did not have the money; that is, not that much. And Mr. Johnson then said, 'Well, you can cash one and I will cash the other.' I finally consented to accommodate them, and I cashed one check for Mrs. Lemke."

Law spoke carefully, as though to be sure the jury understood the complicated truth. "At that time, did you see both the checks? Were they presented to you there in the restaurant?"

"Yes, sir," Powers assured him. "Mr. Johnson said he would cash one . . . and Mrs. Lemke would endorse those checks and turn them over to me, and then I could give Mr. Johnson, at a future day, a check for his amount."

The tale accommodated Powers: he alone would deal directly with the bank, reimbursing himself with one check, for which he'd already advanced Mrs. Lemke cash, and collecting cash on the other check, with which he would supposedly reimburse Cecil Johnson. Emily looked at Eric. "Can he be serious? Is this really his story?"

Law offered both checks into evidence. "Mr. Powers, I will ask you which of the checks you advanced the money on."

"This one right here," Powers said.

Law held up the check. "That is for the sum

of one thousand, five hundred and thirty-three dollars and one cent?"

Yes, Powers asserted. Emily wondered that anyone might believe Powers carried such a sum in his wallet; $1,500 approached an average year's income for those earning a decent wage. And Mr. Cecil Johnson had cash, in excess of $2,750, to cover the other check.

"This Johnson is well heeled," Emily whispered, "and no vocation mentioned."

"Perhaps he's a con man." Eric gave her a wide-eyed look.

Powers would bank all the money from Lemke's checks while Johnson would hold Powers' postdated check: a check made out to Johnson. Powers would reimburse him after the bank paid; they would tear up the check, and so Powers could not be asked to produce it. It was bewildering, a sort of parlor game that netted Powers over four thousand dollars.

Law was presented the second check. "Whose endorsement is that, of 'A. R. Weaver'?"

"That is my handwriting and my endorsement," said Powers, admitting to fraud.

Why did he write the name A. R. Weaver? Well, he did not want to be responsible in case the checks were not paid, and endorsed them with a false name suggested by Mr. Johnson.

No, he did not see Mrs. Lemke again after

July 30. He drove to Hagerstown, Maryland, to see a friend with whom he'd been acquainted four years, whose address he did not know, for whom the post office there had no information; then he drove back to Uniontown to present the checks for payment the next day, August 1, just as the Uniontown bank tellers had testified. And yes, he returned to Uniontown on August 7 to collect on the checks, and to pay Mr. Johnson the amount due him. Powers' only contact with Mrs. Lemke consisted of the note she left in his car before "disappearing" in Uniontown.

Law began reading the note. *"Connie dear —"*

"That was supposed to be me," Powers informed Law.

Law went on: *"I think it best that we part. . . . So I am leaving you now. Please think as well of me as you possibly can. Best Wishes, Dorothy. P.S. I will write you . . . telling you where to send my things."*

"Best wishes," Emily told Eric. "No 'word of Love.'"

"I don't wonder," he said.

Powers of course knew Mrs. Lemke's handwriting; they had corresponded since the first of the year. At Law's request, Powers read out a second letter, received August 7, postmarked from Uniontown on the third.

He made a show of putting on his gold-rimmed spectacles and holding up the letter: *"I do not know as yet where to tell you to send my things. Please hold them for a while until I know where I will locate."* "Dorothy" did not blame him for getting so mad at her after he found out she had deceived him. Would he forgive her? She meant no harm, but was "so anxious."

The letter implied a hysterical, confused woman living who-knew-where with none of her belongings, for Powers had them.

On the way back from collecting her money in Uniontown, Powers stopped in Fairmont to collect her trunks. He took them to his Quiet Dell garage for safekeeping. Did he open them? He did not, but went into the "shed" on his return, for "it was not a garage," and "found the contents of those two trunks on the floor."

"Imagine," Eric said.

Prompted by Law, Powers confided that he'd often heard "about the neighborhood, being rather suspicious." He took Lemke's trunks home to Quincy Street.

Law referred to the large bloodstain on the concrete floor and asked about the "natural light" in Powers' "shed."

"Well, there was no provision made for any light at all," Powers answered.

No light, Emily knew, for this was his dark place, his hole in the earth, to starve them, hang them, strangle them.

There were four ventilators in the basement, Powers volunteered, "near the overhead, right close." The "ventilators," Emily knew, were merely small grated openings near the ceiling of each cell, barely at ground level outside, fitted with bolts so that boards could be secured over them. All this was known, for a newspaper had commissioned a detailed diagram of the "Murder Farm."

Emily knew the diagram by heart: four four-by-five-foot basement cells with thick, windowless doors and ceilings lined with soundproof board. A trapdoor in the garage covered the rough steps to the basement. A rope tied securely to a rafter dangled over it, broken off as though snapped by a heavy weight.

Dorothy, the last, broke the rope. And so he beat her and used the strap. Emily forced herself to look at Powers, who was saying he saw no stains in the near-dark garage until shown them by police.

And his arrest?

Powers sat back in his chair, relaxing as though to converse. "My wife and her sister told me at once; they were awfully excited . . . that city police had been there that morning asking for C. O. Pierson, that they did not know anyone by that name, and they told him so."

"Luella and Eva Belle," Eric said, "pure as

driven snow."

"And awfully excited," Emily wrote Powers' exact phrase.

Powers said he went along to the police station, "to find out what this is all about."

Law noted that Powers had been held in jail ever since, and faced the audience to ask, "Mr. Powers, have you ever endeavored to find Cecil Johnson or Charles S. Rogers, since your arrest?"

"I have given such information as I knew, to different persons, including officers of this town, but there was not much information that I could give."

"What to do?" Eric asked, writing.

"Did you ever have a letter at any time from Charles Rogers?" Law paused, as though for a reveal.

"Several letters," Powers answered.

Law then gave him a letter "bearing date of 'Fairmont, July 6, 1931,' addressed to 'Dear Pal,' and signed 'Charles.' . . . Are you acquainted with his handwrite, and often saw him write?" Law accepted Powers' affirmation and declared "we now want to offer this letter in evidence."

Finally, Morris objected. "It is self-serving."

Judge Southern examined the letter. "Sustained."

Emily reflected that Powers was quite occupied between calamities, driving from town to town, cashing checks and mailing himself letters.

Law reintroduced the linchpin of Powers' defense. "You spoke of the man Charles S. Rogers. Have you met him at Clarksburg other than the time when he introduced you to Mrs. Lemke?"

"I have. . . . He was out to the garage several times."

"State whether he had a key to the garage."

"Mr. Rogers had a key to that building practically ever since it was finished."

"Tell us about Cecil Johnson, was he ever out there?"

"Not to my knowledge."

And had Powers ever seen Cecil Johnson in Clarksburg?

"Why, yes . . . he was introduced to me by Mr. Rogers. . . . I think it was at the post office." Powers described Johnson as looking "similar to myself"; Rogers was a bit older, and had a joint missing from a finger on his left hand. Powers wasn't sure which finger and didn't know the cause of the injury, but "went to see him quite frequently" in 1925 and '26.

Before he married Luella in 'twenty-seven, was the point. Emily looked up to find William gone from his seat, for it was not his job to listen to Powers' lies.

"I took a liking to Rogers," Powers was saying, "and we became friends."

Morris rose for the cross; what was the purpose of the lists of names shown Powers by Charlie Rogers?

"Well, all I can tell you . . . it was a list used by a correspondence club . . . that went under the name of the American Friendship Society."

So he'd gotten both Asta's and Dorothy's names from an agency that catered to respectable women. Eva Belle Strother corresponded through "Cupid's Columns," but "the American Friendship Society" implied a vaguely charitable or even spiritual mission.

"What was the purpose of a married man," Morris asked, "in corresponding with these women, members of matrimonial bureaus?"

Powers leapt into the breach. "That purpose, to explain it right, would be a story."

"Well," said Morris, "let us have it."

"No," Emily said, into her notes.

But Powers obliged. "During the four years that we were married there was a good many domestic troubles. I had made up my mind that I would obtain a divorce. . . . I had frequently told [Rogers] about my troubles. . . . One day, January of this year . . . I met Mr. Rogers . . . and he pulled out several sheets . . . of these names, and he said, 'I know what I would do if I was in your place.' And I said, 'What would you do, Charlie?' "

Powers was actually doing the voices, pitching his own part in a slightly higher register.

"He says, 'I would get someone else.' My troubles had nearly driven me crazy at that time." Powers allowed his voice to tremble, and wiped at his eyes.

Morris looked skeptical. "And as a result . . . you did correspond with several women throughout the country?"

"I then, in my frame of mind, jumped at that suggestion that Mr. Rogers made to me."

"And among the women," Morris demanded, "was one Mrs. Asta Buick Eicher, of Park Ridge, Illinois?"

"Objected to!" Law shouted, for the noise in the hall suddenly increased. "That is not cross-examination!"

"Overruled!" Judge Southern declaimed.

Morris pressed on. "You had an understanding with Mrs. Lemke that you would be married?"

"No understanding whatsoever."

No understanding? Yet, Morris observed, Powers sent his picture to Lemke, and to other women, including Asta Eicher.

"Just a small picture," Powers said.

And he described himself, C. O. Pierson, as a man of wealth who owned property, a civil engineer . . . who built bridges?

Powers did not remember.

"Let us come to your trip to Northborough on Monday evening, July twenty-seventh. . . . You all talked over the situation together, you and Mr. and Mrs. Fleming, Mrs. Lemke, and the two Fleming children. Do you recall that?"

"I absolutely recall that we did not."

Morris reminded him: the large ranch near Cedar Rapids, his own electrical installation, to light the farm and house.

"There was no electricity mentioned by myself." Powers glanced at Law.

Didn't Powers recall the conversation later that Monday night with Mr. and Mrs. Fleming and Mrs. Lemke, about future arrangements? That he was going to give Dorothy all her heart could wish for?

"I did absolutely not say that." Powers tone was cold and flat.

And nothing was said about a honeymoon, Morris persisted, because Powers had no matrimonial ideas; was that correct?

"I did not say that merely; I meant that there was no such thing mentioned on the twenty-seventh day of July in the presence of Mr. and Mrs. Fleming."

"Where were you going then?"

Powers repeated, like an automaton, "Mrs. Lemke was on her way to Paris, Illinois, and Fairmont, West Virginia."

"And you were just very kindly taking her along, without any ultimate intention of marrying her? And brought her all the way from Northborough to Fairmont, and she never told you who she was going to visit in Fair-mont?"

"She did not."

"Now, Mr. Powers, just tell the jury please, how long a vacation Mrs. Lemke was going to take."

"I did not ask . . . that was her affair." Powers was sweating, and wiped his brow quickly.

"She took her bedding with her, didn't she, and a lot of other articles . . . winter clothes . . ."

"I can express my opinion about those things," Powers retorted, "but from real knowledge I would not be able to tell."

Morris went on, clarifying that Powers could not describe their route, did not register under any name at any of the tourist homes where they stayed. And so they arrived at Uniontown, where "the business of the checks" took place. "And without any more ado you took out a roll of bills and counted out one thousand, five hundred and thirty-three dollars and one cent, to Mrs. Lemke, and cashed the check payable to Dorothy A. Pressler?"

"That is right," Powers said.

Morris stood beside the jury box, as though to ascertain the tale for their benefit. "And I suppose Mr. Johnson did the same with the other check?"

Powers was unperturbed. "I did not see him do anything."

"What date did the check bear that you gave Mr. Johnson?"

"It bore the date of August eighteenth."

"That check, of course, was never presented?" Morris looked at the jury.

"It was presented to me," Powers said.

"It was never presented to the bank?"

"No, sir."

"And you merely cashed these checks for Mrs. Lemke, a woman who was leaving you for another man, on July thirtieth, for the purpose of accommodating her?"

"In one sort of way, yes. . . . Mr. Johnson had offered me thirty dollars for doing that."

A tidy fee, Emily reflected, improvised for the jury's benefit.

Morris observed that Powers, making no arrangements by telephone, telegraph, letter, or otherwise, drove five hours from Uniontown, Pennsylvania, to Hagerstown, Maryland, to look for a friend whose address he did not know, despite an "acquaintance" of about four years. And where did the defendant stay in Hagerstown on July 30, since he could not find his friend?

"Stayed in a sort of tourist home," Powers replied shortly.

Morris walked close to Powers, and raised his voice. "Did you see anybody in Hagerstown on that occasion who knew you?"

"No."

Morris turned to slowly pace the stage.

"You haven't the least idea of the name of the place where you stayed . . . and you came down to Uniontown again on July thirty-first . . . arrived after the banks had closed . . . and rather than come back to Clarksburg to leave these two checks for collection, you spent the night in Uniontown?"

"I decided to do that."

"Nor have you made any effort to ascertain where you stayed that night. And you do know . . . that Mrs. Lemke . . . spent the night of July thirtieth at the Gore Hotel in Clarksburg."

"I have seen that a number of times in the paper, yes," Powers said.

Morris asked, as though distracted, "Mr. Powers, where does that road go that passes your garage?"

"Out in the country?" Powers appeared nonplussed. "To Mount Clare, as I understand it."

"In other words," said Morris, "it is the road between Quiet Dell and Mount Clare?"

"That is what I understand."

"Now, as I understand you to say, you spent the night of July thirty-first in Uniontown."

"Yes, I was in Uniontown, or close to Uniontown."

Morris went near him. "Did you or did you not, about nine o'clock in the evening on July thirty-first . . . drive on that road from Mount Clare toward Quiet Dell, and have tire

610

trouble?"

"No, sir, I have never had tire trouble on that road in all my life."

"And didn't you, on that occasion, talk to various members of the Jones family?"

"I don't know the Jones family."

Morris paused, and took his seat.

Law, in the redirect, asked one question. "I will ask you to state, Mr. Powers, whether you were in Clarksburg on July twenty-eighth, twenty-ninth, thirtieth, or thirty-first."

"No, sir."

The gavel sounded. Court recessed for lunch.

The three witnesses seated onstage were surprise afternoon additions: an older man dressed in clean overalls, a young woman in a simple muslin dress and bonnet that hid her face, and a young boy, Mason's age, or Hart's, wearing new trousers. His white shirt showed the faint burn of an iron on one cuff. They refuted Powers' flimsy Hagerstown alibi, placing him at their farm the night of July thirty-first, asking to borrow pliers to fix a flat on his car, stopped below on Quiet Dell road.

Unlike Powers' meandering tale, their chilling account was clear. Morris questioned "the Jones family" one by one, ending with the child, whose open, freckled face was utterly guileless. His very presence onstage, as the tale played out, underscored a sense of horror in the audience.

Emily listened, spellbound: Morris established that Jones' daughter, Ada Thompson, twenty-one, was visiting her father last July. Most country girls were married at her age; this one removed her bonnet to reveal the blond countenance of a milkmaid. She was slender and lovely, perfection itself.

"I seen him on my dad's farm at Mount Clare about the last of July," she repeated, "nine or nine-thirty at night." She added a detail. "He hallued, 'Boys' . . . up through the corn —"

Here there was faint laughter, for she was certainly no boy, but the corn was tall; Powers would only have glimpsed her at first. Emily could feel the men around her entertain visions of meeting this girl in a fragrant cornfield at the height of summer twilight.

Ada Thompson cast her sloe-eyed gaze across the lit assemblage, demanding silence. "I was all in white. . . . He walked right up to us . . . he asked my name . . . and said his name was Pierson."

Emily looked up at William in his box seat and stood to leave, making her way quickly into the aisle. She would cover this story and file it quickly, rather than ramify Powers' lies. No interview required; every quote was in the testimony. Powers' car, broken down on the road, just as on that other night —

William caught up with her in the driven snow, on the street. "Emily, Powers is likely to be recalled. You're leaving? Are you all right?"

She could barely see in front of her but walked on quickly. "Why is everyone asking me if I'm all right? Of course I'm all right. I must write this quickly and file. Law will weep and wail at the end; should the jury recommend mercy, I want this town to finish what they began in September." William took her arm, for the sidewalk was slick with ice, but she turned on him sharply. "You needn't follow me. Go back if you like."

He stopped her. "I'm here for you, Emily, and I pray to God it turns out in whatever way allows you to live beyond it. Will hanging do it? The state, even a mob, can't make him suffer anything comparable to the terror and mayhem he created —"

"But someone, something, must!"

"We can't know. We don't see into any realm but this."

"You'll say next that this is all there is."

"You know I don't quite believe that."

Snow, sharp with ice, flew at them in gusts. She pulled him to her and turned in to the wind. "Come with me, then, and wait in your room until I type this and file. Then I will bring you the words, and read them like the modest prayer they will be."

■ ■ ■ ■

She wrote in a fury, with Mason at his worktable. She told him not to go out in the storm for the evening papers because it would all be over soon.

He looked at her, curious. "I can get them tomorrow."

"Of course you can," she said.

There was no line downstairs and she filed; possibly she would make the late edition. Copy in hand, she passed by Mr. Parrish at Reception.

"Quite a storm," he said to her. "Everything is shut down. I don't know that they'll get the jury back to the Waldo in this. Listen to the wind."

"Yes," she said. "I must go."

She walked up the stairs to William's room and let herself in with her key. The lights were off. Snow, blown against the panes of the big windows, gleamed faintly; all seemed enveloped. She heard the water of the bath; fragrance and heat drew her on. The white-tiled bathroom was fogged with steam. He lay in the deep tub, water drawn to the very brim.

"Are you chilled?"

"No." His wet hair was swept back. "I'm waiting for you." He moved in the water and rested his long arms on the tub's curled edge.

Water sluiced to the floor. "Read to me."

She sat in a small vanity chair he'd drawn up beside the tub. "This is my headline. If I write one, they know to use it."

"What was that child's name?"

"Jones' grandson? Degler, Harry Degler." She read by snowlight:

"Boy Bolsters State's Case Against Alleged Child Killer

"Special to the Chicago Tribune, by Emily Thornhill

"December 9, 1931

"Harry Powers' defense lawyer, J. Ed Law, today attributed five murders to two mysterious acquaintances of Powers, and supplied no witness to corroborate the defendant's statement that he was in Hagerstown, Maryland, on July 31. A farm family today placed Powers, as Cornelius Pierson, on the road to Quiet Dell that night.

"Thirteen-year-old Harry Degler, of Florida, was visiting his grandfather, H. F. Jones, last summer. According to the child's testimony today, a car traveling from Mount Clare to Quiet Dell, a distance of four miles on the Quiet Dell road, stopped on the dirt road below the farm at twilight.

"It was the night of a community corn roast. Farmer Jones rents a farm on the rural road and feared that revelers might raid his crop. He watched the fields behind his house while his grandson and his visiting 21-year-old daughter, Ada Thompson, watched the fields below. 'We heard a car stop,' testified Mrs. Thompson. 'A man walked up through the corn and asked me my name . . . he said his was Pierson.'

" 'Pierson' is known as an alias of alleged murderer Powers. 'Pierson' said he would pay the farmer well for his trouble: 'You just send the boy down so he can bring the pliers back,' he reportedly said.

"Harry Powers is accused of breaking 12-year-old Hart Eicher's skull with a hammer. In fact, as young Harry Degler followed 'Pierson' back through the cornfield to his car, the young boy from Park Ridge, Illinois, was buried in a drainage ditch behind Powers' Quiet Dell garage.

" 'Pierson' changed a flat tire. 'He did not have a flashlight,' young Degler testified, 'and this woman that was in the car with him, struck matches and held them for him to fix . . . the right tire on the back.' Spectators at the trial went silent: the woman in the car was likely Dorothy Lemke, last seen leaving Clarksburg's Gore Hotel with an unidentified man early on July 31.

"Degler said 'Pierson' changed the tire, 'fumbled over some bills in his wallet . . . most of them was twenty-dollar bills,' said young Degler. 'He gave me a one-dollar bill. . . . I bought me a pair of shoes the next day.'

"The car went on toward Quiet Dell, said the three witnesses, for it never came back the opposite way, past their farm.

"A practical child buys a pair of shoes, while another loses his shoes, his family, his life. Police found multiple pairs of shoes in Powers' 'murder garage.' Hart Eicher's muddy brogans were among them, stained with blood.

Emily continued looking at the words and could see no way past them.

"Emily," William said, "come here."

"I cannot. I must . . . just be still."

"No, come here."

She leaned forward and touched her forehead to the lip of the tub. The heat of the water glowed up and his warm wet hand was on her hair.

VERDICT

December 9, 1931

The players were backstage for the morning session; Emily saw Grimm walking to his front-row seat. Quickly, she got up to approach him. Seeing her, he stepped back into the hallway adjacent to the orchestra rows and stood waiting.

Emily reached him, stepping through the velvet curtains that graced each entrance to the hall. She could smell his aftershave and see behind him the five or six steps leading upward to a door off the stage. "You spoke of inquiries, in the crush of mail to police, from relatives of missing women. I must ask if any of those letters mentions Rogers. If so, might I read and quote them?"

"There are no hard facts. It is not evidence."

"I'm quite aware. I will not state facts, only the questions themselves, as represented. It must be in the public record, even if not examined in the trial. My source will be confidential, of course, and I must file today."

Judge Southern was banging his gavel, opening the proceedings. Grimm looked over her shoulder at the lit stage. "There are two letters I can allow you to quote. I will phone the station and have them left for you at the Gore, this noon. You must return them to me personally."

Emily, moving back, stumbled and fell full against him. "Excuse me," she said.

"All right?" he asked, setting her on her feet.

"Sheriff Grimm, I did not intend —"

"I realize. You must wait here a moment though, before coming in. You look . . . your color is high." He walked past her, into the hall.

She turned and began walking up the hallway, all the way round by the lobby, to shake off her embarrassment. Grimm required her guarded awareness, and not only because he was attractive. He loved manipulating his fiefdom, knowing secrets, pulling strings. Her vocation required matching wits with men like him. She paused in the lobby and saw William enter the opera house by the double doors, turning to walk quickly upstairs to the loge. She stopped herself calling out and merely looked after him. Even thinking of him calmed her. She crossed the lobby and walked down the far aisle to the front rows, deftly taking her seat.

"Did you go out?" Eric asked.

"Ladies' room." She opened her notebook and nodded toward the stage; she had no wish to converse.

Gretchen Fleming was back on the stand, wearing the same coat and hat, as though not to confuse the jury.

Morris was establishing that Gretchen had heard Powers' testimony of yesterday afternoon, in which the defendant stated he first met her sister, Dorothy Lemke, in Clarksburg in the fall of 1930. Did her sister visit Clarksburg at that time?

"No, sir . . . she would have told me so." Dorothy was working that year, Gretchen explained, all but weekends, as a nurse companion. And no, she had no friends or acquaintances at Clarksburg.

"Were you familiar with your sister Dorothy's handwriting?"

"Yes, sir."

Morris described Powers' "Exhibits No. 1 and 2," purporting to be a note and letter "from your sister to Powers." Would Mrs. Fleming look at the writing, and tell if the handwriting was that of her sister?

"Question objected to!" Law exclaimed. He asserted that Mrs. Fleming was not a qualified handwriting expert.

"Overruled!" Judge Southern replied.

Gretchen, the letters in her hands, looked up, emphatic. "It is not her handwriting! It is not!"

Law stated, "Exception." He waited a moment, as though to adjust his tone, and rose for the cross. "Now, Mrs. Fleming," he began, as though calming a skittish horse. He pointed out that Gretchen had identified her sister's endorsement on the two Massachusetts bank checks, and held out the checks.

"Yes, sir, and that is her handwriting."

Law gave the audience an exasperated look, and moved on. Now, did Mrs. Fleming have personal knowledge as to whether Mrs. Lemke was in Clarksburg . . . in the fall of 1930? The truth was, hadn't Mrs. Lemke done a good deal of traveling?

Yes, she traveled about with the lady, part of her job as companion. But no, Mrs. Lemke would not go away for a long trip; the lady needed her. For the trip with Pierson, she gave the lady two weeks' notice.

Law drew near to Gretchen. "You state she never told you about having known a man by the name of Rogers . . . or a man by the name of Cecil Johnson . . . though she might have known them both and not mentioned it to you."

Gretchen paused and said clearly, "I doubt that."

Yet, Law pointed out, Mrs. Lemke had corresponded with Cornelius Pierson beginning in January 1931, and did not mention him to her sister until late June. "Then," he concluded, "she did *not* tell you everything that she was doing, did she?"

"Everything, almost everything!" Gretchen shouted the words, defiant, tears in her eyes.

Dismissed, Gretchen moved toward the wings. Emily saw her expression assume a beseeching sadness.

Law called Powers back to the stand. "Mr. Powers, I will ask you to state if you did kill Mrs. Lemke at any time or place, as charged against you in this indictment."

"No, sir."

"Did you ever see her in Harrison County, West Virginia, at any other time except in the fall of 1930, when you met her, as you say, on the street?"

Powers blinked. "That was the only time I saw Mrs. Lemke in this county."

Would this be the lunch recess? No, for the

621

state called a Mr. Hufford, owner of a gas station, who testified that Powers had purchased gasoline from him at Wilsonburg, evening of July 31. On the paved part of the road, Hufford asserted, that leads to Mount Clare and Quiet Dell. Another witness to refute Powers' flimsy alibi, but Emily must go to the Gore. The letters from Grimm would be there at noon. The witness was saying he noticed the Chevy coupe, a nice one. Powers bought chewing gum and cigarettes, Hufford said. A heavyset woman was in the passenger seat.

It was very cold, nine degrees according to the ornate thermometer by the hotel entrance. Emily went directly to Reception. "Mr. Parrish, good day. Is there a package for me?"

"Miss Thornhill, let me see. No, doesn't appear so." He saw her concern and turned to search again. "Ah, yes, in the wrong place, but safely delivered." He gave her an envelope marked, "Emily, Room 127."

She sighed with relief, went to the elevator, and let herself into her room. The dog barked his breathy noise in greeting, and she threw off her coat, looking through to see Mason, cutting clippings at his table. "There you are. So much to file, yes?"

"An awful lot." He came to her room and sat on the bed. "Is it the noon break?"

"No, but I must quickly write something crucial, to file this afternoon." At her desk, she spilled two letters from the envelope and put her hand upon them. She turned to him. "Sorry I've been here so little. Hope you haven't been lonely."

"It's all right," he said. "I ordered lunch, and I'll get it when they knock." He gave a shy wave and went back to his room.

"Thank you, Mason." She must be more astute: deprivation of her presence was nothing to sleeping behind a hotel. Grief opened one to the true meaning of loneliness. She felt it in the letters: both from Iowa fathers whose daughters had disappeared. Had Powers, in his travels to Chicago, foraged through Iowa, not so far from Oran and Sumner, from Wilko Drenth? Only one letter mentioned Charlie Rogers.

She fell to writing, but would file at the close of today's session, when there might be more to include on the topic of Rogers.

She returned to the trial, the completed story in her valise. Powers was on the stand, to refute Hufford.

Eric leaned toward her, to catch her up. "Powers purchased no gasoline from Hufford, and no chewing gum. Surprised?"

Law paced the stage, affecting irritation. "He states also that you purchased some cigarettes from him at that time."

"I do not use cigarettes," Powers said.

Dorothy did, then, in private. Confident, relaxed, she smoked in Powers' car, riding along country roads where no one would see.

Morris began the cross and stood just below Powers, as though to engage in conversation. "How much money did you have on your person when you left Clarksburg to go up to see Mrs. Lemke and bring her back?"

"I had something like one thousand, eight hundred and seventy-five dollars. . . . I had that money . . . I had saved that money from my work."

"What was your business or occupation at the time, Mr. Powers?"

"I was working at home."

"And you were carrying that money in cash about your person. . . . I presume you must have been afraid of the bank?"

"I certainly was," Powers said.

Then why, Morris questioned, had Powers deposited two thousand dollars cash on August 11, and seventeen hundred sixty dollars on August 21, a total of three thousand, seven hundred and sixty dollars?

"Well, we intended to use that money . . . that was only to be there temporarily, just for a few days."

Morris looked at the jury. "And it was there until you were arrested, wasn't it?"

"That is true."

"And then what was left in that account

you turned over by check to your wife?"

"I did."

Morris persisted. "And that was a check for three thousand, six hundred and fifty-seven dollars and sixty-three cents?"

Emily rounded the figures: five hundred plus of Dorothy's money for their expenses, Northborough to Clarksburg, including her last night at the Gore; one hundred or so to Law, for his services did not come cheap, and the rest, over thirty-six hundred, windfall for Luella and Eva Belle.

"I reckon that is correct," Powers was agreeing. "I haven't the cents, the amounts."

"The fact of the matter is, Mr. Powers, you have gone under the name of Rogers."

Emily sat forward. The entire press section was still.

"Never have," Powers said.

"Do you remember when they had the Boyd Robinson trial out at West Union, some time ago?" Morris looked up at him.

"No, I don't recall that."

"Did you attend the trial of Boyd Robinson?"

"No."

"Wait a minute." Morris held up a hand, as though to caution him. "In the circuit court of Doddridge County, at West Union?"

"I have never been in that courthouse in all my life," said Powers.

He was fond of that phrase, Emily noted.

Morris seemed to abruptly change course. He restated Powers' testimony concerning the contents of Mrs. Lemke's trunk, scattered around his Quiet Dell garage on August 20 or 21. "I presume you thought some person had unlawfully entered the garage and done that?"

Powers said, oddly, "I did not know what to think of it for a little while."

Morris walked to center stage. He faced Powers only to deliver questions, turning to the jury as Powers answered. "It was not done with your permission?"

"No, I did not give any permission for that."

"You did not change the lock on the garage?"

"No, I had my opinion as to who done it and that was all."

"Who did you think had done that?"

"I think either Rogers or Johnson."

"Johnson did not know where the garage was, as far as you know?"

"No, but that was my opinion."

"And Rogers was the only one that had a key to the garage?"

"Yes, sir."

"And you did not notify officers that someone had burglarized your garage?"

"I did not know that it had been done," Powers said. "Rogers had a key to it and he could get in any time he wanted . . . he had some things to store."

"Who stored the Eicher things in there?" Morris moved close to him. "The fact of the matter is, you took them out there."

"I did not," said Powers, like a child.

Morris leaned in, nearly shouting. "Did you meet Rogers or anyone else, or give them permission to store them there?"

"He could store anything he wanted," Powers said.

"Did you have an agreement of some kind with this man, Rogers?"

"Just a verbal understanding was all."

Morris turned away, speaking rapidly. "I asked you earlier if you attended the Boyd Robinson trial in Doddridge County. I ask you now if you attended the trial of the case of *State versus Boyd Robinson* at the March term, 1930, of the criminal court of Doddridge County in the old courthouse building?"

"I don't recall that I did . . ."

"Well, answer yes or no if you can."

"I will say no." He seemed slightly fatigued.

Morris called out, "Is Mrs. Alice Bartlett here?"

Sheriff Grimm spoke from the right side of the stage, behind the wings. "Yes, sir, she is here."

A short, full-figured woman walked onto the stage. Her calf-length dress, apricot brocade or satin, too celebratory for a court appearance, shone in the lights. She was fifty or so, very fair, with the blue eyes and pink cheeks of a bisque doll, her hair completely covered with a black cloche hat. The ruched V-neck of the dress drew the eye to her full, well-supported breasts. She gazed at Powers.

Morris addressed him. "Mr. Powers, I will ask you if you know Mrs. Alice A. Bartlett, who is standing at your right."

Powers glanced at her. "I do not believe I am acquainted with the lady."

"Did you ever see her without knowing who she was?" persisted Morris.

"I don't recall," Powers said.

"I will refresh your memory . . . and ask you again if you attended the Boyd Robinson trial . . . and if you sat next to or near Mrs. Bartlett at that trial."

Powers looked about him, sensing that he must tread carefully. "What was this man, Robinson, charged with, and maybe I could recall it better."

Sheriff Grimm, standing just out of sight of the stage, called in, "Stealing chickens."

"I don't recall," Powers said, though Morris hadn't asked.

Morris dismissed him, and called Mrs. Bartlett to the stand. She waited as Powers took his chair, watching him openly, then moved forward to put her hand on the Bible and be sworn. She sat as though pleased, shrugging her cropped, dark coat to her shoulders. Her ample breasts moved in the dress. She wore a large oval locket on a beaded gold chain.

Morris walked about the stage, asking her to recall the trial of the *State versus Boyd Robinson,* Criminal Court of Doddridge County, in the neighboring town of West Union, March term, 1930.

Yes, Alice Bartlett answered. She did recall.

Morris reminded her: this trial was one in which Mr. Robinson was accused of stealing chickens from the farm of C. O. Young.

Law pushed back in his chair at the counsel table. "Objection! What have we to do with a chicken thief?" He opened his arms to Judge Southern, provoking ripples of laughter in the gallery.

Southern glowered. "The court will be the judge of that. Overruled! Proceed."

"Exception!" proclaimed Law, writing.

Morris established that Alice Bartlett lived in West Union, and asked why she took an interest in the Robinson trial.

She went by herself to the trial that afternoon, Mrs. Bartlett said, "because I met Boyd Robinson's sister on the street and she remarked to me that she felt so bad that none of her neighbors, or none of the women she knew, was taking any interest in the trial."

And where was Mrs. Bartlett sitting in the courtroom? Morris asked.

"I was not sitting very far back," she said, "in the place reserved for the audience."

Morris approached her, his hands clasped behind his back. "I will ask if you know the defendant, Harry F. Powers?"

"Well," she replied, her hand at her neck. The gold locket gleamed up at her clavicle. "I saw him there that day; I recognized him from the newspapers, as being at the trial."

Did she mean that she saw Powers in March 1930, at the Boyd Robinson trial? And recognized Powers in his newspaper photo, and so came forward, to testify here today?

"Yes." She looked at Powers, across the room. "He is the same man, and he was at the trial that day."

"Where did he sit, with reference to where you were?"

"He came in and sat right down by the side of me."

"Mrs. Bartlett, I will ask if either of you started a conversation."

Alice Bartlett leaned forward. "He did. The first thing he said, he asked me if I was a witness, and I said, 'No,' and then he said, 'Rogers is my name.' He says, 'I am very well acquainted with the Youngs.' He says, 'I buy lots of stock of them.' He says, 'I have a big stock farm and store, and I am manager for an electric sweeper company.' And I turned around and remarked to him, 'That is nice,' and when I turned around to make him that answer I saw he had laid his arm on the back of my seat, and I moved toward the edge of the seat, and then he reached over and asked me my name. I replied by asking him to take his arm down off of the back of my seat, and I said, 'See now that you do it.' "

"Did either of you move away from the other?" Morris asked.

Alice Bartlett pulled at the fingertips of one gloved hand with the other. "He took his arm down then and only remained a very short time . . . until he got up and stepped to the back in the courtroom, or went out, I don't know where. I did not see no more of him." She touched her throat. The gold locket winked as she moved; it was large, nearly two inches round, and set with a stone, a diamond, from the catch of the light.

"Mrs. Bartlett," Morris said. "Are you sure of your identification of the defendant?"

"Yes, sir. I identified him in the papers, and he looks like the man today."

Powers would have noticed the locket, Emily knew, and Alice Bartlett was the right age and weight, and dressed expensively, despite her country grammar. She'd married up; perhaps she was widowed, with the time and inclination to attend a trial on a weekday afternoon, a favor to a female friend, an entertainment for herself.

Morris paused and said he had one more question. Her locket was lovely. Did she wear it every day?

Why yes, she told him, it was her late

husband's gift, a family heirloom —

"Objection!" Law thundered. "Immaterial!"

"Sustained," Judge Southern replied. "You may cross-examine the witness."

But Morris had made his point. The locket had attracted Powers' attention, if her breasts did not. And Emily thought not.

Law stood and walked back and forth across the stage, fixing the attention of the crowd. He spoke in clipped, angry phrases, as though insulted. "Were you summoned as a witness in the case, and if so, when?"

"Yes, sir, I was summoned today."

"To whom have you talked with regard to this conversation before you were summoned?"

"Oh, to several people . . ." Alice Bartlett looked about her, as though to find them on the stage.

Law stopped before her. "How did the information get out, and how were the prosecution told, that you recognized Rogers?"

"Why," she said, "I let the law here know it."

"Who did you let know it?"

"Sheriff W. B. Grimm."

Law turned to face the audience. "Where did you talk to him?"

"To let him know? I just wrote it to him." She looked at Law as though he lacked sense.

"What purpose did he have, this defendant here, in giving you a name, Rogers?"

"I don't know." Alice Bartlett widened her blue eyes. "You will have to ask him that."

There was murmuring, even applause, in the audience. Law stalked back to his table, shouting, "Dismissed!"

The gavel banged. Emily put her hand to her forehead, and turned to Eric. "I must file. I have the story nearly written." She stood and stepped past a number of male reporters, to the end of the row, and moved quickly up the carpeted aisle to the lobby. She went to the press corps office, across the street, rather than to the Gore, and approached the counter. No one was in line; the trial was still in session.

She sat to handwrite several sentences incorporating Bartlett into the first graph. Her headline was interrogative, for she could only insinuate. She read the words over quickly:

Killer Powers Cites "Charlie Rogers" as Friend and Love Mentor: Are "Rogers" and Powers the Same Man? Clarksburg, WV, Special to the Chicago Tribune, by Emily Thornhill:

In breaking developments today, witness Mrs. Alice A. Bartlett, local resident, testified that a man she identified as Harry F. Powers introduced himself to her as "Rogers" in March of last year "owner of a large stock farm and manager of an electric sweeper company." Accused killer Harry F. Powers has cited his friend Charlie Rogers as acquainted with Asta B. Eicher, murdered widow, and testified that Rogers introduced him to Northborough, Massachusetts, victim Dorothy P. Lemke, pointing out her name as the most suitable correspondent listed by the Friendship Society of Detroit, a matrimonial agency.

Clarksburg police have received numerous letters suggesting that other unsolved cases of missing women may be traced to Powers. One in particular mentions Charlie Rogers by name. The letter comes from C. S. Brown of Iowa Falls, Iowa, concerning the death of his daughter, Miss Golda Brown, 37, a trained nurse working in Cleveland, Ohio; her father expresses the belief she was murdered and that Powers was involved. Official records state that Golda Brown died after taking poison on July 26, 1929. At her death, her father received a night message alerting him to the tragedy, signed by "Rogers." No "Rogers" turned up when the father went to Cleveland to identify his daughter's body, but Brown says that a short, stocky man fell into step beside him as he emerged from the morgue: "He asked me if he could do anything and I inquired if he knew of a man in Cleveland by the name of Rogers, who was from Pittsburgh. He advised me to take the body and 'get to hell out of here.' "

Brown's letter claims the supposed suicide note left by his daughter "is no more her handwriting than that of a two-year-old child." Golda Brown's father believes Rogers and Powers are the same man.

Arrest halted Powers' correspondence with over 200 women. Letters arrived to Cornelius O Pierson's P.O. Box 227, Clarksburg, West Virginia, at the rate of 20 a day. Dozens of women's photographs found in Powers' possession were simply inscribed to "Connie, dear," a pet name Powers employed. The names of other possible victims will likely remain unknown, and their lives go unremarked, but in the grieving hearts of those who still search for them.

Emily went to the counter and called to the dispatcher. "Sir? Would you send this immediately, please, to the *Chicago Tribune*?" She handed over her copy and stood by the window to wait. Crowds, discouraged by yesterday's storm, were back in front of the opera house; closing arguments were expected today. She saw the crowd jostle, and police holding up billy clubs, directing human traffic. It was the lunch recess. Hundreds were making their way outside. She saw William striding free of the throng, crossing the street, and flung open the door of the press office. "Mr. Malone! Over here!" She was about to rush into the street, but he saw her and walked toward her.

"Miss," called the dispatcher. "Your copy!"

The opera house was packed for closing arguments. Law swept his gaze over the aisles, the balconies and gallery, questioning the motives of the state's witnesses, one by one. He condemned the public's sad fascination with gruesome detail and clutched the sides of the counsel table, decrying the base desire for public spectacle, even when a man's life hung in the balance. The lights onstage seemed to dim.

"Law has paid someone to dim the border lights," Emily told Eric. "Why doesn't Morris object?"

"Best not to interrupt. Morris will use the trick to his own ends." Eric put a finger to his lips.

Law spoke in ringing tones of the love of mankind. Even the state admitted to a wholly circumstantial case, he claimed, and reasonable doubt must always exist in the absence of hard evidence. He pleaded that the jury "remain firm in their convictions," for the true consideration here was the question of the sane men in the jury killing another, less fortunate, misbegotten man, a man mired in ill fate and bad judgment. Law stood before the jury box to quote the Gospels from memory: cast the first stone; judge not lest ye be judged. There but for God's grace, he intoned, lifting his long arms; the jury alone might exercise compassion and pity, for compassion, so desired by all of us in our darkest hour, was the epitome of human blessing. Tears streaming down his face, he urged the jury to apply the spirit of Jesus: "sympathy, justice, and mercy." Powers, as though moved by Law's plea, looked pointedly at the painted backdrop of the church behind the judge, and lifted his face to display the tracks of tears.

"Well played," Eric whispered.

But Morris did not disappoint. He appealed first to reason, pounding on the stenographer's desk, reviewing the state's inexorable chain of evidence point by point, for nearly an hour. Then he took his turn at center stage, declaiming like a town crier. Indicted but not charged! He pointed at Powers, and called the names: Asta Buick Eicher. Her children: Grethe Eicher, fourteen years old; Hart Eicher, twelve years old; Annabel Eicher, nine years old. Indicted and charged! Dorothy. Pressler. Lemke.

Morris had silenced the hall. There was no Johnson, no Rogers, he told them. Harry Powers, after Dorothy Lemke helpfully struck match after match to light his mechanic's chore on a darkening road, drove her, in the same car, less than two miles to his death chamber. Mercy? Her death was not quick, he reminded the jury. Let us walk with her, every step; surely she was owed that much, for she found no compassion, no help in that long night.

Certainly, he was using the lights, which seemed to have dimmed further. Emily heard women softly weeping. She only hoped Gretchen Fleming was not here, that she'd left after her grueling testimony.

Morris went on, commanding the hushed crowd. She died not once but twice, for the rope broke and she plunged deeper into darkness . . . before he wielded the strap.

There were gasps and stifled cries.

Morris finished: "The state demands nothing less than a verdict carrying the death penalty for the first mass slayer the county has ever known!"

It was 3:20. The jury retired to a guarded opera house dressing room.

Emily and Eric walked out onto the snowy streets, away from the crowd, and waited for William. The three drifted slowly into the lightly falling snow. A mere two blocks away on a parallel street, the city was quiet. Few came and went.

"How long?" William asked.

"They will stay out an hour at least," Eric said, "to be taken seriously in such a publicized capital case."

"What a show." William pulled his scarf up about him. "Morris had final say, at least, to offset Law's histrionics. He made the truth dramatic, but I wonder if he went too far."

Emily brushed the snow from his shoulders. "Too far, my darling? As you say, it was every word the truth. And he didn't cry."

"The state does not cry, Emily." Eric smiled. "Not Morris' style, in any case."

"Powers, weeping," Emily scoffed. "I didn't think he could. Perhaps they practiced."

"Cousin, I remind you. He sniveled and cried in fear of the lynch mob, in September."

"I don't believe it's genuine." Emily led them toward the park. "He does not feel fear; he calculates and postures. He will show no emotion at his hanging. I would bet money on it."

"Law's appeal was staged philosophy and biblical allusion, and the jury are likely religious." William stopped and looked into the snow. "Might they actually recommend mercy?"

"We will know immediately," Eric said. "The verdict will read 'guilty as charged in the indictment,' which means he hangs, or they will add the phrase 'further find that he be confined in the penitentiary,' which means life in prison, because that is what Southern will sentence him."

"No," Emily said, "it must be over."

Eric pulled off his gloves and took a ciga-rette from his pocket. He signaled them to stand near while he lit a match.

"Eric, you're smoking." Emily watched the fire in his cigarette glow bright orange in the blue afternoon.

"Settle my nerves. I filched a few from the complimentary box in the Gore smoking room. I knew I'd want one just now."

"Give me one then," Emily said. "William?"

"No, though I'd like a bourbon. I'll have a stiff one when it's over."

"So shall we all." Eric leaned in to light her cigarette with his own, and caught her eye.

Charles. The drop moment. "Thank you, cousin," she said.

"In any case," Eric continued, "Law will gather up his overruled exceptions and request a new trial. He will appeal beyond Southern, but he will fail."

"The sentence must be carried out no sooner than thirty days after sentencing," Emily said. "The execution should be mid-January, at the latest."

William pulled her to him as they walked, for they were out of sight of the crowd. "And these other cases, brought to attention. In the unlikely event that he is not hanged, might other charges be filed?"

"No." She drew in, watching the languid

smoke of her cigarette ascend. "It is all hearsay, and much weaker circumstance, and the trail is cold."

"He is strangely contemptuous of it all," William said, "and no real alibi, as though he might exonerate himself with lies alone."

Eric threw down his cigarette, burning a hole in the snow. "That is freedom, that a killer might range over a territory for years, no one watching. And with Luella and her sister the perfect cover on home ground, asking no questions, he maintained anonymity."

"He didn't plan on getting caught," Emily said. "Lone women might disappear with a man, and their relations seek information, but until Powers was famous, no one knew whom to ask, or where to write. He was caught because he killed the Eichers. Whatever he's done or would have done, their deaths have ended it."

"That at least is true." William pulled her closer.

Emily held her gloved hands open, catching flakes that fell on a slant, like soft rain. "Such snow. It stops and starts at intervals, as though looking away and coming back to us, dancing or raging. Is it always like this here in winter?"

"Parrish says such heavy snows are not usual so early in December, but he is my only authority." Eric leaned across her, toward William. "Emily, William and I have made plans. The sentencing will be tomorrow morning, Thursday."

"You do want to go home, don't you, Emily?" William looked at her as though truly asking. "We made train reservations, two days ago, for Friday, to be sure there is room for the four of us, as scores will be leaving at once."

"I hadn't thought, but of course. We're going together?" She smiled at the thought.

"No, but on the same train, three compartments, and we shall meet for meals, like acquaintances who have survived the same peril." He touched her hair that trailed down from under her hat.

"And take separate cabs on arrival," Eric said. "William must see to his bank in Park Ridge, but I will go home with you, to help you with the luggage, and the three of us will dine."

Emily looked at Eric in his lamb's-wool fedora and realized that he would take them to a celebratory dinner somewhere near, and go home to Charles O'Boyle.

"I've bought Mason a trunk; he knows to expect it this afternoon, at the hotel." William looked at his watch. "The jury has been out . . . forty minutes."

They stood and began walking back, silent, quickly, until they could see, from the end of the street, the opera house marquee lights glowing pale pink in the snow.

"William, please sit with us for the verdict. I want you near." Emily pulled them both to her and linked her arms in theirs. She could not imagine who she was before she stood between them, these tall men in their big coats and snow-covered shoulders. Life was merciless, and then briefly miraculous, for all was so brief. Their own lives, together and apart, would last the blink of an eye.

"Whatever happens," William said, "you both must know — no one could have done more, so constantly, than you have done."

The statement was oddly mournful. Emily was suddenly afraid. "We must get back. We should not have left. We —"

"Emily, we are a block away." Eric was ushering them through groups of spectators that seemed to flow from one end of the street to the other.

Emily supposed the car to whisk Powers away was waiting as usual at the rear of the opera house. Police drove through the Central Garage, up Fifth Street to the jail, avoiding drifted snow, crowds, and enterprising photographers at the stage door.

Inside, time crawled. Emily waited, William to her left, Eric to her right, watching Powers, who sat with his back to them and occasionally looked around like a man waiting for a bus. Law paced, or sat by Powers, legs crossed, shaking his foot nervously. He borrowed a newspaper from a reporter in the front row and perused it intently with Powers, as though reviewing the coverage.

It was nearly five; the audience had begun to dwindle. Rumor had officers bringing in supper and bedding for the jury, and the jury requesting a minister, or summoning the minister who'd counseled Powers after his "confession" in August.

Another half hour; nearly two hours. Judge Southern came to the bench, seemingly to adjourn for the night. Three loud raps suddenly rang out, almost like a theatrical effect.

The jury was signaling their entrance from the dressing room. Powers remained expressionless. The jury walked in. They didn't look at him, and took their seats.

The court clerk intoned: "Harken to your verdict, gentlemen."

The jury foreman read: "We, the jury, find the defendant, Harry F. Powers, alias Cornelius O. Pierson, guilty of first-degree murder as charged in the indictment within."

Emily listened for the additional phrase, but the clerk read the verdict again immediately, inserting the indictment number. Cheers rang out from the lobby and the crowd in the street. She felt William take her hand as state troopers rushed the prisoner from both sides of the stage. Powers merely waited as his various chains were fastened. Law stood to make a formal motion for a new trial as the audience raced for the exits and the lobby doors opened wide to applause and shouting. A wild glee seemed to pour down the aisles. Emily looked behind her. Spectators rushed out as others rushed in, finally allowed entrance.

"We will not embrace," Emily said, "we will not shake hands." She felt William pulling her to her feet.

"No, but we must leave by the back." Eric led them toward a rear exit as the houselights flashed rapidly. All was confusion until they were through a narrow passage onto a metal fire escape. Others had cleared the snow, and they walked down into an alley.

"I must file immediately at the Gore." Eric set off.

William caught her arm. "Emily, this will take time to be over." He touched his warm mouth to her forehead. "You must try to push the sadness away, for Mason."

For you, she thought, looking up into his warm brown eyes.

Snow fell in the gathering dark. All was before them, but she pulled him back, under the snow-shrouded fire escape, against the sheltered wall of the opera house. They must end in embraces after all.

■ ■ ■ ■

XVI.

■ ■ ■ ■

State Prison, Moundsville, March 18 —
Harry Powers went to the gallows here
tonight protesting his innocence. . . . It is
reported that [he] received $600 for the
story to be "sold to the highest Bidder" after
his death. . . . A half-smile played on the
lips of the man who lured women to their
deaths with love correspondence. . . . A few
seconds later, the black death hood was
placed over his head.

Among the men crowded at the foot of
the gallows were Sheriff W. B. Grimm, Chief
Deputy Simeon C. Bond, Police Chief C. A.
Duckworth. . . .

Powers' body was not claimed by his

widow, and will be buried . . . in the prison Potters Field.

— *The Clarksburg Telegram,*
March 19, 1932

March 18, 1932
Moundsville and
Quiet Dell,
West Virginia

An Execution

Annabel, borne up, sees lantern light amidst the valleys and rumpled mountains. The prison potter's field is marked, a name and a box for the murderer, but those gathered above Quiet Dell are nameless. Taken, they fell apart like fruit in muck and water, barely hidden or never found. Now they lift and swirl, a cumulus of air and cloud, a charged flow drawn to that place, below. Night furls down over the dirt road and abundant hills, the runnel of creek, the hunched garage.

The black hood over his head eclipses the fixed blue stare, the cunning shift of gaze. The spring of the trapdoor, the click of the hinge, the taut drop of the rope are like claps of thunder.

Annabel sees him falling in his own dark hole. He plummets in air that tosses and whirls like water dredged with earth, thick air dense with the soil of the ditch. He drowns, never to stop falling or drowning. No pain, only terror; he remembers this thickened water and reaches, thrashing, lungs bursting, for his father. He is in that moment: his father hesitates, plunges toward him in the lake. He reaches, flailing, and the fire in his hands ignites. Now he burns, long and bright in the black air, for the speed of his descent feeds the flames, lengthens the crackling roar. He cannot die and so he burns.

He burns through winter's end and a slow cold spring, through summer and harvest and another winter of ceaseless storm, into spring and summer and a clear October week.

The blond grandson walks home from the field. Annabel walks with him to the white farmhouse. She sees smoke curl from the upstairs window, a winding tendril like a scrap of slow-burned curtain; the boy, nearly a man, runs up the stairs to his grandfather's room, into the acrid smell.

Instantly, the plummeting fire is taken up: the endless fire is nothing, only smoke, curling from a window in Iowa.

Annabel hears a cold storm of many whispers, a sea of drifting, flurried tears. The snow on the giant trees is falling. Slides and shifts, a pounding fall, a cloud released, white as the long silk scarf she pulls about her.

He brought them here, all of them, even those who never saw this place, who slipped from him elsewhere and were found or never found; all are gone beyond him and are only aware of some disturbance ended, folding into itself in endless penance.

The stream meanders, shines with snow-melt; the water, shaken in ripples, warms suddenly, as though some seismic shift deep in the earth moves time forward. The air breathes and the trees stir, tossing their limbs, opening every bud and folded leaf.

The bells on the wind are calling her, and she goes.

■ ■ ■ ■

XVII.

■ ■ ■ ■

People come and people go
The earth goes on and on

the wind blows round, round and round
it stops, it blows again

these things make me so tired
I can't speak, I can't see, I can't hear

what happened before will happen again

I forgot it all before
I will forget it all again
— "again (after ecclesiastes),"
words and music by David Lang

That which is Below corresponds to that which is Above, and that which is Above corresponds to that which is Below, to accomplish the miracle of the One Thing.

— Hermes Trismegistus,
The Emerald Tablet, translated from the
Latin by Dennis W. Hauck

For love is strong as death . . .
like a seal upon thine arm . . .
like the best wine for my beloved
that goeth down sweetly,
causing the lips of those that are asleep to
    speak.

— "for love is strong,"
words and music by David Lang

OCTOBER 18, 1933
CHICAGO AND PARK RIDGE, ILLINOIS

CODA: THE WORLD IS AIR

Emily meant to stop in the office only briefly, and so had Duty with her on the leash. She paged through her *Tribune* mail to find a special delivery letter from Marta Baertman, postmistress, Oran, Iowa. It was a clipping from the Sumner paper; the note enclosed said simply, "I thought you would want to know. He was much respected and the funeral well attended." Emily read the clipping through once, and then again, conscious of the floor beneath her feet; she was so taken aback that the room seemed to swim around her.

Sumner Gazette, *Sumner, Iowa*
12 October 1933
A Suicide by Using
.38 Caliber Rifle

Fires Shot into Chest
at Home of Son-in-Law
in Leroy Township, Friday

Wilko Drenth, 71, who has made his home with his son-in-law, Evert Schroder in Leroy Township for the past four years, committed suicide Friday afternoon by discharging a .38 caliber rifle bullet through his chest. First intimation that he had taken his own life was gained about 3:15 when Evert Schroder, Jr., who was returning home from a field, noticed smoke coming from one of the upstairs windows. He rushed upstairs and found the body of his grandfather slumped on the floor and clothing surrounding the wound smoldering from being ignited from the shot, which was apparently fired at close range. Coroner F. C. Koch of Waverly was called, but considered there was no need for an inquest, the circumstances being clearly that of suicide. The aged man came in for some notoriety about two years ago when his name was connected with that of Harry Powers of West Virginia, who was accused of numerous killings of wives whose bodies Powers is said to have buried under the floor of his garage. It was quite definitely established at the time that Powers was Mr. Drenth's son, who he had not seen for a number of years after the boy ran away from home. While Mr. Drenth is said to have brooded somewhat over the waywardness of his son, relatives do not believe that this had any connection with his suicide. He had been enjoying good health and had experienced no financial difficulties. He and his son-in-law had been planning a trip to Michigan with the expectation of leaving Saturday. Drenth had been a widower for five years, living in the vicinity of Oran until he moved to the Schroder home about four years ago. Surviving are his son-in-law and two grandsons. His daughter, Mrs. Evert Schroder, preceded him in death. Funeral services were held Monday afternoon from the Schroder home.

He'd waited two years since the September she found him, a year and a half since the execution. No one would bother the family now or address the facts. Private misfortune, private grief, and the glorious flat land bathed in Indian summer. News of Wilko's death was front page in Sumner, the larger town near Oran, but Marta Baertman knew no one would hear of it from Emily.

She looked up from her desk to see Eric at his, across the room.

He saw her expression and came over immediately. "Emily? I'm surprised to see you in the office. Aren't you and William going to Paris tomorrow?"

"Yes, but I wanted to check the mail. I've had a letter from Iowa." She held it out. "I don't want it known. Here, pull a chair next to me. There, Duty."

He read the clipping through. "I would not

have thought —"

"Eric, we started the clock ticking."

He put his hand on her wrist, as though to delay an action already begun. "We do not start clocks, Emily, or stop them."

"It's dated October twelfth, last Thursday, and happened on Friday, the sixth."

"The date is not in question," Eric said, "but why."

"We will not know," Emily said.

He looked up at her. "I will say what you're thinking. For a man so concerned with shame — he said that word, in Dutch — to do this. Small towns know such histories for generations."

"The town will not blame him, or the family. See her words, there? The whole town, towns around, I shouldn't wonder, went to the funeral . . . at the home. Respect. They did not believe him guilty of anything. He was visited by misfortune."

"He believed himself guilty. That is clear." Eric paused, as though to be certain. "He said, 'I knew it then,' but what did he know?"

"Wasn't it 'God help me, I knew' — or words to that effect?"

"Yes. As though he knew things he should have told, or could not tell. But the phrase implies not what Wilko did, but what the son did, before Wilko saved him that day in the lake, and afterward. He didn't send the boy to the Midwest until Harm was eighteen."

Emily let the dog jump down to his basket under her desk, and moved her hand across the page. "A suicide cannot repent, in most religions. It's as though he sacrificed himself, in shame or despair or —"

"Or he simply couldn't live with what he knew, and took the burden with him." Eric folded the clipping and note back into the envelope, and held it out to her. "What will you do with this? You will tell William?"

"Of course, but not today." She put the envelope in her purse. "Oh, Eric, it's quite odd. William and I are meeting at the children's graves in Park Ridge. The footstones, with their names and dates, have been set. It seemed long enough after, that the graves might be quietly marked."

He took her hand. "Have you been there, since the service? No need to answer; I see it in your eyes. Not often, I hope."

"No, but I have no church but St. Luke's graveyard. I take Duty there, near Christmas, in thanks for Mason. And on her birthday."

"You mean, Annabel's birthday. Which is?"

"It is today." She was putting on her hat, a straw hat with a brim, and a light sweater, for the warm afternoon was cloudy.

"Emily, let me take you for a drink, or a coffee. Don't rush off, into all this."

"I must. We have an appointment. William will be waiting."

"Then I'll walk you to the train, and ride

out with you, and take the next train back."

"Eric, not necessary. But you may walk us to the train, and if we have time, there's that outdoor place in the Loop, just by the station." She gave him Duty's leash, and the dog ran before them.

The station in the Loop was a mere three blocks. They tied the leash on a café chair and Duty claimed his own cushion. Eric insisted on coffees with shots of whiskey. They sat with steaming cups and doll-size glasses.

"It's a beautiful day, really, just brisk enough." Emily looked above them, at the lifted canopy of a fenced tree. "A day with such news must be windblown, to give one hope, to compensate."

"Emily, what we cannot know, we must accept. It is the end of the story." The dog rested his head on the table. "You see? Duty rests. Coffee, Emily, but first the whiskey, together."

They touched glasses and drank, one go.

"It's good that you're leaving tomorrow, Emily. The timing couldn't be better. You remember we have a date at nine tonight; Charles and I will be collecting Duty and his baggage."

"Oh yes. The visit to the graves is a brief ceremony, of sorts. It's very pretty, the graveyard, wooded and small."

"If I remember, it's just across the park from William's several acres. You've never seen his wife, or the house?"

"Nor do I need to. Catherine is his first obligation. I benefit by the man he became, in loyalty to her."

"It's a bit too Mr. Rochester for comfort."

"Not at all, Eric. He says she's very placid, like a child, doesn't know him, doesn't speak, anymore; it's the course of the disease."

"He's lucky in that, at least." Eric took her arm. "Don't listen to me. It's no one's luck; it just is. What happened to her could happen to any of us. He's lucky in you, and Mason, and he knows it. You'll stop off to visit Mason at school, on the way to New York, and the crossing?"

"Yes. A train to Mason, then on to New York. William has business in Paris. We'll take Mason for a month, in the summer. You and Charles must come and stay."

"We shall, cousin." He leaned back in his chair. "As for school, I feel responsible, as the alum who suggested the place. Mason does like it, doesn't he? He tells me so."

"Are you surprised?"

He clasped his hands. "I try not to have expectations. We can't imagine what it's like for him, or where he came from."

"I know exactly where he came from." She saw for a moment, very clearly, the snowy alley behind the Gore. "And you were there,

Eric, with us."

"That was our passage, one world to another."

"Perhaps. I've come to believe it is one world, as they say. Mason worked very hard with his tutors. And thank you again for coming with us to the interview, when he applied." She tapped Eric's shoe with hers. "And your pistons helped, of course."

"Pistons should be good for something, other than turning crankshafts."

"We agreed he'd give it a year, and he's thriving. He never had friends, boys his age. A Chicago classmate of William's teaches Latin there; we hear they've already moved Mason up a class."

"And with Paris . . . French will come." Eric shrugged, playful, and grew serious. "I know you wanted him nearby, but I think the school will serve him."

"He does write descriptive letters; I save them, and phone him once a fortnight. I miss him, of course." She drank her coffee. "Eric, I must go."

"I know you must, but truly, this interlude is my comfort." He lifted Duty down, gave Emily the leash, and kissed her, both cheeks. "I'll see you this evening. That's a lovely dress, by the way. It so suits you."

She only smiled, and took his hand for a moment.

■ ■ ■ ■

She walked from the Park Ridge station, enjoying Duty's familiarity with the streets, fences, corners. They walked past the Eicher house, though Duty no longer stopped there, and two blocks on, to the parklike cemetery opposite St. Luke's. It was always quiet and empty, well tended by invisible hands, for she'd never seen anyone here but William and herself. She reflected that she was wearing her wedding clothes, the only wedding clothes she might ever wear, and was quietly happy. It was private between them; they'd agreed not to plan their vows, but to say the words that came to them, and to size in advance the rings they would exchange, both family possessions that required no purchase. She could see him the moment she came in through the gate. The graves were not far along the little road. He stood to meet her.

Nearly a year ago, William had arranged that a simple stone bench be placed under a tree near the graves. They sat there now, Duty at their feet, and turned toward one another.

William took her hands.

"Emily, I saw you there, at the edge of a dark place. I loved you then but could not dare hope. There was no time, yet you stood to meet me, in that office where years of my life have disappeared, and I knew that every passion within me would find answer." He slipped the ring onto her finger. "This sapphire ring was my mother's, and I choose it for you because the star within it, always visible, is so like you, the reason for my life, and the truth within me."

She kissed him once. She'd thought words might elude her, but they came easily. "William, I shall stay with you forever. Mason is ours; we will make a chance for him, a life. I will help you uphold your responsibility to Catherine. If she dies before you, we will marry. If you die before her, I will not attend your funeral, nor will Mason. We will grieve together, for we love you deeply, abidingly, always. How strange life is, that goodness might assert itself, insist on existing, begin from such a terrible thing, in such a dark field." She saw him through tearful eyes and put the ring on his finger, a man's gold band with an onyx stone. "This was my grandfather's ring. It is yours, that we may lead long lives together, in a heartland of our own."

He gathered her to him, his forehead against hers. "Shall I kiss the bride?"

"Yes, please."

A sprinkling rain began. Sheltered under the pine, they looked into the woods. Old gravestones carved with illegible words stood amongst the trees, leaves and vines trailing near. Not speaking, they stood and walked a few steps to the children's graves. The small footstones were white marble, fitted to the earth, and the grass upon the graves a paler green, the soil still slightly raised. Duty dashed forward, rustling the fallen leaves. Emily, her eyes blurred with rain and tears, saw wafting movement in the trees opposite, a flash of white. She thought of a child playing, but of course no child was here. Duty ran into the thicket, where the younger growth left patches of clearing, as though to follow.

They called for the dog, and began walking through the woods, among the gravestones. They could hear him nearby, running through layered leaves. Emily glimpsed again some white scrap amongst the young trees, moving weightlessly as though blown about. Then nothing, only the lovely thicket itself, full of wild growth and saplings the wind had planted. The trees' thin, wandlike branches nearly met overhead, intermingled greens barely tinged with color.

"There," William said, and took her arm, for the ground was wet and the leaves slick with moisture.

Duty sat, as though waiting for them, half upon a dirtied piece of white cloth. William bent down to retrieve it. "It's a scrap of something. See here, it was hemmed once, along this edge."

Emily took it from him. It was silk, so worn she could see her fingers through it. She held it to her throat, then folded it in half and tied it to the limb of a young birch.

"A flag to mark our way," she said.

He took her hand, and they turned to go.

ACKNOWLEDGMENTS

Only four characters in *Quiet Dell* are wholly invented. Lavinia Eicher, beloved grandmother, proponent of "dreams that see past us," and Emily Thornhill, modern professional woman, are homage to my own loving, intrepid mother, Jane Thornhill (Phillips), who first told me the story of Quiet Dell. She was six years old when her own mother walked her past the scene of the murders: "a dirt road in the hot sun, lined with cars on both sides as far as I could see, and people taking the place apart piece by piece for souvenirs." Randolph Mason Phillips, imagined orphan gifted with a new life, is offered in loving remembrance of my father, Russell Randolph Phillips, whose Randolph County grandparents gave the land for Phillips Chapel and Phillips Cemetery in Coalton, West Virginia. Eric Lindstrom, journalist whose (then necessary) secret life in no way impedes his perceptions, is inspired by dear friends and by my own niece, Amy Phillips, lawyer and Cornell grad, who continues to shelter many and live her life courageously.

Deepest thanks to Yaddo, in whose summer refuge this book was mostly written, and to Yaddo's founder, Katrina Trask, who lost her own children and created good from grief. Thanks to the MacDowell Colony, the Rockefeller Foundation and Bellagio, the Bogliasco Foundation, and the Liguria Study Center, for time, support, and encouragement. Thanks to my literary agent and friend of thirty years, Lynn Nesbit, who found this book a home with the miraculous Nan Graham at Scribner. Thanks to the late Robert "Red" McQuain, family friend, who knew I referenced the Quiet Dell crime in my first novel, *Machine Dreams,* and gave me a small envelope he found in an antique dresser at his home in Rock Cave, West Virginia: *Piece of soundproof board, used by Harry Powers during his notorious Murdering in the fall of 1931, Aug. 28.* Thanks to excellent book person Bill Long, of Chicago, who helped me locate Reta and Paul Kikutani, of Park Ridge, Illinois, whose home, purchased by Reta's parents in 1932, was the Eicher home for so many years. Thanks to Reta for showing me the Eicher playhouse and barn/workshop, for sending photographs of the playhouse mural Asta painted for her children, and for telling me, "This is where they were happy." Thanks to my friends from childhood, the late Susan Harper Hitt, and Elizabeth Randall, who insisted we stop by the Clarksburg library on one of my visits home, helped me copy dozens of newspaper accounts, and walked with me in the green woods at Quiet Dell.

Special thanks to the invaluable David Houchin, Special Collections Librarian at the West Virginia Collection, Clarksburg-Harrison Public Library, who helped locate 1930s newspaper sources and advised me on contacting permissions. Thanks to Robert Sayre and Deborah Sayre Stoikowitz, grandchildren of West Virginia photographer Floyd E. Sayre, for permission to reprint his beautiful images pertaining to the crime at Quiet Dell. Thanks to the West Virginia Division of Culture and History for allowing me to purchase copies of the Powers trial documents and portions of transcript quoted in the trial. Thanks to Brian Jarvis, publisher of the locally owned *Clarksburg Exponent Telegram,* who allowed me to quote numerous short excerpts from 1931–32 coverage of the Quiet Dell case. Thanks to Martha Mendoza, who guided efforts to credit AP sources, to the Associated Press, *The Mason City Globe-Gazette, The Sumner Gazette,* and *The Ames Tribune,* for permission to quote original articles, and to King Features Syndicate, for permission to reprint the photograph of

Duty. Thanks to Seek Publishing for permission to quote from *Remember When, 1931, A Nostalgic Look Back in Time*. Thanks to David Lang, extraordinary composer of *The Little Match Girl Passion and Other Works*, for permission to quote lines from *"again (after ecclesiastes)"* and *"love is strong."* Thanks to Dorothy Gosse and Elvira Hebell, who researched 1930s documents in Iowa. Grateful acknowledgment to E. A. Bartlett, author of the 1931 account *Love Murders of Harry F. Powers (Beware Such Bluebeards)*, published in 1931 by the Sheftel Press.

Special thanks to my first readers, Pamela Rikkers, Annabel Lee, Anita Ruthling Klaussen, the late Irene McKinney, Marcelle Clements, and to my husband, Mark Stockman, who lovingly encouraged this "secret book" over years of research and writing.

CREDITS

Quotes used on pages 13, 249, 255, 332-3, 337, 338, 345-6, 347, 365, 423, 463-4, 467, 486, 498-9, 500, 547-8, and 647-8 reprinted with permission of the Clarksburg Publishing Company; the quote used on page 422-23 reprinted with permission of the *Mason City Globe-Gazette;* the quote on page 431 reprinted with permission of the Associated Press; the quote on pages 655-57 reprinted with permission of the *Sumner Gazette.*

Lyrics on pages 653 and 654 are from "again (after ecclesiastes)" and "for love is strong," words and music by David Lang, and appear courtesy of the composer.

Page 237: Image appears courtesy of www .925-1000.com; Pages 252-253, 547: Images appear courtesy of Clarksburg-Harrison County Public Library, Special Collections; Pages 340, 348, and 465: Photographs by Floyd E. Sayre courtesy of Robert Sayre, Deborah Sayre Stoikowitz, and the

ABOUT THE AUTHOR

Jayne Anne Phillips is the author of *Lark and Termite, MotherKind, Shelter,* and *Machine Dreams,* and the widely anthologized collections of stories *Fast Lanes* and *Black Tickets. Lark and Termite,* winner of the Heartland Prize, was a finalist for the 2009 National Book Award, the National Book Critics Circle Award, and the Prix Médicis Étranger. Phillips' works are published in nine languages. She is the recipient of a Guggenheim Fellowship, two National Endowment for the Arts Fellowships, a Bunting Fellowship, and an Academy Award in Literature from the American Academy and Institute of Arts and Letters. She is Distinguished Professor of English and Director of the MFA Program at Rutgers-Newark, the State University of New Jersey, where she established the Writers at Newark Reading Series. Information, essays, and text source photographs on her fiction can be viewed at www.JayneAnnePhillips

.com. She divides her time between Boston, New York, and Newark, New Jersey.

The employees of Thorndike Press hope you have enjoyed this Large Print book. All our Thorndike, Wheeler, and Kennebec Large Print titles are designed for easy reading, and all our books are made to last. Other Thorndike Press Large Print books are available at your library, through selected bookstores, or directly from us.

For information about titles, please call:
 (800) 223-1244

or visit our Web site at:
 http://gale.cengage.com/thorndike

To share your comments, please write:
 Publisher
 Thorndike Press
 10 Water St., Suite 310
 Waterville, ME 04901